Simisola

SIMISOLA

Ruth Rendell

Crown Publishers, Inc.
New York

Originally published in Great Britain by Random House UK in 1994.

Published by Crown Publishers, Inc., 201 East 50th Street, New York, New York 10022.
Member of the Crown Publishing Group.

Random House, Inc. New York, Toronto, London, Sydney, Auckland

CROWN is a trademark of Crown Publishers, Inc.

Manufactured in the United States of America

Design by Jennifer Harper

Library of Congress Cataloging-in-Publication Data
Rendell, Ruth.
Simisola / Ruth Rendell.—1st American ed.
1. Wexford, Inspector (Fictitious character)—Fiction.   2. Police—
England—Fiction.   I. Title.
PR6068.E63S56   1995b
823'.914—dc20   95-8428

ISBN 0-517-70073-5

10 9 8 7 6 5 4 3 2 1

First American Edition

To Marie

Simisola

one

There were four people besides himself in the waiting room and none of them looked ill. The olive-skinned blonde in the designer tracksuit bloomed with health, her body all muscles, her hands all golden tendons, apart from the geranium nails and the nicotine stains on the right forefinger. She had changed her seat when a child of two arrived with its mother and homed on the chair next to hers. Now the blonde woman in the tracksuit was as far away as she could get, two seats from himself and three from the very old man who sat with his knees together, his hands clutching his checked cap in his lap and his eyes on the board where the doctors' names were printed.

Each of the GPs had a light above his or her name and a hook underneath it on which colored rings hung: a red light and rings for Dr. Moss, green for Dr. Akande, blue for Dr. Wolf. The old man had been given a red ring, Wexford noticed, the child's mother a blue one, which was exactly what he would have expected, the preference for the senior man in one case, the woman in the other. The woman in the tracksuit hadn't got a ring at all. She either didn't know you were supposed to announce yourself at reception or couldn't be bothered. Wexford wondered why she wasn't a private patient with an appointment later in the morning and therefore not obliged to wait here fidgeting and impatient.

The child, tired of marching back and forth on the seats of the row of chairs, had turned her attention to the magazines on the table and begun tearing off their covers. Who was ill, this little girl or her overweight pallid mother? Nobody said a word to hinder the tearing, though the old man glared and the woman in the tracksuit did the unforgivable, the outrageous, thing. She thrust a hand into her crocodile-skin handbag, took out a flat gold case, the function of which would have been a mystery to most people under thirty, removed a cigarette, and lit it with a gold lighter.

Wexford, who had been successfully distracted from his own anxiety, now became positively fascinated. No fewer than three notices on the walls, among the exhortations to use a condom, have children immunized, and watch your weight, forbade smoking. What would happen? Was there some system whereby smoke in the waiting room could be detected in reception or the dispensary?

The child's mother reacted, not with a word to the woman in the tracksuit but by sniffing, giving the little girl a vicious yank with one hand and administering a slap with the other. Screams ensued. The old man began a sorrowful head-shaking. To Wexford's surprise the smoker turned to him and said, without preamble, "I called the doctor, but he refused to come. Isn't that amazing? I was forced to come here myself."

Wexford said something about GPs no longer making house calls except in cases of serious illness.

"How would he know it wasn't serious if he didn't come?" She must have correctly interpreted Wexford's disbelieving look. "Oh, it's not *me*," she said and, incredibly, "It's one of the servants."

He longed to know more, but the chance was lost. Two things happened simultaneously. The blue light for Dr. Wolf came on and the door opened to admit the practice nurse. She said crisply, "Please put that cigarette out. Didn't you see the notice?"

The woman in the tracksuit had compounded her offense by dropping ash on the floor. No doubt she would have ground her butt out there too but for the nurse taking it from her with a little convulsive grunt and carrying it off into hitherto unpolluted regions. She was unembarrassed by what had happened, lifting her shoulders a little, giving Wexford a radiant smile. Mother and child left the waiting room in quest of Dr. Wolf just as two more patients came in and Dr. Akande's light came on. This is it, thought Wexford, his fear returning, now I shall know. He hung up the green ring and went out without a backward glance. Instantly it was as if those people had never been, as if none of those things had happened.

Suppose he fell over as he walked the short corridor to Dr. Akande's room? Already twice that morning he had fallen. I'd be in the best place, he told himself, the doctors' surgery—no, he corrected himself, must move with the times, the Medical Center. The best place to be taken ill. If it's something in my brain, a growth, a blood clot . . . He knocked on the door, though most people didn't.

Raymond Akande called, "Come in."

This was only the second time Wexford had been to him since Akande joined the practice on Dr. Crocker's retirement, and the first visit had been for an anti-tetanus injection when he cut himself in the garden. He liked to believe there had been some sort of rapport between them, that they had taken to each other. And then he castigated himself for thinking this way, for caring, because he knew damned well he wouldn't have involved himself with likings or dislikings if Akande had been other than he was.

This morning, though, these reflections were nowhere. He was concerned only with himself, the fear, the horrid symptoms. Keeping calm, trying to be detached, he described them, the way he fell over when he got out of bed in the morning, the loss of balance, the floor coming up to meet him.

"Any headache?" said Dr. Akande. "Any nausea?"

No, there was none of that, Wexford said, hope creeping in at the door Akande was opening. And, yes, he had had a bit of a cold. But, you see, a few years ago he'd had this thrombosis in the eye and ever since then he'd . . . well, he'd been on the alert for something like it, a stroke maybe, God forbid.

"I thought maybe Ménière's syndrome," he said unwisely.

"I'm no believer in banning books," said the doctor, "but I'd personally burn all medical dictionaries."

"Okay, I did look at one," Wexford admitted. "And I didn't seem to have the right symptoms, apart from the falling bit."

"Why don't you stick to the judges' rules and leave diagnosis to me?"

He was quite willing. Akande examined his head and his chest and a few reflexes. "Did you drive yourself here?"

His heart in his mouth, Wexford nodded.

"Well, don't drive. Not for a few days. Of course you can drive home. Half the population of Kingsmarkham's got this virus. I've had it myself."

"Virus?"

"That's what I said. It's a funny one, it seems to affect the semi-circular canals in the ears and they control the balance."

"It's really just that, a virus? A virus can make you fall down like that, out of the blue? I measured my length in the front garden yesterday."

"It's quite a length to measure," said Akande. "Didn't have any illuminating visions, I suppose? No one to tell you to stop kicking against the pricks?"

"You mean visions are another symptom? Oh, no, I see. Like on the Road to Damascus. You're not going to tell me that was all Paul had, a virus?"

Akande laughed. "The received view is that he was an epileptic. No, don't look like that. This is a virus, I promise you, not a case of spontaneous epilepsy. I'm not going to give you anything for it. It'll get right in a day or two on its own. In fact, I'll be surprised if it doesn't get right immediately now you know you haven't got a brain tumor."

"How did you . . . ? Oh, well, I suppose you're used to patients with irrational fears."

"It's understandable. If it's not medical books, it's the newspapers never letting them forget about their health for five minutes."

Akande got up and held out his hand. Wexford thought it a

pleasant custom, that of shaking hands with patients, the way doctors must have done years ago when they made house calls and sent bills.

"Funny creatures, people," the doctor said. "For instance, I'm expecting someone this morning who's coming on behalf of her *cook*. Send the cook, I said, but that apparently wouldn't do. I've a feeling—without foundation, I must tell you, mere intuition—that she's not going to be too overjoyed when she finds I'm what my father-in-law's boss used to call 'a man of color.' "

For once, Wexford was speechless.

"Have I embarrassed you? I'm sorry. These things are always just under the surface and sometimes they bubble up."

"You haven't embarrassed me," Wexford said. "It was only that I couldn't think of anything to say that would be—well, a refutation or a consolation. I just agreed and I didn't care to say that."

Akande gave him a pat on the shoulder, or one that was aimed at the shoulder but landed on his upper arm. "Take a couple of days off. You should be fine by Thursday."

Halfway down the corridor Wexford met the blonde woman heading toward Akande's room. "I know I'm going to lose my cook, I can just see it coming," she said as she passed him. A miasma that was a mix of Paloma Picasso and Rothman Kingsize hung in her wake. Surely she hadn't meant the cook was going to *die?*

He went jauntily out, pushing open both of the double doors. Only one of the cars in the car park could possibly be hers, the Lotus Elan with the personalized number, AK 3. She must have paid a lot for that, it was one of the earliest. Annabel King, he speculated. Anne Knight? Alison Kendall? Not all that number of English surnames begin with K, but then she certainly wasn't of English origin. Anna Karenina, he thought, being silly.

Akande had said he could drive home. In fact, Wexford would have enjoyed walking home, he loved the idea of walking now he had stopped falling over or being afraid of falling over. The mind was a funny thing, what it could make the body do. If he left the car here he'd only have to come back for it later.

The young woman waddled and the child skipped down the Medical Center's shallow steps. Full of good cheer, Wexford wound down his window and asked them if they'd like a lift. Somewhere, anywhere, he was in the mood to drive miles out of his way if need be.

"We don't take lifts from strangers." To the child she said very loudly, "Do we, Kelly?"

Snubbed, Wexford withdrew his head. She was quite right. She had behaved wisely and he had not. He might be a combined rapist and child molester cunningly disguising his nefarious motives by a visit to the doctor. Leaving, he passed a car he recognized coming in, an old Ford Escort that had been resprayed bright pink. You hardly ever saw a pink car. But whose was it? He often had a brilliant eidetic memory, faces and townscapes recorded in full color, but the names got lost.

He drove out into South Queen Street. It was going to be nice telling the news to Dora and he indulged himself by thinking what might have been, the horror, the communicated dread, the putting of two brave faces on it, if he'd had to tell her he'd an appointment at the hospital for a brain scan. None of that was going to happen. Would he have been brave if it had? Would he have *lied* to her?

In that case he'd have had to lie to three people. Turning into his own garage drive, he saw Neil's car already there, thoughtfully parked on the far left to allow his own passage. Neil *and* Sylvia's car, he had better learn to say, for they had just the one between them now, since hers had been given up when her job went. They might not even be able to afford this one, the way things were now.

I ought to be gratified, he thought, I ought to be flattered. Not everybody's children come flying to the bosom of mum and dad when misfortune strikes. His always did. He ought not to have this reaction, this immediate response to the sight of the Fairfax car, which was to ask: what now?

*   *   *

A dversity is good for some marriages. The warring couple put aside their strife and stand united against the world. Sometimes. And the marriage has to be in a pretty bad way before this happens. Wexford's elder daughter's marriage had been bad for a long time and it was different from other people's bad marriages chiefly in that she and Neil stayed doggedly together, ever seeking new remedies, for the sake of their two sons.

Once Neil had said to his father-in-law, "I do love her. I really love her," but that was a long time ago. A lot of tears had fallen since then and a lot of cruel things had been said. Many times Sylvia had brought the boys home to Dora and just as often Neil had taken himself to a motel room on the Eastbourne Road. Her educating herself and working for the Social Services had solved no problems, nor had their lavish foreign holidays or moves to bigger and better houses. At least, money or the lack of it had never been an issue. There was enough, more than enough.

Until now. Until Neil's father's firm of architects (two partners, father and son) felt the recession, then its bite, then was punched and undermined by it into collapse. Neil had been without work for five weeks now, Sylvia for nearly six months.

Wexford let himself into his house and stood for a moment, listening to their voices: Dora's measured and calm, Neil's indignant, still incredulous, Sylvia's hectoring. He was in no doubt they were waiting for him, had come expecting to find him there, ready to be diverted from his brain tumor or embolism by their catalog of troubles: joblessness, no prospects, increasing mortgage debt.

He opened the living room door and Sylvia fell upon him, throwing her arms round his neck. She was a big tall woman, well able to embrace him without finding herself clutching his middle. For a moment he thought her affection occasioned by anxiety for his health, his very life.

"Dad," she said, she wailed, "Dad, what d'you think we've come to? I mean, *us*. It's unbelievable but it's happening. You won't believe it. Neil's *going on the dole*."

"It won't exactly be the dole, darling," said Neil, using an endearment Wexford hadn't heard on his lips for many a year. "Not the dole. Benefit."

"Well, it amounts to the same thing. Welfare, social security, unemployment pay, it comes to the same. It's all unbelievably ghastly, happening to *us*."

It was interesting how Dora's quite soft voice could penetrate this stridency. It cut through it like a fine wire splitting a chunk of extra-strong Cheddar. "What did Dr. Akande say, Reg?"

"A virus. Apparently, there's a lot of it about. I'm to take a couple of days off, that's all."

"What a relief," Dora said lightly. "A virus."

Sylvia made a snorting sound. "I could have told you that. I had it myself last week, I could hardly keep on my feet."

"Then it's a pity you didn't tell me, Sylvia."

"I've got more things to think about, haven't I? I'd be laughing if feeling a bit giddy was all I had to contend with. Now you're back, Dad, perhaps you can stop Neil doing this. I can't, he never takes any notice of what I say. Anybody's got more influence with him than his own wife."

"Stop him doing what?" said Wexford.

"I've *told* you. Going to the—what's it called?—the ESJ. I don't know what that stands for but I know what it is, the combined dole place and labor exchange—no, they don't call it that anymore, do they?"

"They haven't called it that for years," said Neil. "The Job Center."

"Why should I stop him?" Wexford said.

"Because it's hateful, it's degrading, it isn't the kind of place people like us go to."

"And what do people like us do?" Wexford asked in the voice that should have warned her.

"Find something in the Appointments section of *The Times*."

Neil began to laugh and Wexford, his anger swiftly changed to pity, smiled sadly. Neil had been studying the Situations Vacant daily for weeks now, had written, he had told his father-in-law, over three hundred letters of application, all in vain.

"*The Times* doesn't give you any money," said Neil, and Wexford could hear the bitterness in his voice, if Sylvia couldn't. "Besides, I have to know where I stand on our mortgage. Maybe they can do something to stop the Building Society repossessing the house. *I* can't. Perhaps they can advise me what to do about the kids' schools, if it's only to tell us to send them to Kingsmarkham Comprehensive. Anyway, I'll get money—don't they call it a giro that they send you? One thing, I shall soon know. And I'd better, Reg, I'd better. We've got just two hundred and seventy pounds left in our joint account and that's the only account we've got. Just as well, I expect, since they ask you what savings you've got before they pay out."

Wexford said quietly, "Do you want a loan? We could let you have a bit." He thought, swallowed. "Say a thousand?"

"Thanks, Reg, thanks very much, but it had better be no. It'll only postpone the evil day. I'm very grateful for the offer. A loan ought to be paid back and I can't see how I'd ever repay you, not for years." Neil looked at his watch. "I must go," he said. "My appointment with the new claims adviser is for ten-thirty."

Dora must have spoken without thinking, "Oh, do they give you an appointment?"

It was odd to see how a smile could sadden a face. Neil hadn't quite winced. "You see how being unemployed demotes you? I no longer belong among those who can expect social grace. I'm one of the queuers now, the waiters in line who are lucky to be seen at all, who get sent home with nothing and told to come back tomorrow. I've probably lost my style and my surname too. Someone'll come out and call, 'Neil, Mr. Stanton will see you now.' At ten to one, though I'm due there at ten-thirty."

"I'm sorry, Neil, I didn't mean . . ."

"No, of course you didn't. It's unconscious. Or, rather, it's a shift the consciousness makes, an adjustment in the way you think about a prosperous architect with more commissions than he can handle and someone who's out of work. I have to go now."

He didn't take their car. Sylvia needed it. He would walk the half mile to the ESJ, and later on . . .

"Get the bus, I suppose," said Sylvia. "Why not? Half the time I have to. If there are only four a day that's too bad. We have to watch our petrol consumption. I expect he can walk five miles. You used to tell us your grandfather walked five miles to school and five back when he was only ten."

There was a settled despair in her voice Wexford didn't like to hear, much as he deplored her self-pity and her petulance. He heard Dora offering to have the boys for the weekend so that Sylvia and Neil could get away, if only to London where Neil's sister lived, and he seconded that rather too heartily.

"When I think," said Sylvia, who was given to doleful reminiscence, "how I slaved to get to be a social worker." She nodded to her husband as he left, resumed while he was still in earshot, "Neil didn't exactly adapt his lifestyle to help. I had to arrange to get the boys looked after. I'd still be working at midnight sometimes. And what has it all come to?"

"Things must get better eventually, dear," said Dora.

"I'll never get another job with the Social Services, I *feel* it. Do you remember those children in Stowerton, Dad? The 'home alone' kids?"

Wexford thought. Two of his officers had met the parents at Gatwick coming off a plane from Tenerife. He said, "Epson, weren't they called? He was black and she was white . . ."

"What's that got to do with it? Why bring racism into it? That was my last job as a child-care officer before the cuts. Little did I dream I'd be a housewife again before those kids went back to their parents. Will you really have the boys for the weekend, Mother?"

That was the woman he had seen driving the pink car. Fiona Epson. Not that it was important. Wexford debated whether to go upstairs and lie down or defy the doctor and return to work. Work won. As he left the house he could hear Sylvia lecturing her mother on what she called acceptable forms of political correctness.

two

When the Akande family had moved to Kingsmarkham a year or so earlier, the owner-occupiers on either side of 27 Ollerton Avenue put their houses up for sale. Insulting as this was to Raymond and Laurette Akande and their children, from a practical point of view it was to their advantage. Recession was at its height and the houses took a long time to sell, their asking prices regularly falling, but when the newcomers arrived they turned out to be nice people, as friendly and as liberal-minded as the rest of the Ollerton Avenue neighbors.

"Note my choice of words," said Wexford. "I said 'friendly,' I said 'liberal,' I didn't say 'non-racist.' We're all racist in this country."

"Oh, come on," said Detective Inspector Michael Burden. "I'm not. You're not."

They were in Wexford's dining room, having coffee, while the Fairfax boys, Robin and Ben, and Burden's son Mark watched Wimbledon on television in the room next door with Dora. It was Wexford who had begun this topic of conversation, he hardly knew why. Perhaps it had arisen out of Sylvia's accusation when they discussed the Epsons. He had certainly been thinking about it.

"My wife's not and nor is yours," Burden said, "nor our children."

"We're all racists," said Wexford as if he hadn't spoken. "Without exception. People over forty are worse and that's about all you can say. You were brought up and I was brought up to think ourselves superior to black people. Oh, it may not have been explicit but it was there all right. We were conditioned that way and it's in us still, it's ineradicable. My wife had a black doll called a golliwog and a white one called Pamela. Black people were known as Negroes. When did you ever hear anyone but a sociologist like my daughter Sylvia refer to white people as Caucasians?"

"As a matter of fact, my mother referred to black people as 'darkies' and she thought she was being polite. 'Nigger' was rude but 'darky' was okay. But that was a long time ago. Things have changed."

"No, they haven't. Not much. There are just more black people about. My son-in-law said to me the other day that he no longer noticed the difference between a black person and a white one. I said, you don't notice the difference between fair hair and dark, then? You don't notice if one person's fat and another's thin? What possible help to overcoming racism is that? We'll be getting somewhere when one person says to another of someone black, 'Which one is he?' and the other one says, 'That chap in the red tie.' "

Burden smiled. The boys came in, banging the door behind them, to announce that Martina had won her first set and Steffi hers. Surnames scarcely existed as far as they and their contemporaries were concerned.

"Can we have the chocolate biscuits?"

"Ask your grandmother."

"She's gone to sleep," said Ben. "But she said we could have them after lunch and it's after lunch now. It's the ones that are chocolate *with* chocolate chips and we know where they are."

"Anything for a quiet life," said Wexford, and he added gravely, with a hint of scolding in his voice, "but if you start on them you must finish the whole packet. Is that understood?"

"*Kein Problem,*" said Robin.

After Burden and Mark had gone Wexford picked up the

booklet his son-in-law had left him to look at, the ES 461. Or rather, the photocopy of the booklet. The original had gone back with Neil to his interview with the Employment Service. Neil, whose method of handling his misfortunes was to wallow in them, with the maximum self-created humiliation, had gone to the trouble of photocopying all nineteen pages of what the Employment Service chose to call a "form." He had taken the collection of turquoise-blue, green, yellow, and orange papers to Kingsmarkham Instant Print where they had a color copier so that Wexford could see an ES 461 in all its glory (his words) and read the demands a beneficent government made of its unemployed citizens.

A new word had been coined for the first page: "jobsearch." There were three pages of notes to be read before completing the "form" and then forty-five questions, many of them multiple inquiries, which made Wexford's head spin to read. Some were innocuous, some desperately sad, some sinister. Does your health limit the work you can do? asked number 30 following 29's, What is the lowest wage you are willing to work for? Sights were set humbly for the inquiry, Do you have any academic qualifications (for example, O Levels, GCSEs, City and Guilds)? Do you have your own transport? asked number 9. Number 4 wanted to know, If you have not worked for the past 12 months, how have you spent your time?

This last made his anger rise. What business was that of these Client Advisers, these small-time civil servants, this *government* department? He asked himself what answers they expected apart from "looking for work." Having a fortnight on Grand Bahama? Dining at Les Quat' Saisons? Collecting Chinese porcelain? He pushed the colored pages aside and went into the living room where Navratilova was still battling it out on the Center Court.

"Move up," he said to Robin on the sofa.

"Pas de problème."

Doctors used to tell you to come back and see them next week or "when the symptoms have cleared up." These days they are mostly too busy to do that. They don't want to see patients

without symptoms, not if they can help it. There are too many of
the other kind, the ones that really ought to be in bed and visited
at home, but who are obliged to stagger down to the Medical Center and spread their viruses round the waiting room.

Wexford's virus had apparently flown away at the moment Dr.
Akande spoke his magic words. He had no intention of going back
for a mere checkup and even disobeyed the doctor in taking no
days off. From time to time he thought about that question, the
one that asked how the victim of "jobsearch" had spent his or her
time, and he wondered how he would answer. When he wasn't at
work, for instance, when he was on leave but hadn't gone away.
Reading, talking to grandchildren, thinking, drying the dishes,
having a quick one in the Olive with a friend. Would that satisfy
them? Or was it something quite other they wanted to hear?

But when Dr. Akande phoned him a week later, he was first
guilty, then apprehensive. Dora took the call. It was getting on for
nine in the evening, a Wednesday in early July, and the sun not
yet set. The French windows were open and Wexford was sitting
just inside them, reading Camus's *The Outsider*, thirty years after
he had first read it, and swiping at mosquitoes with the *Kingsmarkham Courier*.

"What does he want?"

"He didn't say, Reg."

It was just remotely possible that Akande was so thorough and
painstaking a general practitioner that he troubled to check up on
patients who had been no more than marginally unwell. Or else—
and Wexford's heart gave a little hop and a thud—that "falling
sickness" he had had wasn't the minor matter Akande had diag-
nosed, wasn't the result of a generalized but petty plague, was in
fact much more serious, its symptoms the forerunner of . . .

"I'm coming."

He took the receiver. From Akande's first words he knew he
wasn't to be *told* anything but *asked* something; the doctor wasn't
dispensing wisdom but coming cap in hand; this time it was he, the
policeman, who must make the diagnosis.

"I'm sorry to trouble you with this, Mr. Wexford, but I hoped you might help me."

Wexford waited.

"It's probably nothing."

Those words, no matter how often he heard them, always caused a small shiver. In his experience, it was nearly always something and, if brought to his attention, something bad.

"If I was really worried I'd get in touch with the police station, but it isn't on that scale. My wife and I don't know many people in Kingsmarkham—of course, we're relatively new here. You being my patient . . ."

"What has happened, Doctor?"

A small deprecating laugh, a hesitation, and Akande said, using a curious phrase, "I'm trying in vain to locate my daughter." He paused. He made another attempt. "I suppose what I mean is, I don't know how to find out where she is. Of course, she's twenty-two years old. She's a grown woman. If she wasn't living at home with us, if she was somewhere on her own, I wouldn't even know she hadn't come home, I wouldn't . . ."

Wexford cut in, "Do you mean your daughter is missing?"

"No, no, that's putting it too strongly. She hasn't come home and she wasn't where we expected her to be last night, that's all. But as I say, she's grown up. If she changed her mind and went somewhere else—well, she has that right."

"But you would have expected her to let you know?"

"I suppose so. She's not very reliable about that kind of thing, young people aren't, as you may know, but we've never known her to—well, it looks as if she's deceiving us. Telling us one thing and doing another. That's the way I personally see it. My wife, on the other hand, is worried. That's an understatement, she's very anxious."

It was always their wives, Wexford thought. They projected their emotions onto their wives. *My wife is rather anxious about it. It's bothering my wife. I'm taking this step because, frankly, the whole thing is affecting my wife's health.* As strong men themselves, *macho* men, they would like you to believe they were prey to no fears, no anxieties, and to no desires either, no longings, no passions, no needs.

"What's her name?" he asked.

"Melanie."

"When did you last see Melanie, Dr. Akande?"

"Yesterday afternoon. She had an appointment in Kingsmarkham and then she was going over to Myringham on the bus to her friend's house. The friend was having a twenty-first birthday party last evening and Melanie was going to it and afterward to stay the night. They have their majority at eighteen, so what they do is have two parties, one for eighteen and one for twenty-one."

Wexford had noticed. He was more interested in the suppressed terror he could detect in Akande's voice, a terror he overlaid with a pathetic optimism. "We didn't expect her home till this afternoon. If they don't have to they don't get up before noon. My wife was working and so was I. We expected to find her at home when we got in."

"Could she have been in and gone out again?"

"I suppose she could. Of course she has her own key. But she was never at Laurel's—that's the friend. My wife phoned them. Melanie hadn't turned up. And yet I can't see that that's too much to worry about. She and Laurel had had a row—well, a disagreement. I heard Melanie say on the phone to her, I can remember her very words: 'I'm going to ring off now and don't count on seeing me on Tuesday.' "

"Has Melanie a boyfriend, Doctor?"

"Not any longer. They broke up about two months ago."

"But there might have been a—a reconciliation?"

"I suppose there might." He sounded grudging. When he said it again he sounded hopeful. "I suppose there might. You mean, she met him yesterday and they've gone off somewhere together? My wife wouldn't like that. She has rather . . . strict ideas on these matters."

Presumably, she'd prefer fornication to rape or murder,

thought Wexford rather sourly but he didn't, of course, say this aloud. "Dr. Akande, you're probably right when you say this is nothing. Melanie is somewhere where she has no access to a phone. Will you give me a ring in the morning, please? As early as you like." He hesitated. "Well, after six. Whatever happens, whether she appears or phones or doesn't appear or phone?"

"I've got a feeling she's trying to get through to us now."

"In that case let's not occupy the line any longer."

H is phone rang at five past six.
He wasn't asleep. He had just woken up. Perhaps he awoke because he was subconsciously troubled about the Akande girl. As he picked up the receiver, before Akande spoke, he was thinking, I shouldn't have waited, I should have done something last night.

"She hasn't come back and she hasn't phoned. My wife is very anxious."

I expect you are too, Wexford thought. I would be. "I'll come and see you. In half an hour."

Sylvia had married almost as soon as she left school. There had been no time to worry about where she was or what was happening to her. But his younger daughter Sheila had caused him sleepless nights, nights of terror. Home in the holidays from drama school, she had made a specialty of disappearing with boyfriends, not phoning, giving no clue to her whereabouts until, three or four days later, she phoned from Glasgow or Bristol or Amsterdam. And he had never got used to it. He would tell reassuring stories of his own experience to the Akandes, he thought, as he showered and put his clothes on, but he would also report Melanie as a missing person. She was female, she was young, therefore they would mount a search for her.

Some days he walked to work, for his health's sake, but it was usually two hours later than this that he started off. The morning was hazy, everything very still, the sun a brighter whiteness in a white sky. Dew lay on the roadside turf high summer had burnt straw color. He didn't see a soul in the first two streets, then as he turned out of Mansfield Road, he met an old woman walking a minuscule Yorkshire terrier. No one else. Two cars passed him. A cat carrying a mouse in its mouth crossed the road from 32 Ollerton Avenue to 25 and dived through a flap in the front door.

Wexford didn't have to knock at 27. Dr. Akande was already waiting for him on the step.

"It's very good of you."

Resisting the temptation to say "no problem" in one of Robin's polyglot versions, Wexford stepped ahead of him into the house. A nice, dull, ordinary sort of place to live in. He couldn't recall having been into any of the detached four-bedroomed houses of Ollerton Avenue before. The street itself was tree-lined, heavily tree-*shaded* at this time of the year. It would rob the interior of the Akande house of light until the sun came round and for a moment, until he was inside the room, he failed to see the woman who stood at the window, looking out.

The classic stance, the time-honored position, of the parent or spouse or lover who waits and waits. Sister Anne, sister Anne, do you see anyone coming? I see only the green grass and the yellow sand. . . . She turned round and came toward him, a tall slender woman of about forty-five dressed in the uniform of a ward sister at Stowerton Royal Infirmary, short-sleeved navy blue dress, navy belt with a rather ornate silver buckle, two or three badges pinned at the left breast. Wexford hadn't expected someone so handsome, so striking to look at, such an elegant figure. *Why* hadn't he?

"Laurette Akande."

She held out her hand. It was a long slender hand, the palm corn-colored, the back deep coffee. She managed to smile. He thought, They always have these wonderful teeth, and then the blood rushed up into his face the way it hadn't done since he was a teenager. He *was* a racist. Why, from the instant he'd walked into this room he'd been thinking, How odd, it's just the same in here as in anyone else's house, same sort of furniture, same sweet peas in the same sort of vase. . . . He cleared his throat, spoke firmly.

"You're worried about your daughter, Mrs. Akande?"

"We both are. I think we've cause for worry, don't you? It's two days now."

He noted she didn't say it was nothing, she wasn't saying it was just the way young people behaved.

"Sit down, please."

Her manner was peremptory, a little offhand. She lacked her husband's *Englishness*, perhaps his bedside manner. This was no time, he thought, for tales of the adolescent Sheila's truancy. Laurette Akande spoke briskly.

"It's time we did this officially, I think. I mean, we have to report her missing. Aren't you too high up to take care of it?"

"I'll do for now," Wexford said. "Perhaps you'll give me some details. We'll start with the name and address of these people she was supposed to spend the night with. I'll have the boyfriend's name too. Oh, and what was this appointment she had in Kingsmarkham before she was due to leave for Myringham?"

"It was at the Job Center," said Dr. Akande.

His wife corrected him with precision. "The Employment Service Job Center. The ESJ, as it's now called. Melanie was looking for a job."

She was trying to find work long before she finished her course," said Laurette Akande. "That was at Myringham. She graduated this summer."

"The University of the South?" Wexford asked.

Her husband answered. "No, Myringham University, the old Polytechnic that was. They're all universities now. She was studying music and dance, 'performance arts,' it's called. I never wanted her to do that. She got a good history A Level—why couldn't she have read history?"

Wexford thought he knew what the objection was to music and dance. "They make such wonderful dancers," "They have these great singing voices . . ." How often had he heard those seemingly generous remarks?

Laurette said, "You may or may not know that black Africans are the most highly educated members of British society. Statistics show that. In view of this, we have high expectations of our children, she should have been preparing herself for a profession." She seemed suddenly to recollect that it wasn't Melanie's education or the lack of it that this crisis was about. "Well, it doesn't matter now. There were no openings for her in what she wanted to do. Her father had told her there wouldn't be but they never listen. You'll have to retrain in business management or something, I said to her. She went to the ESJ and picked up a form and got an appointment to see a new claims adviser there at two-thirty on Tuesday."

"So when did she leave here?"

"My husband had his afternoon surgery. It was my day off. Melanie took an overnight bag with her. She said she expected to get to Laurel's by five and I remember I said, Don't count on it, having that appointment at two-thirty doesn't mean she'll see you then, you could easily wait an hour. She left here at ten past two to give herself plenty of time. I know that because it's a fifteen-minute walk to the High Street from here."

What an admirable witness Laurette Akande would make! Wexford found himself hoping she would never be called upon to be one. Her voice was cool and controlled. She wasted no words. Somewhere, under the accent of Southeast England, was a hint of the African country she had come from perhaps as a student.

"You had the impression she was going straight from the ESJ to this place in Myringham?"

"I *know* she was. By bus. She hoped to catch the four-fifteen, which was why I said that about having to wait to see the new claims adviser. She wanted to take my car but I had to say no. I needed it in the morning. I was due at the hospital by eight when the day shift starts." She looked at her watch. "I am today. The traffic at this hour makes a ten-minute journey into half an hour."

So she was going to work? Wexford had waited for a sign of that anxiety Dr. Akande had been so insistent his wife was a prey to. There was none. Either she wasn't worried or she was under an iron control.

"Where do *you* think Melanie is, Mrs. Akande?"

She gave a small light laugh, a rather chilling laugh. "I very much hope she isn't where I think it most likely she is. In Euan's flat—room, rather—with him."

"Melanie wouldn't do that to us, Letty."

"She wouldn't see it as doing anything to *us*. She has never appreciated our concern for her security and her future. I said to her, Do you want to be one of those girls these boys get pregnant on purpose and are *proud* of it? Euan's already got two children with two different girls and he's not twenty-two yet. You know that, you remember when she told us about those children."

They had forgotten Wexford was there. He coughed. Dr. Akande said miserably, "That's why she split up with him. She was just as shocked and upset as we were. She hasn't gone back to him, I'm sure of that."

"Dr. Akande," said Wexford, "I'd like you to come down to the police station with me and report Melanie missing. I think this is a serious matter. We have to search for your daughter and keep on searching till we find her."

Alive or dead, but he didn't say that.

There was nothing Caucasian about the face in the photograph. Melanie Elizabeth Akande had a low forehead, a broad rather flat nose, and full, thick protuberant lips. Nothing of her mother's classical cast of feature showed in that face. Her father was an African from Nigeria, Wexford now discovered, her mother from Freetown in Sierra Leone. The eyes were huge, her thick black hair a mass of tight curls. Wexford, looking at the photograph, made a strange discovery. Though she was not beautiful to him, he could see that by the standards of others, of millions of African people, Afro-Caribbean people, and African Americans, she might be considered very lovely. Why was it always the white people who set the standard?

The missing persons form, filled in by her father, described her as being five feet seven, hair black, eyes dark brown, and gave her age as twenty-two. He had to phone his wife at the hospital to be reminded that Melanie weighed nine stone two (or 128 pounds) and had been wearing blue denims, a white shirt, and a long embroidered waistcoat when last seen.

"You also have a son, I think."

"Yes, he's a medical student at Edinburgh."

"He can't be there now. Not in July."

"No, he's in Southeast Asia. So far as I know. He went off in a car about three weeks ago with two friends. They were making for Vietnam, but of course they can't be there yet . . ."

"At any rate, his sister couldn't have gone to him," said Wexford. "I have to ask you this, Doctor. What sort of terms were you and your wife on with Melanie? Were there disagreements?"

"We were on good terms," the doctor said quickly. He hesitated and then qualified that statement. "My wife has strict ideas. No harm in that, of course, and there's no doubt we had high expectations for Melanie, which perhaps she couldn't fulfill."

"Does she like living at home?"

"She really doesn't have much choice. I'm not in a position to provide accommodation for my children and I don't think Laurette would much care for . . . I mean Laurette expects Melanie to live at home until she . . ."

"Until what, Doctor?"

"Well, take this idea of retraining. Laurette expects Melanie to live at home while she does that and perhaps not move away until she's earning enough and she's responsible enough to buy somewhere for herself."

"I see."

She was with the boyfriend, Wexford thought. She had met him, according to her father, when they both found themselves in their first term at what was then Myringham Polytechnic, before such institutions were elevated to university status. Euan Sinclair came from the East End of London, had graduated at the same time as Melanie, though by then the quarrel with its anger and insults had divided them. One of Euan's children, now nearly two, had been born when he and Melanie had been going out together for over a year.

Akande knew his present address. He spoke as if it was written in bitterness on his heart. "We've tried to phone him but the number is unobtainable. That means it's been cut off for non-payment of his bill, doesn't it?"

"Probably."

"That young man is a West Indian." Snobbery raised its head in these areas as well, did it? "An Afro-Caribbean, as we're supposed to call them. Her mother sees him as someone who could potentially wreck Melanie's life."

It was Detective Sergeant Vine who went to London to seek Euan Sinclair in his rented room in a Stepney street. Akande told him he wouldn't be surprised if Euan was living there with one of the mothers of his children and perhaps the child as well. This would make it very unlikely that Melanie was there too, but Vine didn't say so. Myringham Police had undertaken to send an officer round to the home of Laurel Tucker.

"I shall look in at the ESJ myself," Wexford said to Burden.

"The what?"

"The Employment Service and Job Center."

"Then why isn't it the ESAJC?"

"Maybe it's really Employment-Service-Job-Center, all one word. I'm afraid that those civil servants who remodel our language have made Job Center into one word as they have 'job-search.'"

For a moment Burden said nothing. He was trying to read, with increasing incredulity, a PR handout from a company guaranteeing to make private cars thief-proof.

"It shuts them up in a metal cage. After two minutes it stops and nothing will start it. Then it makes these blood-curdling howls. Imagine that on the M2 at five-thirty, the obstruction, the safety hazard . . ." Burden looked up. "Why you?" he said.

"Archbold could do that, or Pemberton."

"I daresay they could," said Wexford. "They go there often enough when someone's assaulted an admin. officer or started taking the place apart. I'm going because I want to see what it's like."

three

I t was going to be a fine day, if you could stand the humidity. The air was still, not so much misty as with a thick feel to it. You wanted to fill your lungs with fresh air but this *was* fresh air, all you were going to get. A hot sun was filtered through meshes of cloud behind which the sky must be a rich dark blue but which looked like a pale opal and was covered with an unmoving thready network of cirrus.

Fumes from traffic were trapped under the cloud ceiling and by the still air. Along the pavement Wexford found himself passing through areas where someone had stopped to talk while smoking. The smell that still hung there was of cigarettes, in one spot a French cigarette, in another a cigar. Though it was still early, not quite ten, a reek of stale seafood swung out from the fishmonger's. To pass a woman from whose skin came light floral scent or musky perfume was a pleasant relief. He paused to read the menu inside the window of the new Indian restaurant The Nawab: Chicken Korma, Lamb Tikka, Chicken Tandoori, Prawn Biryani, Murghe Raja—all the usual stuff, but you might say that about roast beef and fish and chips. It all depended on the cooking. He and Burden could try it for lunch, when they had a lunchtime, when they had a moment. Otherwise, it would be takeaway from the Moonflower Instant Cantonese Cuisine.

The Employment Service Jobcenter was this side of the Kingsbrook Bridge, a little way down Brook Road between the Marks and Spencer foodstore and the Nationwide Building Society. Not a particularly sensitive location, Wexford thought, considering this for the first time. The people who came to sign on would be made to wince at anything that reminded them of burdensome mortgages and repossessed houses and hardly cheered by the sight of shoppers coming out of the doors on the other side with carrier bags full of food specialties they could no longer afford. Still, nobody who had a say in it had thought of that and perhaps the ESJ came there first. He couldn't remember.

A car park at the side—"strictly ESJ staff only"—had access into the High Street. Steps with chipped stone balustrades led up to double doors of aluminum and glass. Inside, the atmosphere smelled stale. It was hard to say what it smelled of, for Wexford could see two notices that forbade smoking ("strictly prohibited") and no one was disobeying. Nor was it the smell of bodies. If he were to be fanciful, and he decided he had better not be, he would have said it was the odor of hopelessness, of defeat.

The large room was divided into two sections: one area, the larger, was the Benefit Office, where you went to give proof of life, proximity, and continuing unemployed status, by signing on; the other offered jobs. On the face of it, an abundance of jobs. One freestanding notice board advertised Receptionists, another Housekeepers and Catering, a third Shops, Managerial, Drivers, Bar Staff, and Miscellaneous. A closer look showed him that in all cases only the experienced need apply, references were required, CVs, qualifications, skills, yet it was obvious that only the young were wanted. None of the cards actually said "Up to age 30," but energy was stressed as a requirement, or a vigorous and youthful outlook.

People sat about on three rows of chairs. All must have been under sixty-five but the older ones looked more. The young ones looked particularly hopeless. The chairs they sat on were a neutral shade of gray and now he noticed there was a color scheme here, a rather unfortunate combination of a buttery-cream shade, navy blue, and this gray. At the end of each row of chairs, on the mottled carpet, stood a plastic houseplant in a plastic Grecian urn. Several doors at the side were marked "private" and one, which seemed to lead to the car park, "strictly private." They had a passion for strictness in here.

Apparently, when you arrived you took a card with a number on it from a kind of ticket machine. When your number and the number of one of the desks came up in red neon you went up and signed your claim. That was the way it looked, a bit like the doctor's. Wexford hesitated between the "jobseekers" counter (another new composite word) and the numbered desks. At each one of these someone stood or sat, discussing complications of his or her claim with a staff member. The gray and navy badge the one nearest to him wore on her blouse proclaimed her as *Ms. I. Pamber, Admin. Officer.*

The next desk was temporarily free. Wexford went up to Ms. W. Stowlap, Admin. Officer, and asked politely if he could see someone in authority. She glanced up, said gruffly, "You have to wait your turn. Don't you know you're supposed to take a card from the machine?"

"This is the only card I have." She had riled him. It was his warrant card he produced as he snapped, "Police."

She was a thin freckled woman with white eyebrows and blushing didn't become her. The pink tide spread to the roots of her pale ginger hair. "Sorry," she said. "You'll want the manager—Mr. Leyton, that is."

While she was away finding him Wexford wondered what the reason could be for all this formality, the "Ms." and "Mr." stuff, the initials instead of Christian names. It seemed out of tune with contemporary attitudes. Not that he minded that, recalling the way Ben and Robin called everyone by first names, even Dr. Crocker, nearly sixty years their senior.

Discreetly, not staring, he surveyed the people who waited. Quite a lot of women, at least half. Before his wife laid into him, calling him a sexist, a chauvinist and antediluvian as well, Mike Burden had been in the habit of saying that if all these married women didn't take the jobs the unemployment figures would be halved. A black man, someone vaguely Southeast Asian, two or three Indians—Kingsmarkham was becoming more cosmopolitan daily. Then, in the back row, he spotted the fat young woman who had been in the waiting room at the Medical Center. Wearing red and green floral leggings and a tight white T-shirt, she slumped in her chair with her legs apart, gazing at the poster that, under a drawing of a gaily colored gas balloon, advertised the "Jobplan Workshop" and advised candidates for it to "give your jobhunting a lift."

It was with unseeing eyes, Wexford thought, that she gazed. She looked as if sledgehammered into apathy, without thoughts, without even resentment, in utter despair. Today Kelly wasn't with her, the little girl who had run along the chairs and torn up magazines. Left with a mother or a neighbor probably, not, he hoped, in one of those toddler farms, where they strapped the infants into pushchairs in front of videos of rampaging monsters. Better that, though, than left alone. Next to her, in fact two empty seats away, a trim handsome girl provided a cruel contrast. Middle-classness stamped her, from her long corn-colored hair, shining clean and cut as evenly as a curtain hem, her white shirt and blue denim skirt, to the brown loafers she wore. Another Melanie Akande, Wexford thought, a new graduate who had found a degree doesn't automatically confer a job . . .

"Can I help you?"

He turned around. The man was about forty, red-faced, black-haired, with big features, the kind who looks as if his blood pressure would be high. To his gray tweed sports jacket was pinned the badge with his name and status: Mr. C. Leyton, Manager. He had a harsh grating voice, an accent from somewhere north of the Trent.

"Do you want to go somewhere private?"

Leyton asked the question as if expecting the answer "no" or "no, don't bother."

"Yes," said Wexford.

"What's all this about then?" He asked it over his shoulder as he led Wexford past the counter and the New Claims booths.

"It can wait till we're in your somewhere private."

Leyton shrugged. The heavyset bullet-headed man who stood outside the door moved off as they approached. The Benefit Office was more in need of a security guard than most banks and it was the regular haunt of members of the uniformed branch. Desperation, paranoia and indignation, resentment, fear and humiliation all breed violence. Most people who came here were either angry or afraid.

Rather late in the day the manager said, "I'm Cyril Leyton." He closed the door behind them. "What's the trouble?"

"I hope there won't be any. I want you to tell me if a certain—er, claimant came here on Tuesday to see one of your new claims advisers. Tuesday, July the sixth, at two-thirty P.M."

Leyton curled his lip and put up his eyebrows. His expression would have been appropriate for the Head of MI5 when asked by some minion, a cleaner or driver perhaps, for access to Top Secret papers.

"I don't want documentation," said Wexford impatiently. "I only want to know if she came here. And I'd like to talk to the new claims adviser she saw."

"Well, I . . ."

"Mr. Leyton, this is a police investigation. I suppose you know I could get a warrant in a couple of hours. Is there any point in delaying things?"

"What's her name?"

"Melanie Akande. A-K-A-N-D-E."

"If she came on Tuesday," said Leyton grudgingly, "it should be on the computer by now. She would have met with either Miss Bystock or Mr. Stanton. Just wait a minute, will you?"

His manner was unfortunate, cold, sour, rebarbative. Wexford guessed that the greatest pleasure he got out of life was derived from putting spokes in wheels. What effect must he have on claimants? Perhaps he never saw them, perhaps he was too "high up" (as Laurette Akande put it) for that.

The room was all gray, lined with filing cabinets. There was a gray chair like those the claimants sat on, a small gray metal desk and on it a gray telephone. The view from the window seemed a riot of color, though it was only of the shoppers' pickup bay at the back of Marks and Spencers. Cyril Leyton came in, holding a millboard with papers attached to it by an elastic band.

"Your Miss Akande came in for her appointment at two-thirty and brought back her ES 461. That's the form required by . . ."

"I know what it is," Wexford said.

"Right. The NCA she saw—that is, new claims adviser—was Miss Bystock, but you can't talk to her, she's off sick." Leyton unbent an inch. "One of these viruses."

"If she's off sick how do you know it was Miss Bystock Melanie Akande saw and not Mr. Stanton?"

"Come on. Her initials are on the claim. See?"

Ostentatiously covering up everything but the bottom right-hand corner of the sheet, Leyton showed Wexford the penciled initials: A.B.

"Did anyone else see her? Any of the other NCAs? The administration officers?"

"Not that I know of. Why would they?"

Wexford said suddenly, with extreme sharpness, "Don't ask me. It doesn't help to be obstructive."

Leyton's mouth opened but no sound came.

"Mr. Leyton, it is an offense to obstruct the police in their duties. Did you know that? Melanie Akande is missing from home. She hasn't been seen since she left this building. This is a very serious matter. I suppose you read the newspapers? You watch television? You know what happens in the world we live in? Have you some reason for jeopardizing this inquiry?"

The man went a darker red. He said slowly, "I didn't know. I'd have been—well, I had no idea."

"You mean that what I've been treated to is your normal manner?"

Leyton said nothing. Then he seemed to take hold of himself.

"I'm sorry. I'm under a lot of pressure here. Has—has something happened to her? This woman?"

"That's what I'm trying to find out." Wexford showed him the photograph. "Will you ask your staff, please?"

This time he waited outside that stuffy gray room. He thought of the hymn line: "Frail children of dust . . ." That room was like a cell spun and carved out of dust. He read the other posters, the one advocating work trials, whatever they were, and the one that asked employers: "Do you always choose the right person to fill your vacancy?" He decided to fill his own vacancy by reading one of the leaflets that lay about.

It was curiously apposite. "Be Alert," it said. "Be safe when jobseeking." Inside he read, "DO: tell a friend or relative where you are going and what time you expect to be back . . . arrange to be collected from the interview if it takes place outside working hours . . . find out as much as you can about the company before the interview, especially if there are no details in the job advert . . . make sure that the interview takes place at the employer's premises or, if not, in a public place. DON'T: apply for a job that seems to offer too much money for very little work . . . agree to continue the interview over drinks or a meal, even if it seems to be going very well . . . let the interviewer steer the conversation toward personal subjects that have nothing to do with the job . . . accept a lift home from the interviewer . . .

Melanie hadn't been offered a job, she hadn't been sent for an interview—or had she? Cyril Leyton came back with the Admin. Officer labeled Ms. I. Pamber, a dark-haired pretty girl with dazzling blue eyes, in her late twenties, wearing a gray skirt and pink shirt. None of the staff wore jeans, Wexford had noticed, everyone was dressed in a neat, rather outdated way.

"I saw her, this girl you're looking for."

Wexford nodded. "Did you speak to her?"

"Oh, no. I'd no call to. I was on the counter. I just saw her go up and talk to Annette—er, Miss Bystock."

"Can you remember what time that was?"

"Well, her appointment was for two-thirty and no one's allowed more than twenty minutes. I suppose it must have been twenty to three, something like that."

"If she was able to see Miss Bystock on time. Was she? Or did she have to wait half an hour?"

"No, she couldn't have done. A claims adviser's last appointment is at three-thirty, and I know Annette had three to see after her."

So Laurette Akande had been wrong about that. He asked Leyton for Annette Bystock's address. While the manager was away finding it, he said, "Did you see her leave the building? Go out through those doors?"

"I just saw her talking to Annette."

"Thank you for your help, Miss Pamber. By the way, tell me something, in these days of universal first names, why do you all have Ms. or Mr. and your surname and an initial on your name tags? It seems very formal."

"Oh, it's not that," she said. She had a charming manner, he thought, warm and just a touch flirtatious. "Actually, I'm Ingrid. No one calls me Ms. Pamber, not anyone. But they say it's for our protection."

She looked up at him through long dark eyelashes. Her eyes were the bluest he had ever seen, the blue of a gentian or a Delft plate or a star sapphire.

"I don't follow."

"Well, most clients are okay, I mean they're nice, most of them. But you do get some nuts—crazy people, you know? I mean, we had someone in here threw acid at Cyril—Mr. Leyton, that is. He didn't hit him but he had a go. Don't you remember?"

Vaguely, Wexford did, though he'd been on leave at the time.

"Hopefully, there's very few that would do that. But if we had our full names on our tags, like 'Ingrid Pamber,' say, they could look us up in the phone book and—well, you might get someone who thought he was in love with you or someone—and that's more likely—who hated you. You know, we've got jobs and they haven't, that's what it's about."

Wexford wondered how many "I. Pambers" there were in the Kingsmarkham and District telephone directory and guessed at just one. Still, as a safety measure keeping first names a secret was wise. The thought came to him that quite a lot of people might fancy themselves in love with Ingrid Pamber. Another poster caught his eye, this one warning those seeking jobs not to pay anyone money for finding them work. The system seemed open to many abuses.

With Annette Bystock's address in his pocket, he went out and down the steps. In the half hour since he had gone in there several young men had arrived to seat themselves on the stone balustrades, two of them smoking, the others staring vacantly at nothing. They took no notice of him. Lying on the pavement where someone, perhaps one of them, had discarded it was an ES 461, the highly colored questionnaire form. It was open at page three and when Wexford bent to pick it up he saw that the egregious question 4—"If you have not worked for the past 12 months, how have you spent your time?"—had been answered. Carefully printed in the allotted space was the single word "Wanking."

That made him laugh. He began trying to retrace what might have been Melanie Akande's footsteps on leaving the ESJ. According to Ingrid Pamber, she would have been in plenty of time for the 3:15 bus to Myringham, no more than five minutes' walk away.

Wexford timed himself to the nearest bus stop. These periods of time were nearly always shorter than you anticipated and he found it took him, not five minutes, but three. However, there was no earlier bus she could have caught. He studied the timetable in its frame, somewhat vandalized, with a diagonal crack across the glass, but still readable. The buses went once an hour, on the first quarter. She would have had to wait at least twenty minutes.

It was during that sort of enforced waiting, he thought, that women accepted lifts. Would she have done that? He must ask the parents if she ever, for instance, hitched lifts. Wait, though, until Vine's report came in and there was some information from the Myringham end. Meanwhile, had anyone in the neighborhood of this bus stop seen anything?

In the dry cleaner's he drew a blank. You couldn't see the street from the interior of the wineshop. Its windows were too densely stacked with bottles and cans. He went into Grover's the newsagents. They were his newsagents, the shop that supplied his daily paper and had done for years. As soon as she saw him the woman behind the counter began apologizing for the recent late deliveries. Wexford cut her short, said he hadn't noticed, and anyway he didn't expect some schoolboy or schoolgirl to get up at the crack of dawn to bring his *Independent* by seven-thirty. He showed her the photograph.

Melanie Akande's being black was to their advantage. In a place where there were very few black people, she was known, remembered, even by those who had never spoken to her. Dinny Lawson, the newsagent, knew her by sight but, as far as she knew, Melanie had never been into the shop. As to bus queues, she sometimes noticed them and she sometimes didn't. It was Tuesday afternoon Wexford was talking about? One thing she could tell him was that no one, black or white, got on the 3:15 to Myringham bus, no one at all.

"How can you be so sure?"

"I'll tell you. My husband said to me, it must have been Saturday or Sunday, he said it was a wonder they went on running that bus in the afternoons on account of no one went on it. Mornings, yes, specially the eight-fifteen and the nine-fifteen, and the ones that come back in the evening, they're busy. So I said, I'll keep an eye open and see. Well, we've kept the shop door open all day this week, it's been so hot, and I could see without even going to the door. And he was right, it's a fact, no one's got on the two-fifteen, the three-fifteen, or the four-fifteen Monday, Tuesday, or yesterday. My husband said to have five pounds on it and was I glad I didn't take him up on that . . ."

So she had disappeared somewhere between the Benefit Office and the bus stop. No, "disappeared" was too strong a word—yet. No matter what she told her parents, perhaps she had never intended to take that bus. Perhaps she had arranged to meet someone as soon as her appointment with the new claims adviser was over.

In that case, was there a chance she had mentioned this to Annette Bystock? For all he knew, Annette Bystock might be one of those warm friendly people whose effect on others is to invite confidences, and confidences that have no apparent connection with the matter in hand. It was quite possible Annette had asked her if she'd be available for an interview that day and Melanie had said no, she was going to meet her boyfriend . . .

Or there had been no meeting with a boyfriend, no confidences, nothing to confide, and Melanie had accepted a lift to Myringham from a stranger. After all, Dinny Lawson hadn't said there had been no one in the vicinity of the bus stop all afternoon, only that she had seen nobody get on the bus when it came.

Dora Wexford had got into the habit of preparing large and quite elaborate quantities of food for her daughter and her daughter's family when they came to meals. Her husband had pointed out to her that though Neil and Sylvia were unemployed, they weren't poverty-stricken, they weren't on the breadline, but this had little effect. He came home that evening just in time to share in the servings of carrot and orange soup before a main course of braised lambs' kidneys, spinach and ricotta cheese in filo pastry, new potatoes, and French beans. Dessert spoons on the table indicated the arrival later of that rarity, that luxury that never happened when the two of them were alone, a pudding.

Pale weedy Neil ate hugely, as if for comfort. As Wexford joined them and sat down, he was describing to his mother-in-law his abortive visit to the Benefit Office. No payments could be made to him because, before losing his work, he had been self-employed.

"What difference does that make?" Wexford asked.

"Oh," he explained quite carefully. "As a self-employed person I didn't pay Class One National Insurance contributions during the two tax years prior to the tax year in which I'm making my claim."

"But you paid them?"

"Oh, I paid them but in another class. The adviser explained that too."

"Who was it?" Wexford said. "Ms. Bystock or Mr. Stanton?"

Neil goggled at him. "How do *you* know?"

Enigmatically, "I have my reasons." Wexford relented. "I was there today about something else."

"It was Stanton," Neil said.

Wexford wondered suddenly why Sylvia was looking so smug. Anxious not to put on weight, she had eaten the kidneys, refused the pastry, and had now laid her knife and fork precisely down diagonally across her plate. A little smile lifted the corners of her mouth. One after the other, Ben and Robin asked for more potatoes.

"You promise to eat every bit then."

"*Problem yok,*" said Robin.

"So what are you going to do? They must do something for you."

"Sylvia has to claim, if you can believe it. She was only parttime but she got in just enough hours to claim, so she's doing it for herself and me and the boys."

Having told Ben to chew his food properly and not swallow in lumps, Sylvia said with undisguised triumph, "I sign on every other Tuesday. It's A to K on Tuesdays, L to R on Wednesdays, and S to Z on Thursdays. I get benefit for all of us. *And* they'll pay the mortgage. Neil hates me doing it, don't you, Neil? He'd rather I went out cleaning."

"That isn't true."

"It is true. I won't pretend I don't enjoy it, because I do. How d'you think I feel after years of my husband telling me first that I wasn't capable of earning and then when I was, that what I earned wasn't worth the trouble of working, it'd all go in tax."

"I never said any of that."

"It feels *great,*" Sylvia said, ignoring him. "The whole lot of them depend on *me* now. All the money, quite a lot of it, will be paid to me personally. So much for sexism, so much for chau-vinism . . ."

"They won't pay the mortgage," Neil interrupted her. "Almost everything you say is wildly inaccurate. They'll pay the *interest* on the mortgage and they're putting a ceiling on the amount of mort-gage they'll pay up to. We shall put the house on the market."

"We shall not."

"Of course we shall. We have no option. We shall sell it and buy a semi in Mansfield Road—if we're lucky. That looks like Eve's Pudding, Dora, one of my favorites. You don't improve the situation, Sylvia, by telling a pack of lies as a vindication of the rights of women."

Ben said, "You know men have Adam's apples, don't you?"

Silently blessing him for the distraction, Wexford said yes, he did know, he supposed everyone knew.

"Yes, well, d'you know why they're called that? I bet you don't. It's because when the snake gave Eve the apple she could swallow it all right but a lump of it stuck in Adam's throat and that's why men have got that bit sticking out . . ."

"If that story isn't rank sexism, I don't know what is. Are you ever going to eat up those potatoes, Robin?"

"*No pasa nada.*"

"I don't know what that means," said Sylvia crossly.

"Come on, Mum. Can't you guess?"

Refusing pudding and coffee, Wexford went out into the hall to phone Detective Sergeant Vine.

It had taken Barry Vine a long time to find Euan Sinclair. He had only just got back from London. After he had eaten he was going to write his report. It would be on Wexford's desk by nine in the morning.

"Give me a résumé now," said Wexford.

"I didn't find the girl."

Vine had gone first to the address provided by Dr. Akande. It was a fairly large Victorian house in the East End of London, occupied by three generations of the Sinclair and Lafay families. An old grandmother, though domiciled there for thirty years, spoke only a version of the patois. Three of her daughters also lived in the house and four of their children, though not Euan. He had moved out some three months earlier.

Deeply distrustful of the police, the women spoke to him with a kind of laconic suspicion. Euan's mother Claudine, who occupied the ground floor with her partner and father of her two younger children, a man called Samuel Lafay, the brother incidentally of the elder sister's ex-husband . . .

"Oh, get on with it," Wexford said.

It was clear that Vine was expounding with relish on the complexities of this intricate family. He seemed to have enjoyed his day. After asking rhetorically why she should tell him anything about her son, who was a good, clean-living, and honorable man, an intellectual, Claudine Sinclair or Lafay had sent him to a council flat in Whitechapel. This turned out to be the home of a girl called Joan-Anne, mother of Euan Sinclair's daughter. Joan-Anne never wanted to see Euan again, if he came into a million she wouldn't accept a penny of it in child support for Tasha, if he went on his knees to her she wouldn't, she had a good man now who had never been without so much as a day's work in his life. She gave Vine an address in Shadwell, home of Sheena ("poor cow, lets him walk all over her") who was the mother of Euan's son.

Euan had gone to sign on, Sheena told him. Thursday was his day. After signing on he usually went for a drink with some friends, but he'd turn up sometime, she couldn't really say when. No, Vine couldn't wait for him, she couldn't have that. The idea made her nervous, Vine could see, probably on account of the neighbors. The neighbors would have identified him in the mysterious way some people can always spot a policeman and they'd make a note of how many hours Vine spent in Sheena's flat. All this time Euan's son was screaming his head off in the next room. Sheena went to attend to him and came back with a handsome angry boy who already looked too big for his diminutive mother to carry.

"Oh, stop your noise, Scott, stop your noise," she said ineffectually, over and over. Scott roared at her and roared at the visitor. Vine left and went back at four.

Sheena and her son were still alone. Scott was still intermittently roaring. No, Euan hadn't been back. Phone her? What did he mean, phone her? Why would he? Vine gave up. Sheena gave Scott a bag of salt and vinegar crisps and stuck him in front of a video of what appeared to be *Miami Vice*. When he was quiet, Vine asked her about Melanie Akande but it was plain Sheena had never heard of her. While Vine probed a bit, Euan Sinclair came in.

Tall, handsome, very thin, Euan had the sort of looks that reminded Vine of Linford Christie. His hair was very short, a week's growth, Vine guessed, after a total shave. He walked with the peculiar grace of the young black man, all movement from the hips, the torso erect and still. But it was his voice that surprised Vine. Not Creole English, one generation removed, not East End Cockney, not Estuary, but nearer Public School.

Wexford said, half joking, half serious, "So you're a snob as well as a racist, Barry."

Vine didn't deny it. He said he'd had the impression Euan Sinclair had taught himself to talk like that for some unknown reasons of policy. It suddenly struck him—for the first time—that Euan might deny knowledge of Melanie in Sheena's presence.

"That would have been the first thing I'd have thought of," said Wexford.

"He didn't, though. That was the funny thing. I could see it was all news to her and she didn't like it. He couldn't have cared less."

He'd seen Melanie the previous week. At the Myringham graduation ceremonies. They had a talk and she agreed to meet him the following Tuesday in Myringham. By this time Sheena was staring at him with a kind of horror. Melanie was going to Laurel Tucker's party, Euan said, and he could come too.

Vine asked where they were meeting and Euan named a pub in

Myringham. At around four. The Wig and Ribbon in the High Street opened from eleven A.M. till eleven P.M. She hadn't turned up, though Euan waited till five-thirty. At this point he saw a man he knew, another alumnus of Myringham University. The two of them got together, went to another pub and then another, and Euan spent the night sleeping on the floor in this man's room.

Sheena could contain herself no longer. "You told me you were at your grandma's."

He said to her, in the sort of voice a man uses to say it's raining, "I lied."

Sheena stalked to the door. Just before it closed behind her Euan called out, "You'd better not leave me alone with him. I'm no baby-minder. That's women's work, right?"

"I'll check it out with this bloke he says he met," said Vine, "but I believe him. He gave me the fellow's name and address without turning a hair."

"It looks as if Melanie never reached Myringham," Wexford said. "Something happened to deflect her in Kingsmarkham High Street. Somewhere on about two hundred yards of pavement. We have to find out what it was."

four

The Tucker family, Laurel and Glenda Tucker, their father and stepmother, had little that was new to offer. They were plainly unwilling "to get mixed up in anything." It was true that Laurel had expected Melanie on the late afternoon of July the sixth and had been displeased when it was clear she wasn't coming. But she hadn't been all that *surprised*. After all, they had quarreled.

The detective sergeant from Myringham who had been asking the questions said, "What was that about then?"

Laurel had been at the graduation ceremony, witnessed the meeting between Melanie and Euan Sinclair, and seen the two of them go off together. Melanie phoned her the next day, said she was thinking of getting back with Euan, he was lonely, there had been no one in his life since they split up, and she'd told him she'd bring him to Laurel's party on Tuesday. I don't want him, Laurel said, I don't like him, I never did. I'm not surprised he hasn't been seeing anyone else—who'd want him? Melanie said if Euan couldn't come to the party she wasn't coming either, and they had a row.

"She did tell her parents she was going to this party," Burden said to Wexford. "She was going to the Tucker house first and then on to this party."

"Well, she wouldn't tell them she had a date with this Euan, would she? They can't stand him, haven't got a good word to say for him. Mother's something of a formidable woman, I'd almost say she'd be capable of locking a daughter up. By this time Melanie had obviously decided she wasn't going to the party. She was going to stick to what she'd said and not go if Euan wasn't also welcome. She was going to meet Euan in the Wig and Ribbon and there's not much doubt she meant to stay with him, spend the night with him . . ."

"Yes, but where? Not at this Sheena's place. People that age don't hire hotel rooms, do they?"

Wexford laughed. "Not if they're living on the I.S. they don't."

"The what?"

"Income Support. If Melanie thought about that aspect at all I expect she thought they'd go to Euan's mother's place in Bow. She'd very likely been there before. And the next day she'd come home."

"Amazing, isn't it?" said Burden, looking down his nose. "They've got no jobs, they're living on what-d'you-call-it, I.S., and they still splash out on drinks and dates with girls and God knows what for train fares."

"It doesn't matter much, Mike, because we know she didn't go to London. She didn't even go to Myringham. She didn't meet Euan because Euan"—Wexford had another look at Vine's latest report—"spent the evening with someone called John Varcava in the Wig and Ribbon, the Wild Goose, and Silk's Club before returning to Varcava's rented room in Myringham at three in the morning. It's all confirmed by a barman, a barmaid, the manager of Silk's, and Varcava's landlady, who nearly came to blows with Varcava and Euan Sinclair over the mayhem they were making in her house in the small hours."

"So what happened to Melanie in those few minutes after she left the unemployment place? The last person she saw, according to you, was this Annette Bystock, the new claims adviser. Is there any point in talking to her?"

"She was off sick," said Wexford. "She may be back at work by now, though people don't usually go back on a Friday, they take the whole week. But what are we saying, Mike? That Melanie Akande confided the details of some secret appointment to a complete stranger? A woman she'd talked to for fifteen minutes and talked to surely only about filling in a form and job prospects? Come to that, what secret appointment? She'd already got one of those with Euan. Now she's having another with some other chap just an hour before she meets Euan?"

Burden shrugged. "Well, you said all that. I didn't. My imagination hasn't traveled that far. All I'm saying is, we ought to talk to Annette Bystock, solely on the grounds that she was the last person to see Melanie . . ." He hesitated.

"You were going to say 'alive,' weren't you?"

There but for the grace of God go I, was not a reflection Michael Burden was ever likely to quote. He neither said it to himself when he saw famine victims on television, nor if he passed the half-dozen or so homeless who slept on the street in Myringham. He didn't say it now, entering the Benefit Office and contemplating the jobless who sat about waiting on the gray chairs.

That he wasn't among them had nothing to do with God's grace in his opinion, and everything to do with his own industry, determination, and hard work. He was one of those who ask the unemployed why they don't get a job and the homeless why they don't find a place to live. If he had been in Paris in the 1780s he would have told the starving who begged for bread to eat cake. Now, wearing his immaculate beige trousers and new jacket of beige linen with a navy fleck—one thing, as Wexford sometimes said, no one would have taken him for a policeman—he contemplated the unemployed and reflected on what a hideous garment the shellsuit was. Marginally worse than the tracksuit. It had never occurred to him that these clothes are cheap, warm in cold weather and cool in hot, easy to wash, resistant to creases, and very comfortable, and he didn't consider the matter now. He turned his attention to the administrative assistants behind their desks, deciding which one he should approach.

Jenny Burden said of her husband that if he had a choice, he would always inquire of a man rather than a woman, ask a man the way somewhere, go up to a male assistant in a shop, take the seat in a train next to a man. He hadn't liked that, he said it made him sound homosexual, but that wasn't what she meant at all. In the Benefit Office he had a choice, for behind the desks sat a man and three women. The man, however, had a brown skin and wore a label with the name Mr. O. Messaoud. Burden, who hotly denied that he was a racist in any degree, nevertheless rejected Osman Messaoud on the grounds (of which he was only subliminally aware) of his skin color and his name, and went up to freckled, ginger-haired Wendy Stowlap. She happened to be briefly free and this was the reason Burden would have given for choosing her.

"Is it about that girl who's missing?" she asked after he had inquired for Annette Bystock.

"Just routine inquiries," said Burden blandly. "Is Miss Bystock back yet?"

"She's still off sick."

He turned away, almost colliding with Wendy Stowlap's next client, a big heavy woman in a red shellsuit. She smelled powerfully of cigarettes. They can always afford to smoke, Burden said to himself. Two of the boys sitting on the stone balustrade were smoking, their feet dabbling in a litter of ash and cigarette ends. Burden gave them a long severe look, drawing his brows together. His eyes lingered particularly on the black boy with the Rastafarian hair, a mountainous crest of matted dreadlocks, on top of which rested a woolly cap, knitted in concentric circles of color. It was the sort of hat he called a tam-o'-shanter, as his father would have done and his grandfather before him.

The boys took absolutely no notice of him. It was as if his body was transparent and their eyes penetrated it to the stonework behind him, the pavement, the corner where Brook Road turned into the High Street. They made him feel invisible. With an angry shrug he went back to the car he had parked in the "strictly private" area for ESJ staff only.

The address Wexford had given him was in south Kingsmarkham. It was formerly one of the best parts of the town, where in the late nineteenth century the most prosperous of its citizens had built themselves large houses, each standing in an acre or two of garden. Most of them were still there but partitioned now, and their gardens "infilled" with new houses and rows of garages. Ladyhall Gardens had come in for this treatment, but the Victorian relics were smaller and each one was divided into two or three flats.

Someone had pretentiously named number 15 Ladyhall Court.

It was a gabled house on two floors, built of the "white" brick that was the fashionable building material here in the 1890s. A screen of copper sycamores hid much of the ground floor from the road. Burden guessed there were two flats on each floor, the two at the rear accessible from a side door. Above the bell for the upper floor a card read: John and Edwina Harris, and above the bell for the lower flat: Ms. A. Bystock.

When there was no answer from Flat 1, he rang the Harrises' bell. No answer there either. The front door had a lock at the top, a lock in the middle, and a brass knob, now tarnished black. On the off chance Burden tried the handle and to his surprise—and disapproval—it came open.

He found himself in a hallway with plaster scrollwork on the ceiling and uncompromisingly modern vinyl tiles on the floor. The staircase had an iron balustrade and gray marble steps. There was only one door, dark green with the figure 1 painted on it in white. The knocker was brass and so was the knob, but polished brass, and the bell push bright as gold.

Burden rang the bell, waited. She might be in bed. If she was ill she might well be. He listened for sounds of movement, for footsteps or the creak of a floorboard. He rang the bell again. The little knocker was almost useless, it made a frenzied clack-clack, like a child trying to make its small voice heard.

Probably she was simply not answering the bell. If he was ill in bed, alone in the house, and some unexpected caller rang the bell, he wouldn't answer it. There might be someone looking after her, of course, some neighbor perhaps, and that person would have a key.

He knelt down and looked through the letter box. Inside it seemed quite dark, darker than in the corridor. Gradually, through the small open rectangle, he made out a shadowy hallway with red fitted carpet, a small console table, dried flowers in a little gilded basket.

He stood up, rang the bell again, banged on the baby knocker, squatted down, and called her name through the aperture: "Miss Bystock!" and, louder, "Miss Bystock! Are you at home?"

For one last time he called her name and then he went out of the house and round the side, pushing aside the sycamore branches with their leathery leaves that made everything so dark. This little window would be the kitchen, this one the bathroom. No sycamores here, only waist-high goldenrod on either side of a concrete drive. Behind the last window by the side door the curtains were closed. For some reason he looked behind him, the way we do when we think we are being watched. On the opposite side of the street, in a 1900-ish house with a short front garden, someone was looking at him from an upstairs window. A face that looked as old as the house, crinkled, frowning, glaring.

Burden turned back to the window. He thought the drawn curtains a bit strange. How ill was she? Ill enough to need a darkened room to sleep in mid-morning? The thought came to him that perhaps she wasn't ill at all, that she was skiving off work and had gone out somewhere.

He wouldn't have been surprised if the old watcher at the window had come downstairs and crossed the road and tapped him on the shoulder. In the expectation of this he turned round once more. But the face was still there, its expression unchanged, and it was perfectly still, so much so that for a moment Burden asked himself if this was a real person or some sort of facsimile, a wooden cutout of a glaring and evil-countenanced observer, placed there by the occupier as some people keep a painted chipboard cat in their gardens to frighten real ones.

But this was nonsense. He squatted down and tried to see between the curtains but the gap was infinitesimal, the merest line. In defiance of what the watcher over the way might think or do, he knelt down on the concrete paving and tried to look under the hem of the curtains. Here was a gap of perhaps half an inch between curtain hem and lower window frame.

It was dim in there. He couldn't see much. At first he could see scarcely anything. Then, as his eyes grew accustomed to the subfusc interior of the room, he made out the edge of a table, possibly a dressing table, the polished wooden foot of something on blue carpet, a segment of flowered material touching the floor. And a hand. A hand, which hung down against those printed lilies and roses, a white immobile hand, the fingers extended.

It must be made of china, of plaster, of plastic. It couldn't be real. Or it could be real and she asleep. What sort of sleep was maintained through all that shouting? Almost involuntarily, forgetting possible watchers, he drummed on the glass with his knuckles. The hand didn't move. The hand's owner didn't leap up with a cry.

Burden ran back into the house. Why had he never learned how to pick a lock? Opening this one would be child's play to a lot of the men and women he encountered in a day's work. Doors in the movies cave in with ease at the pressure of a shoulder. It always made him laugh angrily when he saw actors on television run up against stout doors and send them crashing in at one shove. It was so silent too, the way they did it. He knew his own efforts would be noisy and very likely bring the neighbors. But it couldn't be helped.

He ran up against the door, applying his shoulder. It juddered and creaked but his action hurt him more than it hurt the door. He rubbed his shoulder, took a deep breath, and hurled himself at it— once and again and once more. This time he kicked it, more of a

punch with his foot, and the door groaned. Another foot-punch—
he hadn't kicked like that since on the soccer field at school—and
the door split and flew open. He stepped over the broken wood and
paused to get his breath.

The hallway was tiny. It turned the corner and became a passage. All five doors were shut. Burden went down it, guessed at the
bedroom door, opened it and found a broom cupboard. Next to it
must be the bedroom, its door not quite closed, half an inch ajar.
First taking a deep breath, he pushed it open.

She lay as if asleep, her head on the pillow, her face turned
into it and hidden by a mass of dark curly hair. One shoulder was
bare, the other and the rest of her body covered by the bedclothes
and the flowered quilt. From the naked shoulder extended her
rather plump white arm with the hand he had seen, trailing almost
to the floor.

He touched nothing, not the curtains, not the bedclothes, not
that buried head, nothing but the hanging hand. One finger he put
out to feel it, the back of it above the knuckles. It was stiffening as
if frozen and as cold as ice.

five

They filled the place, it was so small; the pathologist, the photographers, the scene-of-crimes officers, everyone indispensable, each with a specific task. Once the windows had been photographed and the curtains drawn back it was better, and when the body was taken away most of them went with it. Wexford lifted the lower sash in the bay and watched the van bearing Annette Bystock's remains disappear in the direction of the mortuary.

There would have to be formal identification but he had identified her from the passport he found in a dressing table drawer. The passport was a newish one, in the dark red and gold binding of the European Community, issued just over twelve months earlier. It gave the holder's name as Bystock, Annette Rosemary, her status as a British Citizen, and her date of birth, 22.11.54. The photograph was plainly of the dead woman, clearly identifiable, in spite of the effects on her face of strangulation, the swelling, the cyanosis, the tongue protruding between the teeth. Her eyes were the same. She had stared into the camera with almost the same degree of horrified apprehension as she had looked into her killer's face.

They were round dark eyes. Her hair was dark and fuzzy, a dense bush of it which must have made a wide frame for her face unless she had somehow confined it. When Burden found her she had been wearing a pink nightdress patterned with white flowers. Across the quilt had lain a white wool cardigan that had evidently done duty as a bedjacket. There were no rings on the hands, no earrings in her ears. On the left-hand bedside cabinet were her watch, gold with a black strap, a gold ring with a red stone, probably a ruby, that looked valuable, a comb, and a half-empty bottle of aspirins; on the right-hand cabinet were a novel by Danielle Steel in paperback, a glass of water, a packet of throat pastilles, and a Yale key.

A bed lamp stood on each cabinet, each one a simple white vase-shaped base with a pleated blue shade. The one on the right of the bed, farthest from the door, was intact. The other had a chip out of its base and its cord torn from the base. This cord, with plug still attached, had gone now, had been removed in a plastic bag by DC Pemberton, but when they first came into the bedroom it had been lying on the floor within inches of Annette Bystock's hanging hand.

"She's been dead at least thirty-six hours," Sir Hilary Tremlett, the pathologist, had said to Wexford. "I'll be able to tell you more precisely when I've had a closer look. Let me see, it's Friday, isn't it? On the face of it, I'd say she died on Wednesday night, certainly before midnight on Wednesday."

He left before the van bearing the body was out of sight. Wexford closed the bedroom door.

"A confident killer," he said. "An experienced killer, I'd say. He must have been very sure of himself. He didn't bother to bring a weapon with him, he was sure he'd find one at hand. Everyone has electric leads in their home, but if by chance he couldn't find a suitable one, everyone has knives, heavy objects, hammers."

Burden nodded. "Or he was familiar with the place. He knew what was on offer."

"Must it be a he? Or are you just being politically incorrect?"

Burden grinned. "Old Tremlett may be able to help us there. I can't somehow imagine a woman breaking into a place and tearing a lead out of a lamp to strangle someone."

"You're well known for having quaint ideas about women," said Wexford. "He or she didn't break in, though, did they?"

"There's no sign of a break-in. They were let in or they had a key."

"Someone she knew, then?" Wexford shrugged. "How's this for a scenario? She started to feel ill on Tuesday evening, went to bed, felt worse in the morning, so she phoned the Benefit Office to say she wasn't coming in and then she phoned a friend or a neighbor and asked them to fetch something in for her. Look at this."

Burden followed him into the kitchen. It was too small to contain a table but on the narrow counter, on the left side, was a grocer's cardboard box, twelve inches by nine and about nine inches high. The items inside seemed untouched. On top of them lay a supermarket printout, dated July 8. Beneath it were a packet of cornflakes, two small pots of strawberry yogurt, a carton of milk, a small wholemeal loaf wrapped in tissue paper, a packet of presliced Cheddar cheese, and a grapefruit.

"The friend that was shopping for her brought that in yesterday," Wexford said. "If the friend works, the likelihood is it was yesterday evening . . . Yes, Chepstow, what is it?"

The fingerprint man said, "I haven't done in here yet, sir."

"We'll clear out of your way then."

"There's a key on the bedside table. Why not give the friend a key?" Burden asked as they moved into Annette Bystock's living room. "The front door was unlocked when I got here. Did she leave her own front door on the latch? Why do that in this day and age?" If Wexford winced Burden didn't notice. "It's just inviting a burglar."

"She couldn't give the friend a key if the friend wasn't there, Mike. Man hasn't yet mastered the technique of sending solid objects by phone, radio, or satellite transmission. If she didn't want to get out of bed to let him or her in she could only leave the door on the latch. Once the friend had come she could hand over a key."

"But someone else came in while the door was on the latch?"

"It looks like it."

"We have to find the friend," said Burden.

"Yes, I'm wondering if it was a neighbor or if she only made one phone call on Wednesday morning, if she killed two birds with one stone, so to speak. After all, Mike, who are our friends? Mainly, the people we were at school with or trained with or met at work. I think it's very likely the Good Samaritan who brought the yogurt and grapefruit works at the Benefit Office."

"Karen and Barry are doing the neighbors now, but most of them are at work."

Wexford had been standing at the window, but now he turned around and surveyed the room. He looked at Annette Bystock's pictures on the wall, a bland and innocuous pen-and-ink drawing of a windmill, a bright watercolor of a rainbow over green hills; at her framed photographs, one in black and white of a girl of about three in a frilly dress and white socks, one of a couple in a suburban garden, the woman with her hair in sausage curls, her dress full-skirted and tight-waisted, the man in floppy gray flannels and pullover. Her mother as a child, Wexford guessed. Her parents newly married.

The furniture was a three-piece suite, a lacquered coffee table, a useless-looking two-tiered table, a bookcase that contained few books and the middle shelves of which were used to display china animals. On the bottom shelf were perhaps twenty compact disks and the same number of cassettes. The red hall carpet extended to cover the floor of this room but otherwise the color scheme was unexciting, mostly beige and brown. Her parents probably had a beige living room and a blue bedroom. There was nothing to show that Annette had been comparatively young, not yet forty, no break-away from convention, nothing minimally adventurous.

"Where's the television?" Wexford asked. "Where's the VCR? No radio, no cassette player, no CD player? None of those?"

"That's funny. Maybe she didn't have them, maybe she was some sort of fundamentalist who didn't believe in those things. No, but wait a minute, she had CDs . . . See that table there? The one with the two tiers. Don't you reckon there's been a TV on the top and a VCR underneath?"

The marks were clearly visible, a rectangle of dust in the polished surface above and a slightly larger one below.

"It looks as if her invitation to the burglar was accepted," said Wexford. "I wonder what else she had. A computer maybe? A microwave in the kitchen? Though it's hard to say where it would have fitted in."

"She was killed for *that?*"

"I doubt it. If our perpetrator killed her for what she had in the flat, he'd have taken her watch and her ring. That ring looks valuable to me."

"Or it could be that the TV and the VCR have gone off somewhere to be repaired."

"Oh, sure, it could be. All sorts of things could be. There's been one single case recorded of successful self-strangulation, so she might be the second one. And she sold the best part of her consumer goods first to pay for her funeral. Come *on*, Mike."

Returning to the bedroom, now free for any kind of arbitrary examination, Wexford opened the cupboard door and, without comment, though Burden was behind him, eyed the garments inside. Two pairs of jeans, a pair of cords, cotton loons, several not very short mini-skirts size twelve and two longer skirts size fourteen, which seemed to indicate that Annette had recently put on weight. Folded sweaters on the shelves, blouses, all of them ordinary, safe, quiet. Behind the other door hung a navy winter coat, beige raincoat, two jackets, one dark red, one black. Had she never dressed up, gone out in the evenings, been to a party?

Wexford picked the ring off the bedside cabinet and held it out on his palm to Burden. "A fine ruby," he said. "Worth more than all your TVs and Nicam video-pluses and cassette players put together." He hesitated. "Which of us is going to be the first to ask the question?"

"It's been on the tip of my tongue ever since I knew she'd been murdered."

"And mine."

"Okay," said Burden, "I will. Is there any connection between this death and the fact that she seems to have been the last person to have seen Melanie Akande alive?"

Edwina Harris came home while they were still there. She pushed the door open, entered the hall, saw Flat 1 sealed off with yellow tape, and was standing staring when DS Karen Malahyde came out to her.

"Did I leave the door on the latch? I mean, I always do when I go out and nothing's ever happened." She realized what she had said. "What *has* happened?"

"Can we go upstairs, Mrs. Harris?"

Karen broke it to her carefully. It was a shock but no more than that. She and Annette Bystock had been neighbors, not friends, never close. After a few minutes she was able to tell Karen that Annette's parents were dead, she had no brothers or sisters. She thought Annette had once been married but she knew no more than that.

No, she hadn't heard or seen anything untoward in the past few days. She lived in the upper flat with her husband and he hadn't heard anything or he would have told her. In fact, she hadn't known Annette was ill. She wasn't the friend who had brought in the groceries.

"Like I said, I wasn't her *friend.*"

"Who was?"

"She never had any boyfriends to my knowledge."

"Women friends, then?"

But Edwina Harris couldn't say. She had only once been inside Flat 1, but couldn't remember noticing whether or not Annette had a television.

"But everyone has a TV, don't they? She had a radio, a little white one. I know that because while I was in there she showed it to me. She'd spilled red nail varnish on it and she couldn't get it off, wanted to know what would get it off, and I said remover, but she'd tried that."

"There's someone lives opposite," Burden said. It was a bit

awkward, he found he couldn't tell whether it was a man or a woman. "A very old person," he said carefully, and with equal tact. "They look as if they'd see everything. Did they know Annette?"

"Mr. Hammond? He's never been over here. He hasn't left that room for—well, it has to be three years."

Edwina Harris wasn't prepared to identify the body. She had never seen a dead person and didn't want to start now. Annette had had a cousin somewhere, she had heard her mention a cousin. Jane something. A birthday card had come from this woman and the postman had put it in her box instead of Annette's. That was when Edwina Harris heard about the cousin, when she took the birthday card to Annette.

It was Wexford who asked her about the front door to the house.

"It was never left unlocked overnight."

"Are you sure?"

"Well, I'm sure I never left it unlocked."

"Strange, isn't it?" said Burden, after they left her. "Women in ground-floor flats are supposed to be sleepless with dread about intruders. They have alarms, they have bars on all the windows—or that's what I read."

"Appearance and reality," said Wexford.

Sometime later in the day they found Annette's cousin, a married woman with three children living in Pomfret. Jane Winster agreed to come to Kingsmarkham and identify the body.

Told what had happened, Cyril Leyton at first refused to believe. Incredibly, "You're having me on," he had said roughly when phoned, then, "Is this some sort of trick?" Finally convinced, he repeated over and over, "My God, my God . . ."

Tomorrow would be Saturday, but in name only, as Wexford said to Burden. There wouldn't be any time off and all leave would be canceled. Burden's remarks about women in ground-floor flats reminded him of the meeting scheduled for Saturday night at Kingsmarkham Comprehensive School. He wondered if he would still be able to take part. The talk he was planning he had given twice before at Women, Aware! meetings, and he had enjoyed speaking. He wouldn't miss it this time, not unless he absolutely had to; unless, for instance, someone had been arrested for this murder.

The young men—Wexford disliked the word "youth" and re-fused ever to use it—were still sitting on the stone balustrade of the Benefit Office steps. Perhaps they weren't the same ones but they looked the same to him. This time he took particular note of them so that he would know them again: a boy with a shaven head in a gray T-shirt; a boy in a black leather jacket and track-suit bottoms with rat's-tail hair tied back in a ponytail; another very short one with fair curly hair; and a black boy with dreadlocks and one of those big floppy knitted caps. Assessing them like this, he realized what he had done, what he had told Burden racists did, so he changed the description to: a *boy* with dreadlocks and a knit-ted cap.

They looked at him with indifference, or three of them did. The one with the ponytail didn't look at him at all. For all that, he expected some muttered remark as he passed them, an insult or a quip, but there was nothing. He went up the steps to find the door locked but a young girl coming toward him behind the glass to open it.

He hadn't seen her before. She was small with pointed features and reddish hair, the label pinned to her black T-shirt identifying her as Ms. Ann Selby, Admin. Assistant. He said good afternoon to her and something about being sorry to detain them all like this after hours but she was too shy to reply. He followed her between counters to the back, where she opened a door marked not only "Private" but "Keep Out" as well.

He hadn't intended it to be like this. Cyril Leyton—for it was surely he who had fixed this up—was evidently a headmaster *manqué*. The chairs, normally those on which clients waited to sign on, were arranged in five rows with gray metal tables in front of each. On these chairs the staff sat. There were more of them than Wexford had realized. He saw to his rather horrified amusement that Leyton had seated them according to rank: the two supervisors and the remaining new claims adviser, all executive officers, in the first row; administrative officers behind; then the administrative assistants, those who worked on the switchboard, saw to the post, operated the copier, at the back.

In the last row, on the extreme left, possibly the seat of the lowliest, was the bullet-headed security officer.

On each table, in front of each member of staff, was a notepad. All that was lacking, Wexford thought, was a blackboard—and perhaps a ferrule for Leyton to hold and use for rapping knuckles. The manager looked busy and important, enjoying himself now the first shock was past. His red face was shiny. Since Wexford had last seen him he had had his hair cut cruelly short and the clippers had left an angry-looking crimson rash on his neck.

"All present and correct, I trust," he said.

Wexford merely nodded to him. Ridiculous as this regimentation was, the notepads might be useful. So long as they understood they weren't to write down what *he* said but what *they* knew.

"I'll try not to detain you long," he began. "You'll all have heard by now of Miss Bystock's violent death. It will be on our local television news at six-thirty and in the papers tomorrow so there's no reason why I shouldn't tell you now that it was a case of murder."

From somewhere in the audience he heard the sound of an indrawn breath. It might have come from Ingrid Pamber, whose blue eyes were fixed earnestly on him, or the wispy fragile blonde sitting next to her who must have been twenty-five but looked no more than fifteen. Her label was too far away for him to read. In the row in front of them Peter Stanton, the other new claims adviser, sat like an important young executive at a seminar, one long elegant leg crossed over the other, ankle on knee, his elbows on the chair arms, his head flung back. He was very good-looking in a dark brooding way and he seemed to be enjoying himself.

"She was murdered in her own home, Ladyhall Court in Ladyhall Avenue. We don't yet know when. We shan't know until the postmortem is over and the other forensic tests have been done. We shan't know how she died or when or why. But as far as that goes the help of the people who knew her will be invaluable to us. Miss Bystock had very little family, few friends. The people she knew are the people she worked with and that means *you*.

"One of you or several of you may between you have all the information we need to find Miss Bystock's killer and bring him— or her—to justice. Your cooperation will be invaluable. I should like you all to agree to be interviewed by my officers tomorrow, either in your own homes or at Kingsmarkham Police Station if you prefer. Meanwhile, if any of you has anything to tell me now, anything that might be important or urgent, I shall be in Mr. Leyton's office for the next half hour and I'd be grateful if you'd come to me there and pass this information on. Thank you."

Cyril Leyton said importantly as they walked into the little gray office, "I can tell you anything you want to know. There's not much goes on here that I don't know about."

"I've already told everyone that if they have something to tell me that's urgent they should do it now. Have you anything to tell me?"

Leyton grew redder. "Well, no, not specifically, but I . . ."

"What time did Miss Bystock phone on Wednesday to say she wouldn't be coming in? Can you tell me that?"

"I? No, I can't. I'm not a switchboard operator. I can find someone who will . . ."

"Yes, Mr. Leyton," Wexford said patiently, "I'm sure you can, but all your staff will be questioned tomorrow. Didn't you hear me say that? I'm asking you what you can tell me."

Leyton was saved from answering by a tap on the door. It opened and Ingrid Pamber came in. Wexford, who always noticed—as most men do—if a woman is specially good-looking, had taken good note of this girl. Her looks were the kind that most appealed to him, the fresh wholesomeness of her, her glossy dark hair sleekly held back by a barrette, her fine features and smooth pink and white skin—what his father would have called her "complexion"—her shapely figure that was slim but a long way from today's anorexic ideal. The clothes she wore were in his opinion the most flattering to any pretty woman: a short straight skirt, a clinging knitted sweater—in this case cream cotton and short-sleeved—low-cut shoes with heels, as unlike a man's shoe as could be.

She leveled at Wexford a rueful smile that was almost laughter through tears. It looked natural but he thought it was calculated. Her eyes were the kind whose irises are such a strong color that they seem to shed their own blue light.

"I was—I was looking after her," she said. "Poor Annette, I was taking care of her."

"You were friends, Miss Pamber?"

"I was her only friend."

Ingrid Pamber said it quietly but dramatically. She sat down opposite Wexford, and sat with care, but her skirt was too short not to rise six inches above her knees. The sideways attitude she sat in, knees and ankles close together, seemed designed to show off a woman's legs to best advantage—but a modest woman's, not the Hollywood starlet kind who crosses one leg over the other, extending the toe in its high-heeled shoe. He thought he understood Ingrid Pamber as a girl whose sexual success depended on a contrived reserve, discreet revelations, an almost shy appeal. In another age she would have managed excellently the manipulation of petticoats to give a sight of ankle or the handling of a shawl that when it slipped allowed a glimpse of cleavage.

"It was you who took the call from Miss Bystock on Wednesday morning?"

"Yes. Yes, it was. She asked the switchboard to put the call through to me."

"Which was most improper," said Leyton. "I shall be speaking to Mr. Jones and Miss Selby about that. The call should have come to me."

"I told you about it," said Ingrid. "I told you within about thirty seconds."

"Yes, maybe, but that's not the—"

"Mr. Leyton," Wexford said, "I'd be grateful if you'd leave us. I'd like to talk to Miss Pamber alone."

"Look here, this is my office!"

"Yes, I know, and very obliging it is of you to let me use it. I'll see you later."

Wexford got up and opened the door for Leyton. He had scarcely gone through it before Ingrid Pamber giggled. One of the hardest things we are ever called on to do is feign sorrow when we are happy, or pretend happiness when we are in grief. Ingrid remembered too late that, as Annette's only friend, she was supposed to be sad. She looked down, biting her lip.

He waited a moment, then asked her, "Can you tell me what time this call came?"

"It was nine-fifteen."

"How can you be so sure of the time?"

"Well, we start at nine-thirty and we're supposed to be in by nine-fifteen." She opened her eyes wide as she looked at him and he felt the force of that blue beam. "I've been getting in a bit late lately and—well, I was pleased with myself for making it on time. I'd looked at the clock and seen it was nine-fifteen and at that moment the call from Annette came for me."

"What did she say, Miss Pamber?"

"That she thought she had a bug and felt awful and wouldn't be in and I was to tell Cyril. And she said would I take her in a pint of milk on my way home from work, that was all she wanted, she couldn't eat anything. She said she'd leave the door on the latch for me. It's the kind of door that's got a handle like a door—well, an inside-door if you know what I mean."

Wexford nodded. This then was the friend he had guessed at.

"So I said I would and the minute I put the phone down a man phoned and asked for her. He didn't give his name but I knew who it was." She gave him a sidelong look, rather a roguish look. "Anyway, I said she was at home ill."

"And you did take her the milk?"

"Yes. It was about five-thirty I went in."

"She was in bed?"

"Yes, she was. I was going to stay for a bit, have a chat, you know, but she said not to come too near in case I caught it. She'd made a list of things she wanted me to get her the next day and I took that with me. She said she'd give me a ring at work in the morning."

"Did she?"

"No, she didn't but it didn't matter." Ingrid Pamber seemed quite unaware of what she was saying. "I'd got her list. I knew what she wanted."

"So she'd given you a key?"

"Yes, she had. She had two keys on her bedside table. I got the things, cornflakes and grapefruit and stuff, and I went in with them at the same time last evening. I left them in the box. I thought she'd put them away."

"You didn't go in to see her?"

"Last evening? No, I didn't. I couldn't hear anything. I thought she must be asleep."

He detected the guilt in her voice. Friend she might have been but she hadn't wanted to be bothered with Annette the night before, she had been in a hurry, so she had dumped the box of groceries and left without looking into the bedroom . . . or wasn't it like that at all?

"Now when you left the flat on Wednesday evening you had a key, so of course you didn't leave the front door on the latch? It was locked behind you?"

"Oh, yes."

How blue her eyes were! They seemed to grow bluer, to become neon-like Day-Glo peacock eyes, as they gazed earnestly into his. "So when you returned on Thursday evening, last evening, you found the door locked and let yourself in with your key?"

"Oh, yes. Absolutely."

He switched to another subject. "I suppose Miss Bystock had a television? A VCR?"

"Yes." She looked surprised. "I remember when she bought the VCR. It was around last Christmas."

"Now when you went there on Wednesday and yesterday, did you see the television set?"

She hesitated. "I don't know, I . . . I'm sure I saw it on Wednesday. Annette said to draw the curtains as I was leaving. She wanted the curtains drawn to stop the sun fading the carpet or something. Funny, wasn't it? I'd never heard of that before. Anyway, I did draw them and I saw the TV and the VCR."

He nodded. "And yesterday?"

"I don't know. I didn't notice." In too much of a hurry, Wexford thought, in and out, no messing. Something in his look seemed to touch her. "You don't mean . . . she was dead then, she was already dead . . . you can't mean that!"

"I'm afraid she was, Miss Pamber. It looks very much as if she was."

"Oh, God, and I didn't know. If I'd gone in there . . ."

"It would have made no difference."

"They didn't . . . they didn't kill her for a telly and a VCR?"

"It wouldn't be the first time such a thing has happened."

"Poor Annette. That makes me feel terrible."

Why did he have the distinct impression she didn't feel terrible at all? She spoke the conventional words in the conventional way and her face wore a conventional mask of woe. But those eyes danced with life and vitality and happiness. "The man who phoned here and asked for her? Who did you think that was?"

She lied again. He marveled that she thought he couldn't tell. "Oh, just a friend, one of her neighbors actually."

"Who did you think it was, Miss Pamber?" he said.

She looked him straight in the eye. "I don't know, I honestly don't know."

"You knew who it was just now and now you don't? I'll ask you again tomorrow."

The light inside her head had gone out. He watched her go, leave the room, then let an indignant Leyton back into it. She had lied a great deal, he thought, and he could pinpoint the moment at which the lying began: it was when he first uttered the word "key." He looked beyond the grayness at Marks and Spencers' loading bay, at a bright green carrier bag the summer wind was tossing to and fro. A woman was lifting carriers from a trolley into her car boot. She belonged to the same type as Annette, dark, stocky with an hourglass figure, a high color, excellent legs. Why had Ingrid lied about the man who phoned? Why had she lied about the key? And in what respect had she lied?

She had been dead while Ingrid was in the flat on Thursday evening. Ingrid had locked the door behind her. Who then had unlocked it during the night before Burden arrived?

six

Those who had jobs and went to them every day were the lucky ones. Looking back a few years, Barry Vine wondered what he would have thought of such a sentiment then. It was true today, no denying it. He was surprised when he found that the occupants of Flat 3 and Flat 4 in Ladyhall Court all had work.

The Greenalls, however, had not been at their jobs during the previous week; they had been away on holiday, returning home some five hours after the discovery of Annette's body. The occupant of Flat 4, Jason Partridge, a solicitor just six months over the Law Society's exams, had lived there for only a matter of weeks and could not remember ever having seen Annette. Vine, who knew all about how seeing policemen as younger and younger was a sign of middle age, wondered what it meant when solicitors looked like A-Level candidates.

On the opposite side of Ladyhall Gardens were an old house divided into three flats, three red brick bungalows, and an empty site where six houses like the old one had been demolished. The new ones would be in nineties trend, a Port Meirion–like arrangement of a Gothic weatherboard house at angles to a brick house, joined to a plaster-rendered Georgian house, all the roofs at different levels, all the windows different shapes. So far only the foundations were there, the "infrastructure" and walls built to a height of six feet. That limited those likely to have had a view of Ladyhall Court to the bungalows and the old house.

It was Saturday, so the occupants of the bungalows were at home. Vine talked to a youngish couple, Matthew Ross and his partner Alison Brown, but neither of them had so much as looked out of their front windows on the night of July 7. They knew nothing of Annette Bystock and could not remember ever having seen her.

Next door was shared by two women, Diana Graddon, in her mid-thirties, and Helen Ringstead, twenty years older. Mrs. Ringstead was lodger rather than friend. Diana Graddon couldn't have afforded to live there without her contribution, she frankly said, though since she had lost her own job the Social Security paid her rent. She had once known Annette well. In fact, it ws she who, about ten years before when herself a newcomer to Ladyhall Avenue, had told Annette of the flat for sale on the other side of the street.

"We'd lost touch, though," said Diana Graddon. "She dropped me, as a matter of fact. I don't know why. I mean, it was silly really, living opposite and all that, but she never seemed to want to know me after she came here."

"When did you last see her?"

"It must have been Monday. Last Monday. I was going away for a few days. I saw her coming home from work as I was going to get the bus. We just said hallo, we didn't really speak."

She had been away from home until Thursday morning. Helen Ringstead said she never noticed who came and went across the road.

The wrinkled face that Burden had for a wild moment thought might be a mask or a cutout belonged to a man of ninety-two called Percy Hammond. It was four years, not three, since he had come down the stairs from his first-floor flat, and most days he remained in the bedroom that overlooked Ladyhall Avenue. Meals-on-Wheels were brought to him and twice a week a home helper came in. For thirty years he had been a widower, his sons were dead, and his only friend was the tenant of the ground-floor flat who, though eighty and blind, made her way upstairs to visit him every day.

It was she who let Burden in. Having introduced herself as Gladys Prior, asked him for his name twice, and then made him spell it, she walked up the stairs ahead of him, surefooted on the treads, her hand touching the banister more from convention than for support. Percy Hammond was in a chair by the window, staring into an empty street. The face that was dinosaur-like in close-up was turned on Burden's and its owner said, "I've seen you somewhere before."

"No, you haven't, Percy. You've made a mistake there. He's a police detective that's come to make inquiries. He's called Burden, Inspector Burden, B-U-R-D-E-N."

"All right. I don't want to write to him. And I *have* seen him before. What do you know? You can't see at all."

This on the face of it cruel taunt seemed to amuse rather than distress Mrs. Prior. She sat down, giggling. "Where have I seen you?" said Percy Hammond. "Now *when* have I seen you?"

"Yesterday morning, over on the other . . ." Burden began but was interrupted.

"All right, don't tell me. Don't you know a rhetorical question when you hear one? I know who you are. You were trying to break into the house, or that's what I thought. Yesterday morning. Ten, was it? Or a bit later—eleven-ish? I'm not as good on time as I used to be. I don't suppose you were breaking in, *looking* in, more likely."

"Of course he wasn't breaking in, Percy. He's a *policeman.*"

"You're naive, Gladys, that's what you are. I suppose Inspector B-U-R-D-E-N was looking through the curtains at our murder."

That was one way of putting it, if somewhat cold-blooded. "That's right, Mr. Hammond. I really want to know, not if you saw me, but if you saw anyone else. I think you watch the street from your window quite a bit, don't you?"

"Never leaves that window all blessed day long," said Mrs. Prior.

"And how about the night?" said Burden.

"It's light at night this time of the year," Percy Hammond said, a gleam of pleasures in his hooded eyes. "Doesn't get dark till ten and it starts getting light again at four. Generally, I get in my bed at ten and out of it at half-past three. That's as long as I can sleep at my age. And when I'm not in my bed I'm at my window, I'm at my watching place. Do you know what Mizpah means?"

"I can't say I do," said Burden.

"The watching place that overlooked the Plain of Syria. You youngsters don't know your Bible, more's the pity. This window is my Mizpah."

"And have you seen anything on the—er, Plain of Syria these past two nights, Mr. Hammond?"

"Not last night but the night before . . ."

"Two tomcats came knocking at the door!" crowed Mrs. Prior, laughing.

Percy Hammond ignored her. "A young chap came out of Ladyhall Court. I'd never seen him before, I knew he didn't live there. I know them all by sight, the ones that live there."

"What time would that have been?"

"It was dawn," said Percy Hammond. "Four. Maybe a bit later. And I saw him again, I saw him come out carrying something, like a big wireless set."

"Wireless set!" said Gladys Prior. "I may not have my sight but I do move with the times. They call them tellies and radios."

"He went in again and came out with something else in a box. I couldn't see what he did with it. If he had a car it was parked round the corner. I thought to myself, He's moving house for someone, getting it done early before the traffic gets bad."

"Could you describe him, Mr. Hammond?"

"He was young, about your age. About your height. Had quite a look of you. It was still darkish, you know, the sun wasn't up. Everything looks black and gray at that hour. I couldn't tell you the color of his hair . . ."

"He gets confused," said Mrs. Prior.

"No, I don't, Gladys. As I said, it was about four-thirty to five, and I saw him come out and go in again and come out, carrying these boxes, a young chap of maybe twenty-five or thirty, six feet tall, at least six feet."

"Would you know him again?"

"Of course I would. I'm an observant man. It may have been dark but I'd know him anywhere."

Percy Hammond turned on Burden the fierce scowl, down-turned mouth, heavy dewlaps, that was his normal expression, an intense gleam in his saurian eyes.

W omen, learn to be streetwise," the program text began. "Come and hear what the experts have to say about making yourselves aware. In your car, walking home alone after dark, in your home. Do you know what to do if attacked in the street? Can you protect yourself if your car breaks down on the motorway? Can you defend yourself against rape?"

It listed the speakers: Chief Inspector R. Wexford, of Kingsmarkham CID, to talk on "Crime on the Streets and in Your Home"; PC Oliver Adams on "Driving Alone and Safe"; WPC Clare Scott, the Rape Adviser, on "Changed Attitudes to Reporting Rape"; Mr. Ronald Pollen, self-defense expert and judo black belt, to show his enthralling and informative video and talk on "How to Fight Back." Questions would be invited from the audience for the team of experts to answer. Organizer: Mrs. Susan Riding, President, Kingsmarkham Women Rotarians; Chairperson, Mrs. Anouk Khoori.

"Have you ever heard of a woman called Anouk Khoori? Curious name, isn't it? Sounds Arabic."

Dora didn't hesitate. "Oh, Reg, you never listen to me. I told you all about her coming to the Women's Institute and talking about women's lives in the United Arab Emirates."

"There you are, I was right. She is an Arab."

"Well, she doesn't look like one. She's a blonde. Very good-looking in a showy sort of way. Very rich, I should think. Her husband owns a lot of shops, Tesco or Safeway or something. No, it's not those, it's Crescent. You know the ones, they're springing up everywhere."

"You mean those supermarkets you see from motorways that look like palaces from the Arabian Nights? All pointed arches and moons on the roof? What's she got to do with not getting raped or mugged? Is she going to tell the women to wear the veil?"

"Oh, she's just there because she wants to get herself in the public eye. She and her husband have built a vast new house where Mynford Old Hall used to be. She's standing for the council in the by-election. They say she'd like to get into Parliament, but she can't surely, she isn't even English."

Wexford shrugged. He didn't know and cared less. The task ahead of him, the immediate task, he dreaded and would have avoided if he could. On the way he was going to meet Burden in the Olive and Dove for a drink, but after that, after it could be postponed no longer, the Akandes.

The Olive stayed open from and until all hours now. You could drink brandy at nine in the morning if you wanted to, and a surprising lot of European visitors did want to. Instead of being cleared out pell-mell at two-thirty you could drink on through the afternoon and evening till the Olive finally closed its bars at midnight. It was ten past eleven when Wexford got there and found Burden sitting outside at a table in the shade.

There were almost too many tubs, barrels, vases, and hanging baskets spilling out fuchsias and geraniums and other unnameable brilliant flowers. But all were scentless and the air smelled of petrol fumes and also of the river, its waters low from drought and scummed with algae. A few yellow leaves had fallen onto the table. In July they were too early for the autumnal shedding but their presence warned that autumn would come.

Burden had a half of Adnams in a tankard that the Olive called a jug. "I'll have the same," said Wexford. "No, I won't, I'll have a Heineken. I need some Dutch courage."

Returning with it, Burden said, "The old man definitely saw

someone. Those trees don't block the view from up there. He saw the thief of the TV and the VCR."

"But not Annette's killer?"

"Not if it was four-thirty in the morning. Annette had been dead five hours by then. He says he'd know him again. On the other hand, he says the man he saw was about my age and then that he was between twenty-five and thirty." Burden looked down modestly. "Of course, it wasn't very light."

"I don't suppose it was, Dorian."

"Yes, well, you may laugh, but if this character looks like me we may be getting somewhere."

"It's a killer we want, Mike, not a burglar." The sun had moved round and Wexford shifted his chair into the shade. "So—Melanie Akande, where does she come into it?"

"We haven't looked for her body."

"Where would you start, Mike? In the High Street here? In the cellars of the Benefit Office? If it has a cellar, which I doubt. On British Rail's inter-city line to Victoria?"

"I talked to those layabouts, you know, the ones who hang about outside the Benefit Office. They're always there, always more or less the same ones. What attracts them to the place? They only have to sign on once a fortnight but they're there every day. It would be different if they went inside asking about jobs."

"Maybe they do."

"I doubt it. I very much doubt it. I asked them if they'd ever seen the black girl. You know what they said."

Wexford made a guess. " 'I don't know, I might have.' "

"Exactly right. That's what they said. I tried to get them to cast their minds back to last Tuesday. Correction, what *passes* for minds with people like that. The way they went about it, I mean the *process*, it was like three very old men trying to recall something. It went something like this, Well, yeah, man, that was the day I like, you know, I come here early on account of me mum was, you know, going to . . . mumble, mumble, scratch scalp, and then the next one says, No, man, no, you got it all wrong, that was Tuesday 'cos I said like . . ."

"Spare me."

"The black one, the one with the hair in sort of plaits, only not, sort of matted up, he's the worst, he sounds brain-damaged. You know you can have senile and juvenile diabetes? Well, d'you reckon there's such a thing as juvenile Alzheimer's?"

"I suppose they knew nothing about her?"

"Not a thing. You could have a girl abducted on those steps by three characters from *Jurassic Park* and they wouldn't notice. All I got was that the one with the ponytail says he thinks he saw a black girl on the other side of the street on Monday. I'll tell you something, we aren't going to find anyone who saw Melanie after she left the Benefit Office. We'd have done so by now if we were going to. All we've got is the connection between her and Annette Bystock."

The sun had moved round. Once again Wexford pushed his chair into the shade. "But what exactly is that connection, Mike?"

" 'Exactly' is what I don't know. 'Exactly' is what Annette was killed for, to stop her telling. It's obvious, isn't it? Melanie told her something before she left on Tuesday afternoon and whatever it was was overheard. Either that, or some meeting was arranged which the killer of both girls decided must not at all costs take place."

"You must mean overheard by someone in the Benefit Office, an employee."

"Or a client," said Burden.

"But what was it that was overheard? What sort of thing?"

"I don't know and for our purposes it basically doesn't matter. The point is that whoever heard it was worried by it, more than that, felt that his or her life or liberty was endangered by it. Melanie had to die and because she had passed this secret on, the woman to whom it was spoken had to die too."

"D'you want another one? The other half for the road before we walk round and see them?"

"We?"

"You're coming with me." Wexford fetched their drinks. When he came back with them he said, "When someone mentions terrible secrets to me I always need to be given some inkling of what they might be. I'd like an example. You know me, I always want examples."

They were no longer alone. A number of the Olive's clientele were finding it more pleasant out in the open air. A touring American with a camera posed the other members of his party at a table under a sunshade and began taking shots of them. Wexford moved his chair again.

"Well, this man she was going to meet," Burden began. "I mean, she could have told Annette his name."

"She was going to meet *another* man? That's the first I've heard of it. What was he, a white slaver?"

Burden looked genuinely puzzled. "A what?"

"Before your time. You've really never heard the term?"

"I don't think so."

"It must have been used at the beginning of the century and maybe a bit later. A white slaver was a sort of pimp, specifically one who procured girls for prostitution abroad."

"Why 'white'?"

Wexford felt himself approaching dangerous ground. He lifted the "jug" to his lips and as he did so blinked at the sudden flash. The photographer—not the same one—said something that might have been "thanks" and dived back into the Olive.

"Because slaves were always thought of as black. It wasn't that long after emancipation in the United States. The girls were taken against their will, I suppose, like slaves, and forced into servitude abroad, again like slaves, only it was brothels for them. Buenos Aires was the favorite place in the popular imagination. Shall we go? Akande's surgery will be over by now."

It was and he was back at home. The days gone by had aged him. Hair doesn't turn gray in a matter of days from shock or anxiety, whatever the sensation merchants may say, and Akande's was the same as it had been on Wednesday, black with a white sprinkling at the temples. It was his face that had become gray, drawn and gaunt, all the protrusions of the skull showing.

"My wife is at work," he said as he showed them into the living room. "We've tried to carry on as usual. My son phoned us from Malaysia. We didn't tell him, there seemed no point in spoiling his trip. He would have felt he had to come home."

"I'm not sure that that was a good idea." Wexford noticed what he hadn't noticed before, a framed photograph of the whole family. It stood on the bookcase and it was obviously a studio portrait, posed and rather formal, the children dressed in white, Laurette Akande in a low-cut blue silk dress and gold jewelry looking beautiful and very unlike a ward sister. "He might have been able to help. His sister may have confided in him before he went away."

"Confided what, Mr. Wexford?"

"Possibly that there was a man in her life apart from Euan Sinclair."

"But I'm sure there wasn't." The doctor sat down and fixed Wexford with his eyes. He had a rather disconcerting way of doing this. Wexford had noticed it when their roles were reversed, when he so to speak was the client and the other man the omniscient adviser, and in his surgery, confronting each other across the doctor's desk, Akande's black penetrating eyes had stared deep into his own. "I'm sure she had never had any boyfriend but Euan. Apart, that is, from—I'm not quite sure how to say this . . ."

"Say what, Dr. Akande?"

"My wife and I—well, we wouldn't care for the idea of Melanie taking up with a—well, a white man. Oh, I know things are changing every day, they don't even use words like 'miscegenation' anymore and, of course, there was no question of *marriage* but still . . ."

Wexford could imagine Sister Akande being as magisterial about this as any country gentlewoman whose daughter was attracted by a Rastafarian. "Melanie had a white boyfriend, Doctor?"

"No, no, nothing like that. It was just that his sister was at the college too, that was how Melanie met him, and she told us they'd had a drink together—with the sister. I mention him because he's the only other boy Melanie told us about apart from Euan. Laurette said at once that she hoped Melanie wouldn't get to know him better and I'm sure Melanie never did."

How much did he know, this parent, of his children's lives? How much does any parent know? "Melanie didn't meet Euan last Tuesday evening," Wexford said. "That's been established beyond doubt."

"I knew she didn't. I knew it. I told my wife she'd too much sense to go back to that boy who had no respect for her." Akande seemed calm but his hands gripped the arms of his chair and the knucklebones showed white. "Do you—" he began. "Do you have any news for me?"

"We've nothing specific, sir." Wexford read a lot into that emphatic "sir," probably a good deal more than Burden was aware of. He heard in the stress a real effort on the inspector's part to treat this man just as he would any other man in the doctor's position. And he could tell that Burden, who had encountered very few black people, was ill at ease, not at a loss but nervous, unsure how to proceed. "We've done all we can to find your daughter. We've done everything that's humanly possible."

The doctor must have thought, as Wexford did, that this was meaningless. His knowledge of psychology, and perhaps of white men, enabled him to see through Burden. Wexford thought he could detect the ghost of a sneer on Akande's unhappy face. "What are you trying to say to me, Inspector?"

Burden didn't like that "trying." There had been a faintly sarcastic emphasis on the participle. Wexford took over, rather too hastily.

"You must prepare yourself, Dr. Akande."

His short bark of laughter was shocking in that context. It was a single "Ha!" and then it was gone, the doctor's face wretched again—worse than wretched now, distraught. "I am prepared," he said in a stoical voice. "We are prepared. You're going to tell me to accept that Melanie must be dead?"

"Not quite that. But, yes, there's a very strong probability."

Silence fell. Akande put his hands into his lap and forced himself to relax them. He gave a heavy profound sigh. To his horror, Wexford saw a tear fall from each of those tragic eyes. Akande was unembarrassed. He removed the teardrops with the forefingers of each hand, wiping them across his cheeks, then contemplating the fingertips with bent head.

To keep his face hidden, without looking up, he said quietly, in an almost conversational tone, "There is something I've wondered about. Since I saw the television news last evening and read this morning's paper. The murdered woman in Ladyhall Avenue, her name is the same as the one Melanie had her appointment with last Tuesday: Annette Bystock. The paper called her a civil servant and I suppose that's what she was. Is it a—coincidence? I've wondered if there could be a connection. As a matter of fact, I was awake all last night thinking about it."

"Melanie had no previous knowledge of Annette Bystock, Doctor?"

"I'm sure she didn't. I remember her exact words. 'I have to see the new claims adviser at two-thirty,' she said, and then, a while later, 'a Ms. Bystock,' she said."

Wexford said gently that the doctor had not told him that before. Mrs. Akande hadn't told him that on the single occasion he had talked to her.

"Maybe not. It came back to me when I saw the name in the paper."

Wexford deeply distrusted evidence that "came back to" witnesses when they saw a name in the paper. Poor Akande said he was prepared, he could accept, but he hoped just the same. Hope may be a virtue but it causes more pain, Wexford thought, than despair. He considered asking the doctor if he knew of anything Melanie might have said to Annette Bystock that would have put both their lives in jeopardy, and then he thought how pointless such a question was. Of course Akande didn't know.

He said instead, "What is the name of this white boy she had a drink with?"

"Riding. Christopher Riding. But that was months ago."

Akande, seeing them to the door, struggled not to say it. He lost the fight, wincing before he spoke. "Is there any—is there the slightest hope she may be—still alive?"

Until we find her body we can't regard her as dead. Wexford didn't use those words. "Let's just say you must prepare yourself, Doctor." He couldn't give hope, knowing almost for sure that in a day or two he would snatch it away again.

The women filled the school hall, at least three hundred of them. With ten minutes still to go before the meeting started, they were still arriving and one of the organizers was bringing in more chairs.

"It's not us they're coming for," Susan Riding whispered to Wexford. "Don't flatter yourself. And finding out how to blind and maim a rapist is only part of it. No, they've come for *her*. To see *her*. It was a good move getting her in the chair, wasn't it?"

Wexford looked across the platform at Anouk Khoori. He had a feeling he had seen her somewhere before, though he couldn't remember where. Perhaps it had only been a photograph in a paper. She was a big fish in a small pond, he thought, on her way to becoming Kingsmarkham's First Lady. Presumably, that suited her. If it was true that most of these women had come for a sight of her in the flesh, to see what she wore and hear how she talked, their aspirations were not high. In her small way she was like one of those international celebrities whose pictures are always in the papers, whose names are household words and who are favorites for TV chat shows, but of whom it would be hard to say what they *did* and impossible to know what they had achieved.

"She doesn't look Middle Eastern," he said and immediately wondered if that was a racist remark.

Susan Riding only smiled. "Her family is from Beirut. Anouk is a French name, of course. We knew them slightly when we were in Kuwait. His young nephew needed a minor op and Swithun did it."

"They left because of the Gulf War?"

"*We* did. I don't think they ever left. They've a house there and one in Mentone and an apartment in New York, or so I've heard. I knew they'd bought Mynford Old Hall so I plucked up my courage and asked her if she'd do this and she was charming about it. Swithun's here, by the way, and it looks as if he's going to be the only man down there. Still, he won't mind, he takes that sort of thing in his stride."

Wexford spotted the pediatric surgeon sitting one row from the back, looking as urbane as his wife had suggested he would be. Why was it that when women sat with their legs crossed they rested calf on kneecap but when men did it they placed ankle on femur? Out of modesty in the women's case, presumably, but that wouldn't apply now they wore trousers all the time. Swithun Riding was sitting with his ankle on his femur and clasping it with a long elegant hand. Next to him sat a girl with corn-colored hair so like him she must be his and Susan's daughter. Wexford recognized her. The last time he saw her she had been waiting to sign on at his first visit to the Benefit Office.

"Your son couldn't bring himself to give his father moral support?" said Wexford.

"Christopher's away for a week. He went off to Spain with a bunch of friends."

So much for another tentative theory.

Across the room Mrs. Khoori laughed, a long musical peal. The man she was talking to, an ex-mayor of Kingsmarkham, smiled at her, evidently already smitten. She gave him a light pat on the arm, a delightful and strangely intimate gesture, before moving back behind the table to the central chair. There, she adjusted her microphone with the ease of someone accustomed to public speaking.

"I'll introduce you," said Susan Riding.

Wexford expected an accent but there was none, only the faintest French intonation, the ends of her sentences rising instead of falling. "How do you do?" She held his hand a little longer than was necessary. "I knew I should meet you here, I felt it."

Not surprising, he thought, since his name as a speaker was in the program. He was a little disturbed by her eyes, which seemed to be assessing him, calculating something about him. It was as if she was speculating how far she could go with him, at what point she would need to draw back. Oh, nonsense, imagination . . . They were black eyes, and that must be what disconcerted him, such dark eyes in contrast to that creamy-olive skin and very fair hair.

"Are you going to tell us poor creatures how to fight big strong men and protect ourselves?"

Anyone less like a poor creature it would be hard to find. She was at least five feet nine, her body sinuous and strong in the pink linen suit, arms and legs muscular, her skin glowing with health. On the hand he hadn't held was a huge rock of a diamond, a single uncluttered stone on a platinum band.

"I'm not a martial arts expert, Mrs. Khoori," he said. "I shall be leaving that to Mr. Adams and Mr. Pollen."

"But you are going to speak? I shall be *so* disappointed if you aren't going to speak."

"A few words."

"Then you and I must have a chat afterward. I'm worried, Mr. Wexford, I am seriously worried about what is happening to us in this country, child murders, all these poor young girls assaulted, raped, and worse. That's why I'm doing this, to do what I can in my small way to—well, turn the tide of crime. Don't you think we each and every one of us ought to do that?"

He wondered about that "us." How long had she been living here? Two years? He wondered if he was being unreasonable, resenting her claims to Englishness while he honored Akande's. Her husband was an Arab multi-millionaire. . . . He was saved from making any reply to her earnest, though oddly vague, remarks by a whispered, "Anouk, we're ready to start," from Susan Riding.

With great confidence Anouk Khoori stood and surveyed her audience. She waited for their silence, their total silence, holding up her hands, the great ring catching the light, her head very slightly to one side. When they were quiet she began to address them.

An hour later, if he had been asked to give a résumé of what she had said, he couldn't have recalled a word of it. And at the time he was aware that she had that great gift, on which so many politicians have founded their success, of being able to say nothing at length and in a flowing sequence of polysyllabic fashionable words, of talking meaningless nonsense in fine mellifluous phrases with absolute self-confidence. From time to time she paused for no apparent reason. Occasionally she smiled. Once she shook her head and once she raised her voice on an impassioned note. Just when he thought she would go on for half an hour, that nothing but physical force would stop her, she ceased, thanked her audience, and, turning to him graciously, began to introduce him.

She knew a lot about him, Wexford heard, to his amusement rather than dismay, his whole curriculum vitae reeled off. How did she know he had once been a copper on the beat in Brighton? Where did she find out he had two daughters?

He got to his feet and talked to the women. He told them they must learn to be streetwise but told them too that they must cultivate a balanced attitude to what they heard and read about crime on the streets. With a glance of mild displeasure at the *Kingsmarkham Courier* reporter, taking notes from the front row, he said that newspapers were to blame for a great deal of the hysteria over crime in this country. An example would be an account he had read recently of pensioners in Myfleet afraid to leave their homes for fear of the mugger who stalked the village and was responsible for numerous attacks on women and elderly people. The truth, on the other hand, was that one old lady, walking home from the bus stop at eleven P.M., had had her purse snatched by someone who asked her the way. They must be sensible, avoid taking risks, but not become paranoid. In the rural areas of the police district the chances of a woman being attacked in the street were ninety-nine percent against, and that they should remember.

Oliver Adams spoke and then Ronald Pollen. A video was shown in which actors simulated an encounter on the street between a young woman and a man with a stocking over his face. When grasped from behind, her attacker's hands at her waist and her throat, the actress showed how to draw the high heel of her shoe down the man's calf and grind it into his instep. This drew delighted cheers and clapping from the audience. They recoiled a little from a demonstration of how to stick one's thumbs in an assailant's eyes, but shocked gasps soon became sighs of pleasure. Everyone, Wexford decided, was enjoying herself a lot. The atmosphere became grimmer when WPC Clare Scott began to talk about rape.

How many of these women, if raped, would report it? Half, maybe. Once you could have said no more than ten percent. Things had changed for the better but he still wondered if the pictures now coming up on the screen of the comfortable "suite" at the new Rape Crisis Center in Stowerton would go far in enticing women to be open about the only crime in which authority often treated the victim worse than the perpetrator.

They were applauding now. They were writing down their questions for the four speakers. In the sea of faces he spotted Edwina Harris and, a dozen seats along from her, Wendy Stowlap. A quarter of an hour, he thought, and he could go home. There was no way he was going to become involved in a chat with Anouk Khoori about crime waves and dangerous Britain.

The first question was for PC Adams. Suppose you hadn't a car phone and your car broke down after dark on an A road where there were no roadside phones? What should you do? After Adams had done his best to answer this PC Scott, the rape adviser, was asked a difficult question about so-called date rape from someone who sounded like a victim. Clare Scott did her best to answer the unanswerable and Mrs. Khoori, having opened the next folded paper, handed it to her. The rape adviser read it, shrugged, and after a small hesitation handed it to Wexford.

He read the question aloud. "If you know a member of your family is a rapist, what should you do?"

There was a sudden silence. Women had been whispering to each other, one or two at the back were gathering their things preparatory to leaving. But now all was still. Wexford saw Dora's face in the second row from the front with Jenny beside her. He said, "The obvious answer is: tell the police. But you know that already." He hesitated, then said in a strong voice, "I would like to know if this question is simply academic or if the member of the audience who wrote this had a personal reason for asking."

Silence. It was broken by three women in the back row leaving. Then someone broke into prolonged coughing. Wexford persisted.

"You've been told you remain anonymous when you ask these questions, but I should like to know who asked this one. Outside the hall, behind the stage here, there's a door marked Private. I'll be inside that door for half an hour after the meeting with PC Scott. You only have to come round the side of the hall and knock on that door. I very much hope you will."

After that there were no more questions. The youngest girl pupil at Kingsmarkham Comprehensive came up to the stage and presented Mrs. Khoori with a bouquet of carnations. She thanked her effusively, she bent over and kissed her. The audience began filing out, some lingering in groups to talk over what had been discussed.

Although smoking was banned from the hall, Anouk Khoori was evidently unable to wait a minute longer for a cigarette. When Wexford saw her put the king-size to her lips and bring the lighter to it, he remembered who she was. He recognized her. She had looked very different then, in her tracksuit and without makeup, but there was no doubt she was the woman in the Medical Center who had come to see Dr. Akande about some malady suffered by her cook.

He walked out into the car park, saw Susan Riding step into a Range Rover, saw Wendy Stowlap toss her holdall into the boot of a tiny Fiat, and then he retreated by the side door into the room at the back, a storage place for chairs and trestle tables. Clare Scott unfolded a couple of chairs, he sat on one and she on the other. A clock on the wall with a large face and a loud tick gave the time as five past ten. He and Clare talked about the morality of betraying family members in aid of the greater good, whether one never should but keep silent out of loyalty or whether one always should and whether there were exceptions. They talked about the heinousness of rape. Perhaps it was right to betray the perpetrator only in the case of a crime of violence. You wouldn't report your wife's shoplifting, would you? The time went by and no one knocked at the door. They gave it another five minutes but when they came out of the room at twenty to eleven the hall was empty. There was no one outside. The place was deserted.

seven

His face looked back at him from the front page of the Sunday paper, a so-called quality Sunday paper. And not only his face. The photograph showed himself and Burden at the table outside the Olive and Dove, only there wasn't much of Burden. Burden would be unrecognizable except to those who knew him well. His, on the other hand, was an excellent likeness. He was smiling—well, laughing, to tell the truth—as he raised to his lips the brimming tankard of Heineken. In case there was any doubt, the caption said: *Wexford hunts Annette's killer*, and underneath was the legend: *Chief Inspector in charge of Kingsmarkham murder has time to relax with a pint.*

There hadn't been a moment, he reflected bitterly, when his thoughts hadn't been occupied with Annette Bystock and her death. But to whom could he tell that without seeming absurdly defensive? He could do nothing but pretend he didn't care and thank God the Deputy Chief Constable bought *The Mail* on Sunday.

Things were not improved by the arrival of Sylvia with Neil and the boys. His daughter, having forgotten which newspaper he took, had brought her own copy of the offending one to show him on the grounds that he would "want to see it." And no amount of arguing on the part of her mother and her husband could persuade

her that there was any irony in the caption. In her eyes it was
"nice," the best photograph she had seen of her father in years and
did he think the newspaper would let her have a copy?

Sylvia dominated the conversation at lunch. She was fast
becoming an expert on the provisions made by government for its
jobless citizens and their dependents. Wexford and Dora had to
listen to a lecture on Unemployment Benefit and who was entitled
to it, the differences between it and Income Support, and the
amenities of something called a "Job Club" which she was engaged
in pulling strings for Neil to join.

"They have all the main newspapers there and free use of the
phone, which has to be taken into consideration. And they supply
envelopes and stamps."

"Sounds a breeze," said her father sourly. "Somebody once
took me to lunch at the Garrick and there weren't any free stamps
there."

Sylvia ignored him. "After he's been unemployed another
three months he can go on a training course. An TFW course
might be best . . ."

"A *what?*"

"Training For Work. And I think I might do one for computers. Robin, be a love, and get the leaflets from my handbag,
will you?"

"*Nitchi vo,*" said Robin.

Unable to bear another run-through of the most boring brochures he had ever seen in his life, Wexford made an excuse and
resorted to the living room. Sport dominated the television pro-
grams and he balked at switching to the news in case, mysteriously,
his own portrait had found its way to the screen. It was paranoia
but he knew no way of conquering it. He even speculated if it
could be a journalist's revenge for what he had said the previous
night about the press fomenting people's fears of violence.

He was still smarting, though less painfully, when he came into
his office very early next morning. His team's reports were already
on his desk and no one was going to say a word about that photo-

graph. Burden had seen it. That particular newspaper wasn't his choice but Jenny's.

"Funny how you get used to it," Wexford said. "I mean the way the passage of time eases things. I don't feel as bad about it today as I did yesterday and tomorrow I won't feel as bad as I do today. If only we could live by that instead of just coming to the knowledge afresh each time, if we could be aware at the time that it's not going to matter a lot after a couple of days, life'd be a lot easier, wouldn't it?"

"Hm. You are what you are and that's about it. You can't change your nature."

"What a depressing philosophy." Wexford began going through the reports. "Jane Winster, the cousin, identified the body. Not that there was much doubt. We should get something from old Tremlett today or maybe tomorrow morning. Vine interviewed Mrs. Winster at her home in Pomfret but he doesn't seem to have learned much. They weren't close. So far as she knows, Annette had no boyfriends and, oddly, no close woman friend. It sounds a very lonely life. Ingrid Pamber seems to have been the only person she was friendly with."

"Yes, but would the Winster woman know? She hadn't seen Annette since April. That would be understandable if she lived in Scotland, say, but she lives in *Pomfret* and that's all of three miles. They can't have liked each other much."

"Mrs. Winster says, I quote, 'I had my own family to think about.' They spoke to each other on the phone. Annette always went to them on Christmas Day and was apparently with them when they celebrated a twentieth wedding anniversary. Still, as you say, it's a bit distant." He worked through the pages, pausing occasionally to read something twice. "He also saw that Mrs. Harris we talked to—remember? Edwina Harris, the woman upstairs? She said she heard nothing at night, but she admits she and her husband are heavy sleepers. Another thing she insists on is that she never saw any friend call on Annette or Annette leave the building or come into it with someone accompanying her.

"Neither of the supervisors at the Benefit Office, that's Niall Clarke and Valerie Parker, seems to know anything about Annette, her private life, that is. Peter Stanton—he's the other new claims adviser, the one who looks like the young Sean Connery— he seems to have been very open with Pemberton, told him he took Annette out a couple of times. And then Cyril Leyton told him it wouldn't do. He didn't want staff getting into 'intimate relationships.' "

"And Stanton accepted that?"

"It doesn't sound as if he was bothered. He told Pemberton they hadn't much in common, whatever that means. Hayley Gordon, she's the young administrative officer, the fair one, she hardly knew Annette, she's only been on the staff a month. Karen saw Osman Messaoud and Wendy Stowlap. Messaoud was very nervous. He was born and brought up in this country but he's uneasy around women. He told Karen he didn't want to be interviewed by a woman, he wanted, again I quote, 'a police*man*' and he said if Karen questioned him about a woman, Annette that is, his wife would be suspicious. However, he seems to know less than nothing about Annette's life outside the Benefit Office.

"Apart from Ingrid Pamber, Wendy Stowlap appears to be the only member of staff to have been to Annette's flat. She herself lives fairly near, in Queens Gardens. It was a Sunday and she wanted someone to witness a document—doesn't say what kind of document—something she apparently didn't want the neighbors to know about, so she took it round to Annette. Annette was watching a video and told Wendy she'd just bought a new video recorder, some special kind that you punch a code into. That was six or seven months ago. All this circumlocution seems just to prove she did in fact have a VCR. Now let's have a look at what Barry has to say about Ingrid Pamber . . ."

But at that moment Detective Sergeant Vine came into the room. Vine wasn't really a short man but he looked short beside Wexford, and Burden too towered above him. He had the extraordinary combination of red hair on his head and dark hair on his upper lip. If he was in Barry Vine's shoes, Wexford had often thought, he'd shave off that mustache. But Vine—though this was unexpressed seemed to enjoy the bi-colored effect, appearing to believe it gave him distinction. He was sharp and watchful and clever, a man with a prodigious memory that he crammed with all kinds of information, useful and otherwise.

"Have you looked at my report yet, sir?"

"I'm reading it now, Barry. This Ingrid really was Annette's only friend, wasn't she?"

"Not exactly. How about this married man?"

"What married man? Ah . . . wait a minute. Ingrid Pamber told you Annette had confided in her she'd been having an affair for the past *nine years* with a married man?"

"That's right."

"Why didn't she tell me this on Friday?"

Vine sat down on the edge of the desk. "She said she'd lain awake all night, wondering what was the right thing to do. She'd promised Annette faithfully, you see, that she'd never tell."

The man who had phoned the Benefit Office, Wexford thought, the man Ingrid had said was a neighbor. "All right. Yes, I can imagine. Spare us the schoolgirl heart-searching, will you?"

Vine grinned. "I gave her the usual stuff, sir. Annette's dead, promises to a dead person weren't valid, didn't she want to help find whoever killed her, all that. She told me a bit and then she said she'd tell you. I mean, she'd only tell you."

"Really? What have I got that you haven't, Barry? Must be age." Wexford concealed the mild embarrassment he felt by pretending to read from the report. "We'll gratify her, shall we?"

"I thought you'd say that, so I asked her if she'd be at the Benefit Office, but no, she won't be. She starts two weeks' leave today and she and her boyfriend can't afford to go away. She'll be at home."

Burden stepped over the yellow scene-of-crime tape, unlocked the door of the flat, and went inside. Starting at the living room, he walked from room to room, slowly studying every object, looking out of the window into reddish-brown foliage, the concrete drive, the red brick side of the house next door. He took down what few books there were and shook their pages in case there were sheets enclosed but with no particular purpose in mind. In the living room he looked carefully at Annette Bystock's music on a shelf of the bookcase, the compact disks for the missing CD player, the cassettes for the missing cassette player which was also a radio.

Her taste seemed to have been for popular classics and country. *Eine Kleine Nachtmusik*, Bach's *Mass in B Minor*—Burden had heard that this was among the top sellers in classical music—highlights from *Porgy and Bess*, a complete *Carmen Jones*, Beethoven's *Moonlight Sonata*, Natalie Cole's album *Unforgettable*, Michelle Wright, k.d. lang, Patsy Cline . . . Without Wexford breathing reproof over his shoulder, Burden was quick to notice that Natalie Cole was a black woman and that *Porgy and Bess* and *Carmen Jones* were about black people. Was that significant?

He was trying to find points of connection between Annette and Melanie Akande. There was no desk in the flat. The dressing table up against the bedroom window had served as a desk. Her passport had been taken away. Burden looked at the other papers in the drawer. They were contained in one of those folders made of clear plastic: certificates showing Annette's O and A Level results, a certificate or diploma showing that she had gained a Bachelor of Arts pass degree in Business Studies at Myringham Polytechnic. That was where Melanie Akande had completed her education, only they called it Myringham University now. Burden looked at the date: 1976. Melanie was only three in 1976. Yet there might be a link there. . . .

Edwina Harris had told them she thought Annette had once been married. There was no marriage certificate in the top drawer. Burden tried the bottom one and found a decree of divorce, dissolving the marriage of Annette Rosemary Colegate née Bystock, and Stephen Henry Colegate, the divorce having been made absolute on June 29, 1985.

No letters. He had hoped for letters. A brown envelope, eight inches by five, contained a photograph of a man with a high fore-head and dark curly hair. Under it was a stack of pamphlets in-structing purchasers how to operate a Panasonic video recorder and an Akai CD player. The middle drawer held underclothes. He had already had a good look at the clothes in the wardrobe when he and Wexford came here on Friday. They were safe, dull clothes, the sort bought by a woman who can afford few and must put warmth and comfort before style. Therefore the underclothes sur-prised him.

They weren't quite what Burden would have called indecent. There were no bras with cutouts, no crotchless pants. But all the—lingerie, he supposed, was the word—all of it was black or red and most of it transparent. There were two suspender belts, one black, one red, ordinary black bras and black platform bras, one strapless; a thing he called a corselet but Jenny said was a "bustier" in red satin and lace, several pairs of black stockings, plain, fishnet, and lacy, red and black knickers the size of the bottom part of a bikini, and a kind of body stocking of black lace.

Had she worn that stuff under those jeans and sweaters, that beige raincoat?

Instead of clearing, as the meteorologists had said it would, the summery mist thinned and turned to rain. A gray drizzle began to fall and cool things down. Vine, driving the car, began speculat-ing as to why rain in England is always cold while in other parts of the world it is warm and why, which he said was more to the point, it doesn't warm up again here afterward as it does abroad.

"Something to do with being an island, I expect," said Wex-ford abstractedly.

"Malta's an island. When I was there on holiday last year it rained but the sun came out afterward and we were dry in five min-utes. Did you see that picture of yourself in the paper yesterday?"

"Yes."

"I cut it out to show you but I seem to have mislaid it some-where."

"Good."

Vine said no more. They drove in silence to Glebe Lane, where Ingrid Pamber lived in two rooms over a pair of lock-up garages with her boyfriend Jeremy Lang. Vine gave it as his opinion that as it was the first day of her holiday and only ten to ten in the morning she would still be in bed.

The neighborhood was one of the charmless areas of Kingsmarkham. All you could say for it was that beyond the shabbiness, the waste ground and squat buildings, green hills rose skyward, topped with tree rings and behind them the sweep of downs. The district was vaguely commercial or industrial, some of the little houses converted to business premises, a good many buildings of the small factory or workshop kind. Gardens had become yards filled with used cars, scrap iron, oil drums, unidentifiable metal parts. The garages had one door painted black, the other green. At the side, approached by a narrow passage between chain-link fencing, was the front door to the flat. There was no shelter from the rain. Vine rang the bell.

After rather a long time, during which there was some banging about and creaking from the upper floor, feet drummed on the stairs and the door was opened by a young man with wild black hair wearing nothing but black-framed glasses and a bath towel round his waist.

"Oh, sorry," he said when he saw them. "I thought you were the post. I'm expecting a parcel."

"Kingsmarkham CID," said Wexford, who wasn't usually so brusque. "To see Miss Pamber."

"Oh, sure. Come up."

He was a small man, no more than five feet six, and fine-boned with it. The girl was no doubt, as Vine had predicted, still in bed. He closed the door behind them with perfect trust.

"You're Mr. Lang?"

"That's me, though I'm mostly known as Jerry."

"Mr. Lang, are you in the habit of letting strangers into your home without question?"

Jeremy Lang peered at Wexford and pushed his right ear at him as if he had been addressed inaudibly or in a foreign language. "You're police, you said."

Neither Wexford nor Vine said anything. Each produced his warrant card and held it under Lang's nose. He grinned and nodded. He began to go upstairs, gestured to them to follow him, suddenly yelling at the top of his voice: "Hey, Ing, you going to get up? It's the cops."

Upstairs was a surprise. Wexford hardly knew what he had expected, but not this pleasantly furnished clean room with a big yellow sofa, blue and yellow floor cushions on a big brightly colored woven mat, the walls entirely concealed under draped lengths of cloth, posters, and a huge faded tapestry bedspread. Everything had obviously been perks from a parent or else bought very cheaply but it made a harmonious and comfortable place to be. Houseplants in a yellow-painted wooden trough filled the floorspace between the windows.

The door to the bedroom opened and Ingrid Pamber came out. She too wasn't yet dressed but there was nothing frowsty about her, nothing to suggest she had just risen from a long lie-in. She wore a dressing gown or robe of white broderie anglaise that came to her knees. Her small shapely feet were bare. The satiny dark hair, which had been confined by a barrette when Wexford had talked to her on Friday evening, was now held back by a red Alice band. Without makeup her face was even prettier, the skin glowing, the blueness of her eyes startling.

"Oh, hallo, it's you," she said to Wexford, sounding delighted to see him. On Vine she bestowed a friendly smile.

"Would you like some coffee? If I ask him very nicely, I'm sure Jerry will make us some coffee."

"Ask me nicely then," said Jeremy Lang.

She gave him a kiss. A highly sexual kiss, Wexford thought, in spite of being planted in the middle of his cheek and with closed lips. The kiss lingered, she withdrew her mouth an inch, whispered, "Make us some coffee, my love, please, please. And I'm going to have a huge breakfast, two eggs and bacon and sausages if we've got any and—yes, fried potatoes. You'll cook it for me, won't you, angel? Please, please, mmm?"

Vine coughed. He was exasperated rather than embarrassed. Ingrid sat down on a floor cushion and gazed up at them. She was, Wexford thought, immeasurably more confident and in control here, on her home ground.

"I've already told him a bit of it," she said, glancing at Vine. "I've saved the important part for you. It's an amazing story."

"All right," Wexford said, and in the manner of Cocteau to Diaghilev, "Astound me."

"I never told anyone before, you know. Not even Jerry. I think people should keep their promises, don't you?"

"Certainly they should," Wexford said. "But not beyond the grave."

Ingrid Pamber evidently enjoyed this kind of conversation. "Yes, but if you'd promised somebody something and they died it wouldn't be right to break your promise and tell their children, would it? Not if it affected the children? I mean, it might be something about them that would ruin their lives."

"Let's not get on to moral philosophy now, Miss Pamber. Annette Bystock hadn't any children. She had no relatives apart from a cousin. I'd like to hear what she told you about this love affair she was having."

"He might be affected though, mightn't he?"

"Who do you mean?"

"Well, Bruce. The man. The man I told *him* about." She pointed a forefinger at Vine.

"Leave that to me," said Wexford. "I'll worry about that."

Jeremy Lang came back with coffee in three cups and on a plate, like a waiter in certain kinds of restaurant displaying to clients the raw materials of their meal, two eggs still in their shells, two rashers of bacon, three pork sausages, and a potato.

"Thank you." Ingrid looked into his eyes and said it again, "Thank you, thank you, that will be lovely," the words apparently having some special or secret meaning for the two of them, for the effect on him was to make him roll his eyes while she began to giggle. Wexford coughed. He could manage to get a good deal of reproach into a cough. "Oh, sorry," she said, and she stopped laughing. "I must be good. I shouldn't laugh. I'm really very, very sad about poor Annette."

"How long had you known her, Miss Pamber?" Vine asked.

"Since I started working for the ES three years ago. I've *told* you all this. I was a teacher before that, only I wasn't much good. I couldn't get on with the kids and they hated me."

"You didn't tell me that," said Vine.

"Well, it's not exactly relevant, is it? I had a place quite near where Annette lived. That was before I met Jerry." She cast Jeremy Lang a loving look and pursed up her lips in a kissing shape. "We used to walk home together, Annette and I, and sometimes we'd have a meal somewhere. You know, if we didn't feel like cooking or getting anything in. I went to her flat once or twice but she came to mine much more and I just had a room. I got the feeling she didn't like asking people to her place.

"Then—well, I met someone and we started—" A rueful look this time for Jeremy, who returned it with a pantomime frown. "We started going about. I didn't live with him or anything," she added, not making clear what "anything" might signify. "That was what made Annette tell me, I think. Or it might have been that one evening when I did go into her place and while I was there the phone rang and it was *him*. That was when she made me promise not to tell anyone what she was going to tell me.

"She'd been so jumpy before the phone rang. I'd guess he'd promised to phone at seven and it was nearly eight. She grabbed that phone like it was—well, a matter of life and death. Afterward she said, 'Can you keep a secret?' and I said of course I could and she said, 'Well, I've got someone too. That was him,' and then it all came out."

"His name, Miss Pamber?"

"Bruce. His name's Bruce. I don't know Bruce *What*."

"This was the man you thought had phoned the Benefit Office after Miss Bystock phoned to say she wouldn't be coming in?"

She nodded, untroubled by that earlier lie. "You know where he lives?" Vine asked.

A sip of the coffee, hotter than she had expected, made her squeeze her eyes tight shut for a moment. "My boyfriend and me, we were going to Pomfret one day and we gave Annette a lift. She was going to see her cousin. It was sort of Christmas, the day before Christmas Eve, I think. Annette was sitting in the back and as we passed this house she tapped on my shoulder and said, 'Look at that, that house with the window in the roof, that's where you-know-who lives.' That was what she said, 'you-know-who.'"

"I don't know the number. I could show you." Furious faces of discouragement made by Jeremy weren't lost on Wexford. Ingrid saw them and sighed happily. "I could describe it. I will. You mustn't make silly faces, lovey. Now run away and cook my breakfast."

"What did you do with the key to Miss Bystock's flat," Wexford asked, "when you left on Thursday?"

She answered promptly—too promptly.

Sitting in the car outside 101 Harrow Avenue, a biggish Victorian house on three floors to which a fourth had been added with a dormer window in the mansard roof, Wexford gave Burden an account of what Ingrid Pamber had told him. They had already been to the house and found no one at home. It was about as far from the street in which Annette lived as was possible and still be in Kingsmarkham.

The electoral roll had shown its occupants to be Snow, Carolyn E.; Snow, Bruce J.; and Snow, Melissa E. Wife, husband, and grown-up daughter, Wexford guessed. No hint, of course, was given in the list of those eligible to vote as to how many other children the Snows might have.

"She'd been having this affair with him for nine years," Wexford said. "Or so she told Ingrid Pamber, and I can't think of any reason why even a liar like her should lie about that. It was one of those situations in which the married man tells his mistress he'll leave his wife for her as soon as the children are off their hands. Nine years ago Bruce Snow's youngest child was five, so you could say if you were a cynic like me that he was on to a good thing."

"Right," said Burden in a heartfelt way.

Wexford cast up his eyes. "Wait for it. It gets better. They had to meet somewhere but he never took her to a hotel, he said he couldn't afford it. After that trip past the house in the boyfriend's car Ingrid asked her what Bruce had given her for Christmas and Annette said nothing, he never gave her anything, she'd never had a present from him. He needed everything he had for his family. Mind you, according to Ingrid, Annette wasn't resentful, she never criticized him. She *understood*."

"I take it that after the first confidings there were more on other occasions?"

"Oh, yes. Once she'd started, there was no stopping her. It was Bruce this and Bruce that whenever she and Ingrid were alone together. I imagine it was a relief to the poor woman to have someone she could talk to." Wexford took another look at the house, at the signs of prosperity about it, the evidently recent rooftop extension, the new paint, the satellite dish outside an upper window. "As I said," he went on, "Snow never took her to a hotel and of course they couldn't go to his house. She had her flat but he refused to go there. Apparently, there was some friend or relative of his wife living opposite. So he summoned her to his office after hours."

"You're joking," said Burden.

"Not unless Ingrid Pamber is and I doubt if she'd have the imagination. Snow never wrote to her, which is why we found no letters. He gave her nothing, not even a photograph of himself. He phoned, at appointed times, 'when he could.' But she loved him, you see, and that was why all that was okay, was reasonable in her eyes, was prudent. After all, it would only go on so long as the children were young."

Burden used his small son's currently favorite word, "Yuck!"

"I couldn't put it better myself. When he wanted to meet her, or let's say when he wanted his bit on the side"—Wexford ignored Burden's pained expression—"he'd ask her to come to his office. He's an accountant with Hawkins and Steele."

"Is he now? In York Street, aren't they?"

"In one of those very old houses that overhang the street. The back way has access into Kiln Lane, that sort of alley that comes out in the High Street the other side of St. Peter's. There's never a soul about down there after the shops close and Kiln Lane is just an alley between high walls. Annette could sneak down there and he'd let her in by the back door. The best part of this—or the worst part, depending on how you look at it—is that he explained his choice of venue by saying that if his wife phoned the office he'd be there to answer it and she'd know he was working late."

Lights were coming on in the houses but 101 remained in darkness. Wexford and Burden left the car again and walked up the drive. A side gate was unlocked and they went into the rear garden, a large area of lawn and shrubs whose end was lost in a cluster of tall trees, darkening as the dusk came.

"She did that for nine years?" said Burden. "Like a call girl?"

"A call girl would expect a bed, Mike, and probably a glass of something stimulating. Call girls, I'm told, expect bathrooms. And very definitely to get paid."

"It explains the underwear." Burden described what he had found at the flat in Ladyhall Court. "She'd always be ready for him. I wonder what's going through his mind now?"

"Is he the guy in the photo, d'you think? What I'm wondering is if he's away on holiday."

"He won't be, Reg. Not if his youngest is only fourteen. He'll wait for the school term to end and that won't be for a couple of weeks."

"We have to see him and soon."

Burden considered. "What makes you say this Ingrid's a liar?"

"She told me she left the key Annette gave her behind in the flat after she left on Thursday. If she did, where is it?"

"It was on the bedside table," said Burden promptly.

"No, it wasn't, Mike. Not unless she was lying when she said there were two keys there on Wednesday. One of those statements of hers has to be a lie."

eight

 nly two samples of fingerprints had been found in Annette Bystock's flat. Most were those of Annette herself; the other set of women's prints, on the surface of the grocer's box, the kitchen door, the front door, and the hall table, were those of Ingrid Pamber. Not another print had been found in the whole place. It seemed as if Annette's home had not only been her castle, it had been the cell where she passed her solitary confinement.

The thief of the electronic equipment had worn gloves. Her killer had worn gloves. Bruce Snow had never set foot or finger inside the home of the woman who had been his mistress for nearly a decade. No friend, apart from Ingrid, had come there. It was likely, Wexford thought, that Annette had discouraged potential friends. Such visitors might overhear one of her conversations with Snow, might betray her; more to the point as she saw it, might by some indiscretion destroy Snow's carefully planned cover. So, for love's sake, she lived this lonely life. It was the saddest story . . .

The one friend she had she must have trusted to be discreet. And if Ingrid was to be believed her trust was not misplaced, for Ingrid had told no one until after Annette was dead. It seemed that her death had occurred about seven months after she had first confided in Ingrid, so it was hardly likely to be the result of her divulging the secret or divulging more details.

Wexford sighed. Annette had died in the region of thirty-six hours before Burden found her body on Friday morning. Not earlier than ten P.M. on the Wednesday and not later than one A.M. on the Thursday. By the time Ingrid Pamber went into the flat at five-thirty on Thursday evening, Annette had been dead for nearly a day. Death was due to strangulation with a ligature, in this case a length of electric lead. He knew that already and such medical details were always incomprehensible. Tremlett offered his opinion that a strong woman might have been the perpetrator. Until her death Annette had been a normal healthy woman with no distinguishing marks, not a scar on her body, no peculiarities or minor deformities. She was of normal weight for her height. There was no disease of any kind present.

The flat had been clean but still a considerable amount of hairs and fibers had been gathered from the bed, the bedside tables, and the floor. How helpful it would be, Wexford thought as he often did, if one of the investigating officers had picked up a spent cigarette end in the vicinity of the body, as happened in detective stories. Or if a button torn from the killer's jacket and obligingly retaining a fragment of tweed on its shank had been found clutched in poor Annette's lifeless hand. Such clues never came his way. Of course it was true that nobody goes anywhere without leaving a vestige of himself behind and taking a vestige of where he has been away with him. That was only useful if you had a clue who and where he might be . . .

He was leaving for the local studios to make his television appeal for help from the public when his phone rang. The switchboard said it was the Chief Constable for him, calling from his home in Stowerton.

Freeborn, a cold man, always went straight to the heart of things. "I don't want to see pictures of you carousing."

"No, sir. It was unfortunate."

"It was more than that, it was bloody disgraceful. And in a *good* newspaper too."

"I can't see it would have been any better in a tabloid," said Wexford.

"Then that's just one of the many things you ought to see and don't." Freeborn went on for quite a long time about the need to catch Annette's murderer fast, about the increase in violent crime, about this lovely, safe, once secure place in which they lived, quickly becoming as dangerous as some inner suburb of London. "And when you go on TV try not to have a glass in your hand."

They allowed him only two minutes and that, he knew, would be cut to thirty seconds. Still, it was better than nothing. His appeal would call forth from a public who longed to be important its members' imagined and fantasized sightings of a killer in the vicinity of Ladyhall Avenue, confessions to the crime, offers from clairvoyants, claims to have been at school with Annette, at college with her, to have been her lover, her mother, her sister, to have seen her in Inverness or Carlisle or Budapest after she was dead, and, perhaps, one genuine and valuable piece of information.

He got to bed late. But he was up early just as the post came. Dora came down in her dressing gown to get his breakfast, an affectionate but unnecessary move as he was only having cereal and a piece of bread.

"One letter and it's for both of us. You open it."

Dora slit the envelope and drew out a card, deckle-edged. "Goodness, Reg, she must have taken a fancy to you."

"Who must? What are you talking about?" Strange that his thoughts ran straight to pretty Ingrid Pamber.

"Invitations to this party are like gold dust, Sylvia says. She'd *love* to go."

"Let's have a look." What a fool! Why did he take these fancies into his head at his age? He read aloud what was on the card. " 'Wael and Anouk Khoori request the pleasure of the company of Mr. and Mrs. Reginald Wexford at a Garden Party at their home, Mynford New Hall, Mynford, Sussex, on Saturday, July seventeenth, at 3 P.M.' " At the foot of the card was the addendum: "In aid of CIBACT, the Cancer in Babies and Children Trust."

"They're not giving us much notice. It's the thirteenth today."

"No, well, that's what I mean. We obviously weren't on the guest list. And then she took a shine to you last Saturday night."

"I bet Freeborn's on the list," Wexford said gloomily. "Everyone will be expected to fork out at least a tenner, which is a bit of a nerve when you consider Khoori's a millionaire. He could underwrite this CIBACT himself without fund-raising bonanzas. Anyway, it doesn't matter since we shan't go."

"I should like to go," Dora said as her husband disappeared out of the door. She called after him, "I said I should like to go, Reg."

There was no answer. The front door closed quietly.

The inquest on Annette Bystock opened at ten A.M. and was adjourned pending further evidence at ten past. Jane Winster, who was Annette's cousin, though not attending it, was waiting for Wexford when he got back to the police station. Somebody— some fool, he thought—had put her in one of the bleak interview rooms, where she sat on a tubular metal chair in front of the chipboard table, looking puzzled and a little alarmed.

"You have something you want to tell me, Mrs. Winster?"

She nodded. She looked about her, as well she might, at the cream-painted brick walls, the uncurtained window.

"Come upstairs to my office," he said.

Someone's head ought to roll for this. What did they take her for, this small middle-aged woman buttoned up in her raincoat, a damp scarf tied round her head? A shoplifter? A bag-snatcher? She looked like a school dinner lady who could have done with a good helping of what she purveyed. Her face was thin and pinched, her hands bony and veined, prematurely aged.

Once in the comparative comfort of his office, carpeted and with seats that were almost armchairs, he expected her to complain of her treatment, but she only gave the room the same wary look. Perhaps all new places overawed her, so sheltered and circumscribed was her life. He asked her to sit down and he repeated what he had said to her downstairs. For the first time she spoke, having seated herself on the edge of the chair, her knees pressed together.

"The policeman who came, there was something I forgot to tell him. It was a bit . . . I mean, I was . . ."

Vine's briskness had intimidated her, he supposed. "It doesn't matter, Mrs. Winster. You've remembered now, that's the main thing."

"It was a shock, you see. I mean, we weren't . . . well, we weren't close, Annette and me, but . . . well, she was my *cousin*, my own auntie's daughter."

"Yes."

"And having to go to that place and see her—well, dead like that, that was a shock. I've never had to do anything like that before and I . . ."

A woman who left sentences unfinished through self-doubt and perhaps uncertainty that anyone would ever take her seriously. He realized that all this was in the nature of an apology. She was apologizing for having emotions.

"I did tell him we phoned each other. I mean, I said we spoke on the phone but he was—well, he was more interested in when I'd last seen her. I hadn't seen her since she came to our wedding anniversary, and that was April, April the third."

"But you had spoken on the phone?"

She was going to need a lot of prompting and of the kind Vine wasn't the man to give. She looked at him appealingly.

"She phoned me on the Tuesday before she . . . last Tuesday, I mean . . ."

The day Melanie Akande had spoken to her. "Was that in the evening, Mrs. Winster?"

"In the evening, about seven. I was getting my husband's meal on the table. He doesn't—well, he doesn't like to be kept waiting. I was a bit surprised she phoned, but then she said she wasn't feeling too good, she thought she'd go to bed early." Mrs. Winster hesitated. "My husband—well, my husband was making signs to me, so

I put the phone down for a minute and he said—I know you'll think this sounds awful . . ."

"Please go on, Mrs. Winster."

"My husband—it's not that he didn't like Annette, it's really that he doesn't care for any outsiders. Our own family's enough for us, he always says. Of course, Annette *was* family in a way, but he always says cousins don't count. He said to me, I mean when Annette was on the phone, he said, don't get involved. If she's ill she'll expect you to go over there getting her shopping and all the rest of it. Well, I suppose she did expect that, that's why she phoned, and I felt awful saying I was busy, I couldn't talk then, but I have to put his wishes first, don't I?"

If this was all, he was wasting his time. He had to be patient. "You rang off?"

"Well, no. Not at once. She said, could she call me back later? I didn't know what to say. Then she said there was something else, something she wanted to ask me about, maybe ask Malcolm too—Malcolm's my husband—it was whether she ought to go to the police."

"Ah." This was it, then. "She told you what this was about?"

"No, because she was going to call me back. But she didn't."

"You didn't phone her?"

Jane Winster flushed. She looked defiant. "My husband doesn't like me making unnecessary phone calls. And it's up to him, isn't it? He earns the money."

"Tell me exactly what your cousin said to you about going to the police."

Wexford was beginning to understand Vine's impatience with her as a witness, even understand whoever it was who had incarcerated her in that grim interview room. His sympathies were fast diminishing. Here was just another person who had rejected Annette Bystock. She was fidgeting with her handbag, pursing her lips; a woman, he guessed, who though an expert at putting herself down would deeply resent anyone else's criticism.

"I can't do the exact words, or I don't . . . well, it was some-

thing like, 'There was something happened through work and
I think maybe I should go to the police, but I want to see what
you think and maybe Malcolm too.' That was all."

"You mean 'at' work, don't you?"

"No. 'Through work' is what she said."

"You never spoke to her again?"

"She never phoned back and I . . . no, I . . . I hadn't any call to
speak to her."

He nodded. Her cousin having failed her, Annette had called
on the slightly more sympathetic Ingrid to come in, do her shopping, pay her the small attentions needed by someone with "the
falling sickness." As for the police, she had changed her mind, or
more likely, postponed the phone call she should have made until
she was better. But she was never better, she was much, much
worse and it was too late.

"Did your cousin ever mention a man called Bruce Snow?"

She looked up with indifference. "No. Who's he?"

"You'd be surprised to learn he was a married man Miss Bystock had been in a relationship with for several years?"

Jane Winster was more shocked than she had been by her
cousin's death, more shocked than when she saw Annette's dead
face in the mortuary. "I'll never believe that. Annette would never
have done a thing like that. She wasn't that sort of person." Astonishment had made her articulate. "My husband would never
have had her in the house if there'd ever been a suspicion of any of
that. Oh, no, you've got it wrong there. Not Annette, Annette
wouldn't have done that."

When she had gone, Wexford had a call put through to Hawkins and Steele and asked to speak to Mr. Snow. Waiting while a
tape played "Greensleeves," he thought about Snow and wondered how appalling a shock hearing who was calling him would
be. Annette, after all, had been found dead on the previous Friday,
it had been on television on Friday, in the papers on Saturday. But
no one knew of their liaison except Annette and himself, did they?
And Annette was dead. He must think he had got away with it.

Got away with exactly what, though, Wexford asked himself.

"Mr. Snow is on his other line. Will you hold?"

"No, I won't. I'll call back in ten minutes. You can tell him it's Kingsmarkham Police."

That should stir him up a bit. Wexford wouldn't have been surprised if Snow had called back himself, unable to wait to know the worst, but no call came. He gave it a quarter of an hour before dialing the number again.

"Mr. Snow is in a meeting."

"Did you give him the message?"

"Yes, I did, but he had this meeting straight after he came off the phone."

"I see. How long will this meeting last?"

"Half an hour. Mr. Snow has his next meeting at eleven-fifteen."

"Give him another message, will you? Tell him to cancel his other meeting as Chief Inspector Wexford will see him in his office at eleven."

"I can't possibly . . ."

"Thank you." Wexford put the phone down. His temper had started to rise. He remembered his blood pressure. Then he had a good idea that made him laugh to himself before he picked up the phone again and asked DS Karen Malahyde to come up and see him.

Karen Malahyde was very much the new woman. Young, fairly good-looking, she did nothing to enhance her looks. Her face was always without makeup of any kind, her fair hair was very short as were her fingernails. Many with fewer advantages than she had made themselves into beauties. She could do nothing, however, to disguise the excellence of her figure. Karen was a beautiful shape and had the sort of long legs that looked as if they started at her waist. She was a feminist and almost a radical one, a good police officer but one who had sometimes to be cautioned not to lean too hard on men or favor women.

"Yes, sir?"

"I want you to come with me on a visit to a gallant lover."

"Sir?"

Wexford told her some of Annette Bystock's love story. Instead of castigating Snow as a bastard, which was what he expected, she said rather gloomily, "These women are their own worst enemies," and then, "Did he kill her?"

"I don't know."

They entered the old house by the front door in York Street. Inside it was poky and low-ceilinged but authentically ancient, the kind of place that is generally said to be full of character. There was no lift. The receptionist left her desk and took them upstairs, up a narrow creaking oak staircase, winding to a passage at the top. She knocked on a door, opened it, and said rather cryptically, "Your eleven o'clock appointment, Mr. Snow."

The man in the photograph Burden had found came up to them with outstretched hand. Wexford pretended not to have seen it. For a moment he thought Snow hadn't been told who his callers were. Surely if he had known he could hardly have been so confident, would hardly have smiled so winningly.

"I'm happy to tell you it's turned up," he said.

They were evidently at cross-purposes, but how and why Wexford couldn't tell. He thought that if he didn't keep a watch on himself he might start enjoying this. It was going to be good.

"What has turned up, sir?"

"My driving license, of course. There were five places it could have been, I looked in them and there it was in the fifth and last." Snow realized that something was wrong but he was only disconcerted, not fearful. "I'm sorry. What did you want to see me about?"

Karen was looking offended at being taken for a traffic cop. Wexford asked, "What do you *think* we want to see you about, Mr. Snow?"

A wariness in his eyes showed that realization was dawning. He put up his eyebrows, his head a little on one side. He was a tall thin man, his bushy dark hair graying, not good-looking but with an air of distinction. Wexford thought he had a mean mouth. "How should I know?" he said in a voice that was a little shriller than it had been.

"May we sit down?"

Karen, when she was seated, couldn't help showing a lot of leg. Even in those awful brown lace-ups with their Cuban heels, her legs were spectacular. Snow gave them a swift but significant glance.

"I'm surprised you don't know why we've come, Mr. Snow," Wexford said. "I'd have thought you'd be expecting us."

"I was. I told you, I thought you were here because I couldn't produce my license when I was stopped on Saturday." He knew, Wexford could tell. Was he going to brazen it out? Snow's fingers fidgeted with objects on his desk, straightening a sheet of paper, replacing the cap on a pen. "So what is it then?"

"Annette Bystock."

"Who?"

If it hadn't been for those restless fingers, now busy with the telephone lead, those eyes that held a gleam of real panic, Wexford might have doubted, might have thought the dead woman a paranoid fantasist, Jane Winster an oracle, and Ingrid Pamber queen of the liars. He glanced at Karen.

"Annette Bystock was murdered last Wednesday," said Karen. "Don't you watch television? You haven't seen the papers? You and she had a relationship. You'd been having a relationship with her for nine years."

"I *what?*"

"I think you heard me, sir, but I don't mind repeating it. You had been having a relationship with Annette Bystock for . . ."

"That is absolute nonsense!"

Bruce Snow got to his feet. His thin face had gone a dark red and a pulse beat in a bluish vein on his forehead.

"How dare you come into my office and make these totally false suggestions!"

For some reason Wexford thought suddenly of Annette coming here, hiding in the alley, tapping on the back door, being brought up that winding stair by Snow to this office where there wasn't even a couch, where there was not the means to produce a drink or even a cup of tea. The phone was there, though, in case his wife called him.

He got up and Karen, taking her cue from him, also rose to her feet.

"No doubt it was a mistake coming to your office, Mr. Snow," he said. "I apologize." He watched Snow relax, breathe again, gather up his energy for a final blustering. "I'll tell you what we'll do. We'll come to your home this evening and talk about it there. Shall we say eight? That'll give you and your wife a chance to have your evening meal first."

I f it hadn't worked it would have shown he was wrong, one or both of the women were fantasists, he'd imagined every sign he'd detected in Snow, and he'd be for the high jump. Freeborn would like this a lot less than newspaper photographs of merry-making.

But it worked.

Snow said, "Sit down, please."

"Are you going to tell us about it, Mr. Snow?"

"What is there to tell? I'm not the first married man to have a girlfriend. As it happens, Annette and I had decided to break up. It was over." Snow paused, cleared his throat. "There is no point in my wife's knowing now. I may as well tell you I went to great lengths to conceal my relationship from my wife. I was anxious not to cause her pain. Annette understood that. Our relationship was, not to put too fine a point on it, purely physical."

"Then you never intended to leave your wife and marry Miss Bystock once your youngest child was off your hands?"

"Good heavens, no!"

Karen said, "Where did you meet, Mr. Snow? At Miss By-stock's home? At a hotel?"

"I can't see that that's relevant."

"Perhaps you'd answer the question just the same."

"At her home," said Snow uncomfortably. "We met at her home."

"That's odd, sir, because we didn't find any fingerprints in Miss Bystock's flat apart from her own and those of a woman friend. Perhaps you wiped surfaces clean of prints." Karen seemed to rack her brains. "Or—yes, that would be it—you wore gloves."

"Of course I didn't wear gloves!"

Snow was growing angry. Wexford watched the beating pulse, the bloodshot eyes. Had he no grief for Annette Bystock at all? After all that time was there no sorrow, no nostalgia even, no regret? And what did the man mean with his "purely physical" relationship? What did anyone ever mean? That there had been no words exchanged, no endearments, no promises? One at least he had extracted from the dead woman, that she tell nobody. She had very nearly kept it.

"When did you last see her?"

"I don't know. I'll have to think. A few weeks ago, I think it was a Wednesday."

"Here?" said Karen.

He shrugged, then nodded. Wexford said, "I'd like you to tell me where you were between eight P.M. and midnight last Wednesday. Wednesday, July the seventh."

"At home, of course. I've always got home by six."

"Except when you were meeting Miss Bystock."

Snow winced and coughed as if screwing up his face was a normal preliminary to clearing his throat. "I got home by six last Wednesday and I stayed at home. I didn't go out again."

"You spent the evening at home with your wife and—your children, Mr. Snow?"

"My elder daughter doesn't live at home. The younger one, Catherine, she's—well, she's not often in in the evenings . . ."

"But your wife and your son were with you? We shall need to talk to your wife."

"You can't bring my wife into this!"

"You have brought her into it yourself, Mr. Snow," Wexford said quietly.

Bruce Snow's 11:15 appointment had been canceled and now he was obliged to postpone the one he had with a tax inspector at 12:30. Wexford didn't think his misery had anything to do with guilt, or rather, with any responsibility for Annette's death. It was terror, the fear of his orderly world falling to pieces. But he couldn't be sure.

"Now you last saw Miss Bystock on a Wednesday some weeks ago. How many weeks, sir?"

"Do you really want me to be precise about it?"

"Certainly I do."

"Three weeks, then. It was three weeks."

"And when did you last talk to her on the phone?"

Snow didn't want to admit it. He screwed up his eyes like someone in a smoky room. "It was Tuesday evening."

"What, the Tuesday before her death?" Karen Malahyde was surprised. "Tuesday, the sixth?"

"I phoned her from here," Snow said in a rush. "I phoned her from this office just before I went home." He rubbed his hands together. "To make a date, if you must know. For the next night. God, this is my private life you're putting on the line. Anyway, it wasn't important, there was nothing, she just said she wasn't well. She was in bed. She'd got flu or something."

"Did she mention a girl called Melanie Akande? Did she say anything about giving information to the police?"

This gave Snow a sort of hope. Here was something else. The heat had, at least temporarily, gone off his long and suddenly reprehensible affair with Annette. But he gave a heavy sigh.

"No, I don't—wait a minute, did you say Akande? There's a doctor called that in the same practice as my doctor. Colored chap."

"Melanie is his daughter," said Karen.

"Well, what about her? I don't know anything about her. I

don't know him, I didn't know he had a daughter."

"Annette did. And Melanie Akande has disappeared. But no, of course not, Annette wouldn't have mentioned anything to you because yours was a purely physical relationship, you said, conducted in silence."

Snow was too wretched to lash back. He did ask when Wexford intended to speak to his wife.

"Oh, not yet, Mr. Snow," Wexford said. "Not today. I'll give you a chance to tell her yourself first." He dropped the faintly bantering tone and became serious. "I suggest you do that, sir, at the first possible opportunity."

William Cousins, the jeweler, took a good look at Annette Bystock's ring, pronounced it a fine ruby, and valued it at two thousand five hundred pounds. Give or take a little. That was around the sum he would be prepared to pay for such a ring if it was offered to him. He could probably sell it for much more.

It was one of Kingsmarkham's two market days, the other being Saturday. As a matter of routine, Sergeant Vine cast his eye over the goods for sale on the stalls in St. Peter's Place. The stolen stuff either turned up here or at the car boot sales in gardens or on waste ground that had become a regular weekend feature. He generally went round the stalls first, then headed for the sandwich bar to collect his lunch.

Leaving Cousins's, he began his investigation of the market, and on the second stall he looked at he saw for sale a radio-cassette player. It was made of a hard white plastic substance and across the top of it, just above the digital clock, was a dark red stain someone had tried in vain to eradicate. For a moment or two Vine thought the stain was blood and then he remembered.

nine

The worst thing, Dr. Akande told Wexford, was the way everybody asked them if there was any news of their daughter. All his patients knew and they all asked. At last, unable to keep the truth from him any longer, Laurette Akande had told her son when he telephoned from Kuala Lumpur. Immediately he said he would come home. As soon as he could get a cheap flight he would come back.

"The death of that other girl made me believe Melanie must also be dead," Akande said.

"I should be raising false hopes if I told you not to think that way."

"But I've told myself there's no connection. I have to keep hoping."

Wexford had come to them as he did most mornings on his way to work or evenings on his way home. Laurette, changed out of her sister's navy and white uniform into a linen dress, impressed him with her handsome looks, her dignified demeanor. He had seldom seen a woman with a straighter back. She showed less emotion than her husband, was always under control, cool, steady-eyed.

"I wonder if you can tell me what Melanie did the day before she . . . disappeared," he said. "On the Monday. What did she do that day?"

Akande didn't know. He had been at work but it was Laurette's day off. "She wanted a lie-in." Wexford got the impression that here was a mother who disapproved of staying in bed late. "I got her up at ten. It's no good getting into those habits if you want to get on in life. She went down to the shops, I don't know what for. In the afternoon she went for a run—you know, jogging that they all do. She always took the same route, Harrow Avenue, Eton Grove, uphill all the way, horrible in this heat, but it would have been pointless saying so. The world would be a better place if they thought as much about their responsibilities as they do about their figures. My husband came home, we had our meal, the three of us . . ."

"She talked about getting a job," said the doctor, "about this appointment she had and the possibility of getting a grant to do a business training." He made an effort at a laugh. "She got cross with me because I said she'd have to think about working her way through college the way they do in America."

"Well, we couldn't afford to pay," Laurette said sharply. "And she'd had one grant. It wasn't as if her first degree was any good, they do take that into account, I told her. She got sulky about it. We all watched some television. She phoned someone, I don't know who, possibly that Euan, God forbid."

"My wife," said Dr. Akande, in almost reverential tones, "had a degree in physics from University College, Ibadan, before she studied nursing."

Wexford was beginning to pity Melanie Akande, a seriously pressurized young woman. The irony was that it looked as if she had had no more chance of escape from forcible education than a Victorian girl had from its denial. And like that Victorian, she was obliged to live at home for an unforeseeable future.

He referred back to her afternoon's jogging. "She told you nothing of what she had seen while she was out, anyone who had spoken to her, anything at all?"

"She didn't tell us anything," said Laurette. "They don't. They're experts at that. You'd think she'd taken a course in secrecy."

Wexford got into the car, driving himself, but instead of heading for home, took the Glebe Lane direction. Asking himself if it was possible either of the Akandes was responsible for Melanie's disappearance, perhaps Melanie's death, he had to face the chance that it was. But he still went and talked to them. To allege that Akande might be guilty of such a crime was to presuppose him mad or at least a fanatic. The doctor appeared neither of those things and not at all obsessed about Euan Sinclair's association with his daughter. Wexford had never checked out Akande's alibi, hardly knew if he *had* an alibi. But he could see that there was one car Melanie would have got into while she was on her way from the Benefit Office to the bus stop—her father's.

Then had Akande lied? As Snow had, as surely Ingrid Pamber had? It was strange how he knew she had been lying without knowing what she was lying about. He drove into Glebe Lane, over the cobbles. She came down to let him in and said she was at home alone. Lang had gone to see his uncle, a strange excuse that immediately made Wexford suspicious, though he hardly knew of what. Her eyes met his. It spoke of a sublime self-confidence, or an ability to lie effectively, when someone could look you so boldly in the eye and hold the gaze. She wore a long patterned skirt, blue with paler blue flowers, and a silk sweater. Her dark shiny hair was twisted up on top of her head.

"Miss Pamber, you'll think I have a bad memory but I wonder if you'd tell me all over again just what happened when you called on Miss Bystock last Wednesday? When you took her a pint of milk and she asked you to fetch her some shopping on the following day?"

"You haven't really got a bad memory, have you? You're just testing me to see if I'll say the same things."

"Perhaps I am."

The blue she wore made him think all blue-eyed women should wear that shade. She was an ornament to the room so that it seemed to need no other. "I bought the milk at the corner shop where Ladyhall Avenue crosses Lower Queen Street. Did I say that before?" She must know she hadn't. He said nothing. "It's easy to park there, you see. It was just a bit after five-thirty when I got to Annette's. The front door to those flats has been unlocked every time I've been there—I don't think that's very secure, do you?"

"Evidently not."

"I think I said Annette had left her door on the latch. I put the milk straight in the fridge and then I went into the bedroom. I knocked on the door first." All these details were being given to tease him. He realized that but didn't mind. Any detail, however small, might be relevant in a case like this. "She said, 'Come in.' I think she said, 'Come in, Ingrid.' I went in and she was in bed, sort of half sitting up, but she looked quite ill. She said not to come near her because she was sure she was infectious, but would I get her the things on this list she'd made. It was a loaf and cornflakes and yogurt and cheese and grapefruit and more milk."

Wexford listened, deadpan. He didn't move.

"She had two keys on the bedside table. She gave me one— that was the nearest I got to her, I really didn't want to catch it— and she said, Now you'll be able to let yourself in tomorrow. So I said I would, yes, I would, and I'd get the things and to get well soon, and she said would I draw the curtains in the living room on my way out. So I did that and I called out good-bye and . . ." Ingrid Pamber looked at him ruefully, her head on one side. "I may as well come out with it. You're not going to eat me, are you?"

Had he looked as if he wanted to? "Go on."

"I forgot to lock the door after me. I mean, I left it on the latch like it was. I just *did*. It was awful of me, I know, but it's easy to do with those sort of doors."

"So the door was left unlocked all night?"

Before replying, she got up, walked across the room, and felt for something behind the books on a shelf. Over her shoulder she smiled at him. Wexford repeated what he had said.

"I suppose so," she said. "It was locked when I got there on Thursday. Are you very, very angry with me?"

She hadn't seen. She had no realization of what she had done.

Her eyes were warm and full of happy light as she handed him Annette Bystock's key.

Carolyn Snow was out. She was taking her son Joel to school,
the cleaning woman told Wexford. He decided to take a walk
round the block, though "block" was not the word for it. "Park"
would have been better, or "enclave." The Snows' house, though
twice the size of Wexford's own, was one of the smallest in this
neighborhood. Houses seemed to get bigger and be farther apart as
he reached the corner and turned into Winchester Drive. He
couldn't remember the last time he was in this part of Kingsmarkham, it must have been years, but he did now recall that he was in
the vicinity of the route Laurette Akande said her daughter took
when she went running.

The hallmark of desirability in dwelling places is when a suburb looks like a stretch of woodland and no houses are visible,
where there are no gates and all that shows that people live somewhere in there are the letter boxes, discreetly positioned at gaps in
the hedge. It was very high up, a green thickly treed ridge, beyond
which, far below, he could catch glimpses of the winding Kingsbrook. In Winchester Drive, green lawns terminated in high
hedges or low walls at the pavement and, because you knew it must
be there, you fancied you caught the faintest glimpse of mellowed
brick between the great gray beech trees, the delicate silver bir-
ches, and the branches of a majestic cedar.

The presence of two people on one of these lawns, a woman
with a basket of shiny dark red fruit, a young man a little over
twenty putting a ladder up against a cherry tree, did a little more to
damage this image of wooded countryside. Wexford was surprised
to identify the woman as Susan Riding, though he hardly knew
why he should be. She must live somewhere and was reputed to be
well-off. The young man was startlingly like his father with the
same straw-colored hair and Nordic looks, the high forehead,
blunt nose, long upper lip.

Wexford said good morning.

She came a little way toward him. If you didn't know who she was and had encountered her away from her own environment, you would have taken her for one of the dossers who slept on Myringham High Street. She wore a cotton skirt with half the hem coming down and a T-shirt that must have originated with one of her children, for "University of Myringham" was printed across the faded red material. An elastic band held back her grayish frizzy fair hair.

He thought how her smile transformed her. In an instant she was almost beautiful, beggarwoman into earth mother.

"The birds take most of our cherries. I wouldn't mind if they ate them but they just pick a bit out and drop the rest on the ground." The boy had gone up the tree, his back toward them, but she introduced him just the same. "My son, Christopher." He took absolutely no notice. She shrugged as if this was no more than she had expected. "You really need to be bird scaring from morning till night. We did last year but I had help then. How do people get staff in this country?"

"I understand it's difficult."

"Do it yourself is what you're saying, isn't it? That's not so easy when you've got six bedrooms and four children all living at home most of the time. My au pair's just left me too."

Christopher suddenly let out a string of startling obscenities and the wasp that had been annoying him zoomed out of the tree and headed for Susan Riding. She ducked, flapped at it with her hand.

"I *hate* them. Why on earth did God make wasps?"

"To clean it up, I suppose." Her puzzled face made him explain. "The earth."

"Oh, yes. I really must thank you for giving up your Saturday night to us vulnerable women. I have written to you, but I'm afraid I didn't post the letter till this morning."

"Come on, Mum," said the boy in the tree. "We're supposed to be picking the buggers."

Wexford called out to him, "Do you know a girl called Melanie Akande?"

"*What?*"

"Melanie Akande. You once had a drink with her. Perhaps you saw her more than once."

Susan Riding laughed. "What is this, Mr. Wexford? An interrogation? Is that the girl that's missing?"

Christopher came down the ladder. "Is she missing? I didn't know."

He was at least as tall as Wexford. His hands were big and his feet were big, his shoulders ox-like.

"Melanie disappeared last Tuesday afternoon," Wexford said. "Had you seen her recently?"

"Not for months. I went away last Tuesday morning. I can give you the names of the people I went with if I need an alibi. You can see my air ticket or what remains of it."

"Christopher!" said his mother.

"Well, why ask me? I'm the last person. Can I get on with picking these cherries now?"

Wexford said good-bye and walked on. At the corner he looked back and between a gap in the trees could see the house quite clearly, the back of an Italianate villa, white walls, green roof, a tall turret. He could even see the bars on the ground-floor windows. Well, Susan Riding was a Women, Aware! woman, one who would no doubt be prudent. The place looked as if it contained a lot worth stealing. He turned into Eton Grove and went back down the hill. The Riding house was momentarily clearly visible from the road and then, suddenly, it disappeared behind a dense plantation of shrubs in white blossom. He stepped back to look at it once more and lingered for a while before turning left back into Marlborough Gardens and walking the few hundred yards to Harrow Avenue.

Donaldson in the driving seat of the parked car was reading the *Sun* but folded it up when he saw the boss. Wexford read his own paper for ten minutes. A young man with a camera hung round his neck appeared from round the corner and Wexford put his paper away, although this passerby was clearly not interested in photographing him, hadn't even noticed him or taken his camera from its case.

"I'm getting paranoid."

"Sir?"

"Nothing. Ignore me."

The car suddenly appeared from nowhere, driven much too fast, sweeping into the drive of 101 and coming to a stop with a squeal of brakes. He had a good look at her as she left the car and went quickly to the front door, her door key on the same ring as the car keys. She was a tall slim woman, fairish, wearing black trousers and a sleeveless top. Two minutes after she had gone inside he went up to the front door and rang the bell. She answered it herself. She was younger than he had expected, probably forty but looking less. It struck him that she looked a lot younger than poor Annette.

No wedding ring. That was one of the first things he noticed and saw too that she had been used to wearing a ring, for there was a band of white skin on that brown finger.

"I've been expecting you," she said. "Won't you come in?"

Her voice was cultivated, pleasant, with the sort of accent associated with a select girls' boarding school. Wexford was suddenly and surprisingly aware of how very attractive she was. Her hair was so cut as to transform it into a cap of flaxen feathers. She wore no makeup and her skin was good, smooth, light golden brown, only faintly lined about the eyes. The top she wore was the same sea-blue as her eyes and the brown arms it exposed might have been those of a young girl.

He began to ask himself why a man who had this at home, legitimately and honorably, would chase after Annette, but he knew such questions were always in vain. Some of it was due to the legitimate and honorable being less attractive than the illicit and forbidden, and some of it to a strange lusting after the sordid and the naughty, after soft porn made flesh. He would guarantee, for instance, that Mrs. Snow didn't wear see-through black and scarlet camisoles, but Calvin Klein briefs and Playtex sports bras.

She took him into a large living room with a green velvet carpet, enough sofas and armchairs to accommodate twenty people, and a fireplace of Cotswold stone with a copper hood over it. It was clear she knew why he had come and that she had her answers ready. She was confident but grim, her movements deliberate, her expression fixed and resolute.

He said carefully, "I am sure your husband has told you he has been questioned in connection with the death of Annette Bystock."

She nodded. She put her elbow on the arm of her chair and rested her cheek against her hand. It was a pose of controlled exasperation.

"That evening, Wednesday, July the seventh, your husband spent the evening at home with you and your son? Is that correct?"

She delayed answering so long that he was on the point of repeating what he had said. Her reply, when it came, was stiff and cold. "Whoever gave you that idea? Did he tell you that?"

"What do you mean, Mrs. Snow? That he wasn't here?"

The sigh she gave was as heavy and deliberate as the inhaling and exhaling prescribed for the exerciser, a deep intake of breath, a full expulsion of breath.

"My son wasn't here. He, my son, Joel, was upstairs in the playroom. He always is in the week evenings, he has a lot of homework, he's fourteen. We often don't see him between the time he has his meal and bedtime—and sometimes not then."

Why was she telling him all this? No one was accusing the boy of a crime.

"So you and your husband were alone together? In here?"

"I asked who gave you that idea. My husband wasn't here." Her expression became unearthly, dreamy, she seemed to gaze into the middle distance as if looking at a perfect sunset, her lips just parted. Suddenly she turned on him. "He often wasn't on a Wednesday. He worked late on Wednesdays, or didn't you know?"

This was not at all what he had expected. If he hadn't been at home with his wife, why had Snow mentioned her? If his dearest wish was to keep the knowledge of his affair with Annette secret from her, why had he produced his wife as his alibi? Surely because he had no choice. The last thing he wanted to do was enlighten

Carolyn Snow himself as to her husband's philandering, but it looked as if he would have to. Snow then had chickened out, had lost his nerve, had evaded confession. Or had he?

"Mrs. Snow, you have been told of your husband's relationship with Annette Bystock?"

No one can whiten under a tan, but her skin contracted and aged her. It hadn't been a revelation, though. "Oh, yes. He told me." She stopped looking at him. "You understand that I didn't know until yesterday. I was in the dark, I'd been kept in the dark." A little cold laugh summed up her feelings about such men as Snow, their values, their cowardice. "He had to tell me."

"And asked you perhaps to tell me you were with him last Wednesday?"

"He didn't ask me anything," she said. "He knew better than to ask for favors."

There was nothing more to say for the moment. It was all very different from what he had anticipated. Until this moment he had never seriously considered Snow as a suspect, as a candidate for murderer. After all, Snow hadn't been inside the flat at Ladyhall Court. But by that reckoning no one had been in the flat except Annette herself and Ingrid Pamber. There had been no evidence of Edwina Harris's visit or, more to the point, of the thief who came in at some point and took the television, the VCR, and the radio-cassette player. If that thief had worn gloves, so might Bruce Snow have done.

He had spoken to Annette on the Tuesday evening but he might have been lying when he said she told him she was ill and couldn't meet him the following night. She loved him, she never refused him, she put him first. It was one thing not to go to work, to tell Ingrid she would need shopping done for her, but quite another to cancel a longed-for meeting with Snow on the dubious grounds that she might still be ill twenty-four hours later.

But they always met in Snow's office. Always except for just this once? I'm not well enough to go out, she had perhaps said, but you could come here—won't you just for once come here? And he had agreed, had gone there, had stayed and stayed, and quarreled with her at last and killed her. . . .

Bob Mole had no intention of telling Vine where the radio came from. All he would say at first was that it had been among a job lot saved from a fire. That there were no burn marks on it meant nothing. These rugs, for instance—had Vine even bothered to look at them?—weren't burnt. The three dining chairs weren't burnt. There was plenty of stuff that was and no one was going to buy that from a stall. What did he think, the public were daft?

Where did that stain come from, Vine wanted to know. Bob Mole couldn't account for it. Come to that, why should he account for it and what was Vine getting at? When Vine told him, things changed. It was the word "murder" that did it, specifically the murder of Annette Bystock, Kingsmarkham's own local murder that was in the daily papers and even on telly.

"It was hers?"

"Looks very much like it."

Bob Mole, who had gone putty color, curled back his upper lip. "Not blood, is it?"

"No, it's not blood." Vine wanted to laugh but didn't. "It's red nail varnish. She spilled it. Now tell me where you got it from."

"It's like I said, Mr. Vine. It was what come out of this fire."

"Sure. I heard you. But who was it rescued it from the flames and put it in your sticky hands?"

"My supplier," said Bob Mole as if he were a respectable retailer talking about a wholesaler of nationwide repute. "You're sure it's hers, this Annette that's dead?" He dropped his voice on the name and looked from side to side.

"There's a TV and a VCR too," said Vine.

"I never got them, Mr. Vine, and that's the absolute honest truth." With another glance to the right and one to the left, Bob Mole leaned toward Vine and whispered, "They call him Zack."

"Does he have another name?"

"If he does I don't know it, but I can tell you where he lives."

Not an address but a description of a place. Bob Mole didn't know the address. His directions were to go all the way down to the bottom of Glebe Lane, turn down that passage by that place, that sort of church, the Methodists used to have but was now a sort of store, go round the back of the used car dump, and he lives in the farthest away of the two cottages facing Tiller's paintbrush works.

When Burden heard about it he went on the hunt for Bob Mole's supplier himself, taking Vine with him. He expected something like Ingrid Pamber's place, but this back corner of Kingsmarkham made hers look like a smart mews. Confusion could hardly have arisen as to which cottage Zack lived in as the nearer to the lane of the two was derelict, its door and windows boarded up. It scarcely seemed like a dwelling house any longer, but more a shed for neglected animals, a dirty brownish hut, the broken tiles on its roof yellow with stonecrop.

Zack's wasn't much better. Years ago someone had put a pink undercoat on the front door, never painted on top but apparently wiped a brush laden with different colored paints against its surface. Perhaps this was the work of an employee at the little factory opposite. A broken window had been mended with masking tape. From a rickety trellis hung the tendrils of a climbing plant that had apparently died some years before.

"The council should do something about this dump," Burden said crossly. "What do we pay our rates for, I should like to know."

The young woman who came to the door was thin and pale, no taller than a child of twelve. She carried on one puny hip a boy of about a year who was crying loudly.

"Yes, what is it?"

"Police," said Vine. "Can we come in?"

"Oh, shut up, Clint," she said to the child, shaking him in a halfhearted way. She looked with a kind of apathetic distaste from Barry Vine to Burden and back again. "I'll want to see some identification before I let you in."

"Who are *you*, then?" said Vine.

"Kimberley. Ms. Pearson to you. He's not here."

Warrant cards were produced and she scrutinized them as if to check they weren't forgeries. "Look at the funny photo of the man, Clint," she said, pushing the child's head nearly into Vine's chest.

When Clint understood he couldn't have the pictures he began crying even more loudly. Kimberley moved him to her other hip. Burden and Vine followed her into what Burden afterward called one of the worst tips he'd ever been into. Analyzing the smell, he declared it to be compounded of soiled diapers, urine, fat that chips had been cooked in fifty times, meat kept too long without a refrigerator, cigarette smoke, and canned dog food. The linoleum that covered the floor was worn into holes and covered with sticky, hairy patches and dark ring marks. Ashes from last winter's fires were tumbled about the grate, which was piled high over them with waste paper and cigarette ends. Two deck chairs faced a huge television set. It was too large to have been Annette's but the video recorder next to it might have been hers.

Kimberley put the child into one of these chairs and gave him a bag of crisps that she produced from one of the many cardboard grocer's boxes that stood about and served as cupboard, sideboard, and larder. Another box provided her with a packet of Silk Cut and matches.

"What d'you want him for?" she said, lighting her cigarette.

"This and that," said Vine. "Maybe something serious."

"What's serious mean?" said Kimberley. She had the very pale green eyes of a white cat. Her skin and hair were luminous with grease. "He never done nothing serious." She corrected herself. "He never done nothing."

"Where is he?"

"It's his signing-on day."

All ways, as Wexford had thought, led back to the Benefit Office.

"Where did the VCR come from, Miss Pearson?" Burden asked, refusing to have any truck with that "Ms." stuff.

"My mum give it me." Her answer came quick as a flash. That, of course, meant nothing. "And it's Mrs. Nelson."

"I see. Miss Pearson to him and Mrs. Nelson to me. That his name, is it? Nelson?"

She didn't answer. Having finished the crisps, Clint set up a renewed roaring. "Oh, piss off, Clint," she said. Taken from his deck chair and placed on the floor, he crawled over to one of the grocer's boxes, pulled himself into a standing position, and began removing its contents, item by item. Kimberley took no notice. Apropos of nothing that had gone before, she said, "They're going to pull it down, this place."

"Best thing they can do," said Vine.

"Oh, yes, sure, it's the best bloody thing they can do. What's going to happen to us? You don't think of that, do you, when you say"—she mimicked his voice in an exaggerated way—"it's the best thing they can do."

"They'll have to rehouse you."

"You want to bet? In a bed and breakfast maybe. If you want to be rehoused you have to do it yourself. One thing you can say for this dump, the DSS pays the rent. He'll lose that, won't he? He's not had a job in months."

Outside, Burden inhaled the air, somewhat contaminated though it was with the fumes from paintbrush manufacture. "Doesn't stop them having kids, does it, being out of work? You'll notice they can always afford to smoke."

If I lived in that midden I'd smoke myself to death, thought Vine, but he didn't say it aloud.

"Did you see them in the paper, it'd have been around last Christmas? I remember the name, Clint. He had something wrong with his heart and they operated on it at Stowerton Infirmary. There were pictures of him and Kimberley Pearson all over the *Courier*."

But Burden couldn't remember. He was sure that somehow they would miss Zack Nelson, that he was a genius at slip-giving. Kimberley had no phone, even if it was possible to phone people waiting to sign on. Burden didn't know whether it was or not and he was sure Vine didn't. But when they came into the Benefit Office, Zack was still there.

He was one of a dozen people waiting, sitting on the gray chairs. Burden had made what he thought was an intelligent guess at which one of the seven or eight men he was and got it wrong. The first person he approached, a boy of perhaps twenty-two with a blond crew cut, three rings in each ear and one in a nostril, turned out to be a John MacAntony. The only other man who could possibly be Zack Nelson admitted it first with an exaggerated shrug, then a nod.

He was tallish and of all the men in there, in the best condition. It looked as if he worked out with weights, for his body was lean and hard and he had no need to flex his bare arms to show the large round muscles that stretched the sleeves of a dirty red polo shirt. His long hair, as greasy as Kimberley's, was plaited for an inch or two before being tied with a shoelace. Inside the open neck of his shirt, under the fuzz of dark hair, could be seen the greenish-blue, red, and black inks of an elaborate tattoo.

"A word," said Burden.

"It'll have to wait till my number comes up," said Zack Nelson without irony.

Burden was baffled, then saw that he referred to the neon signs that hung from the ceiling. When the number on his card appeared he would go up to a desk to sign on.

"How long is that going to be, then?"

"Five minutes. Maybe ten." Zack made the sort of face at Vine that he himself had made when he smelled the inside of the cottage. "What's the hurry?"

"No hurry," said Burden. "We've got plenty of time."

They moved away and sat on a pair of gray chairs. Burden fingered one of the leaves of the houseplant in the tub next to him. It had the faintly sticky, rubbery texture of polythene.

Vine said in a low voice, "He looks like you, you know. I mean, if you grew your hair and didn't wash much. He might be your young brother."

Incensed by this, Burden said nothing. But he remembered what Percy Hammond had said, that the man he had seen in the night coming out of Ladyhall Court looked like him. If it was true, and here was Vine absurdly confirming it, it said a lot for the old man's powers of observation. It meant that the old man could be trusted.

He looked about the big room. Behind the counter were Osman Messaoud, Hayley Gordon, and Wendy Stowlap, this last apparently suffering from an allergy, for she kept wiping her nose on a succession of colored tissues pulled from a box in front of her. All were occupied with clients. Cyril Leyton stood outside the door of his office deep in conversation with the security officer.

Messaoud's client finished her business and moved away from the desk. A number came up in red neon and the boy with the rings in ears and nose went up. You couldn't see the new claims officers from where Burden sat, only the sides of their booths. He got up and began walking about, apparently aimlessly, but avoiding confrontation with Leyton. The new claims officer sitting in the booth next to Peter Stanton's must be a replacement for Annette but was too far away for Burden to read the name tag he wore. In the light of increased knowledge, Burden made a mental note to subject Stanton to a second interview. After all, the man had admitted to taking Annette out. Was she, in his company, trying to find herself a better option than Bruce Snow? And if so, what had gone wrong?

He was alerted by a woman shouting and he turned round. This was the first instance of "trouble" there had been since they began calling at the Benefit Office. The woman, fat and unkempt, was complaining to Wendy Stowlap about a lost giro and Wendy seemed to be checking on the computer screen that it had been sent to her. The answer wasn't apparently acceptable and the torrent of complaint became a stream of abuse, culminating in a yell of, "You're a whore!"

Wendy looked up, unmoved. She shrugged. "How did you know?"

There came a faint snigger from Peter Stanton, who was passing the counter on his way to pick up a leaflet. The woman turned her invective on him and there was a moment when Burden considered intervening. But the staff seemed competent to deal with verbal abuse, and the woman soon deflated.

Zack Nelson's number appeared in red neon at last and he went up to Hayley Gordon. Vine thought her a little like Nelson's girlfriend Kimberley to look at, only cleaner and better dressed and—you had to face it—better fed. Zack would get—what? Nothing here, of course, but when his giro arrived he would collect from the Post Office unemployment benefit for himself of around £40 and the DSS would provide the Income Support for Kimberley and Clint—or did Kimberley herself collect Clint's Child Benefit? It was always the mother, wasn't it? Vine had to confess he didn't know. But no doubt they didn't live in poverty because they liked it.

These were private thoughts that would not affect his attitude to Zack, who was a thief, he reflected, and a villain. They weren't permitted to arrest him in here, not unless requested to do so by the ES staff. "We'll talk in the car," he said when Zack returned, having assured himself of support for another fortnight.

"About what?"

"Bob Mole," said Burden, "and a radio with blood on it."

It was, as he said to Wexford later, as easy as taking peppermints from a baby who didn't like them. "That was never blood," said Zack. He realized immediately what he had said, rolled his eyes, and clapped one hand over his mouth.

"Why not blood?" said Vine, leaning close.

"She was strangled. It was on telly. It was in the papers."

"So you admit you were in Annette Bystock's place, that the radio was hers?"

"Look, I . . ."

"We'll go back to the police station, Sergeant Vine. Zack Nelson, you need not say anything in answer to the charge but anything you do say will be taken down and may be given in evidence . . ."

ten

N ot with murder?" said Zack in the interview room.

Wexford didn't answer. "What *is* your name, anyway? Zachary? Zachariah?"

"You what? No, it's fucking not. It's Zack. There was some singer called his son Zack what is where my mum got it from. Okay? I want to know if you're charging me with murdering that woman."

"Tell us when you went into the flat, Zack," said Burden. "It was the Wednesday night, was it?"

"Who says I ever went in the flat?"

"She didn't bring that radio round to you and give it to you for a birthday present."

This was a lucky shot on Wexford's part, not even intelligent guesswork. If it had been December instead of July he would have said "Christmas present." Zack stared at him in a kind of horror, as he might have at some clairvoyant possessed of proven supernatural powers.

"How d'you know Wednesday was my birthday?"

Wexford held back his laughter with difficulty. "Many happy returns. What time was it you went into the flat?"

"I want my lawyer," said Zack.

"Yes, I expect you do. I would in your position. You can phone him later. I mean, you can find one later and phone him." Zack gave him a suspicious glare. Wexford said, "Let's talk about the ring."

"What ring?"

"A ruby ring worth two grand, give or take a bit."

"I don't know what you're talking about."

"Was she dead, Zack, before you took that ring off her finger?"

"I never took no ring off her finger! It wasn't on her finger, it was on the table!" Once more he had dropped himself in it. "Fuck it all," he said.

"You'd better start at the beginning, Zack," said Burden. "Tell us all about it." Silently he blessed the recording device that had all this on tape. There was no arguing with it.

Zack made a few more attempts at argument before caving in. Finally he said, "What's in it for me if I tell you what I found in there and what I saw?"

"How about you come up in court tomorrow instead of Friday, you only get one night in a cell, and Sergeant Camb'll bring you a Diet Coke for a nightcap."

"Don't give me that crap. I mean, if I tell you what I know I could help you find her killer."

"You'll do that anyway, Zack. You don't want a charge of obstructing the police as well as burglary."

Zack, who had an impressive record of petty offenses, the computer had informed Wexford, knew all about it. "It wasn't burglary. It wasn't dark. I never did no breaking and entering."

"A figure of speech," Burden said. "I suppose you found the door unlocked and just walked in?"

A cunning look came into Zack's face, making it slightly lopsided. There was something sinister about him, something a person with a wilder imagination than Wexford's might have called evil. His eyes narrowed. "Couldn't believe me eyes," he said, his tone becoming conversational. "I tried the handle and the door come open in me hand. I was amazed."

"I'm sure. Carrying housebreaking tools, were you, just on the off chance? What did you mean just now when you said it wasn't dark?"

"It was five in the morning, wasn't it? It'd been light an hour."

"Up with the lark, were you, Zack?" Burden couldn't help grinning. "You always an early riser?"

"The kid woke me up and I couldn't get back to sleep. I went out in the van to clear me head. I was just passing sort of slow—keeping in the speed limit, right?—and the front door was open, so I reckoned I'd pop in and see what was going."

"D'you feel like making a statement, Zack?"

"I want my lawyer."

"I tell you what, you make a statement and then we'll get the yellow pages and find you a lawyer. How's that?"

Zack yielded quite suddenly. He seemed to collapse without warning. One moment he was truculent, the next he had given in. "I don't mind," he said and gave a huge yawn. "I'm dead tired. I don't never get enough sleep, not with my kid."

A t approximately five a.m. on Friday, July ninth," Zack Nelson's statement ran, "I entered Flat 1, 15 Ladyhall Avenue, Kingsmarkham. I had no housebreaking tools and did not break the door or the lock. I was wearing gloves. The front door was unlocked. It was not dark. The curtains were drawn in the living room but I could see. I saw a television set, a video recorder, a CD player, and radio–cassette player, and these I removed from the flat, making two trips to do so.

"I came back to the flat and opened the door to the bedroom. To my surprise there was a woman in the bed. At first I thought she was asleep. Something in her attitude made me suspicious. It was the way her arm was hanging. I approached nearer but did not touch her, as I could see that she was dead. On the table by the bed was a ring and watch. I did not touch these but left the flat quickly, making sure the door was locked behind me.

"I put the television set, the video recorder, and the radio–cassette player into the van I had borrowed from my girlfriend's father and drove home. I am a dealer in secondhand electronic equipment. I had some of the said equipment salvaged from a factory fire and, included as one lot with some of the salvaged goods, I sold the radio–cassette player to Mr. Bob Mole for the sum of seven pounds. The television set and video recorder are at present in my home at 1 Lincoln Cottages, Glebe End, Kingsmarkham."

"I like the virtuous touch about locking the door behind him, don't you?" Wexford said when Zack had been taken to one of the only two cells Kingsmarkham Police Station possessed. "At least it explains how the door came to be locked when you got there. If anyone from the Employment Service reads an account of tomorrow's proceedings in the magistrates' court, Zack's going to lose his UB. The *Courier* will describe him as a dealer in electronic goods."

"He won't need it where he's going," Burden said.

"No, but Kimberley and Clint will. I don't know what happens in a case like this. Do they cut off his dependents' Income Support? Still, he'll not get more than six months and he'll serve four and a bit." Wexford hesitated. "You know, Mike, there's something odd in all this, there's something I don't like."

Burden shrugged. "Like him finding the door unlocked and the place all open for him? Like him not taking the ring?"

"Well, yes, but not that so much. The front door to the house is usually unlocked and we know Ingrid Pamber left Annette's door unlocked. He says he was afraid of taking a ring and a watch that lay beside a dead body and I believe him. What bothers me is his apparently not knowing anything about the flats or their occupants before going in there. According to him, he just slipped in without bothering to shut the door behind him. He couldn't sleep, but he didn't go out on foot, he went out in his *van*. He just happened to be wearing gloves. In a heat wave in July? According to him, he had no housebreaking tools with him, yet how many people could he count on having feckless friends and leaving their front door unlocked overnight?"

"There are only two flats in there," Burden said. "He'd nothing to lose. All he had to do was try Annette's door and then go upstairs and try the Harrises'. If they were both locked he was no worse off than he had been."

"I know. That's what he says himself. Piece of amazing luck for him, wasn't it, that the first door he tried was unlocked?"

"Maybe it wasn't the first door."

"He says it was. So we come to the next odd thing. If what he says is true, he had no means of knowing whether there was any-one in the flat or not. What are we to think? That because he'd seen from outside—and remembered, calculated, worked it out—that all the curtains in Flat One were closed, then discovered that the front door was unlocked, he concluded there was no one at home? That would be on the theory that no one would stay in a place overnight with the front door unlocked, but they might go away and forget to lock it. It's all a bit tenuous."

"He was taking a risk, certainly. But all burglary is risky, Reg."

Wexford looked unconvinced. He always delved into human motive and the peculiarities of human nature while Burden con-centrated on the facts, seldom disputing them however bizarre they might appear. As he made his way back to the Benefit Office, on foot this time, Burden thought of something Wexford had once said to him about Sherlock Holmes, how you couldn't solve much by his methods. A pair of slippers with singed soles no more showed that their wearer had been suffering from a severe chill than that he had merely had cold feet. Nor could you deduce from a man's staring at a portrait on the wall that he was dwelling on the life and career of that portrait's subject, for he might equally be thinking how it resembled his brother-in-law or was badly painted or needed cleaning. With human nature you could only guess—and try to guess right.

He caught Peter Stanton on his way out to lunch.

"Can we have a chat?"

"Not if it stops me from eating."

"I have to eat too," Burden said.

"Come out this way." Stanton took Burden out through the

door marked "private" that led into the car park. It was a shortcut to the High Street.

His wife or Wexford would probably have described the man as Byronic. He had those dark piratical good looks women are said to find so attractive, the handsome features allegedly ravaged by dissipations, the dark wavy hair that by Burden's own exacting standards was tousled, the gleam in the eye that may denote a penchant for cruelty or merely greed. Stanton wore a linen suit, stone-colored and very crumpled, and his tie, which Leyton probably insisted he wear, was loosely tied under the collar of a not very clean shirt whose top button was undone. If it is possible to walk in a laid-back manner, Stanton did so, slouching along, his hands deep in the misshapen pockets of his baggy trousers.

At the doorway of a sandwich bar with four empty tables pushed against the wall opposite the food counter, he paused and cocked a thumb.

"I usually come here. Okay?"

Burden nodded. The last time he had been in one of these places, of which Kingsmarkham now had three, he had eaten "prime freshwater shrimps" and the resulting gastroenteritis had laid him low for three days. So when Stanton picked a prawn salad sandwich he stuck austerely to cheese and tomato. He watched without comment while Stanton emptied the contents of a hip flask into his glass of Sprite.

"I want to ask you about the kind of things you say to your clients."

"Not half what I'd like to."

Rather coldly Burden said, "Specifically, I want to know the kind of thing Annette might have said to Melanie Akande."

"What do you mean exactly?"

"I mean, what happens when a new client brings back a form—is it called an ES something?—and gets given a signing-on day and so on?"

"You want to know what she'd have said to the girl and advised her and all that?"

Stanton sounded deeply bored. His eyes had wandered to the

young woman assistant who now emerged from the back regions to join the man behind the counter. She was about twenty, blonde, tall, very pretty, wearing a white apron over a scoop-necked red T-shirt and the kind of very short tube skirt that is as tight as a bandage.

"Just that, Mr. Stanton."

"Okay." Stanton took a swig of his Sprite cocktail. "Annette'd have taken a look at the ES 461, seen she'd filled it in right. There are forty-five questions to be answered in all and it's complicated till you know how. Let's say it's—well, uncommon for a client to get it right first time on his own. On *her* own, I should say. They've got a funny taste, these prawns, sort of fishy."

"Prawns *are* fish," said Burden.

"Yeah, but you know what I mean, sort of strong, like the smell of outside a fishmonger's. Do you reckon I ought to eat them?"

Burden didn't reply. "Go on about what Annette would have said to her."

"There's often something a bit off about the food here but the crumpet makes up for it. That's why I go on coming, I suppose." Stanton caught Burden's basilisk eye. "Yes, well, once she'd got the form straightened out she'd have given the client, Melanie Whatshername, a signing-on day. It's alphabetical, that. A to K Tuesdays, L to R Wednesdays, S to Z Thursdays. No one signs on on a Monday or a Friday. What did you say she was called? Akande? She'd have had Tuesday. Once a fortnight on a Tuesday.

"Then Annette'd have explained about how signing on is to prove you're still in the land of the living, haven't buggered off somewhere or died, that you're available and actively seeking work, and she'd have said how once you've signed on your giro'll be sent to you. That goes to your home address and you cash it at your post office or you can pay it into your bank if you want. Annette'd have explained all that. Then, I suppose, she'd have asked Melanie if she'd any questions. Melanie'd only have a maximum of twenty minutes with Annette, there wouldn't have been time for much."

"Suppose she'd had a job to offer Melanie? Could she have

had? What would have been the procedure?"

Stanton yawned. He had left his second sandwich uneaten. He was now dividing his eye contact between the girl in the bandage skirt and a sandwich maker who had appeared from some nether region. This woman had waist-length mahogany-colored hair and appeared to be wearing nothing but a white chef's cap and a white cotton coat whose hem reached to two inches below her crotch. At a cough from Burden he dragged his stare away, sighing softly. "There aren't jobs, you know. They're thin on the ground. I suppose Annette just might have had something suitable for this Melanie, client with a degree. Well, once in a blue moon she might have had something."

"What, in a ledger? A file?"

Stanton gave him a pitying look. "She'd have run it up on the computer."

"And if she'd had anything to offer Melanie, what then?"

"She'd have phoned the employer and made an appointment for Melanie for an interview. She didn't, you know," Stanton said unexpectedly. "I can tell you that for a fact. Both the new claims advisers have the same stuff on their computers and there wasn't anything remotely suitable for a girl of twenty-two with a performance arts degree. You can check it out if you want but I can tell you there wasn't."

"How did you know her degree was in performance arts?"

"She told me while I was raping and strangling her, of course." Stanton must have remembered that there is such an offense as wasting police time. He said sullenly, "Oh, come on. I read it in the paper."

Burden fetched himself a cup of coffee. "And that would have been all?" he said. "No advice? You're advisers, aren't you?"

"That *is* advising, telling her how to sign on, explaining about her giro. What more d'you want?"

Hope had sprung for a moment in Burden's heart. A scenario had begun to take shape of Melanie leaving the Benefit Office on her way to a job interview, from which she had never returned.

Only Annette knew where she had gone and why and, absolutely to the point, whom she had gone to see. But his carefully crafted playlet had quickly fallen apart, and when he asked Stanton if he could imagine anything confidential, secret, or sinister Melanie might have said to Annette, something that was a police matter, he wasn't surprised that the man made a dismissive gesture and shook his head.

"I ought to be getting back."

"All right." Burden got up.

"I've got a performance arts degree myself," Stanton suddenly remarked, apropos of nothing. "No doubt that's why I remember she had. All set to be a great actor, I was, a second Olivier and a bloody sight better looking. That was me fifteen years ago and to this favor have I come."

Bored by this, unsympathetic, Burden said as they went out into the street, "Did anyone ever threaten her?"

"Annette? In the office? Bless your policeman's helmet, if you had one, they threaten us all the time. *All the time.* It's worse on the desks. Why d'you think we have a security officer? Ninety-nine percent comes to nothing, it's vague promises to 'get us.' Some of them accuse us of keeping their giros for ourselves, losing their ES 461s on purpose, that sort of thing. And then they're going to 'get' us or 'cut' us.

"Then there's fraud. They know they've been signing on in three or four different names and they think we've reported them to the DSS fraud inspectors, so they're going to get us for that. . . ."

Now Burden recalled Karen Malahyde once being called out to an "incident" at the Benefit Office, on another occasion Pemberton and Archbold had gone. It hadn't meant much to him at the time. He said suddenly to Stanton, "You took her out once or twice?"

"Annette?" Stanton became guarded, cautious. "Twice, to be precise. It was three years ago."

"Why twice? Why no more? Did something happen?"

"I didn't screw her, if that's what you mean." Stanton, who had been slouching along, taking long strides, moving slowly, now stopped altogether. He stood indecisively in the middle of the pavement, then sat down on the low wall that bordered an estate agent's courtyard and took a packet of cigarettes out of one of the baggy pockets. "Cyril the Squirrel called me into his office and said it had to stop. Relationships between staff members of opposite sexes were bad for the image. I asked him if he meant it would be all right for me to fuck Osman but he just said not to be filthy and that was that."

Burden's look was eloquent of heartfelt agreement with Leyton for once, but he said nothing.

"Not that I was all that sorry." Stanton took a long draw on his cigarette and expelled the smoke in two blue columns out of his nostrils. "I wasn't keen on being used as a—how shall I put it?—I don't know, but what it amounts to is she only wanted me around to make this guy she'd got jealous so he'd leave his wife and marry her. Some hopes. She actually told me that, about how she'd tell this chap that I was keen on her and if he didn't want to lose her he'd best get his act together. Charming, wasn't it?"

"You went to her flat?"

"No, I never did. I went to the cinema with her, met her there and we had a coffee after. The next time it was just drinks in a pub and a pizza and we went for a drive in my car. We parked out in the country and there was a bit of how's-your-father but nothing over the top and after that Cyril the doorman put his spoke in."

They walked back to the Benefit Office together and Burden followed him in. He was talking to the security officer, asking if he could remember any specific threats being made to Annette, when a shrill scream from Wendy Stowlap's counter made him jump and spring to his feet.

"I told you I'd scream if you said that just once more," the woman shouted. "If you say that again I'll lie on the floor and scream."

"What else can I say? You can have dental treatment free if

you're on Income Support but you can't get your osteopath's bill paid."

The woman, who was well dressed and spoke in a ringing actor's voice, got down on the floor, lay on her back, and began screaming. She was young and her lungs were strong. The screaming reminded Burden of the noise three-year-olds sometimes make in supermarket aisles. He walked over to her, the security man following. Wendy was leaning over the counter, waving a blue and yellow leaflet with the title "Help Us to Get It Right and How to Complain."

"Come along now," said the security officer. "Up you get. This won't do, all this noise."

She screamed harder. "Stop that," said Burden. He stuck out his warrant card six inches from the screaming face. "Stop. You're causing a breach of the peace."

It was the card that did it. She was middle class and therefore awed by the police and the suggestion she might break the law. The screaming dropped to a whimper. She got awkwardly to her feet, snatched the leaflet from Wendy's hand, and said bitterly to her, "There was no need to call the police."

Husband and wife sat side by side, but not too close to each other, in front of the desk in Wexford's office. He didn't want to frighten Carolyn Snow—not yet. Frightening, if needed, would come later. Meanwhile, though the room was hardly equipped as a recording studio, Detective Constable Pemberton was there with an efficient enough device if it was required.

They had arrived separately, two minutes apart. And Carolyn Snow quickly explained that they *were* apart, she retaining the house in Harrow Avenue—"It's my children's *home*"—the husband she had thrown out resorting to a hotel room. Wexford noticed that Bruce Snow was wearing yesterday's shirt. He looked as if he hadn't shaved. Surely his wife hadn't shaved him as well as laundering his clothes and running round at his beck and call?

"We have to clear up this matter of what you were both doing last Wednesday evening, July the seventh. Mr. Snow?"

"I've already told you what I was doing. I was at home with my wife. My son was at home too. He was upstairs."

"Not according to Mrs. Snow."

"Look, this is rubbish, this is all nonsense. I got home at six and I was all evening at home with my wife. We had a meal at seven, the way we always do. My son went upstairs after that, he had an essay to write for his history homework. The War of the Spanish Succession, it was."

"You have a good memory, Mr. Snow, considering you didn't know you'd have to remember."

"I have been racking my brains, haven't I? I've thought of nothing else."

"What did you do all evening? Watch television? Read something? Telephone anyone?"

"He didn't have a chance," said Carolyn nastily. "He went out at ten to eight."

"That is a damned lie!" said Snow.

"On the contrary, you know it's true. It was *your* Wednesday, wasn't it? The Wednesday evening every couple of weeks you spent bonking that prostitute on your office floor."

"Nice language, thank you, that really becomes you, that terminology. A man can take real pride in hearing his wife talk like that, like someone off the streets."

"Well, you'd know all about those, wouldn't you? Firsthand experience. And I'm not your wife, not anymore. Two years, just two years, and you'll have to say 'my ex-wife,' you'll have to explain you're living in a bedsit because your 'ex-wife' took you to the cleaners, took the house and the car and three-quarters of your income"—Carolyn Snow's normally quiet gentle voice was rising ominously, vibrating with anger—"just because you were hooked on poking that fat floozy through her red knickers!"

For God's sake, thought Wexford, how much of it has he told her? Everything? Because he thought absolute total confession was his only chance? He gave an admonitory cough that nevertheless failed to stop Snow rounding on his wife and shouting, "You shut your mouth, you frigid cow!"

Slowly Carolyn Snow rose to her feet, her eyes fixed on her husband's face. Wexford acted. "Stop this, please. At once. I can't have a matrimonial fracas in here. Sit down, Mrs. Snow."

"Why should I? Why should I be made into some sort of guilty party? I've done nothing."

"Ha!" said Snow, and he repeated it, reinforced with bitterness, "Ha!"

"Very well," said Wexford. "I thought you might be more comfortable talking to me in here but I see I was wrong. We'll go down to Interview Room Two, DC Pemberton, and with your permission"—he looked rather sourly at the Snows, making their permission sound like a formality—"the rest of this interview will be recorded."

It was rather different down there, some distant resemblance to a prison cell being achieved by white-painted walls of unrendered brick and a window set high up under the ceiling. The electronic devices lining the wall behind the metal table Wexford sometimes thought, and thought uneasily, suggested, if not a torture chamber, the kind of place where they kept you standing all night under bright lights.

On the way down he asked Snow, in seemingly casual fashion and out of earshot of his wife, if it was a fact that a friend or relative of theirs lived in Ladyhall Avenue within sight of the flats. Snow denied it. It wasn't true, he said, and he had never told anyone it was.

In the interview room he placed the Snows opposite each other and seated himself at one end. Burden, back from the Benefit Office, took the other. The austerity of the room, its grimness, quieted Carolyn, as he had known it would. Once in the lift, she had kept up a continuous gibing and carping at her husband while he stood with his eyes shut. Down here she was silent. She smoothed the fair hair back from her forehead and pressed fingers to her temples as if her head ached. Snow sat with folded arms, his chin sagging against his chest.

Wexford spoke into the device. "Mr. Bruce Snow, Mrs. Carolyn Snow. DCI Wexford and DI Burden present." He said to the woman, "I should like you to tell me exactly what did happen on the evening of July the seventh, Mrs. Snow."

She gave her husband a sidelong look, deliberate and calculating. "He came home at six and I said, Not working late tonight? I'm going back to the office after I've eaten, he said . . ."

"A lie! Another filthy lie!"

"Please, Mr. Snow."

"Joel said he might want his father to give him some help with this essay he had to do and his father said, Too bad because I'm going out . . ."

"I did not say that!"

"Because I'm going out, and he did go out. At ten to eight. I didn't suspect anything, mind you, not a thing. Why should I? I trusted him. I do trust people. Anyway, I phoned the office. Joel did want help. I said, We'll phone Dad and you can ask him on the phone. But there wasn't any answer. Not that I had any suspicions even then. I thought he just wasn't answering. I was in bed by the time he got home. It was after half-past ten, nearer eleven."

"Oh, let her rave."

"I'm a truthful person, he knows that. Whereas we know the lies *he* tells. Working late! Did you know he screwed her in the office so that if I phoned he'd be there to answer? If she hadn't got her just deserts, getting herself murdered, I could almost feel sorry for the poor fat bitch."

"May I remind you," Wexford said wearily, "that, with your permission, this conversation is being recorded, Mrs. Snow?"

"What do I care? Record it! Put it over the public address system all down the High Street! Let them all know, I'll tell them anyway, I've told all my friends. I've told my children, I've let them know what a bastard their father is."

After they had gone, Burden put on a grave face and shook his head. "Amazing, isn't it?" he said to Wexford. "You'd call her a real lady if you met her socially, quiet, well-mannered, refined. Who'd have thought a woman like that would even know that sort of language?"

"You sound like a policeman in a detective novel circa 1935."

"Okay, maybe I do, but doesn't it surprise you?"

"They get it out of modern fiction," said Wexford. "Nothing to do all day but read. Are we getting anywhere with Stephen Colegate?"

"Annette's ex-husband? He lives in Australia, he's married again, but his mother's in Pomfret and she's expecting him home for a visit on Sunday with his two kids."

"Have someone check that he really was in Australia, will you? What happened to Zack Nelson?"

"Remanded in custody to the Crown Court. Why are you looking like that?"

"I'm thinking of Kimberley and the child."

"You don't want to worry about that Kimberley," said Burden. "She'll know more about claiming benefit than Cyril Leyton does. She's the kind that's got an honors degree in Income Support."

Wexford laughed. "I'm sure you're right. That Snow woman's worn me out." He hesitated, thought. " 'Oh, I am going a long way off, to the island valley of Avilion, where I will heal me of my grievous wound.' "

"Blimey," said Burden, "And where might that be?"

"Home."

eleven

I told her we wouldn't be buying any Oriental rugs," Dora said, "and I was thinking, Chance would be a fine thing, though I didn't say that. Of course, she's quite right, these things are evil and wrong, but it's just that she always throws herself heart and soul into every new project."

Sheila Wexford had become a life member of Anti-Slavery International. On the phone that evening, just before Wexford got in, she had urged her mother not to buy Middle Eastern or Oriental rugs, for these, she said, might well have been woven by children of eleven or twelve or younger. Girls in Turkey went blind from the close work in ill-lit rooms. Children were obliged to work fourteen hours a day and because their parents had put them to this industry as payment of a debt, received no wages.

"I suppose she'll be off to Turkey to see for herself?" said Wexford.

"How did you know?"

"I know my daughter."

"Why 'international,' anyway?" inquired Sylvia in a querulous tone. "International's an adjective. What's wrong with society or association?" Wexford's reference to Sheila as "my daughter" instead of "my younger daughter," thus implying in her estimation that he had only one, was what had set her off, he knew. Much she cared about adjectives. "Sheila wouldn't notice but it's as bad as 'collective,' " she said and glared at her father.

He was swift to make amends, appending to his question a rare endearment. "Any sign of a job, darling?"

"Nothing. Neil's got himself into a workshop that could lead to a retraining program. That's another awful word, 'workshop.' "

"And 'creditable' for 'credible,' " said her father. It was the kind of conversation he usually had only with Sheila. "And 'gender-related' for 'male and female' and 'health problem' for 'ill.' "

Sylvia was happy again. "*Kanena provlima*, which my son tells me is Greek for his favorite phrase. One good thing about being unemployed is I'll be home with them for the summer holidays. School breaks up next week."

It was pouring with rain and Glebe End was awash. With no drainage or what there was long dysfunctional, Lincoln Cottages appeared as if floating on a swamp. A great sheet of water engulfed the brick path and came halfway up the tires of an ancient van, the rear doors of which stood open. A black plastic dustbin bobbed lightly on a puddle by the front door.

Barry Vine had a look inside the van at a damp-looking mattress and an armchair with no seat cushion while Karen Malahyde knocked on the door. It took Kimberley several minutes to come and open it.

"What d'you want?"

"The stuff your boyfriend nicked," said Vine.

She shrugged her thin shoulders but she opened the door wider and stood back. Clint was sitting in a high chair, covering his face and the upper part of his body with a glutinous brown mess from a bowl with a crack in it. The high chair, painted white with pictures of rabbits and squirrels, was quite a respectable piece of furniture, gift perhaps of a comparatively affluent grandparent.

Cocking a thumb back the way he had come, Vine said, "Moving out?"

"What if I am?"

"You gave us to understand you hadn't a hope of being re-housed."

Kimberley picked up a dirty rag from the top of one of her cardboard boxes and began rubbing at Clint's face with it. The child yelled and struggled. Vine went upstairs and fetched the television set. Karen carried the VCR out to the car. Lifting Clint onto the ground, Kimberley said, volunteering information for once, "My nan died."

Not knowing what to make of this, Vine, who hadn't an unpleasant nature, said, "I'm sorry to hear that," and then, because he had cottoned on, "You mean you've come in for her place or what?"

"That's it. Got it in one. My mum don't want it. She says we can have it."

"When did this happen then?"

"What, my nan dying or my mum saying we could have her place?" She didn't wait for an answer. "Mum come round Wednesday and I told her about Zack, so she said, You can't stay here, and I said, Too right we can't, and that was when she said, You better move in your nan's place. Satisfied?"

"It has to be a change for the better."

"Clint," said Kimberley, "you leave them bottles alone or you'll get a smack you won't like."

A father and a conscientious one, Vine disapproved of corporal punishment, he had what he called a "thing" about it, and Clint was very young.

"Is he okay?" he said.

"What d'you mean, okay? You mean he shouldn't be living in this dump? Right, I couldn't agree more. He's moving out, ain't he? You a social worker now, are you?"

"I mean," said Vine, "is he quite recovered from that op he had?"

"For God's sake, that was nearly a year ago." She was suddenly furiously angry, her face bright red, her shoulders and arms trembling. "What the fuck's it got to do with you? Of course he's recovered—look at him. He's bloody marvelous, he's *normal,* he's like he was born that way. Can't you *see?''* She shivered. "Why don't you and her just take the stuff and fuck off?"

She slammed the door behind them. Vine put his foot in the puddle and cursed.

"I've got another child to see," Karen said in the car. "But I'm questioning this one, God help me."

W exford found it odious, the whole thing, the idea of asking a young boy for information about his own father. It re-minded him, by a roundabout route, of the question he had been handed at the Women, Aware! meeting. Having Karen, a nice-looking young woman with a no-nonsense manner, interview Joel seemed the best way. Presumably, her well-known abrasiveness when questioning men wouldn't extend to boys of fourteen.

He went with her and talked to the mother while she sat with Joel in the quaintly named playroom, a place where there was nothing to play with but plenty of equipment conducive to study. Joel had an impressive collection of textbooks and dictionaries, a computer, and a recording device. The posters on the walls were the educational kind, the life of a tree, the human digestive system, a climate map of the world.

Joel looked like his father, dark, thin, already tall, but had his mother's cool manner. Perhaps he too was capable of violent erup-tions. He spoke to Karen before she had a chance to speak to him.

"My mother has told me what you've come for. It isn't any good asking me because I don't know."

"Joel, I only want you to tell me if you were aware of your fa-ther going out just before eight. Were you in this room?"

The boy nodded. He seemed relaxed but his eyes were wary.

"You were in this room which is over the garage? If a car went out you'd hear it."

"My mother keeps her car in the garage. His always stands out."

"Even so. You've got good hearing, haven't you? Or were you concentrating very hard on your essay?" She had noticed that

when the chance came he had not referred to Snow as "my father."
She took the plunge. "Your mother has told you what all this is
about?"

"Please," he said. "I'm not a child. He's been committing adul-
tery and now his woman's been murdered."

Karen blinked. She was seriously taken aback. She took a deep
breath and started again on the car, the garage, the time. Downstairs, Wexford was asking Carolyn Snow if she would care to
amend the statement she had made concerning her husband's
movements on the evening of July 7.

"No. Why should I?" She wore no makeup. Her hair looked as
if she hadn't washed it since she found out about Annette Bystock.
If her clothes were expensive and in good order this was probably
because she had no others. She said suddenly, "There was another
one before her, you know. A Diana something. But she didn't last
long." She put her hand up to her hair. "Is it true that a wife can't
give evidence against her husband?"

"A wife can't be *compelled* to give evidence against her husband," said Wexford. "It's not the same thing."

She thought about this and what she thought seemed to please
her. "You won't want to talk to me again, will you?"

"We might. It's a possibility. Not thinking of going away anywhere, I hope?"

Her eyes narrowed. "Why do you ask?"

He could tell she was thinking of it. "The schools break up
next week. I don't want you going away at present, Mrs. Snow." At
the front door he paused. She was standing behind him but left
him to open the door himself. "You have a relative living in Ladyhall Avenue, I believe?"

"No, I haven't. Where did you get that idea?"

He wasn't going to tell her that her husband had told Annette
that this person's place of residence was his reason for not going to
her flat. "A friend, then?"

"No one." She shook her head fiercely. "My family comes from
Tunbridge Wells."

He left, thinking that if Annette had threatened to expedite a marriage between herself and Snow by divulging all to Carolyn, that would be Snow's motive for murder. Carolyn's reaction to learning of her husband's sustained infidelity was all too evident now. She was as unforgiving and as vindictive as Snow had expected her to be. And he would know; there had been another before Annette.

On the other hand, he might have gone round to Ladyhall Court on that Wednesday evening to beg Annette not to tell. He might have promised her all sorts of concessions. Taking her out to dinner occasionally would have been a start, Wexford thought. Or a holiday somewhere with her or just giving her a present. None of it had worked. Nothing else would do but that he leave Carolyn and come to her. They quarreled, he tore the lead of the bedside lamp out of the wall and strangled her . . . It was that tearing the electric lead part that didn't ring true, Wexford thought. It would have taken some strength. In the heat of rage, wouldn't he have put his bare hands round her throat?

He crossed the pavement to his car where Karen already waited at the wheel, the only exercise he would get that day. Dr. Crocker, and lately Dr. Akande, had told him he should walk more (the best kind of cardiovascular exercise, they both intoned) and he was wondering whether to tell Karen to take the car back alone and leave him to do the mile or two on foot, when he saw the doctor coming toward him. Wexford was immediately aware of that craven reaction that makes us want to pretend we haven't seen someone, makes us cross the road and keep our eyes averted, when the prospective encounter may involve reproach or recrimination. He had committed no offense against Dr. Akande; on the contrary, he had done everything in his and his force's power to find his missing daughter, but in spite of this he felt ashamed. Worse than that, he wanted to avoid the society of someone as unhappy and as despairing as the doctor must be. But he made no attempt to do so. A policeman must confront everything or take some other job (retrain, in ES parlance). It was a maxim he had first uttered to himself some thirty years before.

"How are you, Doctor?"

Akande shook his head. "I've been visiting a patient who's only two years short of a hundred," he said. "Even she asked me if I had any news. They're very kind, very good. I tell myself it would be worse if they stopped asking."

Wexford could think of nothing to say.

"I keep thinking about what Melanie might have done, where she went, all that. It's as if I don't think of anything else. It goes round and round in my head. I've even started wondering if we'll ever have her body. I never could understand that, those people who lost sons in war and craved their—their remains. Or just wanted to know where they were buried. I used to think, What does it matter? It's the person you want, the living creature you love, not the—the outer casing. I understand now."

His voice had broken on the word "love" as unhappy people's voices do break on that particular trigger. He said, "You must excuse me, I try to keep going," and walked off, as if blindly. Wexford watched him fumbling with the key at his car door and guessed his eyes were thick with tears.

"Poor man," said Karen, making Wexford wonder if this was the first time she had ever uttered that adjective and that noun in conjunction before.

"Yes."

"Where are we going now, sir?"

"To Ladyhall Avenue." He was silent for a moment. Then he said, "Ingrid Pamber told us something that seems to have got lost in the general shock-horror over Snow's behavior. Do you know what I'm talking about?"

"Something about Snow?"

"Of course it may not be true. She's a liar and an embroiderer too, I daresay."

"Do you mean about his wife having some relation living opposite Ladyhall Court?"

Wexford nodded. They turned out of Queens Gardens where

Wendy Stowlap lived and passed the corner shop where Ingrid had bought Annette's groceries. A man was banging furiously on the glass side of the phone box in which a woman talked on, unheeding. A blind woman let them into the house. Her eyeballs, in their baskets of wrinkles, were like glass that has been crazed from too much handling. Wexford spoke gently.

"Chief Inspector Wexford, Kingsmarkham CID, and this is Detective Sergeant Malahyde."

"She's a young lady, isn't she?" said Mrs. Prior, staring into the middle distance.

Karen admitted it.

"I can smell you. Very nice too. *Roma*, isn't it?"

"Yes, it is. Clever of you."

"Oh, I know 'em all, all the perfumes, it's how I know one woman from the next. It's no good you showing me those cards of yours, I can't see them, and I don't suppose *they* smell."

Gladys Prior giggled at her own wit. She led them to the staircase and they followed her up. "What's happened to that young chap B-U-R-D-E-N?" It was evidently some kind of in joke and it made her laugh again.

"He's busy somewhere else today," said Wexford.

Percy Hammond wasn't looking out of his window. He was asleep. But the light sleep of the very old was easily broken when they came into the room. Wexford wondered what he had looked like when he was young. There was nothing in that creased, pouchy, stretched, puckered face to indicate the lineaments of middle age, still less youth. It was scarcely human anymore. Only the white, rosy-gummed dentures, displayed when he smiled, hinted at real teeth, lost fifty years before.

He was dressed in a striped suit with waistcoat and collarless shirt. The knees held up the gray worsted as a frame with sharp metal angles might, and the hands that rested on them were like a pigeon's claws. "Do you want me to attend an identity parade?" he asked. "Pick him out from a line of them?"

Wexford didn't. While mentally congratulating Mr. Hammond on his quick-witted assumption, he could only tell him out loud that there was no doubt about who had robbed Annette's flat. They already had someone helping them with their inquiries into this matter.

"You couldn't have gone anyway," said Mrs. Prior. "Not in your state." She addressed Karen, to whom she seemed to have taken a fancy. "He's ninety-two, you know."

"Ninety-three," said Mr. Hammond, thus confirming Wexford's Law that it is only when under fifteen and over ninety that people wish to add years to their true age. "Ninety-three next week, and I could have. I haven't tried going out for four years, so how do you know I couldn't have?"

"An intelligent guess," said Gladys Prior with a giggle in Karen's direction.

"Mr. Hammond," Wexford began, "you've already told Inspector Burden what you saw across the way very early last Thursday morning. Were you looking out of your window on the previous evening?"

"I'm always looking out. Unless I'm asleep or it's dark. In the dark sometimes—you can see with the streetlights if you turn the light off in here."

"And do you turn the light off, Mr. Hammond?" asked Karen.

"I have to think about the electric bills, missy. My lights were off last Wednesday evening, if that's what you want to know. You want to hear what I saw? I've been thinking about it, going back over it. I knew you'd come back."

He was blessed in such a witness, Wexford thought thankfully. "Tell me what you saw, will you, sir?"

"I always watch them come home from work. Mind you, a few of them have gone away on holiday. Most of them ignore me but that chap Harris, he always gives me a wave. He got home about twenty past five and ten minutes after a girl came. She had a car and she parked it outside. There's a yellow line there that means you're not supposed to park till six-thirty but she took no notice of that. I'd never seen her before. Pretty girl she was, about eighteen."

Ingrid would be flattered, for what it was worth. By the time you reach ninety-three, Wexford thought, people of fifty look thirty to you and those in their twenties seem children. "She went into the flats?"

"And came out after five minutes. Well, seven minutes, it was. I'm no good at guessing time but I timed her, I don't know why. Gives me something to do. I do that sometimes, it's a game I play, I bet on it. I say to myself, Ten bob on it, Percy, she comes out before ten minutes are up."

"The young lady doesn't know what ten bob is, Percy. You're not living in the real world, you aren't. Fifty p to you, dear, it's twenty years and more since the changeover but it's like yesterday to him."

Wexford interrupted, "What happened next?"

"Nothing happened. If you mean by that, Did any strangers go in. Mrs. Harris came out and came back with an evening paper. I had my meal then, bit of bread and butter and a glass of Guinness, the same as I always have. I saw the car come that takes Gladys to her blind club."

"Seven sharp," said Mrs. Prior. "And I was back at half-past nine."

"While you were eating, Mr. Hammond," said Wexford, "did you sit at the table over there? Did you watch any television?"

The old man shook his head. He pointed at the window. "That's my telly."

"Don't get much sex and violence on it, though, do you, Percy?" Gladys Prior became convulsed with laughter.

"So you went on watching, did you, Mr. Hammond? What happened after Mrs. Prior had gone out?"

Percy Hammond screwed up his already screwed-up face. "Nothing much, I'm sorry to say." He gave Wexford a shrewd glance. "What do you *want* me to have seen?"

"Only what you did see," said Karen.

"It's around eight I'm interested in, Mr. Hammond," said Wexford. "I don't want to put ideas into your head, but did you see a man go into Ladyhall Court between five to and a quarter past eight?"

"Only that chap with his dog. There's a man whose name I don't know and Gladys doesn't know, he's got a spaniel. He always takes it out in the evening. I saw *him*. I'd think something was wrong if I didn't see him."

Something *was* wrong, thought Wexford, something was very wrong. "No one else?"

"No one at all."

"Not a man or a woman? You saw no one go in at about eight and come out at between ten and ten-thirty?"

"I said I'm no good with times. But I didn't see another soul until the young chap I told Mr. What's-his-name about."

"B-U-R-D-E-N," said Mrs. Prior with a gale of giggles.

"And it was dark then. I was in bed, I'd been asleep, but I got up—why did I get up, Gladys?"

"Don't ask me, Percy. To spend a penny, I daresay."

"I put the light on for a minute but it was so bright, I turned it off, and I looked out of the window and I saw this young chap come out with a big box in his arms—or was that later?"

Karen said gently, "That was in the morning, Mr. Hammond. You saw him in the morning, don't you remember? That's the one you asked us about, if you'd have to pick him out in an identity parade?"

"So it was. I told you I wasn't much good with time . . ."

"I think we've tired you out, Mr. Hammond," said Wexford. "You've been a great help but we'll only ask you one more thing. You and Mrs. Prior. Is either of you related to some people called Snow of Harrow Road, Kingsmarkham?"

Two disappointed old faces turned toward him. Both liked excitement, both hated having to deny knowledge. "Never heard of them," said Mrs. Prior gruffly.

"I suppose you know everyone—er, down this street, do you?" Wexford asked her as they were going down the stairs.

"You were going to say 'by sight,' weren't you? Bless you, I wouldn't have minded. Though it'd be nearer the mark to say 'by smell.' " She waited till she got to the foot of the staircase before letting her laughter escape. "There's a lot of old folks down here, the houses are old, you see, and some of them have lived in them for forty years, fifty. Would they be young or old, this person that's related to Mrs. What-d'you-call-her?"

"I don't know," said Wexford. "I don't know at all."

twelve

T he house was new, just finished, the last coat of paint applied perhaps no more than a week ago. But it still made him feel in a time warp. Not that he saw Mynford New Hall as old but rather that he had gone back two hundred years and, finding himself a character in, say, *Northanger Abbey*, had been brought here to view a brand-new mansion.

It was Georgian, with a pillared portico and a balustrade along the shallow roof, a big house ivory-white, the windows perfectly proportioned sashes, the columns fluted. In alcoves on either side of the front door stood stone vases hung with stone drapery and with living ivy and maidenhair fern. A gravel sweep would have been better but the carriage drive was paved. The tubs and troughs clustered on it held bay trees and yellow cypress, red fuchsias in full bloom, orange and cream arbutus, pink pelargoniums. By contrast, the flower beds were bare, turned earth without a weed showing.

"Give them a chance," Dora whispered. "They've only been here five minutes. They must have hired those tubs for the occasion."

"Where were they before, then?"

"In that place down the hill, the dower house."

The hill was a gentle slope of green lawns descending toward a wooded valley. A gray roof could just be made out among the trees.

Wexford remembered the old hall on the hilltop, a mid-Victorian stucco pile, not old enough or distinctive enough to be listed for preservation. Presumably, the Khooris had encountered no planning difficulties in pulling it down and setting the new hall up.

Their guests thronged the big lawn. In the middle of it stood a large striped marquee. Wexford had referred to it laconically as "the tea tent," a term Dora obscurely felt to be irreverent or even lèse-majesté. Her husband hadn't wanted to come. She told him not altogether truthfully that he had promised, then that it would do him good, take him out of himself. In the end he had come for her sake because she had said she wouldn't go if he didn't.

"Do you know anybody here? Because if you don't we might as well go for a walk. I wouldn't mind having a look at the old dower house."

"No, shh. Here's our hostess and homing on you if I'm not mistaken."

Anouk Khoori was a protean creature. He held in his mind the image of her in her tracksuit, her face *au naturel*, hair in a bouncy ponytail; and that other image, the champagne social worker, the ardent campaigner and political aspirant, power-dressed, up on high heels, her jewelry the solitary solitaire.

It was on her hand now but with many companions, flashing white and blue from her fingers as she walked toward them. And she was different again, not simply altered as women always are by a change of dress and hairstyle, but altogether unrecognizable. If he had met her off her home ground, if Dora hadn't been there to identify her, he doubted if he would have known Anouk Khoori. This time she was the chatelaine in yellow chiffon and a big straw hat piled with daisies, golden tendrils curling on her forehead and escaping to hang to her shoulders.

"Mr. Wexford, I *knew* you would come but I'm delighted just the same. And this is Mrs. Wexford? How do you do? Aren't we lucky to have this glorious day? You must meet my husband." She looked about her, then scanned the horizon. "I don't seem to be able to see him just at the moment. But come, let me introduce you to some very dear friends of ours who I know you'll love." As one of those women who never bother much with women, she turned her full gaze on Wexford and her fullest smile, a radiant beaming from lips painted geranium with a fine brush and teeth capped to Wedgwood whiteness. "And who will love *you*," she added.

The very dear friends turned out to be an aged man, wrinkled and shrunken, with the face of an ancient guru but dressed in denim and Western boots, and a girl some fifty years younger. Anouk Khoori, a genius at picking up and remembering names and one who swiftly dispensed with surnames, said, "Reg and Dora, I've been longing for you to meet Alexander and Cookie Dix. Cookie, darling, this is Reg Wexford, who is a terribly important police chief."

Cookie? How on earth did anyone get a name like that? She was getting on for a foot taller than her husband, dressed like the Princess of Wales at Ascot, but with waist-length black hair. "Is that sort of like a sheriff?" she said.

Anouk Khoori gave a long thrilling peal of laughter and on this laughter, as to a cue provided by herself, floated away. Wexford had astonished himself by his reaction to her, one of physical repulsion. But why should this be? She was beautiful, or many would say so, healthy and strong, extravagantly clean, deodorized, powdered, perfumed. Yet the touch of her hand made him shrink and her scent near him was like a fetid breath.

Dora was making an effort to talk to Cookie Dix. Did she live nearby? What did she think of the neighborhood? He could make small talk as well as anyone but he could no longer see the point. The shrunken old man stood silent and faintly scowling. He reminded Wexford of a horror film he'd watched one night when he couldn't sleep. There had been a mummy in it which the experimenter had unwrapped, succeeded up to a point in reanimating, and brought along to just such a garden party as this one.

"Have you seen Anouk's diamonds?" Cookie said suddenly.

Dora, who had been talking gently about the weather in July, how it never really got warm in England until July, was surprised into silence.

"The ones she's wearing *now* cost a hundred grand alone. Can you believe that? There's ten times that in the house."

"Goodness," said Dora.

"You may well say goodness." She bent forward, necessarily stooping in order to push her face close to Dora's, but instead of whispering spoke in her usual clear tones. "The house is hideous. Don't you think so? Pitiful, really, they think it's based on some Nash design for a house that was never built, but it's not, is it, sweetness?"

The mummy barked. It was exactly what had happened in the horror film, only at this point people had dispersed screaming.

"My husband is a very famous architect," said Cookie. She extended her neck and pushed her face at Wexford. "If we were people in a book, me telling you about the diamonds would be a *clue*, there'd be a robbery while we're out here, and you'd have to question all these people. There are five hundred people here, did you know that?"

Wexford laughed. He rather liked Cookie Dix, her naive manner and her meter-long legs. "At least, I'd say. Still, I doubt if they've left the house unguarded."

"They have but for Juana and Rosenda."

Unexpectedly, the mummy began to sing in a cracked tenor, to a tune from *The Mikado*, "Two little maids from the Philippines, one of them hardly out of her teens . . ."

"I'd have thought they'd have a staff," Dora said faintly.

"They used to have another one, as a matter of fact she was the sister of our one, but the rich are so mean, haven't you noticed? Well, darling Alexander isn't and God knows he's loaded." The mummy's face cracked. At just such a ghastly smile the women in the movie had started screaming. "Mostly they have caterers in," said Cookie. "Their servants don't stay. Well, these two do. The money's rotten but they need it to send home." For some reason Cookie dropped her voice. "Filipinos do."

"Filipi*nas*," said the mummy.

"Thank you, sweet. You're such a stickler. I call him my stickler sometimes. Shall we go and have some tea?"

Together they walked down the green slope, deflected from the prospect of tea by the kind of sideshows considered suitable for this type of charity benefit function. A good-looking dark woman in a kind of ankle-length white sweater was conducting a raffle for Fortnum and Mason hampers. A young man in a smock with an easel and palette was doing instant portraits for a fiver a time. Under a long yellow banner with CIBACT on it in black, a man had his twin daughters on display, little fair-haired girls in white frilled organdy and black patent leather shoes with instep straps. Punters were invited to guess the age of Phyllida and Fenella and whoever came nearest to the correct birth date got the child-size white teddy bear that sat on the counter between them.

"Vulgar, you see," said Cookie. "That's their trouble. They don't know the difference."

Dora glanced at the docile children. "You mean the raffle is all right and perhaps the artist but not the teddy-bear thing?"

"Exactly. That's exactly what I mean. Sad, really, when you've got everything."

At last Alexander Dix expressed himself, otherwise than in song. Wexford thought his voice what a French speaker's would be if he had lived till the age of thirty in, say, Casablanca, and the rest of his life in Aberdeen. "Nothing else is to be expected when you are a child of the gutters of Alexandria."

Presumably he was referring to Wael Khoori. Interested, Wexford was about to ask for more when something happened that always happens at parties. A couple appeared from nowhere and bore down upon the Dixes with cries of astonishment and greeting, and as also is always true, their former companions were forgotten. Wexford and Dora were abandoned, still standing in front of Phyllida, Fenella, and the teddy bear.

"Better do something for CIBACT, I suppose," Wexford said, producing a ten-pound note. "What do you say? I'll guess they're five and their birthday was June the first."

"I don't like to look too closely. They're not animals at Smithfield or something. I see what that Cookie meant. Oh, all right, I'll say they're five but they'll be six in September, September the fifth."

"Older," said a voice from behind Dora. "Six already. Probably six and a half."

Wexford turned round to see Swithun Riding. His wife looked very small beside him. There was a greater disparity in their heights than that between Wexford and Dora or—come to that—between Cookie Dix and the diminutive architect.

Susan said, "Do you know my husband?"

Introductions were made. Unlike his son, Swithun Riding responded. He smiled and uttered the usual archaism that was once an inquiry as to another's health.

"How do you do?"

Wexford handed his money to the twins' father and repeated his estimate of their age.

"Oh, nonsense," said Riding. "Have you no children yourself?"

The question was uttered in a tone both indignant and arrogant. Good manners had swiftly fallen away. Riding seemed to imply the discovery in Wexford of a wanton and antisocial partiality to total contraception.

"He's got two," said Dora rather sharply. "Two *girls*. And he's got a good memory."

"Well, Swithun's a pediatrician, after all," said Swithun's wife in mild reproach.

Her husband ignored her. A twenty-pound note was handed over, no doubt as a sign of social and perhaps parental superiority, and Swithun Riding offered his estimate as six and a half.

"They were six on February the twelfth," he hazarded but in so firm a voice as to suggest that whatever might be Phyllida and Fenella's official birthday, this was what their natural birthday should be.

The Ridings, joined by the burly Christopher in shorts and polo shirt and a fair-haired girl of about ten, set off in the direction of a plant stall. This was enough to turn Dora in the opposite direction toward the tea tent. Tea was a lavish affair, twenty different kinds of sandwiches, scones with raspberry jam and clotted cream, chocolate cake, coffee and walnut cake, passion cake, pecan pie, éclairs, cream slices, brandy snaps, strawberries and cream.

"Just the kind of thing I like," said Wexford, joining the queue.

It was a very long queue, a serpent of guests that wound round the inside perimeter of the yellow and white striped tent, and it was the kind of queue seldom seen, as different as could be from a line of dispirited ill-dressed people waiting for a bus or worse, as Wexford had seen recently in Myringham, at a dossers' soup kitchen. The tea tent at Glyndebourne was probably the nearest you'd get to this one. He'd been there once and, uncomfortable in a dinner jacket at four in the afternoon, had lined up for smoked salmon sandwiches just as he was doing now. But there a good many like himself had dressed themselves in ancient evening clothes, dinner jackets just postwar, old women in black lace from the forties, while here it was as if a *Vogue* centerfold had turned into a video. Dora said the woman in front of them was wearing a suit from Lacroix while Caroline Charles dresses were thick on the ground. She added abstractedly, "Don't eat the clotted cream, Reg."

"I wasn't going to," he lied. "I suppose I can have a bit of pecan pie? And a couple of strawberries?"

"Of course you can but you know what Dr. Akande said."

"Poor devil's got more on his mind at the moment than my cholesterol count."

All the tables in the marquee were occupied. As he had predicted, the Chief Constable was here, sitting at a table with his thin redheaded wife and two friends. Wexford quickly dodged out of the line of sight and he and Dora took their trays outside. They found themselves reduced to a low wall for seats and the top of a balustrade for a table, and were setting out the food when a voice behind Wexford said, "I thought it was you! I'm so pleased to see you because we don't know anyone here."

Ingrid Pamber. Behind her was the wild-haired Jeremy Lang, carrying a tray that sagged under its load of sandwiches, cake, and strawberries.

"I know what you're thinking," said Ingrid. "You're thinking what on earth are that pair doing here up among the nobs."

Fortunately, she didn't know what he was thinking. If he hadn't made it a rule long ago never to admire other women while accompanied by his wife, never to do this even in his own thoughts, he would have been dwelling appreciatively on her pink and white skin, that hair as satiny as a racehorse's coat, that figure, and the charming tilt to her mouth. As it was, he told himself she was ten times prettier in her white top and cotton skirt than Anouk Khoori or Cookie Dix or the woman who ran the hamper raffle. Then he banished covert admiration and said that though this hadn't been the inquiry he had in mind, how did she in fact come to be there?

"Jerry's uncle's a pal of Mr. Khoori. They live next door to each other in London."

The uncle. So the uncle was real. "I see." Since Khoori's London was unlikely to be too far distant from Mayfair, Belgravia, or Hampstead, the uncle must be a rich man.

Up to a little more thought-reading but this time with greater accuracy, Ingrid said, "Eaton Square," and then, "May we join you? It's great to have someone to talk to."

He introduced Dora, who said graciously, "Share our wall."

Ingrid began chatting about the happiness of having a fortnight off work, all the places she and Jeremy had been to, some rock concert, the theater at Chichester. While she talked she managed to mop up a great deal of food. How did the thin eat so much and get away with it? Girls like Ingrid, boys like this bony Jeremy, shoveling in scones plastered with their own thickness in clotted cream. They never seemed to think about it, they just ate it.

Better for him anyway to contemplate food and dwell on its effects than about this charming girl who was now with abundant grace and courtesy complimenting Dora on her dress. This afternoon her eyes seemed a brighter blue than ever, almost the color of a kingfisher's plumage. She wanted to know if they had gone in for guessing the twins' age. Jeremy had said it was silly but she had made him have a go because she did so want to win the teddy bear.

She laid her white hand on his sleeve. "I'm mad about cuddly toys. I can't remember—did we go into the bedroom when you came to the flat?"

The serpent uncoiling in the garden, that was what it was like. Graceful and courteous she might be, but poison was there too, a tiny sac of it under her tongue. Dora was looking surprised but no more than that. Jeremy, taking the second plate of passion cake, said, "Of course he didn't go into the bedroom, Ing. Why would he have? There's not room to swing a cat in there."

"Or a teddy bear." Ingrid giggled. "I've got a golden spaniel my dad bought me in Paris when I was ten and a pink pig and a dinosaur that came from Florida. The dinosaur doesn't sound cuddly but he is, maybe the most cuddly, isn't he, Jerry?"

"Not as cuddly as me, though," said Jeremy and he helped himself to a brandy snap. "You met my uncle Wael yet?"

"Not yet. We spoke to Mrs. Khoori."

"I suppose I still call him uncle. Don't know, really. Until the other day I hadn't spoken to him since I was eighteen. I'll introduce you if you want."

Neither Wexford nor Dora did much want but could hardly say so. Jeremy brushed crumbs off his jeans and got up. "You stay there, Ing," he said kindly, "and finish up the éclairs. You know how you love éclairs."

Finding Wael Khoori took a long time and involved walking all the way round the outside of Mynford New Hall. Wexford spotted the Chief Constable, this time heading in the direction of a rather sophisticated game of coconut shies. It seemed likely that he might avoid an encounter. Jeremy said that when they arrived that afternoon he had expected a house that looked like one of his uncle Wael's Crescent supermarkets with what he called "minaret things" or else something like Abu Dhabi airport. Instead there was this boring Georgian place. Had Mr. and Mrs. Wexford ever seen Abu Dhabi airport? While Dora listened to a description of this Arabian Nights extravaganza and tourist snare, Wexford glanced up at the windows of the new house with a vague idea in mind of seeing the face of either Juana or Rosenda looking out.

It was a big house for two young women to manage. Mrs. Khoori didn't look the sort of woman to make her own bed or wash up the breakfast things. There must be twenty bedrooms and no doubt bathrooms to go with them. What must it be like to be obliged to travel halfway across the world in order to feed your children?

The sky was beginning to cloud over and above the downs had dulled to a threatening purple. A little breeze whistled out of the woodland as they began to descend the slope. Wexford disliked the idea of climbing it again, he was growing weary of this hunting for a host who by rights should have sought them out. And he was thinking of saying so, though in politer terms, when Jeremy suddenly looked around and waved to the people behind them.

Three men, two of them walking arm in arm. It would have looked less odd, Wexford thought, if each had been in a burnoose and djellaba, but all were in Western clothes and one was unmistakably Anglo-Saxon, pink-skinned, fairish, bald. The others were both overweight and tall, taller even than Wexford. Each had the handsome Semite's face, hook-nosed, narrow-lipped, the eyes close-set. Plainly they were brothers, the younger man with a badly pockmarked brown skin, but the other's was no darker than an Englishman's with a tan while his hair, copious and rather long, was white as snow. He seemed about ten years older than his wife but she on the other hand might be older than she looked.

The last thing Wael Khoori wanted at this moment, in the midst perhaps of some business discussion, was to be accosted by this nephew-by-courtesy and introduced to people he didn't want to meet. This was clear from his abstracted and then mildly irritated expression. One thing, he knew Jeremy well, there had been no exaggeration there, though Wexford wouldn't have been surprised if there had been. He called him "dear boy" like some Victorian godparent.

They were presented to Khoori as "Reg and Dora Wexford, friends of Ingrid's," which Dora said afterward she thought a bit much. Khoori behaved as the Royal Family are said to do when meeting strangers. But his manner as he asked his banal questions was impatient rather than gracious, he was in a hurry to get on.

"Have you come far?"

"We live here," Wexford said.

"Like it, do you? Pretty place, very green. Had tea yet? Have some tea, my wife tells me it's tip-top."

"Right," said Jeremy. "I might have some more."

"You do that, dear boy. Kind regards to your uncle when you see him." To Wexford and Dora, he trotted out the old formula, "Nice to have met you. Come again."

Linking arms with both companions, neither of whom had been introduced, he steered them away into a shrubbery as dense as a maze. Jeremy said confidingly as they walked back to the marquee, "Got a funny voice, hasn't he? Did you notice? Estuary English, I suppose, and a hint of Cockney."

"It can't be, though."

"Well, it can actually. His brother that's called Ismail talks the same. They had an English nanny and *he* says she came from Whitechapel."

"So he didn't grow up in the gutters of Alexandria?" said Dora.

"Where did you get that idea? His parents were quite aristocratic, Uncle William says, his dad was a bey or a khalifa or one of those things, and it was Riyadh. Hi, Ing, sorry we've been so long."

"They gave the result of the competition," Ingrid said, "and I didn't get the bear, nor did you. It was three-six-eight got it. Well, they didn't get it, because no one came up with the ticket. Why do people go in for things and then not look to see if they've won?"

Dora said they must be going and, varying Khoori's formula, that she was very glad they had met. Wexford said good-bye.

"We should have offered them a lift, you know. Jeremy told me they hadn't got their car with them, it's in for repairs."

"I bet he did," Wexford said.

That would be a fine thing, driving them back to Kingsmark-ham, perhaps be invited in for a cup of tea and then have Dora in her innocence ask them round next week to spend the evening. "You must meet my daughter Sylvia . . ." He could imagine it all. He took his wife's arm affectionately. She had got out her ticket and was looking at it as they passed the twins' stall, from which the children had disappeared, though their father—and the teddy bear—remained.

"Three-six-seven," she said. "Missed it by one." She turned to look at Wexford. "Reg, you must either have three-six-six or three-six-eight."

He had the winning ticket, of course he had. By some kind of awful intuition he had known it since Ingrid's announcement.

The correct answer to the question of the twins' ages was June 1, on which date Phyllida had been born five years before at two minutes to midnight, and June 2, birth date of Fenella at ten minutes past. No one had come up with that and Wexford was nearest with June 1.

"Let me give it back. You can raffle it for the cause."

"Oh, no, you don't," said the twins' father nastily. "I've had as much of that bloody thing as I can stand. You take it or else chuck it in the river and pollute the environment."

Wexford took it. The teddy bear was as big as a child of two. He knew what he would have to do with it, wanted to do this and didn't want to. Dora said, "You could . . ."

"Yes, I know. I will."

They were eating again, taking Khoori's advice and having some more tea. Most people were leaving, so they had acquired the best table, outside the marquee, under the shade of a mulberry tree. Wexford set the teddy bear on the empty chair between them. Ingrid's brilliant eyes were wide, covetous, yearning. How could eyes that absorbed light and never gave it off produce a beam of peacock blue? Or was it of deep ice?

"He's yours if you want him."

"You don't mean it!"

She had sprung to her feet. "Oh, you're wonderful! You're so kind! I shall call her Christabel!"

Whoever heard of a female teddy bear? He knew what would happen next. It did—before he could get away. She threw her arms round his neck and kissed him. Dora watched enigmatically. Jeremy continued eating coffee walnut cake. Ingrid's body, which was delightfully and distressingly plump and slim at the same time, clung a little too long and a little too closely to his own. He took her hands, removed them gently from his neck, and said, "I'm glad you're pleased."

Since it wasn't in the nature of things that she should be attracted to him—he wasn't rich like Alexander Dix, young like Jeremy, or handsome like Peter Stanton—and nymphomania was a myth, only one possibility remained. She was a flirt. A flirt with the world's bluest glance. "An hundred years should go to praise thine eyes, and on thy forehead gaze . . ." He would *not* offer her a lift.

"Maybe he can be a boy after all," said Ingrid. "I know—your first name's Reg, isn't it?"

Wexford laughed. He said good-bye again, and over his shoulder, "It's not available for christening teddy bears."

A second possibility remained. He thought of it now. She was a liar, he knew that: Was she also a murderer? Was she nice to him, or what she thought of as being nice, to get him on her side? They were coming into the field that was a car park, before Dora said anything. The first drops of rain had begun to fall. The breeze had become a serious wind and a woman in front of them in cartwheel hat and diaphanous dress was having to hold her skirts down.

"She was all over you, that girl," said Dora.

"Yes."

"Who is she, anyway?"

"A suspect in a murder." He never told her more than that about his cases. She looked at him quite cheerfully.

"Really?"

"Really. Let's get in the car, shall we? Your hat'll get wet."

There was a queue to get out but not a long one. The line of cars had to pass through a farm gateway and since Rollses, Bentleys, and Jaguars predominated, progress was slow. Only two cars remained ahead of him to squeeze between the gateposts, when his phone started ringing. He picked up the receiver and it was Karen's voice he heard.

"Yes," he said, "yes," and, "I see."

Dora could hear Karen's voice but not distinguish words. The car slipped and bumped through the narrow gap. Wexford said, "Where did you say?" And then he said, "I'll take my wife home and come straight there."

"What is it, Reg? Oh, Reg, it's not Melanie Akande?"

"Sounds like it. I'm afraid it is."

"Is she dead?"

"Oh, yes," he said. "She's dead."

thirteen

Kingsmarkham lies in that part of Sussex that was once the land of a Celtic tribe the Romans called the Regnenses. To its colonists it was simply a desirable place to live, pleasant to look at and not too cold, the indigenous population regarded only as a source of slave labor. Numerous remains of female infants unearthed by archaeologists near Pomfret Monachorum suggest that the Romans practiced infanticide among the Regnenses with a view to maintaining a male workforce.

As well as this grisly discovery, treasure was found. No one knew how this huge cache of gold coins, figurines, and jewelry came to be buried on farmland a mile or two from Cheriton, but there was evidence that a Roman villa had once stood there. A rather romantic suggestion was made that early in the fifth century the family who lived there, being forced to flee, had buried their valuables in the hope of coming back one day to retrieve them. But the Romans had never come back and the Dark Ages began.

This treasure was found by the farmer himself, digging up a small piece of land, hitherto part of fields on which sheep grazed, with the intention of growing maize on it for fattening pheasants. It was valued at something over two million pounds, most of which he received. He gave up farming and went to live in Florida. The gold statuette he found of a suckling lioness and twin cubs and the two gold bracelets, one chased with a design of a boar hunt, the other of a stag at bay, can now be seen in the British Museum, where they are known as the Framhurst Hoard.

The result was to encourage prospectors. Looking from a distance as if slowly scouring the heathland and the green valley with vacuum cleaners, they came with their metal detectors and worked patiently and in silence for long hours at a time. Farmers had no objection—there was little arable farming in the area—and so long as they damaged nothing and did not frighten the sheep, they were not only harmless but might possibly be a source of untold wealth. Any successful prospector would be obliged to render up half his loot to the landowner.

So far there had been no more. The cache of which the lioness and the bracelets had been part appeared to have been a one-off. But the treasure seekers went on coming and it was one of these who, wandering somewhat outside the favored area, passing and repassing his detector across an area of chalky scree, had come upon firstly a coin, then the body of a girl.

It was where the downland began, between Cheriton and Myfleet. A narrow white road, without fence, wall, or hedge, ran between the foothills, and it was some twenty yards to the left of it, where the woodland began, on the edge of a wood, that she had been buried. While Colin Broadley was plying his metal detector the weather had been fine, the soil fairly damp from recent rains but not wet. The conditions had been ideal for digging and Broadley, once he had found the coin that had so excited his detector, went on with his excavations.

"When you realized what you'd found," Wexford said to him, "why didn't you stop digging?"

Broadley, in his forties, a heavy man with a beer gut, shrugged and looked shifty. He was no archaeologist but an unemployed plumber actuated by greed and hope. It was not he that had called the police but a passerby who, seeing the extensive excavation in progress and thinking it suspicious, had parked his car and gone to look. This public-spirited citizen, James Ranger of Myringham, was paying for his social conscience by being kept at the scene, seated in his car, where he had been for the past two hours.

"It was a strange thing to do, wasn't it?" Wexford persisted.

"She had to *be* dug up," Broadley said at last. "Someone was going to have to do it."

"That was a job for the police," Wexford said, and it was true that the police had finished the job. Of course he knew very well what Broadley had been up to. Having found the coin and not being a sensitive or squeamish man, he had dug down, hoping for more money and perhaps for jewelry on what lay beneath.

There had been none. The body was naked. Nor was it possible to say, at this stage, whether or not there was any connection between it and the coin. In the eyes of Broadley, this coin had been the first sample of a Roman treasure, but a closer look told Wexford it was a Victorian halfpenny, bearing the head of the young queen. The hair was done in a style vaguely suggestive of actresses taking part in Ancient Rome movies. Wexford sent Broadley off with Pemberton to sit in one of the police cars.

It was raining steadily. They had put a tarpaulin up over the grave and the trees provided some shelter. Under here the pathologist was currently examining the body. Not Sir Hilary Tremlett nor Wexford's *bête noire* Dr. Basil Sumner-Quist, both of whom were away on their holiday, but an assistant or surrogate who had introduced himself as Mr. Mavrikiev. Wexford, under an umbrella—there were ten umbrellas at the scene, under the dripping trees—held the coin inside a plastic bag. Not that there was likely to be such a thing as a fingerprint on it after its interment in that fine, chalky, abrasive soil, grains of which clogged the indentations on its surface. Once Mavrikiev was out of there and they had taken the photographs, he was going to have to do what he dreaded: make his way to Ollerton Avenue and tell the Akandes.

He must do it himself, he knew that. He couldn't send Vine or even Burden to do the job for him. Since Melanie had been reported missing he had gone daily to see the doctor and his wife, had missed only the day he had met Akande by chance in the street. He had turned himself into their friend and he knew he had done this because they were black. Their race and their color merited his special attention, yet this was not as it should be. Ideally, if he truly practiced what being unprejudiced was all about, he would have treated them the same as any other parents of a missing child. Later that day the reckoning was coming for him.

Mavrikiev lifted a flap of the tarpaulin and came out. There was some assistant of his at hand to hold an umbrella over him. It was incredible, Wexford could hardly believe his eyes, but the pathologist was going to say nothing to him, was making straight for his waiting Jaguar.

"Dr. Mavrikiev!" he said.

The man was quite young, fair, with a washed-out Nordic look. Forebears from Ukraine probably, Wexford guessed, as he turned round and said, "Mister. Mr. Mavrikiev."

Wexford swallowed his wrath. Why were they always so rude? This one was the worst of the lot. "Can you give me an idea when she died?"

Mavrikiev looked as if he might ask for Wexford's credentials. He pushed out his lips and scowled. "Ten days. Maybe more. I'm not a magician."

No, you're a real bastard . . . "And the cause of death?"

"Nobody shot her. She wasn't strangled. She wasn't buried alive."

He ducked into his car and slammed the door. Didn't like being called out on a wet Saturday night, no doubt. Who did? Wouldn't like doing a postmortem on a Sunday either, but that was too bad. Burden came stumbling across the slippery wet scrub, his coat collar turned up, his hair dripping, no umbrella for him.

"Have you seen her?"

Wexford shook his head. He didn't feel anything anymore about looking on the dead who have met their death by violence, not even on the decomposing dead. He was used to it and you can get used to anything. In some ways, fortunately, his sense of smell wasn't what it had once been. He ducked under the tarpaulin and looked at her. No one had covered her, she wasn't even decently covered with a sheet, but lay sprawled on her back, still in a reasonable state of preservation. The face, particularly, was very nearly intact. Even in death, after days of death and interment, she looked very young.

The black patches on her dark skin, notably the sticky black mass on the side of her hair, might have been decay or they might have been bruises. He didn't know but Mavrikiev would. One of her arms lay at an odd angle and he wondered if it could have been broken before death. Out in the rain he drew a long breath.

"He said ten days or more," said Burden. "That would be about right."

"Yes."

"Back to Tuesday week's eleven days. If whoever brought her here came in a car they didn't bring the car in here off the road. Of course she may have been alive when she got here. He may have killed her here. Want me to attend the postmortem? He says nine in the morning. I will if you like. I just shan't speak to Mavri-Whatsit unless he speaks to me."

"Thanks, Mike," said Wexford. "I'd rather go to the PM than do what I've got to do tonight."

Ten minutes to nine and still light in that grim hopeless way only a wet summer evening in England can be. It was hard to tell whether it was rain falling or just water dripping from the trees. The air was still and heavy and the humidity hung as a cold whitish vapor. No lights were on in the house but that meant nothing. Dusk had barely come. Wexford rang the bell and almost immediately a light came on in the hall and another in the porch above his head. The boy who opened the door he recognized at once as the Akandes' son who had been in the photograph with Melanie.

Wexford introduced himself. The boy being there made things worse, he thought, but better perhaps for the parents. One child was left to comfort them.

"I'm Patrick. My mother and father are in the back, we're finishing supper as a matter of fact. I only got home today and I've been sleeping. I didn't wake up till an hour ago."

To forewarn him or not? "I'm afraid the news is bad."

"Oh." Patrick looked at him, then away. "Yes, well, you must see my parents."

At the sound of their voices Raymond Akande had risen from the table and was standing there, looking toward the door, but Laurette remained where she was, sitting very upright, both hands lying on the cloth on either side of a plate with orange segments on it. Neither of them said anything.

"I have bad news for you, Dr. Akande, Mrs. Akande."

The doctor drew in his breath. His wife silently turned her head in Wexford's direction.

"Will you sit down, please, Doctor? I expect you can guess what I've come to tell you."

The tiny tremor of Akande's head signified a nod.

"Melanie's body has been found," Wexford said. "That is, we are as certain as we can be without a positive identification that this is Melanie."

Laurette beckoned to her son. "Come and sit down again, Patrick." Her voice was quite steady. She said to Wexford, "Where was she found?"

How much he had hoped they wouldn't ask! "In Framhurst Woods."

Leave it there, don't ask any more. "Was her body buried?" Laurette asked relentlessly. "How did they know where to dig?"

Patrick put his hand on his mother's arm. "Mum, don't."

"How did they know where to dig?"

"People go up there with metal detectors looking for treasure like the Framhurst Hoard. One of them found her."

He thought of the bruises and the broken arm, the matted blackness on the skull, but she didn't ask the question so he had no need to lie. Instead, "We knew she must be dead," she said. "Now we really know. What's the difference?"

There was a difference and it lay in the presence of hope and its absence. Everyone in the room knew that. Wexford pulled out the fourth chair from the table and sat down on it. He said, "It is probably no more than a formality but I must ask you to come and make an identification of the body. You'd be the best person, Doctor."

Akande nodded. He spoke for the first time and his voice was unrecognizable. "Yes. All right." He went over to his wife and stood by her chair but he didn't touch her. "Where," he said, "and what time?"

Now? Let them try to get a night's sleep first. Mavrikiev would want to do the postmortem early but it might be a long job. "We'll send a car for you. Say one-thirty?"

"I should like to see her," said Laurette.

You would no more say to this woman that it was better not, that it was an anguish no mother should be put through, than you'd say it to Medea or Lady Macbeth. "Just as you wish."

She said nothing more to him but turned her face toward Patrick, who must have read there some rare sign of weakness or sensed an early warning that her control would break. He put his arms round his mother and held her tightly. Wexford left the room and let himself out of the house.

If those stripped-raw features had been less unmistakable, he would have failed to recognize the pathologist. And this had nothing to do with the grisly disguise supplied by a green rubber gown and cap. Mavrikiev was a changed man. Such violent mood swings are rare in normal people and Wexford wondered what cataclysmic event had so soured him the evening before or piece of good fortune recently cheered him up. One of the oddest things was that he behaved at first as if he had never encountered either policeman before.

"Good morning, good morning. Andy Mavrikiev. How d'you do? I'm not anticipating this being a long job."

He got to work. Wexford wasn't inclined to watch closely. The sound of the saw on a skull, the sight of the removal of organs, though not sickening to him, were not particularly interesting.

Burden watched everything, as he had watched Sir Hilary Trem-lett's operations on Annette Bystock, and asked a stream of questions, all of which Mavrikiev seemed happy to answer. Mavrikiev talked all the time and not only about the remains on the table.

Although he scarcely offered it as an explanation of his contrast in mood, it *was* an explanation. At five on the previous morning his wife had gone into labor with their first child. A difficult delivery was expected and Mavrikiev had hoped to be with her throughout, but the call to Framhurst Heath had come just as the question was being debated: continue to wait and hope for a normal delivery, or perform a cesarean?

"I wasn't best pleased, as you can imagine. Still, I was back in time to see Harriet made comfortable with an epidural and a healthy baby delivered."

"Congratulations," said Wexford. "What was it?"

"A nice little girl. Well, a nice big girl, nearly ten pounds. You see this? Know what it is? It's a ruptured spleen, that's what it is."

When he had finished, the body on the slab—or rather the face, for the poor empty body was now entirely concealed under plastic sheeting—looked a good deal better than when first unearthed. It even appeared as if decomposition was less advanced, for Mavrikiev had done an undertaker's job as well as a pathologist's. The dreadful confrontation awaiting the Akundes would be less harrowing.

He pulled off his gloves. "I'll revise what I said last night. I said ten days or a bit more, didn't I? I can do better than that. Twelve days at least."

Wexford nodded, not surprised. "What did she die of?"

"I told you her spleen was ruptured. There's a fracture of the ulna and a fracture of the radius on the left side—that's the arm, the left arm. She didn't die of that. She was very thin. Could have been a bulimic. Contusions all over her body. And a massive cerebral embolism—blood clot in the brain to you. I'd say the chap beat her to death. I don't think an instrument was used, just his fists and maybe his feet."

"You can kill someone with your fists?" said Burden.

"Sure. If it's a big strong guy. Think of boxers. And then think of a boxer doing to a woman what he does to an opponent, only without gloves. See what I mean?"

"Oh, yes."

"She was just a kid," said Mavrikiev. "Late teens?"

"Older than that," said Wexford. "Twenty-two."

"Really? You surprise me. Well, I must get out of this gear and be on my way as I've a luncheon date with Harriet and Zenobia Helena. It was nice meeting you gentlemen. You'll get my report pronto and soonest."

Burden said when he had gone, "Zenobia Helena Mavrikiev. What does it sound like?"

The question was rhetorical but Wexford answered it. "A maidservant in one of Tolstoy's stories." He cast up his eyes. "Bit better than last night, wasn't he, but what an insensitive bugger! My God, it got up my nose a bit, him on about *his* daughter and the Akandes' daughter's ruptured spleen all in the same breath."

"At least he doesn't make sick jokes like Sumner-Quist."

Wexford found himself incapable of eating any lunch. This departure of appetite, rare for him, seemed to please Dora, who was always trying by subtle or direct means to make him eat less. But it excited wondering comment from Sylvia and her family, who had invited themselves to lunch, as was increasingly their habit on a Sunday. Today he could have done without their company.

Now that the novelty of being, so to speak, the family's bread-winner was starting to wear off, Sylvia had fallen into the irritating habit of pointing out one thing after another on the table and various objects in the room, such as flowers and books, as being beyond the means of those living on seventy-four pounds a week. This was the sum total of UB and IS granted the Fairfaxes by the Employment Service and the Department of Social Security. How quickly she had seized upon that weapon of the disadvantaged most calculated to wound the sensibilities of the better off! Her father sometimes wondered where she had picked up such a catalog of maddening habits.

A tinkly laugh preceded most of these comments. "That's clotted cream, Robin, to put on your raspberries. Make the most of it. You're not likely to get it at home."

Robin, of course, said it was no problem. *"Koi gull knee."*

"I shouldn't have any more wine, Neil. Drinking is just a habit and it's not a habit you can afford the way things are."

"If it isn't there I can't drink it, can I? But it *is here* and I'm making the most of it like you told the boys to do with the clotted cream. Right?"

"Mafesh," said Robin in a heartfelt way.

Wexford felt he was spending his life escaping from things, uncomfortable situations, people's misery, unhappy occasions. It was raining again. He drove himself down to the mortuary, having resisted a masochistic temptation to fetch the Akandes himself.

The car brought them, both of them, at ten past two. Masterful for once, Akande said to his wife, "I'll go in first. I'll *do* it."

"All right."

Laurette was hollow-eyed. Her features seemed to have got bigger and her face smaller. But her glossy hair was still carefully dressed, coiled and pinned to the back of her head. And she was still well dressed. In the black suit and black blouse, she looked as if she was going to a funeral. Raymond Akande's face had been gray for a long while now and he had been losing weight steadily since his daughter first disappeared. That fortnight had made him ten pounds lighter.

Wexford took him into the mortuary, the chilly abode now shared by the bodies of two dead women. He lifted the edge of the sheet in both hands and exposed the face. Akande hesitated for a moment, then came forward. He bent over, looked at the face, and sprang back.

"That's not my daughter! That's not Melanie!"

Wexford's mouth went dry. "Dr. Akande, are you sure? Look again, please."

"Of course I'm sure. That's not my daughter. Do you think a man doesn't know his own child?"

fourteen

S hock suspends everything. There is no thought, only automatic reaction, movement, mechanical speech. Wexford followed Akande out of the mortuary, his mind a blank, his body obeying motor instructions.

Laurette had her back to them. She had been talking, or doing her best to talk, to Karen Malahyde. At the sound of their footsteps she got up, but slowly. Her husband went up to her. His walk was a little unsteady and when he put out his hand to her he seemed to clutch her arm for support.

"Letty," he said, "it isn't Melanie."

"*What?*"

"It isn't her, Letty." His voice shook. "I don't know who it is but it isn't Melanie."

"What are you saying?"

"Letty, it's not Melanie."

He was very close to her. He bowed his head against her shoulder. She put her arms round him and held him, she held his head against her breast and stared at Wexford over his shoulder.

"I don't understand." She was cold as stone. "We gave you a photograph."

The enormity of what had happened, realization of that enormity, was beginning to take over from shock. Wexford said, "Yes," and "Yes, that's right."

Her voice began to rise. "This dead girl, she's black?"

"Yes."

Karen Malahyde, who had seen Wexford's face, said, "Mrs. Akande, if you'd just . . ."

Softly, as if it was a baby she held, so as not to disturb the baby, Laurette Akande almost whispered, "How dare you do that to us!"

"Mrs. Akande," said Wexford, "I am extremely sorry this has happened." He added, with what must have been a lie, "No one regrets it more than I do."

"How dare you do that to us?" Laurette screamed at Wexford. She forgot the baby at her breast. Her hands had ceased to nurse him. "How dare you treat us like that? You're just a damned racist like the rest of them. Coming to our house patronizing us, the great white man condescending to us, so magnanimous, so liberal . . . !"

"Letty, don't," Akande begged her. "Please don't."

She ignored him. She took a step toward Wexford, both fists up now. "It was because she was black, wasn't it? I haven't seen her but I know, I can see it all. One black girl's just the same as another to you, isn't she? A *negress*. A *nigger*, a *darky* . . ."

"Mrs. Akande, I'm sorry. I am deeply sorry."

"*You* regret it. You damned hypocrite! You don't have prejudice, do you? Oh, no, you're not a racist, black and white are all equal in your eyes. But when you find a dead black girl it's got to be *our* girl because we're black!"

Akande was shaking his head. "Not a bit like her," he said. "Not a bit."

"Black, though. Black, isn't she?"

"That's the only way she's like her, Letty. She's black."

"So we don't get a wink of sleep all night. Our son sits up all night and what's he doing? He's crying. For hours and hours. He hasn't cried for ten years but he cried last night. And we tell the neighbors, the nice white liberal neighbors who are bighearted enough to feel sorry for parents whose daughter's been murdered, *even though she was only one of those colored girls, one of those blacks.*"

"Believe me, Mrs. Akande," Wexford said. "It's a mistake that's been made many times before and the dead have been white." It was true but still she was right, he knew she was right. "I can only apologize again. I'm very sorry this has happened."

"We'll go home now," Akande said to his wife.

She looked at Wexford as if she would have liked to spit at him. She didn't do this. The tears she hadn't shed when she thought the body in there was her daughter's now streamed down her cheeks. Sobbing, she hung on to her husband's arm with both hands and he led her out to the waiting car.

A salutary lesson. We think we know ourselves but we don't, and self-discovery of this particular kind of ignorance is bitter. What he had said to Laurette Akande about a similar confusion sometimes occurring between the bodies of white people was factually accurate. It was scarcely true in spirit. He *had* assumed a black girl's body was that of a missing black girl and he had done so *because she was black*. The photograph he had of Melanie Akande had not been referred to. The known heights of the missing girl and the dead girl had not been compared. With a wince, he remembered how only that morning, only about three hours before, Mavrikiev had expressed surprise that the age of the body on the table was twenty-two and not eighteen or nineteen. Now he recalled something learned long ago from a forensic report, that certain important bones in the female anatomy have fused by the age of twenty-two . . .

The worst thing for him was that it had shown him he was wrong about himself. This error had occurred through prejudice, through racism, through making an assumption he could never have made if the missing girl were white and the body white. In such a case he would merely have thought it likely the lost had been found but he would have done a lot more rigorous research into appearance and statistics before summoning the parents to make an identification. Laurette's reproaches were valid, if violent.

Well, it was a lesson and that was how it must be viewed. There was no question of ceasing his visits to the Akandes. The first one, but only the first one, would be uncomfortable for all of them. Unless, of course, they saw to it that the first was the last. He had apologized, and more humbly than he usually did to anyone. He wouldn't say he was sorry again. It came to him, and brought him a wry amusement, that the lesson was having its results already, for from tomorrow he was going to begin treating the Akandes not as members of a disadvantaged minority worthy of special consideration, he was going to treat them as ordinary human beings.

But since the dead girl wasn't Melanie, who was she?

A black girl was missing and a black girl's body had been found but there was no apparent connection between the two.

B urden, untroubled by Wexford's scruples and sensibilities, said it ought to be easy enough to identify her now that police had a national register of missing persons. It would be easier because she was black. Whatever might be the situation in London or Bradford few black people lived in this part of southern England and still fewer went missing. By this time, however, halfway through Monday, he had already discovered that nowhere in the area of the Mid-Sussex Constabulary had the police a missing person approximating to this girl's description on their computer.

"There's a Tamil woman been missing since February. She and her husband had the Kandy Palace restaurant in Myringham. But she's thirty and though I suppose technically she's black, they're very dark, those Tamils . . ."

"Let's not get into that one again," said Wexford.

"I'll get on to the national register," Burden said. "I suppose she could have been brought here, dead or alive, from some place like South London where I've no doubt girls go missing every day. And what happens now to our theory that Annette was killed because of something Melanie told her?"

"Nothing happens to it," Wexford said slowly. "Finding this girl has nothing to do with Melanie. It's irrelevant, it's something else. We still have the status quo. Melanie does something or says

something her killer doesn't want known and he kills Annette because Annette, and presumably Annette alone, has been told what
that is. After all, this girl being dead doesn't mean Melanie's alive.
Melanie is dead too and we just haven't yet found her body."

"You don't think this girl—what shall we call her? We'd better
give her a name."

"Yes, okay, but for God's sake don't come up with something
from *Uncle Tom's Cabin*."

Puzzled, Burden said, "I've never read it."

"Sojourner, we'll call her," Wexford said, "after Sojourner
Truth, the 'Ain't I a Woman?' poet. And maybe—well, I somehow
see her as impermanent, homeless, alone. 'I am a stranger with
thee and a sojourner,' you know."

Burden didn't know. He wore his deeply suspicious uneasy
look. "Sodgernah?"

"That's right. What were you going to say. You said that this
girl . . . ?"

"Oh, yes. You don't think *this* girl—I mean whatshername,
Sojourner—you don't think *she* said something significant to
Annette?"

Wexford looked interested. "At the Benefit Office, d'you
mean?"

"If we don't have a clue who she is she's just as likely to be
signing on or to be a new claimant as not. It's a way of identifying
her, see if they've got someone answering her description among
their claimants."

"Annette was killed on Wednesday the seventh, Sojourner
certainly before that, maybe on the fifth or sixth. It fits, Mike. It's a
good idea. Clever of you."

Burden looked pleased. "We can also check what immigrants
are registered with us. I'll go down to the Benefit Office myself.
Take Barry with me. By the way, where is Barry?"

Sergeant Vine tapped on the door and was in the room before
Wexford had time to answer. He had been in Stowerton, talking to
James Ranger. Ranger was retired, a widower, a solitary man, who

had been on his way to spend Saturday evening baby-sitting his grandsons, when from his car he spotted Broadley digging up a grave.

"He says he won't do that again," said Vine. "Apparently, his daughter and her husband missed their dinner dance. He says next time he sees some peasant, I quote, desecrating the environment he's going to accelerate and drive right on past. D'you know what he thought Broadley was up to? You won't believe this. He thought he was digging up orchids! Apparently there's some rare orchid grows up there and he's its self-appointed guardian."

"Ranger by name and ranger by nature," said Wexford. "Bit unusual, though, wasn't it, quiet elderly chap like him, champion of endangered species, baby-sitter, owner of a ten-year-old but immaculate 2CV, bit odd him having a car phone, isn't it? What does he have it *for*? To call the botanical police when he sees someone pick a primrose?"

"I asked him that. He said it was as well he *did* have it, so he could ring us."

"Not an answer to your question, though."

"No. When pressed, he said—wait for it—it was in case he broke down on the motorway at night."

"There are phones on motorways and in any case he's not permitted to take a *deux chevaux* on them."

"A figure of speech, he said." Vine laughed. "I've got him high on my suspect list. I was coming away from his place, had to park the car half a mile away as usual, when who do I see coming out of that block of flats in the High Street, Something Court, Clifton Court, but Kimberley Pearson."

"Did you speak to her?"

"I asked her how she was getting on in her new home. She had Clint with her all dressed up in a brand-new baby tracksuit sitting in a very smart buggy. She'd tarted herself up a good bit too, red leggings and one of those bustier things and shoes with heels like that." Vine held up thumb and forefinger five inches apart. "A changed woman. She'd told me she was moving into the home of her late grandma. It didn't seem that sort of place. I mean, quite a smart block of newish flats."

Burden gave Wexford a sidelong look. "That'll set your mind at rest," he said not very pleasantly. "You were getting worried about their fate."

" 'Worried' is a strong word, Inspector Burden," Wexford snapped. "Most people not entirely callous would be concerned for a child living in those circumstances."

There was a short uncomfortable silence. Then Vine said, "She seems to be getting on all right without Zack. Glad to see the back of him, I expect."

Wexford said nothing. He had another date with the Snows. Did the death of Sojourner affect his approach to them? Did it perhaps entirely change his attitude? He felt suddenly as if lost in a dark wood. Why had he bitten Mike's head off like that? He picked up the phone and asked Bruce Snow to come to the police station at five.

"I shan't be done here till half-past."

"Five, please, Mr. Snow. And I want your wife here too."

"You'll be lucky," Snow said. "She's going away tonight, taking the kids and going to Malta or Elba or somewhere."

"No, she isn't," said Wexford. He dialed the number of the house in Harrow Avenue and a young girl's voice answered.

"Mrs. Snow, please."

"This is her daughter. Who wants her?"

"Chief Inspector Wexford, Kingsmarkham CID."

"Oh, right. Hang on."

He had to hang on a long time and felt his temper rising. When she finally came to the phone she had regained her coolness. The ice maiden was back in occupation.

"Yes, what is it?"

"I'd like you to come down to the police station at five, please, Mrs. Snow."

"Sorry, but that won't be convenient. My flight to Marseille is at ten to five."

"It will be leaving without you. Have you forgotten I asked you not to go anywhere?"

"No, I haven't but I didn't take it seriously. It's so absurd— what has all this to do with me? I'm the injured party. I'm taking my poor children away from it all. Their father's behavior has broken their hearts."

"Their hearts can wait a few days to be mended, Mrs. Snow. I don't suppose you'd like to find yourself on a charge of obstructing police inquiries, would you?"

He knew better than to believe he could understand people. Why, for instance, did this woman need to lie? She was, as she had just told him, the injured party. Deceiving a wife with a mistress over a period of *nine years* was to do her a serious injury, for it humiliated as well as hurt her, it made her feel a fool. As for Snow, Wexford knew he would never understand the man's conduct. He would hardly have believed it had someone told him that here, in England, in the nineties, a man could enjoy a woman's sexual favors for years on end without paying her, without giving her presents or taking her out, without the use of a hotel room or even a bed, in his office, on the floor, so as to be within reach of his wife's voice on the phone.

And if he couldn't understand that, why should he understand any other aspects of Snow's behavior? It seemed absurd to him that the man might have killed Sojourner because, say, Annette had told her about their affair. But *all* Snow's transactions were incomprehensible to him. So might he have beaten her to death and buried her out there in Framhurst Woods? Kill Annette, kill the woman Annette had told, and all to stop it reaching his wife's ears? Well, they all now knew what happened when it did reach his wife's ears . . .

Sojourner could have been blackmailing him. Perhaps only in a small way. It wouldn't hurt him to give her a bit of money from time to time to keep her from telling his wife. And then she asked for more money, perhaps for a lump sum. Wexford found he disliked thinking this way. Somewhere in his mind, not quite consciously, he had made Sojourner into a good person. Sojourner was the innocent victim of wicked men who exploited and abused her, while she was herself virtuous and gentle, a keeper not a betrayer of secrets, a fearful, simple, trusting soul.

Of course he was sentimentalizing her. Where now was the lesson he should have learned and thought he had learned from that business with the Akandes? He knew nothing about the girl, not her real name, her country of origin, her family if any, not even her age. And Mavrikiev's forensic report, when it came, would tell him very little of that. He didn't even know if she had ever so much as set foot in the Benefit Office.

B ruce Snow sat in Interview Room One with Burden. His wife was with Wexford in Interview Room Two. Putting them in the same room last time had resulted in the slanging match Wexford didn't want to see repeated. He faced a sulky Carolyn Snow across the table, Karen Malahyde standing behind her and wearing a look of unconcealed distaste—for everything concerned with Mrs. Snow, Wexford guessed, her lifestyle, her status as wife without a job or personal income, and, unfortunately, her new position as a betrayed, deceived woman.

"I'd like to put it on record," Carolyn was saying, "that I think it outrageous I'm being stopped from going on holiday. It's an unjustified interference with my liberty. And my poor children—what have they done?"

"It's not what they've done but what you've done, Mrs. Snow. Or, rather, not done. You can put what you like on record. For all your boasts that you don't tell lies, you haven't been truthful with me."

In the other room Burden was asking Bruce Snow if he would like to amend his statement at all or add to it in any way. Would he, for instance, care to tell Burden what he was doing during the evening of July 7?

"I was at home. I was just at home. Reading, maybe, I don't remember. Sitting with my wife. I watched television. But it's no use asking me what I watched, I don't remember."

"Have you ever seen this girl, Mr. Snow?"

Burden showed him a photograph of Sojourner's twelve-days-dead face. It had been skillfully taken but still it looked like the picture of a dead face and a battered one too. Snow recoiled.

"Is that Akande's daughter?"

That mistake again. But Burden wasn't going to let it pass. "What makes you say that?"

"Oh, for God's sake. I've never seen her before anyway."

Her eyes as tragic as if she had suffered a bereavement, Carolyn Snow was asking Wexford to let her go on holiday. Her trip had been booked six months before. When it was made Snow would have been going too but his elder daughter had agreed to take his place. The hotel wouldn't be able to take them next week, there would be no places on flights, the travel agent's fee wasn't refundable.

"You should have thought of all that before," said Wexford, and he showed her the picture of Sojourner, the closed eyes, the bruised skin, the bare patches on the forehead and temples where the hair had begun to fall. "Do you know her?"

"I've never seen her before in my life." Instead of flinching, Carolyn peered more closely. "Is she colored? I don't know any colored people. Look, I've missed my plane but the travel agent says she thinks she could get us on the one tomorrow morning that goes at ten-fifteen."

"Really? Amazing, isn't it, how much more accommodating to passengers' needs air services have become?"

"You make me bloody sick! You're just a sadist. You're enjoying this, aren't you?"

"There's considerable job satisfaction attached to what I do," said Wexford, wondering if the Employment Service would make "job satisfaction" all one word. "I have to get something out of it." He looked at his watch. "All these long hours, unpaid overtime. I'd rather be at home with my wife than stuck in here trying to get the truth out of you."

"Have a good marriage, do you, Chief Inspector? All this has wrecked mine, I hope you know that."

"Your husband has done that, Mrs. Snow. Revenge yourself on him if you like. You won't get revenge on us."

"What do you mean, revenge?"

Wexford drew his chair closer and put his elbows on the table. "Isn't that what you're doing? You're revenging yourself on him for his affairs with two women. Deny he was at home that evening, insist he went out at eight and was out two and a half hours, and maybe you won't only get your house and a big chunk of his income out of him, you'll have the added satisfaction of seeing him on a murder charge."

He had got it exactly right, he could see it in her eyes.

"Was she blackmailing you, Mr. Snow?" said Burden on the other side of the wall.

"Forget it. I've never seen her."

"We know what happens when your wife finds out about your infidelity. We've seen. She's not a forgiving woman, is she? I think you'd have willingly paid up to keep her from finding out and perhaps paid over a long period." Overstepping the bounds once more, he said, "What on earth did Annette Bystock have to make you go on and on with it?" There was no answer, only a scowl. "Still, you did go on. Did you get tired of paying? Did you see there'd never be an end to paying, even if you ended things with Annette? Was killing your blackmailer the only way?"

Beyond the partition, Carolyn Snow said, "Everything I've said was true but, yes, I'd like to see him come to grief—why not? I'd like to see him pay for those two women with years in prison."

"That's frank," said Wexford. "And what about yourself, Mrs. Snow? Do you fancy paying for your revenge?"

"I don't know what you mean."

"You seem to be looking at things upside-down. You've supposed throughout that we've been questioning you to confirm or deny what your husband says were his movements. That it is your *husband* who is the suspect, your *husband* who is the only possible candidate for Annette Bystock's killer. But you're quite wrong. There is yourself."

She said it again, but anxiously this time. "I don't know what you mean."

"We have only your word for it that you knew nothing about Annette's role in your husband's life until after she was dead. I think we know what your word is worth, Mrs. Snow. You had a better motive than he for killing her. You had a better motive than anyone."

She stood up. She had gone quite white. "Of course I didn't kill her! Are you mad? Of course I didn't!"

Wexford smiled. "That's what they all say."

"I swear to you I didn't kill her!"

"You had motive. You had means. You have no alibi for that Wednesday evening."

"I didn't kill her! I didn't know her!"

"Perhaps you'd like to make a statement now, Mrs. Snow. With your permission we'll record your statement. And then I can go home."

She sat down again. She was breathing in short fast gasps, her forehead furrowed, her mouth puckered. Clenching her fists and digging the nails into her palms brought back some of her control. She began to tell the recording machine what had happened, how she had been alone in Harrow Avenue but for her son upstairs, how her husband had gone out at eight and returned at ten-thirty, but she broke off and spoke directly to Wexford.

"Can I go away tomorrow now?"

"I'm afraid not. I don't want you leaving the country. You can have a few days in Eastbourne, I've no objection to that."

Carolyn Snow began to cry.

In the past Sergeant Vine had spent many a long hour sitting at one of these desks in the area at the back, trying to look like an administrative assistant while he waited for a certain person to show up and sign on. Someone he was after for a spot of petty crime, it usually was, and this was a sure way of running him to earth. Whatever their income from theft, from bag-snatching, receiving, shoplifting, they all wanted their UB as well.

So while Wexford and Burden were as newcomers to the Benefit Office, it was familiar territory to Vine. No one got on well with Cyril Leyton, and Osman Messaoud was generally unapproachable, but he had an easy relationship with Stanton and the women. Burden, closeted with Leyton and the security officer, left him to get on with it. Waiting till Wendy Stowlap was temporarily free, he surveyed the waiting claimants and spotted two he knew. One of them was Broadley, the discoverer of Sojourner's body, the other Wexford's elder daughter. He was still trying to think of her name, it must begin with a letter between A and K, when Wendy Stowlap's client moved away from the desk.

She looked up. "All these foreign people coming in here, Italians, Spanish, I don't know what. Why should we keep them on our taxes? The European Union's got a lot to answer for."

"Surely you don't have a lot of black claimants, though, do you?" he said to her. "I mean, not out in this neck of the woods."

"Out here in the boondocks, is that what you're saying?" Wendy was a native of Kingsmarkham and fiercely proprietorial of her home town. "If you don't like it here why don't you go back to Berkshire or wherever you come from that's so lively and sophisticated?"

"Okay, sorry, but do you?"

"Have claimants who are colored people? You'd be surprised. We've more than we did two years ago. Well, we've got more *claimants* than we had two years ago, a lot more. The recession may be ending but unemployment's still very serious."

"So you wouldn't specially notice a black girl?"

"Woman," Wendy corrected him. "I don't call you a boy."

"I should be so lucky," said Sergeant Vine.

"Anyway, I never noticed any black *woman* speaking specially to Annette. I never noticed that Melanie, as you know. I mean, she had new claimants that were black and so did Peter. Frankly, I've got enough on my plate here on the counter without watching what everyone else is doing." Wendy pressed the switch that made the next neon number come up. "So if you'll excuse me I can't keep my clients waiting any longer."

Peter Stanton wanted to know if Sojourner was good-looking. He said frankly that he often fancied black women, they had such fantastic long legs. He liked their long necks, like black swans, and narrow hands. And the way they walked, as if they carried a heavy jar on their heads.

"I only saw her when she was dead," said Vine.

"If she made a claim—that is, if she completed an ES 461, we can find her for you. What's her name?"

Hayley Gordon also asked Sojourner's name. The two supervisors asked a lot of pointless questions about whether she was claiming UB or Income Support, had she ever worked, and what kind of a job was she looking for. Osman Messaoud, off the counter this week and doing his stint at the very desk where Vine had been used to sit and wait, said he closed his mind and sometimes his eyes to young women claimants. If he caught sight of them he forced himself not to look.

"Your wife doesn't trust you as far as she can throw you, is that it?"

"It is proper for a woman to be possessive," said Osman.

"That's a matter of opinion." An idea came to Vine. He felt around it, trying to put the question delicately. "Is your wife—er, Indian like yourself?"

"I am a British citizen," said Osman very coldly.

"Oh, sorry. And where's your wife from?"

"Bristol."

The man was really enjoying this, Vine thought. "And where did her family come from?"

"I am asking myself what all this can be leading up to. Am I perhaps a suspect in the murder of Miss Bystock? Or perhaps my wife is."

"I only want to know"—Vine gave up and said brutally—"if she's colored too."

Messaoud smiled with pleasure at the corner into which he

had driven the sergeant. "Colored? What an interesting term. Red perhaps or blue? My wife, Detective Sergeant Vine, is an Afro-Caribbean lady from Trinidad. But she is not on the dole and she has never set foot in this office."

Eventually Vine was able to extract from the combined Benefit Office staff, at the sacrifice of political correctness on everyone's part, that a total of four of their claimants were black. There were two men and two women and all of them were over thirty years old.

fifteen

D id he know, Sheila asked on the phone, that the BNP had put up a candidate for the Kingsmarkham Borough by-election?

"But that's next week," Wexford said, trying to remember who or what the BNP was.

"I know. But I've only just heard about it. They've already got one Borough Council seat."

Memory returned. The BNP was the British Nationalist Party, committed to a white Britain for the white man. "That's in East London," he said. "It's a bit different out here. It'll be a Tory walk-over."

"Racist attacks in Sussex increased sevenfold last year, Pop. That's fact. You can't dispute statistics."

"All right, Sheila. You don't suppose I want a bunch of fascists getting on the council, do you?"

"Then you'd better cast your vote for the Liberal Democrat—or Mrs. Khoori."

"She's standing, is she?"

"As an Independent Conservative."

Wexford told her about his encounters with Anouk Khoori and about the garden party. She wanted to know how Sylvia and Neil were getting on. For the first time for many years Sheila was without a man in her life. This lack seemed to have made her a calmer, sadder woman. She was to be Nora in an Edinburgh Festival production of *A Doll's House*. Would he and Mother think about coming? Wexford thought about Annette and Sojourner and the missing Melanie and said he was afraid not, he was very much afraid not.

V isiting the Akandes for the first time since that scene in the mortuary, he told himself not to be a coward, to face them, he had acted in good faith if carelessly, but for all that he couldn't eat any breakfast. Coffee he could manage but nothing more. Some lines from Montaigne came into his mind: *There is an old Greek saying that men are tormented not by things themselves but by what they think about them.* Who could tell if he was thinking in the right way?

After the storms of the weekend, warmer less stuffy weather had come back and it was hot today, the air glass-clear, the sky a bright hard blue. Pink and white lilies had opened in the Akandes' front garden. He had been able to smell their funereal scent before he even reached the gate. Laurette Akande came to the door. Wexford said, "Good morning," and waited to have it slammed in his face.

Instead, she opened it wider and asked him to come in, though not very graciously. She seemed chastened. The house was quiet. No doubt, the son Patrick wasn't up yet, it was only just after eight. The doctor was in the kitchen, standing up by the table, drinking tea out of a mug. He put the mug down, came up to Wexford, and for some reason shook hands with him.

"I'm sorry about what happened on Sunday," he said. "Obviously it was a genuine mistake on your part. We hoped it wouldn't mean you'd not come and see us anymore, didn't we, Letty?"

Laurette Akande shrugged and looked away. Wexford thought he might make it one of his laws—he had a mental catalog of Wexford's first law, second law, and so on—that if after the first two or three expressions of regret you stop apologizing to someone you have offended, they will soon start apologizing to *you*.

"As a matter of fact," said Akande, "oddly enough, it's rather cheered us up. It's given us hope. The fact that this girl wasn't Melanie has really given us grounds for hope that Melanie's still alive. Perhaps you think that's foolish?"

He did, but he wasn't going to say so. They were in the worst position parents could be in, worse than that of those whose child is dead, worse than Sojourner's parents, if she had any. They were the parents whose child has disappeared and who may never know what her end was, what torment she suffered, and what was the nature of her death.

"I can only tell you I've no more idea of what may have happened to Melanie than I had two weeks ago. We shall continue to look for her. We shall never give up looking. As for hope . . ."

"A waste of time and energy," said Laurette harshly. "Excuse me, I have to go to my work now. Patients don't stop needing nursing just because Sister Akande's lost her daughter."

"You mustn't mind my wife," the doctor said after she had left. "All this is a terrible strain on her."

"I know."

"I'm just thankful I've got this quite illogical feeling that Melanie's alive. It may be ridiculous but I could almost say I *know* I'll come home from my rounds one afternoon and find her sitting in there. And she'll have a perfectly reasonable explanation for where she's been."

Such as what? "It would be wrong of me to encourage you to hope," said Wexford, remembering his resolve to treat the Akandes just like anyone else. "We've no grounds for believing Melanie is still alive."

Akande shook his head. "Do you know who the—the other girl is, the one you thought might be Melanie? I suppose I shouldn't ask, any more than you'd ask me about a patient."

"I was about to ask you. I was going to ask if you'd ever seen her before."

"You didn't have much chance, did you? We should have been relieved but we were only angry. I'd never seen her before. Surely it won't be hard to find who she is? After all, there aren't many people like us down here. Only one of my patients is black."

Whether they were connected or not, this second death inevitably meant that all the possible witnesses in the first case must be questioned again in reference to the second. If one of them had seen Sojourner in any connection, recognized her face, remembered her however tenuously, this might provide the link they were looking for. It might go some way to establishing her identity. The worst scenario he could construct was the one in which Sojourner's body had been brought by car hundreds of miles, perhaps from some northern place where inner-city prostitutes were as likely to be black as white, had no past, certainly no future, and whose disappearance might pass unnoticed.

He found he was once more thinking of her tenderly and the forensic report did nothing to mitigate his tenderness. Mavrikiev established her age as no more than seventeen. Her injuries were frightful. As well as the arm, two ribs were fractured. Bruising to the inner thighs, old, healed lacerations of the genitals, indicated some previous violent sexual assault and on more than one occasion. The pathologist calculated that a violent blow of the fist had sent her sprawling and that in her fall she had struck her head on some hard, sharp object. This it was that had caused her death.

Fibers found in the head wound had gone to the lab for analysis. Mavrikiev expressed his opinion that these were wool from a sweater not from a carpet but would commit himself no further on this subject, which was not his specialty. Wexford read a lab report that confirmed this.

The fibers were Shetland wool and mohair, typical components of a knitting yarn. More of this mixture had been found under her fingernails along with grains of the soil in which she had been buried. But there was no blood under the nails. She had scratched no one in putting up a fight for her life.

Embassies, High Commissions—African countries all had those. It was a line of inquiry and he put Pemberton on to it. Karen Malahyde set up inquiries at the places of education, many of them closed by now, so that meant contacting head teachers, school administrators, college principals, and accommodation officers. If Sojourner was only seventeen she might have been still at school. The chances of her having stayed in a hotel immediately prior to her death were slight, but inquiries had to be made at all of them, from the Olive and Dove at one end of the scale to the Glebe Road humblest bed and breakfast at the other.

Annette had told her cousin that she had something she ought to tell the police and Wexford asked himself why she hadn't said those same words to Bruce Snow when he phoned her that same Tuesday evening, the evening before her death. He thought of the relative in Ladyhall Avenue whose existence both Snows denied. And he wondered what a girl as young, as vulnerable, and, it seemed, as unwanted as Sojourner could have done to make someone beat her to death. Could he be looking at things back to front? Could the case be, not that Annette had been killed because of what she was told, but that Sojourner was killed because of what Annette said to *her*? Was Annette herself the repository of some secret, unknown to Snow or Jane Winster or Ingrid Pamber?

Meeting Burden outside the Nawab, he said, "I couldn't face breakfast this morning and now I'm feeling that not unpleasant emptiness which is the silent luncheon gong of the soul."

"That's P. G. Wodehouse."

Wexford didn't say anything. This must have been the first time Burden had ever guessed the source of one of his quotations. It was a heartwarming experience, over which the Inspector immediately poured a stream of cold water. He said in the crabbed voice he sometimes used, "Messaoud's got a West Indian wife."

"I've got an English wife," said Wexford inside the restaurant, "but that doesn't mean she knew Annette Bystock."

"It's different. You know it's different."

Wexford hesitated, took a piece of nan from the plate in front of him. "Okay, yes, I do know. It is different. I'm sorry. And, incidentally, I'm sorry about yesterday. I shouldn't have spoken to you like that."

"Forget it."

"Not in front of Barry I shouldn't. I'm sorry." Wexford remembered his new law and changed the subject. "I like Indian breads, don't you?"

"Better than Indians. Sorry, but that fellow Messaoud is really bad news. But I'll go and talk to his wife, shall I?"

The businessman's special they had ordered, the "Quickie Thali," arrived quite quickly. It consisted of practically everything you thought of as Indian food put round the edge of a big plate with a pile of rice in the middle and a puppodum on the side. Wexford poured himself a glass of water.

"I wish that picture we've got didn't make her look so dead, so *long dead*, but it can't be helped. It won't do any harm to show it around in Ladyhall Avenue. We should try it on the shopkeepers in the High Street and the shopping centers, the supermarket checkouts."

"The station," said Burden, "and the bus station. Churches?"

"Black people go to church more than white people, so yes—why not?"

"Stowerton Industrial Estate? They'd be glad to have someone go missing up there—wouldn't have to make them redundant. Sorry, a sick joke. It's worth trying, isn't it?"

"Everything's worth trying, Mike."

"A national register of misspers is only useful if our girl's been reported missing. Suppose she hasn't?"

Wexford sighed. By "everything" he hadn't meant talking to every black resident of the British Isles. He had really meant proceeding as they would have if Sojourner had been a white schoolgirl. But he knew suddenly that he couldn't do that, that this wasn't the way, however apparently ethical.

A quick glance at the fax from Myringham Police awaiting him on his desk told him none of the descriptions matched Sojourner's details. The missing women were categorized according to their ethnic origin, but wasn't such classification inevitable in a case such as this? He remembered a conversation he had once had with Superintendent Hanlon of Myringham CID on the subject of political correctness.

"As far as I'm concerned," Hanlon had said, "PC means police constable."

Four women whose forebears were from the Indian subcontinent and an African were on the list. Myringham, with its industry, though now depleted, had attracted far more immigrants than Kingsmarkham or Stowerton, and its two universities were attended by students from all parts of the world. Melanie Akande was not the only alumna of the former Myringham Polytechnic to have gone missing. Here on the list was Demsie Olish from The Gambia, a sociology student, whose home was in a place called Yarbotendo. One of the Indians, Laxmi Rao, was a graduate student at the University of the South. There had been no sign of her since Christmas but it was known she had not returned home. The Sri Lankan Burden had already mentioned to him as the missing restaurateur. The Pakistani, Naseem Kamar, a widow, had been employed as a seamstress in a garment factory until the company that owned it went into receivership in April. With the loss of her job Mrs. Kamar disappeared. Darshan Kumari, Myringham Police were nearly sure, had run off with the son of her husband's best friend. They suspected that Surinder Begh had been killed by her father and uncles for refusing to marry the man of their choice but they had no evidence to support this theory.

These women's next of kin would have to be fetched to the mortuary and try to make an identification. Well, not Mrs. Kamar's. She was thirty-six. And the age of Laxmi Rao, twenty-two, was an unpleasant reminder of the mistake he had already made. The most likely candidate was Demsie Olish. She was nineteen, had gone home to The Gambia in April and returned, had been seen by her landlady, by the two other students living in the house, by numerous students in her year at Myringham—and then, after May 4, was seen no more. It was a week before she was reported as missing. Everyone who knew her thought she must be somewhere else. The drawback to her being Sojourner was her height, which was given as five feet five. Once these women had been eliminated, they would spread the net farther afield . . .

He called a conference at five for a pooling of discoveries and offered up Demsie Olish himself. A girl who had been her friend and whose home was in Yorkshire was coming to look at the body the next day. To be on the safe side, if no identification was made, Dilip Kumari would be asked to attempt it. His wife was only eighteen.

Claudine Messaoud had been as helpful as her husband was obstructive. It sounded as if Burden had liked her, which was something of a triumph for race relations. Though she knew of no black woman between sixteen and twenty who might have gone missing, she put Burden on to the church she attended, which was also attended by other black people. These were the Kingsmarkham Baptists. The minister told Burden that most of Kingsmarkham's black families had a representative there, usually a middle-aged woman. Even so, they were few.

"Laurette Akande goes there too," Burden said. "So that only leaves four families. I've seen one of them but they're young and their children are only two and four. I thought Karen might feel like talking to the rest."

"Karen?" said Wexford, turning to her.

"Sure. I'll do that tonight. But I suspect I've already seen two of them, that is the ones that have kids at the Comprehensive. Two girls of sixteen and a boy of eighteen, all currently at home and available and seen by me."

"That will leave the Lings, I should think," said Burden. "Mark and Mhonum, M-H-O-N-U-M, in Blakeney Road. He's from Hong Kong, runs the Moonflower restaurant, she's black, and the age of their kids isn't known, or if they have any. She's the one who is Dr. Akande's only black patient."

Pemberton had talked to someone at the Gambian High Commission. They were aware of the disappearance of their national, Demsie Olish, and were "keeping a close eye." The numerous other African embassies had even less to offer him. He had narrowed down the women on the national register who came closest to matching Sojourner's description to five. Next of kin, and, failing that—that often did fail—friends, would have to be fetched to

Kingsmarkham for the weary work of attempting identification.

Wexford had calculated that, as far as he could tell, nineteen black people lived in Kingsmarkham, perhaps half a dozen more in Pomfret, Stowerton, and the villages. That number included the three Akandes, Mhonum Ling, nine people comprising three of the churchgoing families, the two male clients at the Benefit Office, a mother and son who were the other Kingsmarkham Baptists, Melanie Akande who was one of their female clients, and the sister of one of the Baptists who was the other.

The Epsons, who lived in Stowerton, were the family whose children Sylvia had taken into care. He was black, she was white. A year ago they had gone on holiday to Tenerife, leaving their nine-year-old in charge of their five-year-old. Now it appeared they were away again but when Karen phoned, a child-minder answered. The woman sounded jittery and harassed but knew of no missing black girl aged seventeen.

"Those boys, young men, that hang about outside all the time, I don't suppose it's always the same lot, but the day I went there after we found Annette's body, one of them was black. Dreadlocks and a big knitted cap. We seem to be locating and pigeonholing every black person in Kingsmarkham, I don't like it but no doubt it has to be, so what about him? Where does he fit in?"

"He wasn't there today," said Barry, and to Archbold, "He wasn't there, was he, Ian?"

"I didn't see him. You've got a mother and son on the list—he may be the son."

"He's probably my eighteen-year-old," said Karen.

"Not if yours is still at school, he isn't. Not unless he's a full-time truant. He'll have to be found." Wexford glanced from one to the other, suddenly feeling ages older than any of them. The rest of what he was going to say was on the tip of his tongue, but he said it to himself. It's not so easy, is it? Not all their mothers go to church. Most of them don't stay on at school or go on to further education. As for embassies, we forget, we always forget, that most of these people are British, are in the law as British as we are. They aren't on record, they have no dossiers, no cards of identity. And they slip through the net.

She was very young and though dark, with an olive skin and long black hair, looked fragile. This was Demsie Olish's college friend, Yasmin Gavilon from Harrogate, who seemed uncertain what was expected of her, whose shyness was extreme. Wexford would have preferred someone else to take her in there, but this was a task he couldn't delegate. Still fresh in his mind was what had happened last time. And this girl looked so young, looked far less than her twenty years. He had explained three times now that what she was to see might not be Demsie, was even very probably not Demsie. She must only look and tell him the truth. But looking down into her trusting puzzled face, so seemingly innocent, so untouched by experience, he very nearly told her to go home, get the next train back, and he would find someone else to look at Sojourner's body.

The smell of formaldehyde was like a gas. The plastic cover was folded back, the sheet withdrawn. Yasmin looked. The expression on her face changed no more than it had done when she was brought into Wexford's office and introduced to him. Then she had murmured, "Hallo," and now she murmured, "No. No, it isn't." The tone was the same.

Wexford escorted her out. He asked her again. "No," she said. "No, that isn't Demsie," and then, "I'm glad it isn't." She tried to smile, but her face had taken on a greenish pallor, and she said quickly, "I want to go to the toilet, please."

When she had been given hot sweet tea and taken away in a car to the station, Dilip Kumari arrived. If Wexford had seen him in the street, had not been told his name or heard his voice, he would have taken him for a Spaniard. Kumari spoke in the singsong Welsh-sounding but perfect English of the Indian who is Indian-born. He was the assistant manager of the NatWest Bank in Stowerton High Street and he looked all of forty.

"Your wife is very young," said Wexford.

"Too young for me? Is that what you are saying? You are right. But it didn't seem so at the time." He was philosophical, fatalistic, almost jaunty. It was quickly apparent he was as certain as he could be, without having seen her, that Sojourner was not Darshan Kumari. "To the best of my belief, she has run off with a boy of twenty. Of course, if this is she, which I doubt extremely, I will not have the trouble and expense of divorcing her."

He laughed, perhaps to show Wexford he was not entirely serious. They went inside and Sojourner was once more exhibited. "No," he said. "No, indeed," and outside once more, "Better luck next time. Do you happen to know if you can divorce a woman you can't find? Perhaps only after five years, alas and alack. I wonder what the law is on this matter? I shall have to find out."

Which particular net had she slipped through? The same one perhaps as the boy with dreadlocks in the colored cap who wasn't outside the Benefit Office when Wexford got down there ten minutes later. The shaven-headed boy was there, this time in a T-shirt so faded that the dinosaur on it was a ghost of its former self, and the ponytailed boy in tracksuit pants, chain-smoking. And with them was a very short stout boy with golden curls back-combed to make him look taller and a nondescript spotty boy in shorts. But the black boy with dreadlocks wasn't there.

Two sat on the chipped, stained, rough-surfaced balustrade on the right side and two on the left where there was also a small rubbish tip of empty, caved-in Coke cans and crushed cigarette packets. The ponytailed boy was smoking a cigarette he had rolled himself. The spotty boy sat with his feet in a sprawl of cigarette stubs, his toes in the black canvas lace-up boots desultorily making a pattern of circles and loops in the ash. He was chewing the cuticles round his fingernails. His opposite neighbor with the pale dinosaur on his chest, just as Wexford approached, hit on the diverting idea of throwing pieces of gravel, of which he had a handful, at the stack of cans, his aim perhaps being to dislodge the top one and send it rolling into the area below.

He took no notice of Wexford. None of them did. He had to

say who he was twice before getting anyone's attention, and then it was the short boy who looked up at him, possibly because he was the only one not otherwise occupied.

"Where's your friend?"

"You what?"

"Where's your friend? The one in the striped hat?" That was one way of not having to identify him by ethnic origin. Wexford told himself for God's sake to stop being needlessly sensitive. "The black one with the plaits?"

"Don't know what you're talking about."

"He means Raffy." A stone found its target, the can wobbled and fell. "He has to mean Raffy."

"Okay, I do. D'you know where he is?"

No one answered. The smoker smoked, concentrating as if it was a study he was engaged in, involving memory and even powers of deduction. The cuticle biter bit his cuticles and made more rings with his toes in the smoker's ash. The stone thrower threw his handful of gravel over his shoulder and produced a packet from which he took a cigarette. Having given Wexford the kind of look one might give a dangerous dog, at present quiescent, the fat golden-haired boy got off the wall and went into the Benefit Office.

"I asked you if you know where he is?"

"Might do," said the stone thrower in the dinosaur T-shirt.

"So?"

"Might know where his mum is."

"That'll do for a start."

It was the cuticle biter who gave him the information. He spoke as if only a madman, living in a self-created world of schizophrenic fantasy, could be ignorant of this fact. "She sees the little kids across at Thomas Proctor, don't she?"

This sentence, though seemingly obscure, immediately told Wexford without his having to pause and decipher that Raffy's mother was the lollipop lady who, at nine A.M. and three-thirty P.M., conducted the children who attended the Thomas Proctor primary school across the road.

He asked the stone thrower, "Has he a sister?"

The thin shoulders rose and dropped again.

"A girlfriend?"

They looked at each other and started laughing. The golden-haired boy came out and the cuticle biter whispered something to him. He too laughed and the infectious laughter soon had them all convulsed. Wexford shook his head and walked off the way he had come.

sixteen

A full moon loomed behind the distorted branches of a cherry tree on which the blossoms were an improbable shade of bright pink. This picture, painted on a bamboo scroll, was repeated all round the walls of the Moonflower takeaway's waiting room. It was the only place he'd ever been to, Wexford had once said, where they kept the radio and the television on at the same time. The clientele, waiting for their fried rice and lemon chicken, never looked at the moon and cherry blossom pictures and they looked at the television only when sport was on.

This lunchtime the radio was playing Michelle Wright singing "Baby, Don't Start With Me," and the television was showing a rerun of *South Pacific*. Karen Malahyde walked into the Moonflower just as Mitzi Gaynor, in fierce competition with the country singer, had started to wash that man right out of her hair. Karen went up to the counter where a woman was dispensing orders as they came through from the back.

It was a semi-open plan arrangement and Mark Ling, in chef's apron and tall hat and wreathed in steam, could be seen in the gleaming steel kitchen as he conjured with half a dozen woks, while his brother stood talking to him and decanting a sack of rice.

Mhonum Ling was a small sturdy woman whose skin was the color of a coffee bean and whose straightened hair, still faintly crinkled, had the glitter of a seam of coal. Wearing a white coat like a doctor's, she was dispensing foil containers of chow mein and sweet and sour pork to customers whose numbers came up in red neon above her head. It was a bit like a happier version of the Benefit Office, though the Moonflower's clients sat on cane chairs, reading *Today* and *The Sporting Life*.

When Karen told her what she wanted, Mhonum Ling beckoned rather peremptorily to her brother-in-law and cocked her head in the direction of the counter. He came at once.

She looked at the picture. "Who's this?"

"You don't know? You've never seen her before?"

"No way. What she done?"

"Nothing," said Karen carefully. "She's done nothing. She's dead. You've not seen anything about it on TV?"

"We got work to do," said Mhonum Ling proudly. "We've no time for watching that." With a long plum-red fingernail, she prodded her brother-in-law, who was gossiping with a customer and had failed to see an order of fried rice and bamboo shoots come up behind him. She gave the clients a severe glance. "No time for reading papers either."

"Okay, so you don't know her. There's a boy, maybe eighteen, with Rasta hair, always wears one of those floppy cap things, he's the only person that looks like that round here, he's not your son, is he?"

For a moment Karen thought she was going to say she'd had no time for having children. But, "Raffy?" she said. "That sounds like Raffy. Don't forget the fortune cookies, Johnny. They don't like going without their fortune cookies."

"Is he a relative, then?"

"Raffy?" she said. "Raffy's my nephew, my sister's son. He left school two years ago but he's never had work. He never will, there aren't the jobs. My sister Oni, she wanted Mark to give him a job here, just a job helping in the kitchen she said, you could do with another pair of hands, but what's the use? We don't need no other two hands and we're not in the charity business, we're not aid workers in Africa."

Karen asked where Mhonum's sister lived and was given an address. "But she won't be home, she'll be working. *She's* got work."

On the chance of finding Raffy at home, Karen went round to Castlegate, Kingsmarkham's only tower block, where Oni and Raffy Johnson lived at number 24. It wasn't much of a tower, a mere eight stories high, local authority housing that the borough council would have liked to sell off to its tenants, if those tenants had been prepared to buy. Wexford had predicted that soon they would have no option but to pull it down and start afresh. Number 24 was on the sixth floor and the lift was, as usual, out of order. By the time she got up there Karen was sure Raffy wouldn't be at home. She was right.

What made Wexford think this Raffy could help them? He had no grounds to go on, not the least evidence, just a hunch. You could call it intuition and sometimes, she knew, he intuited spectacularly. She had to have faith and tell herself that if Wexford thought Raffy was worth hunting down because the answer lay with Raffy, it quite possibly did. Sojourner—somehow, in some perhaps tenuous way—was connected to this boy his aunt spoke of so contemptuously.

She got back just as Kashyapa Begh's Jaguar swept onto the forecourt in front of the police station and Wexford asked her to take him into the mortuary. Kashyapa Begh was a shriveled elderly man with white hair who wore a pinstriped suit and snow-white shirt. The pin in his red silk tie was a large ruby and two small diamonds. He put Karen's back up by asking her why he was being escorted on this serious business by a woman. She said nothing, remembering that in all likelihood this man and his male relatives had murdered a girl to stop her marrying the man of her choice. Glancing at the body with no attempt to conceal his distaste, Kashyapa Begh said in an outraged tone, "That was a complete waste of my time."

"I'm sorry about that, Mr. Begh. We have to work on a process of elimination."

"Process of folly," said Kashyapa Begh and strutted off toward his car.

It was scarcely out of sight before a police car brought Festus Smith, a young Glaswegian, whose seventeen-year-old sister had been missing since March. His reaction to the body was much the same as Begh's, though he didn't say traveling 400 miles to see it had been a waste of his time. After him came Mary Sheerman from Nottingham, mother of a missing daughter. Carina Sheerman had disappeared on her way home from work on a Friday in June. She was sixteen and she had gone missing once before just before her fourteenth birthday, but she wasn't the dead girl in the mortuary.

On his way to see Carolyn Snow, Wexford told himself that Sojourner was a local girl, she had lived within the town or its environs. It was not that she had slipped through a net but that her disappearance had never been reported. Because it wasn't known? Or because whoever would know wanted to keep her absence concealed, as they had once wanted to conceal her existence?

Carolyn Snow was in the back garden, sitting on a striped sun lounger and reading just the sort of example of modern fiction from which, he had told Burden, her knowledge of obscenities derived. It was Joel who took him out there. Wexford thought it a long time since he had seen such a look of desperate bewildered misery on an adolescent's face.

Carolyn Snow barely looked up. "Yes?" she said. "What is it now?"

"I thought I would give you an opportunity to tell the truth at last, Mrs. Snow."

"I don't know what you're talking about."

Another of Wexford's laws was that no truthful person ever makes this remark. It is exclusively the province of liars.

"I, however, know very well that you weren't telling me the truth when you said your husband went out in the evening on July the seventh. I know he was here all the evening. But you told me he went out and, moreover, you encouraged your son, a boy of fourteen, to support you in this lie."

She laid the book facedown on the seat beside her. Wexford remained standing. She looked up at him and a faint flush came into her face. The twitch of her lips was almost a smile.

"Well, Mrs. Snow?"

"Oh, so what?" she said. "To hell with it. I've given him a few sleepless nights, haven't I? I've punished him. Of course he was at home that evening. It was just a joke saying he wasn't, and it was pretty easy too to fool everyone. I told Joel all the details of what he'd done *and* I told him about that Diana and he would have done anything to support me. There are *some* people who care about me, you know." Her smile was a real one this time, a broad sunny, slightly mad smile. "He's in an awful state, he really thinks he could be done for murdering that bitch."

"He won't be," said Wexford. "It's you I'll be charging with wasting police time."

He had made himself Australian and already had a marked Australian accent. Vine had scarcely shaken hands with him, had said no more than, "Good morning, Mr. Colegate," before the man was off on a diatribe against the Royal Family and the virtues of republicanism.

His mother, whose house in Pomfret this was, put her head round the door to ask Vine if he would like tea. Stephen Colgate said, Not tea, please, what was wrong with coffee, for God's sake?

"Nothing for me," said Vine.

Two children hurtled into the room with a Scottie dog at their heels. They jumped onto the sofa, arms up, screaming. Colgate looked at them with satisfaction. "My daughters," he said. "I got married again in Melbourne. Wife couldn't come, she's got a high-powered job. But I'd made a promise to my mother I'd make it to the U.K. this year and when I say something I stick to it. Take the doggie in the yard, Bonita."

"So you didn't come over for your former wife's funeral?"

"Good God, no. When I got shut of Annette that was for keeps." He gave a loud laugh. "In life, in death, and beyond the grave."

It occurred to Vine that Annette Bystock had had an unfortunate taste in men. The two little girls leapt off the sofa and fled, the younger aiming a kick at the dog as they passed it.

"When did you arrive in this country, Mr. Colegate?"

"Now why the hell would *I* kill Annette?"

"If you would just tell me when you got here, sir."

"Oh, sure. I've nothing to hide. It was last Saturday. I came on Qantas, wouldn't touch a Pom airline with a six-foot pole, rented a car at Heathrow, the kids slept all the way. I can prove all this. You want to see my air ticket?"

"That won't be necessary," said Vine and he showed him Sojourner's picture but it was clear from the indifferent glance Colegate gave it that he had never seen her before. The coffee came, brought by an apprehensive woman who was unused to making it.

Stephen Colegate said, "I never got here till Saturday, did I, Mum?"

"More's the pity. You told me you were coming on the sixth, I still don't know why you changed your mind."

"I *told* you. Something came up and I couldn't get away. If you say that sort of thing he'll think I came over earlier and hid out somewhere so as I could throttle Annette."

Mrs. Colegate gave a little shrill scream. "Oh, Stevie!" She drew breath while her son, wrinkling his nose, skimmed floating grains off the surface of the thin brown liquid in his cup. "I know you shouldn't speak ill of the dead," she said, and was still doing so, dismembering Annette's character and, by extension, that of her parents, when Vine quietly took his leave.

It was far from usual practice in Kingsmarkham local elections to display posters with photographs on them of the candidate. That's because they're so ugly, Dora had said uncharitably, and Wexford had to agree. The bull-necked, red-faced representative of the British Nationalist Party, with his head of gray stubble and small piggy eyes, was no beauty, and the vulture-faced Tory with beaky nose and hooded eyes not much better. Anouk Khoori, on the other hand, in most people's opinion, would be an ornament to any office she might hold and her poster was the best advertisement she could have contrived for herself.

Wexford paused to look at the one displayed on a hoarding in Glebe Road. It was all photograph but for her name and her political status. She smiled down at him and judicious air-brushing had removed the lines such smiling must have created. For the photograph her hair had been done in the ringleted mode. Her eyes were limpid, sincere, earnest. The Thomas Proctor School would be a polling station next week, and this poster was just near enough to it for that face to linger in the mind.

He was early, but cars were already parked at the pavement, waiting to pick up departing children. It was said to be a good school, the choice of certain affluent parents more likely to have opted for private education. His quarry came round from the side of the school, carrying her stop sign. She was evidently also Karen Malahyde's quarry. By some different route from his, Karen must have been led to this school and this crossing, for he suddenly saw her leave a car he had at first taken for that of a Thomas Proctor parent and begin walking toward the woman who had reached the pavement.

She turned when she saw him. "Great minds, sir," she said.

"I hope the great minds think wisely as well as alike, Karen. Her son's called Raffy. Do you know the surname?"

"Johnson. She's Oni Johnson." She risked asking the question. "Why do you think Raffy might identify her?"

He shrugged. "We've no more reason to think Raffy knew her than that old villain Begh did. Or Dr. Akande, come to that. It may be because I think of them both as—well, outcasts. Expendable people that no one cares much about."

"And it's our last chance?"

"There's no such thing as a last chance in our work, Karen."

The school doors opened and the children started coming out. Most of them were carrying bags and packages as well as satchels. It was their last day until school started again in September. Oni Johnson was a stocky black woman, about forty, her navy skirt tight on her, wearing a Day-Glo yellow jacket over her white blouse and a navy peaked cap on her head. She stood at the pavement edge like a shepherd who must gather in her flock without a dog to help her. But the children were obedient sheep, they had done this before, they had done it every day.

She looked to the right, to the left, to the right again, and then she marched into the road, holding up her stop sign. The children streamed after her. Wexford noted the youngest Riding child, the girl who had been at the garden party with her brother. Farther up the pavement a black-haired girl with gold earrings was hauled into a car driven by a woman that Wexford thought might be Claudine Messaoud. He was seeing black people everywhere these days. That was always the way. This time it was a boy of eight or nine opening the door of a car he recognized as the Epsons' but driven by someone whose face he couldn't see. Not exactly black this child, though, light brown with light brown curly hair, black only in the world's uncompromising categorization.

Oni Johnson held up her hand at the fresh throng of children waiting on the pavement. She walked back to them, taking slow deliberate steps, and, back on the curb, beckoned to the traffic to proceed. The Riding girl jumped into her parents' Range Rover. The car that might have been the Messaouds' passed southward and a stream of traffic followed it. Wexford went up to Oni Johnson, showed her his warrant card.

"Nothing to worry about, Mrs. Johnson. Just routine. We'd like to talk to your son. Will you be going home when you've finished here?"

Alarm flashed in her eyes. "My Raffy—what's he done?"

"Nothing, so far as I know. We want to talk to him about something else, some information he may have."

"All right. I don't know when he be home. He come in for his tea. I be going straight there when I'm done here." She let a car pass and then, holding up her stop sign, she marched into the road, but this time, Wexford thought, less confidently.

The first of the cars that waited while she shepherded the children over was, he saw, being driven by Jane Winster. She looked at him and looked away. The child sitting next to her was all of sixteen and must have been fetched from some other school, the Comprehensive probably.

He wasn't far from home. A quick cup of tea in his own house, he thought, and then he'd meet Karen at Castlegate.

The last car to pass was the Rolls-Royce with the AK registration, but driven by Wael Khoori.

Sylvia was there with her sons, sitting round the kitchen table with Dora. For Ben and Robin this too was the last day of term. "I'm thinking of doing a training course. It's to be a counselor in a medical center."

"Enlighten me," said her father.

"They have one at Akande's, Reg. Haven't you seen *Counselor* on the door when you go down the passage to his surgery?"

Robin was temporarily distracted from his video game. "A counselor is what they call lawyers in America."

"Yes, well, it isn't here. I'll have patients referred to me for counseling as a better option than handing out tranquilizers, that's the idea. And don't try to say something else clever, Robin. Just get on with your puzzle."

"*Ko se wahala,*" said Robin.

Long ago the members of his family had stopped asking Robin any questions about his "no problems." Sylvia's theory was that if ignored, he would grow out of it. As phases went, this one had lasted a long time and showed no sign of coming to an end. It was months since parents, grandparents, and brother had laughed or commented or inquired, but now Wexford said, "What language is that, Robin?"

"Yoruba."

"Where do they speak it?"

"In Nigeria," said Robin. "Sounds good, don't you think? *Ko se wahala.* Better than '*nao problema,*' that's practically the same as English."

"Did you get it from someone at school?" Wexford asked, hopeful but of what he hardly knew.

"Yep. I got it from Oni." Robin seemed very pleased to have been asked. "Oni George. She's next to me on the register."

So Oni was a Nigerian name . . . Raymond Akande was Nigerian. He was suddenly sure, for no good reason but instinct, that Sojourner was too. The other Oni, Oni Johnson, had said she would be home by five. He had a strong feeling, an almost excited intuition, that he was on the brink of finding it all out, of finding who Sojourner was, what connection there was between her and Annette, and why they had both been killed. The boy was the answer, the boy in the colored cap called Raffy, who had nothing to do all day but observe, notice, record—or go blindly through his empty days?

Karen was waiting for him when he got to Castlegate at five past. The hoarding outside the block was covered with posters of Anouk Khoori, no fewer than ten of them, pasted up side by side. He and Karen picked their way across the broken concrete forecourt. A dog, or fox, or even, these days, a human being had torn open one of the black plastic rubbish bags piled by the front entrance and left behind a scattering of chicken bones, takeaway containers, frozen vegetable packets. It had become a lot warmer as the day went on and an almost chemical smell of decay emanated from the bags.

Wexford could remember when a Victorian Gothic house with turrets and crenellations had stood on this spot, not very beautiful, grotesque rather, but interesting. And its garden had been an arboretum of rare trees. All of it went in the sixties and, in spite of universal disapproval, petitions, and even a demonstration, the Castlegate had been built on the site. Even those who would otherwise have been homeless disliked it. Wexford pushed open the entrance doors and the cracked glass in them rattled.

"The lift's not working," said Karen.

"Now she tells me. How many flights up is it? If the boy's not home we may as well wait for him here."

"It's only six flights, sir. But if you'd like me to go up and find out I . . ."

"No, no, of course not. Where are the stairs?"

The walls were concrete, painted cream and peeling, the floor laid with gray composition tiles, crazed by wear to the color of coal dust. A graffitist had spray-painted *Gary is a scumbag* on the wall that contained the broken lift.

"They're going to pull the place down," Karen said as if it was her responsibility to apologize for the shortcomings of Castlegate, for its Inner London–style sleaze and dilapidation. "Everyone's been rehoused but the Johnsons and one other family. Round here, sir. The stairs are on the left."

She checked a cry. Her hand flew to her mouth. A split second and Wexford too saw what she had seen.

At the foot of the concrete staircase a woman, or a woman's body, lay spread on the tiles. Her head was in a pool of blood. Oni Johnson had never reached home.

seventeen

I n the Intensive Care Unit at Stowerton Royal
Infirmary, Oni Johnson lay all night between life
and death. In that small world she was the responsibility of Sister Laurette Akande, who had been in
charge of this ward for the past year. Not all Oni's
injuries came from falling downstairs, though it seemed she had
fallen and rolled down all six flights. A bruise on her head was on
the left side while it was the right that had struck the floor, so
there was a policeman stationed outside her door day and night
and Wexford was treating the case as one of attempted murder.

Murder, if she died. Laurette Akande told him she doubted if
Oni Johnson would survive her injuries. Both legs were broken and
the left ankle, there was a fracture of the pelvis, of three ribs and
the right radius, but the most serious injury was a depressed skull
fracture. Cranial surgery was essential if her life was to be saved
and an operation was performed by Mr. Algernon Cozens, the neu-
rosurgeon, on Friday afternoon. The boy who had sat by her bed
for hours on end, who had sat there staring, unchecked tears trick-
ling down his face, had signed the form of consent with slow delib-
eration like a robot whose mechanism is wearing out.

"But why was the attack just before we got there?" Karen asked
Wexford.

He shook his head.

"Do we know what the weapon was?"

"Bare hands perhaps. Whoever did this waited round the corner at the top of the stairs and when she appeared, struck her a blow in the face with his fist, which sent her rolling down those stairs. All he had to do was run down after her, kick her down probably, and make his escape ten minutes before we got there."

"Bare hands were used on Sojourner," said Burden. "I'll never forget that, Mavrikiev telling me how to kill with your fists."

"Yes. It's the only link we have and it's not much of one."

"Where was the boy?"

"When all this happened? He never seems to know where he is at any given time. One thing, he wasn't at Castlegate. That crowd who hangs about outside the Benefit Office says he was with them for part of the afternoon but they don't know which part. They wouldn't. He drifts about. He begs."

"He *begs?*"

"They all do, Mike, if they see a likely benefactor. That's what he took me for. I suppose I should be flattered. We were looking for him—remember?—when his mother was taken to hospital and I met him coming along Queen Street toward Castlegate. He stuck out his hand and said, 'Got the price of a cup of tea, mate?' When I told him who I was and what had happened I thought he was going to faint."

Three hours after that he and Raffy Johnson had had their talk. But Raffy had never seen any black girls in Kingsmarkham. "Only old women," he told Wexford. How about Melanie Akande, Wexford asked, had he ever seen her?

A curious look, part humiliation, part scorn, came into Raffy's face, and Wexford understood before he spoke that these children of immigrants were already infected with the English disease. Their blackness had not saved them.

"It's like, she's a different class, isn't she?" said Raffy. "Her dad's a doctor and all that."

Race and poverty and a hierarchical system had condemned him to a lonely celibacy, for it seemed never to have crossed his mind to speak to, let alone try to befriend, a white girl.

"Your mother is from Nigeria, isn't she?"

"Right."

He looked blankly at Wexford. Raffy had apparently never asked his mother about her native land and no information had been given him unasked. He knew only that she had come here with her sister when they were very young and after her sister had married a Chinese man. Wexford had no interest in the identity of Raffy's father, if indeed the boy knew it. He seemed to know so little, to be without interests or skills, ambition or hope, but to live from day to day, his only wish to stay alive to wander the streets of the town that had given him nothing.

"I asked him," Wexford said, "if he knew why anyone would try to kill his mother. I expected indignation, I expected shock. What I didn't expect was a sort of nervous smile. He looked at me as if I was having him on. He was almost embarrassed."

"But he takes it seriously now?"

"I don't know. I tried to make him understand that someone had attempted to murder his mother. God knows, he must see murder on television every day of his life, but for him telly is fantasy and life is reality—just what they're supposed to be, only we're always being told that young people confuse the two."

Karen said tentatively, "The perpetrator couldn't have been confused, could he? Mistaken Oni Johnson for Raffy? It wasn't very light up there."

"Even if it was dark no one could mistake Oni for her son. He's six inches taller, for one thing. He's as skinny as a rake and she's rather plump. No, it was Oni our killer meant to attack and I haven't the faintest idea why."

The only other people who lived in Castlegate, a married couple, had been at work at the time. No one had been about in the empty parking areas that surrounded the block. It was as if it had already been abandoned to the demolition squad, the fact that four people still lived in it almost forgotten. Oni Johnson's attacker could hardly have found a more propitious place to attempt a silent secret murder.

Karen's suggestion had its final dismissal next day when someone made a second attempt on Oni Johnson's life.

A rchbold was outside her door all night and Pemberton took
over from him in the morning. Nobody could have gone in
without being seen by them, but they had seen only the hospital
staff, doctors, nurses, technicians, and Raffy.

It was the staff nurse who told Wexford, a young woman called
Stacey Martin. He came into the ward at nine and she met him
when he reached the door of Oni's room, where Pemberton was
already waiting.

"Would you come in here, please?"

She took him into the office with *Sister* on the door. "I came
on at eight this morning," she said. "The night-to-day changeover
is at eight. Sister had already come on. I went straight in to look at
Oni and I thought it was funny, the sheet was pulled up over her
hand."

"I don't follow you," said Wexford.

"It's hot in here, as I expect you've noticed. We keep it hot so
patients don't need bedclothes over them. The sheet was covering
the back of her hand where the IV line goes in. Well, I pulled it
back and the line wasn't going in. It had been taken out and a clip
put on to stop it leaking all over the bed."

He looked at her and saw shock still on her face. "You say
'someone' took it out. Could she have done it herself?"

"Hardly. I mean, I suppose it's just possible . . . But why would
she?"

Before he could answer, if he could have answered, the door
opened and Laurette Akande came in. She eyed him like a head-
mistress with a troublesome pupil. He realized for the first time
how deeply she disliked him.

"Mr. Wexford," she said in frosty tones. "Can I help you?"

"You can tell me what goes through the—er, drip on Oni's arm."

"The intravenous line? Drugs. Quite a cocktail of medication.
Why do you want to know that? Oh, I see. Staff Nurse Martin's
been passing on her ridiculous suspicions, has she?"

"But the line was pulled out, wasn't it, Mrs. Akande?"

"Sister. Unfortunately, it was. That is, it *came* out. No harm was done, there was no setback in Mrs. Johnson's condition"—she changed her tune abruptly, sending a beaming smile in Stacey Martin's direction—"thanks to Staff Nurse Martin's prompt action." The tone became mildly satirical. "We must all be very, very grateful to her. Come along now, I'll take you in to see Mrs. Johnson."

She was alone in the room, wearing a white gown, covered only to the waist by a sheet and propped up, not lying flat. One of Raffy's comics was on the bed table, but Raffy wasn't there.

"Is she conscious?" Wexford asked. "Can she talk?"

"She's asleep," said Laurette Akande.

"Could the boy have done it?"

"Nobody did it, Mr. Wexford. Nothing has been done. The IV line came out. It was an unfortunate accident but no harm was done. All right?"

There would be a hospital inquiry, he thought, if he told anyone else of this, if Staff Nurse Martin did. It was clear Sister Akande had no intention of telling anyone, for her job would be on the line. And what was the point now?

"I would like to stay here," he said. "Inside this room."

"You can't do that. You've an officer outside, that's the usual procedure."

"I'll be the best judge of the usual procedure," he said. "There are curtains round that bed. If there are things to be done it would be improper for me to see, you can draw the curtains."

"I've never in all my years of nursing heard of a policeman sitting inside a room in an ICU."

"There's always a first time," said Wexford. He forgot about being polite, sensitive to this woman's feelings, he even forgot his terrible blunder in the mortuary. "I shall create a precedent. If you don't like it you'll have to lump it or I go to Mr. Cozens for permission."

She compressed her lips. She folded her arms and looked down at them, controlling the temper of which he had had a previous sample. Then she advanced a step to the bed and peered closely at Oni Johnson. She agitated the IV line for a second or two, eyed the monitor on the wall, and stalked out without looking at him again.

Either he or Burden must stay there, he thought. Barry Vine, perhaps, and Karen Malahyde. No one else. Until she talked and told them what it was she knew she must never be left. He sat down on the uncomfortable chair and after half an hour a nurse he hadn't seen before, a Thai or Malaysian woman, brought him a cup of tea. They drew the curtains round Oni in the late morning and at one o'clock Algernon Cozens came in with a retinue of housemen, registrars, Staff Nurse Martin, and Sister Akande.

No one took any notice of Wexford. Laurette Akande must have given some prior explanation for his presence, but he would have betted anyone anything it wasn't the correct one. He called Burden on his cellular phone and at three the inspector came in to take over, entering the room simultaneously with a very smartly dressed Mhonum Ling. Her tight high-heeled shoes gave her an added four inches and with her hair elaborately piled on the top of her head, she had become quite a tall woman.

In time-honored fashion, she had brought grapes, useless to Oni, who was still fed intravenously. She seemed glad to see Burden, it was someone to talk to and share the grapes with, though Burden shook his head when they were offered.

She had no idea, she said, why anyone would want to kill her sister. Like Raffy, she seemed embarrassed by the question, and glossed over it as soon as she could to begin on a catalog of Oni's misfortunes and mistakes, how ill luck had dogged her since their arrival in Britain, how she always seemed one of life's victims. She didn't know how her sister managed always to stay so cheerful. Mhonum had no children and perhaps this was why she cited Raffy as the chief of her sister's troubles, a problem since the day he was born—since *before* he was born, since his father disappeared as soon as Oni told him she was pregnant. Raffy had been hopeless at school, had been a chronic truant. He could do nothing, could barely write his name. He would never have a job, would live on benefit all his life. The hardworking and prosperous Mhonum shook her head over Raffy, remarking that the only good thing she could say about him was that he wouldn't hurt a fly.

"Does your sister have any enemies?" Burden asked, rephrasing his question.

Mhonum popped a grape into her mouth. "Enemies? Oni? She don't even have friends." She glanced over her shoulder at the sedated woman as she spoke. "There's only Mark and me and we're busy people. We've a business to run, right?" Her voice went down to a whisper. "Oni had this boyfriend but he was soon gone, she scared him off. Oh, she was so possessive, you wouldn't believe, want to own him, right? But he run off like Raffy's daddy, it's the same old story all over again."

"Can you think of any reason why anyone would want to kill Mrs. Johnson?"

She licked the tips of her fingers delicately. Burden observed her clothes, what he calculated was five hundred pounds' worth of turquoise silk trouser suit and cream-colored Bruno Magli shoes. "No one want to kill her," she said. "They just *kill*, a person like that. They're made that way. She was there and they kill, that's all."

As if he didn't know, as if he needed instruction in that particular field.

Barry Vine took over from Burden in the evening. He brought with him a computer game belonging to his son and a Spanish exercise book. He was learning Spanish when he managed to make it to the evening class. In response to a peremptory summons Wexford drove himself to Stowerton to see the Chief Constable. The traffic was at its worst in the early evening and he found himself in a slow line approaching the roundabout. In his rear mirror he saw the Epsons' pink car behind him but no more than a pale glimmer of the driver's face. It took him all of a further fifteen minutes to get to Freeborn's house.

He had described it to Burden as the only even moderately attractive house in ugly little Stowerton. Once it had been the rectory, a sprawling place with several acres of garden.

"How long is this going to go on, Reg?" Freeborn wanted to know. "Two girls dead and now this woman at death's door."

"Oni Johnson is recovering," Wexford said.

"More by luck than your activities. Come to think of it she's only in the state she is because of your activities."

Wexford thought that hard. He could have rejoined that if he and Karen had been less prompt she would soon have died, lying there in her own blood on the Castlegate's concrete floor. He didn't. A quite arbitrary date came into his head and he said he would have worked the whole thing out by the end of next week. Just give him a week.

"No one been taking any more mug shots of you, I trust?" Freeborn laughed unpleasantly. "I'm scared to look in the paper these days."

Barry sat all night in Oni's room and Wexford took over from him in the morning. Sitting there, he watched a doctor come in and draw the bed curtains, a new staff nurse shake the IV line. How could he tell who meant harm to Oni? How would he know if the injection administered by the surgical registrar was beneficial to Oni—or lethal? All he could do was *be* there and hope the time would soon come when she could talk to him.

Raffy came in at mid-morning, as usual wearing his knitted cap, though it was a hot day and hotter in the ward. He looked at the pictures in his comic, got out his cigarettes and, perhaps realizing smoking would be the ultimate solecism, put them away again. He sat there for half an hour before creeping out. Wexford heard him running down the corridor outside. Karen took over in the afternoon, her arrival timing with Raffy's return. He walked in eating chips out of a greasy paper bag.

"If she comes round, if she talks, let me know at once."

"Of course I will, sir," Karen said.

It happened on Sunday while Vine was in the ward. Raffy was the first person Oni's opening eyes alighted on. She put out her hand, secured his and held it. Wexford found them like that, the boy looking puzzled and somewhat at a loss, Oni clutching his long fingers in her plump stubby ones. She smiled at Wexford and she started talking.

Once she had begun, she spoke a lot, about the room she was in, the nurses, the doctors, she spoke to Raffy about the chances of getting a job as a hospital porter. Of what had happened to her at the top of the stairs in Castlegate she had no memory at all.

It was only what he had expected. The mind is kind to the body and allows it to heal without the setbacks painful and terrible memories may induce. But he dared not leave her until she had told him everything she knew. If only she knew what it was she knew! God help her if what she knew seemed to her trivial or insignificant or, worse, if she had forgotten it. She had emerged as a cheerful and cooperative woman, willing to talk about herself and her life and her son, but whose memory now held two segments of recollections, those of the hospital that went back to her waking in the ward on Sunday, and those of her previous life which ended abruptly as she entered Castlegate on Thursday afternoon, walked past the dysfunctional lift, and began to climb the stairs.

"That lift always out of order," Oni said. "But, you know, I always hope. Always I say to myself, Oni, I say, maybe today they mend it and up you go, sailing up like a bird. But no way and I have to go on my own two feet. These things are sent to try us, I'm telling myself, and then all go black and the floor come up in my face and I wake up in here."

"Before you went into the building, can you remember seeing anyone about? Was there anyone about outside?"

"Not a soul. He was up there, wasn't he, waiting to bop me with his great boxer fist."

"And you've no idea who 'he' might be?"

She shook her head under its thick white bandage. Her own phrase, 'great boxer fist,' which she had used several times, always made her laugh. She had that curious habit, common to Africans and Afro-Caribbeans too but almost incomprehensible to Europeans, of laughing merrily at tragic or terrifying events. Her laughter shook the bed and Wexford looked round, anxious not to alert a nurse who might take Oni's excitement as a sign to terminate their talk for another day.

"Has anyone threatened you? Have you quarreled with anyone?" His questions elicited giggles, then a casting up of eyes. She looked as her son had looked when asked who would want to kill his mother: embarrassed, suspicious of mockery, determined to treat the situation lightly. Sudden inspiration made Wexford ask, "Have you had any quarrel or argument with a car driver, someone you've stopped on the crossing?"

It was mad to think of attempting to kill for such a reason, or he would once have thought it mad. Now he knew people did such things. Sane-looking, ordinary men drove the streets of this town and any other, who if reproved by a traffic warden would think nothing of taking savage revenge—especially if it was a woman who had dared upbraid them. Especially if it was a black woman. But there had apparently been no such violent paranoiac in Oni Johnson's past.

Like her sister, she said, "He's a killer, right? Don't have to have no reason. He kill, he made that way." And her brisk summing up of man's senseless iniquity brought so much fresh cause for laughter that this time the nurse did come over and say that was quite enough for today.

It was possibly quite enough for ever. Leaving Barry Vine in the ward and walking back to the lift down the corridor, Wexford asked himself if there was anything more to be got out of Oni, or if she and Mhonum Ling could be right and this was a virtually unmotivated attack by some psychopath; someone who took against black residents or women or mothers or dwellers in tower blocks or even just other people. Perhaps it had nothing to do with Raffy, nothing to do with the Benefit Office and Annette, perhaps there was no connection between Oni and Annette or, come to that, Oni and Melanie Akande. Perhaps Raffy had plucked the IV line out himself because it frightened him or he thought Oni was hurt by it or he was merely trying to shake it the way he had seen done by the hospital staff. Weren't most killings, after all, committed from motives incomprehensible to ordinary men or from no apparent motive at all?

He had been so deep in thought that he missed his way but, finding a staircase ahead of him, he walked down it. Here, however, he was really lost, in a part of the hospital he had never been before. He had just registered the words "Department of Pediatrics and Diseases of Children" lettered above the open double doors ahead of him when a door opened on his left and Swithun Riding, his white coat open over a fawn fuzzy sweater, came out of it with a baby in his arms.

Wexford expected to be ignored, but Riding instead gave him a cordial smile and remarked that he was glad to see him, he had intended the next time he did see him to congratulate him on guessing the correct age of those twins at the garden party.

"My wife told me. So much for *my* expertise, she said. What do you do with the teddy bear, have a childhood regression and cuddle up to it at night?"

Wexford was too interested in Riding's manner with the baby to think up a clever rejoinder. He said merely, "I gave it away," and marveled at the tender way the pediatrician held the child, with such delicacy for one so big, with such gentle firmness, each of his huge hands large enough to contain it like a cradle. And Riding's expression, normally so elevated and arrogant, the lofty look of the proud possessor of superior intellect and physique, grew soft and almost feminine as he looked down into the tiny round face, the wide blue eyes.

"Nothing wrong with him, I hope?" Wexford hazarded.

"Nothing worse than an umbilical hernia and we've seen to that. Not a him, by the way. A lovely little lady. Don't you adore them? Aren't they gorgeous?"

It might have been a woman talking, and the words, uttered in a strong baritone, which should have been grotesque, sounded only charming. Riding was transformed, he was for a moment a "nice" man. And Wexford felt it would be possible to ask the way out without risking some crushing put-down.

"Oh, back the way you've come and turn left," said the pediatrician. "And now I must take this little sweetheart back to Mother or she'll be fretting and no wonder."

Telling Dora about it later, Wexford was rather surprised to hear it was no surprise to her.

"Sylvia was referred to him with Ben, don't you remember? When Ben broke his arm and had those complications. Oh, it must have been three years ago, soon after the Ridings came here."

"One judges people on the strength of a single unfortunate encounter. It's a pity but there it is."

"She said he was wonderful with Ben and Ben had quite a crush on him."

Three years ago—when Sylvia had a job and Neil had a job and Dora complained they never saw them. "We're not expecting them tonight, I hope. I mean, any of them."

"No. We're not *expecting* them, for what that's worth. We oughtn't to talk about our child like that, ought we? It's wrong of us. I always think I'm tempting Providence and something awful will happen and then think of the guilt I'll feel."

Wexford was starting to say that Providence had been tempted enough times by now to have learned how to resist when the doorbell rang. Sylvia had a key, but she also had the sensitivity not to use it when she came unexpectedly. "I'll go," he said, thinking on his way to the door of another evening of counselor training, job club, and polyglot "no problems."

But it wasn't Sylvia and family. It was Anouk Khoori.

Again he had to look twice to be sure it was she. Her blonde hair was severely drawn back, her makeup light, and she wore the female politician's favored pearl ear studs. The skirt of her dark blue linen dress came well below the knee. Her manner was simple and disarming. At first it appeared the best, the least pompous technique a woman of her sort and her appearance could have used. She stepped inside without waiting to be asked. "You'll have guessed. I've come to ask you to vote for me."

He had guessed but only a matter of seconds before. She reminded him suddenly of Ingrid Pamber, a sophisticated and highly accomplished version of Ingrid. And this was strange because she was far from attractive to him, while Ingrid . . . To his surprise, to his distaste, Anouk Khoori tucked her arm into his and led him through his own house unerringly to where Dora was.

"Now, Dora, my dear," she said. "I've the whole of this street to do tonight and all the next one—politics is *hard* work—but I've come to you first, the very first, because I feel we three have something special, we're what everyone but the English calls *sympathetic.*"

The look on his wife's face he knew well, the smile, the rapid blinking of her eyes, and then only the smile with lips closed, the lifted head. Pretentiousness evoked it and an assumption of intimacy on the part of virtual strangers. Anouk Khoori's hand on his arm, a beige-colored hand with purple vein branches, purple varnish on the long nails, lay there, in his fancy like some exotic crustacean. It was as if his arm, immersed in water, had come up with this thing attached to it, this pentapod or tentacled actiniaria. If he had indeed attracted such a creature while swimming he could have shaken it off. No such recourse was open to him here and his earlier aversion to this woman, his senseless repulsion, returned to him with a shudder.

But she had to sit down and this she could hardly do while clamped to him. Dora offered her a drink, a cup of tea if she preferred. Anouk Khoori, refusing with a smile and an inordinate show of gratitude, launched into her appeal. At first it seemed an exclusively defensive campaign. The idea of fascism, which these days meant racism, coming to a place like Kingsmarkham was horrible in the extreme. She herself was a relative newcomer to the borough but she felt so at home here that it was almost as if she was a natural Kingsmarkhamian, so profound was her sympathy with the hopes and fears of its residents. Racism appalled her and any ideas that might be prevalent of aiming at a white Kingsmarkham. The British Nationalist must be kept off the council at all costs.

"I wouldn't call electing you an action to take 'at all costs,' Mrs. Khoori," Dora said smoothly. "I was going to vote for you anyway."

"I knew it! I knew you'd feel that way. In fact, I said to myself as I came to your door—before going to anyone else, if you remember—I said to myself, I'm wasting my time, they don't need this, they're my supporters already, and then I thought, But I need their boost and *they* need—well, just to see me! Just to know that I appreciate them and I *care*."

She turned the full radiance of her smile on Wexford and, unable to resist the flirtatious gesture, lifted one hand and smoothed her sleek sweep of hair. In spite of what she had said, her raised eyebrows and inquiring tilt of the head implied the expectation of a like support from him. But Wexford had no intention of committing himself. The poll was secret and his vote private. He asked her what positive moves she had in mind should she be elected and was rather amused by signs of ignorance.

"Don't worry," she said. "The first thing I shall work for will be the demolition of that terrible Castlegate where that poor woman was attacked. And then we shall build good new local authority housing on the site from the proceeds of private sales."

Wexford corrected her gently. "Local councils' assets from private sales are frozen and look like being so for some time to come."

"Oh, I ought to know that, I do know it really." She was not a whit put out. "I can see I've a lot of homework to do. But the great thing is to get me there first, don't you agree?"

This Wexford refused to do. Pressed—the hand was back on his arm as he showed her out—he said that he was sure she also really knew his vote was a private matter between himself and his conscience. She entirely agreed, but she was tenacious, she was confrontational, her husband said, it was part of her nature not to shirk the truth, however unpalatable. By this time, Wexford had no idea what she meant, but he managed a fairly gracious good-bye with the usual rider of its having been delightful to see her.

Later on she must have given a similar treatment to the Akandes, for when Wexford called on them next morning, Laurette so far unbent as to complain about the candidate's remarking that black people were her special friends and asserting her affinity with them.

"Do you know what she said to me? 'My skin is white,' she said, 'but oh, my soul is black.' You've got a nerve, I thought."

Wexford couldn't help laughing but it was discreet gentle laughter. Mirth had no place in that house. But Laurette seemed to have forgotten their altercation in the matter of the IV line. She was more cordial than he had ever known her, for the first time offering him something to drink. Would he like coffee? Or she could easily make tea.

"Mrs. Khoori won't get very far if that's her manifesto," said the doctor. "There can't be more than half a dozen of us in the place."

"Nineteen precisely," said Wexford. "That's not families, that's individuals."

He drove himself to the Infirmary and parked his car in the only available space next to the library van. The car on the other side was a curious purplish color and this brought to mind the Epsons' car. Suddenly Wexford understood what had been teasing the back of his mind since driving to the Chief Constable's house. The pink car behind him was being driven by a white man. He hadn't been able to see his face but he had seen that the man was white. The Epsons were a mixed-race couple—no doubt candidates for Laurette Akande's disapproval—but it was *Fiona Epson who was white and her husband black.* Did that mean anything? Was it significant? He had often remarked that everything was significant in a murder case. . . .

The library service was a private concern run by volunteers and last year Dora had persuaded him to donate to it a dozen of his books that she called "superfluous." To his surprise he saw Cookie Dix step down from the driving seat of the library van. It was rather more astonishing that she recognized him.

"Hallo," she said. "How are you? Wasn't that a wonderful party at the Khooris'? Darling Alexander adored it, he's been quite bearable to live with ever since."

She spoke as if they were old, intimate friends, and all the details of her no doubt problematic married life common knowledge between them. Wexford asked her if he could help her load the books onto her trolley. Though nearly as tall as he, she looked fragile with her stick limbs, fairy face, and cloud of black hair.

"You're terribly kind." She stood back to let Wexford lift the trolley out from the back of the van. "I hate Monday and Saturday mornings, I really do, but these are the only good works I ever do and if I give them up my life will be one of pure unbridled hedonism."

Wexford smiled and asked her where she lived. "Oh, don't you know? I thought everyone knew the house that Dix built. The glass palace with the trees inside? The top of Ashley Grove?"

One of the town's monstrosities, one of the places all the visitors stared at and asked about. He helped her load books onto the trolley, inquired where they came from and who selected them. Oh, she did, all her friends gave her books. He should bear her in mind when next he had a clear-out.

"Everyone thinks of romances and detective stories," she said as he parted from her inside the entrance, "but I find horror the most popular." She gave him a beaming smile. "Mutilation and cannibalism actually. That's the stuff if you're feeling really low."

Vine had been with Oni Johnson all night. She was sleeping now and the curtains were drawn round her bed. Wexford said in a low voice, "I know you're going off duty but there's just one thing. Three times now Carolyn Snow has told me Snow's former girlfriend was called Diana. If it rings any bells with you, think about it, will you?"

Half an hour after he had taken Vine's place Raffy came in, gave his mother a kiss, which woke her up, and sat down to look at the pictures in his comic. Today must have been Laurette

Akande's day off and the ICU sister was a red-haired Irishwoman. She brought tea, which Raffy looked at suspiciously and asked if he could have a Coke.

"My goodness, you go down and fetch that for yourself out of the machine, young man. Whatever next!"

"I like him here beside me," said Oni when Raffy had gone outside, having first helped himself to coins from her purse on the bedside table. "I like to know what he's doing." But Wexford remembered her sister's words about Oni's possessiveness. "What we going to talk about today?"

"You're looking a lot better," Wexford said. "I see you've got a smaller bandage."

"Small bandage for a small brain, huh? Maybe my brain smaller now that doctor been cutting it around?"

"Mrs. Johnson, I'll tell you what we're going to talk about today. I want you to think back a few weeks, say three weeks, before last Thursday, and tell me of anything strange that may have happened."

She looked at him without speaking.

"Anything odd or different at home, at work, anything about your son, any new person you met. Don't hurry, just think about it. Go back to the beginning of July and try to remember any unusual thing."

Raffy came back with a can of Coke. Someone had switched on the television and he moved his chair closer to it. Oni couldn't reach his hand. She let hers rest on his arm. She said to Wexford, "You mean, like someone talking to me at the crossing? Like coming to the front door? Like seeing a stranger?"

"All that," said Wexford. "Anything."

"There was someone draw a thing on our door but Raffy clean it off. Like a cross with turning corners."

"A swastika?"

"That was the day the Job Center had a job for Raffy and he go for the interview but it was no go. Then Mhonum, my sister, she had her birthday, she forty-two, though she don't look it, and we go to Moonflower for birthday dinner. I got another job—you know that? School cleaner, three times a week. There was one day I'm cleaning and I find a ten-pound note, they get lot of pocket money these kids, and I hand it in to the teacher. Thought I might get a reward but no way. These things are sent to try us, you know? This the kind of thing you want?"

"Exactly the kind of thing," said Wexford, though he had hoped for something more illuminating.

"This is all the start of July, right? On Sunday the lady come to the door, lady with long blonde hair, saying you vote for me in council elections, but I say maybe, I don't know, I think about it. Though maybe that was the next Sunday. It was a Monday the day after, I know that, what was the date of the first Monday?"

"July the fifth?"

Raffy was laughing at something on the television. He put his empty Coke can on the floor. His mother said, "Come here, Raffy. I like to hold your hand." The boy shifted his chair a fraction without taking his eyes from the screen. Oni made a grab for his hand and gripped it, though this meant stretching her arm to its fullest extent.

"What happened on that Monday?" said Wexford.

"Not so much. The only one thing was in the afternoon and I am at the crossing. Maybe not that Monday but the next. All I am sure is the the day after the election lady come. I thought, Pity Raffy not here. He take you there, poor girl, you won't lose your way if Raffy take you."

Wexford was lost. "I don't quite follow you, Mrs. Johnson."

"I'm telling you, I stand at the crossing before the children come out of school, I just stand there, and a girl come along and stop in front of me, right on the pavement, right in front of me, and she talk to me in Yoruba. I am so surprise you could knock me over with a feather. I never hear Yoruba in twenty years but from my sister and she too proud for it. But this girl is from Nigeria and she say to me in Yoruba, What way is it to where they give you jobs? *Mo fe mo ibit' o gbe wa.* I want to know where it is."

eighteen

Four hours of deep sleep and Barry Vine was up, had taken a cold shower, and phoned Wexford. The Chief Inspector said something incomprehensible to him in an African language. The translation was enough to send him straight off to the Benefit Office.

Ingrid Pamber's holiday was over and she had been back at work for two days, at the desk between Osman Messaoud and Hayley Gordon. She turned the blue beam of her eyes on Vine and smiled at him as if he were a departed lover returned from the wars. Deadpan, he showed her the photograph of Sojourner's dead face and a photograph of Oni Johnson that Raffy had managed to produce from the flat in Castlegate. Sojourner meant nothing to her; Oni she recognized.

Vine's indifference to her charms and smiles made her petulant. "The lollipop lady, isn't she? I'd know her face anywhere. I think she's got it in for me. I only have to be late for work coming down Glebe Road and she's bound to stick that lollipop sign of hers up in front of me."

"Did Annette know her?"

"Annette? How should I know?"

Ingrid alone of the Benefit Office staff failed to ask what had happened to Oni and why he wanted to know. On the other hand, she was the only one who recognized her. No one, to the best of

their recollection, had ever seen Sojourner before. It was Valerie
Parker, one of the supervisors, who voiced what the others perhaps
had hesitated to express in words.

"I'm afraid all black people look much alike to me."

Osman Messaoud, passing her on his way to one of the computers, said nastily, "How peculiar. All whiteys look alike to black
people."

"I wasn't talking to you," said Valerie.

"No, I don't suppose you were. You keep your racist remarks for
like-minded individuals."

A momentary hesitation—should he stand up and be counted?
Should he hotly deny the imputation?—and Vine had left them to
an argument that was developing into a low-voiced hissing match.
Niall Clarke, the other supervisor, a would-be sociologist, said, "I
don't think white people do know black people in a society like
this. I mean, in a place like Kingsmarkham, a country town. After
all, up until about ten years ago there weren't any black people
here. You'd turn round and stare if you saw one in the street.
When I was at school there weren't any black pupils. I doubt if
we've got more than three or four blacks signing on here now."

Valerie Parker, routed by Messaoud and rather pink in the
face, said, "What was her name?"

"I wish I knew."

"I mean we could try checking with the computer if we knew
her name. I mean, there are probably hundreds with the same
name but we could . . ."

"I don't know her name," Vine said, and he had a feeling he
was never going to find out.

Even without a name, it should be easy to identify and locate a
lost black girl in a town like Kingsmarkham where whites over-
whelmingly predominated, but it wasn't. She had been directed to
this place, presumably she started on her way to this place, but
somewhere along the line she had vanished. Or she had reached
here but no one had noticed her. Privately, Vine thought she had
never got here; he would want to know more from Oni Johnson

before he pursued this line. On his way to the door he passed the booth where Peter Stanton was advising a new claimant and he saw that the claimant was Diana Graddon.

Until now he hadn't made up his mind whether to talk to her or not. It seemed unnecessary, even prurient. Of course Wexford's remark had rung a bell and of course he had thought about it, before falling asleep and from the moment he awoke. But what was it to him, or to any of them, if this woman had once been Snow's girlfriend, had been superseded by Annette Bystock? What was its relevance to this case of two murders and one attempted murder? But now he had seen her, Vine sat down on one of the gray chairs next to a plastic pot with its plastic peperomia and waited.

What sort of an impression did that Stanton make on women, eyeing them like that, his eyes rolling? Of course Diana Graddon was quite attractive, but Vine had the feeling that all that would ever matter to Stanton was that she was youngish and a woman. He pulled a leaflet out of the rack called *Income Support: See If You Are Entitled* and read it to pass the time.

It took Burden no more than twenty minutes to arrive at the Infirmary with the photograph of Sojourner. Oni Johnson recognized her at once.

"That's her. That's the girl spoke to me outside Thomas Proctor."

It must have been July the fifth, Wexford thought. She was dead by the evening. Mavrikiev had said she died at least twelve days before she was found on the seventeenth. Oni Johnson had spoken to her a matter of hours before she died.

"I don't suppose she told you her name?" Burden asked.

"She never said her name. Why would she? Never said where she come from, no way. She say to me where she going, to the Job Center, to get a job. That all she say. *Mo fe mo ibit'o gbe wa?*"

"Can you describe her?"

"Someone been beating her, that I do know. I seen *that* before. Her lip's been cut and her eye, you don't get no bruises like that walking into doors, no way. So I tell her where ESJ is, down the road and right and right again, between Nationwide and Marks and Spencers, and then I say to her, Who been beating you?"

"You said that in English or in Yoruba?"

"In Yoruba. And she say to me, *Bi oju ko ba kan e ni, m ba la oran naa ye e.* I tell you what that mean. 'If you are not in a hurry, I would like to explain to you.' "

Wexford's heart did a little bounce. "And did she?"

Oni shook her head vigorously. "I say, Yes, I have the time, the children not coming out for five minutes, ten minutes, yet, but then, when I am saying this, a car pull up right by where I stand, a mother driving a car, right? She come to fetch her child and I say to her, No, you can't park here, you go farther down road, and when I am done with all this I turn round but that young girl, she gone."

"What, gone out of sight?"

"I could see her, long way away, long way off down the road."

"Tell me what she was wearing."

"Had a cloth round her head, a kind of a blue cloth. A dress with flowers, white with pink flowers, and shoes like Raffy wear."

Both policemen looked at Raffy's feet, twisted round the chair legs. Black canvas lace-up half-boots with rubber welt and soles, perhaps the cheapest footwear obtainable in Kingsmarkham's most down-market shoe shop.

"Can you remember which direction she came from, Mrs. Johnson?"

"I never see her till she's there, talking in my ear. I don't see her coming from the High Street, so maybe she come from other end. Maybe she come from Glebe Lane end where there's fields. Maybe she drop from helicopter into field, huh?"

"She talked to you in Yoruba," said Wexford. "But she could speak English?"

"Oh, sure. Little bit. Like me when I come here. I say to her, You go down there, long way down, and you in High Street, you turn right and after little way right again and there's ESJ between Nationwide and Marks and Spencers. It all English words so I say it in English. And she nods her head like this"—Oni Johnson nodded her bandaged head vigorously—"and say what I say, Down here and right and right again, and here it is between Nationwide and Marks and Spencers. And then I ask her who been beating her."

"Mrs. Johnson, can you remember anything about her manner? The way she was? Was she out of breath? Had she been running? Was she happy or sad? Was she nervous?"

The smile that had come back into Oni's face slowly faded. She frowned a little and nodded again, but less energetically. "It was like someone is after her," she said, "someone chasing after her. She was frightened. But after she gone I watch and the place empty, no one is after her, no one chasing. But I can tell you, she very frightened."

"We can discount being dropped from a helicopter," Wexford said in the car. "Though the idea does have its attractions. She came from somewhere in the neighborhood, Glebe Road, Glebe Lane, Lichfield Road, Belper Road . . ." He considered, seeing the topography in his mind's eye. "Harrow Avenue, Wantage Avenue, Ashley Grove . . ."

"Or across the fields beyond Glebe End."

"What, from Sewingbury or Mynford?"

"Why not? Neither of them is that far." Burden considered. "Bruce Snow lives in Harrow Avenue, or he used to. He was living there on July the fifth."

"Yes. But if you can think of some reason for Bruce or Carolyn Snow to be chasing a terrified black girl down Glebe Road at three-thirty in the afternoon, you're a better scenario-maker than I am. Mike, this isn't a very big place even now. She could have come from anywhere north of the High Street and that includes your house and mine."

"And the Akandes'," said Burden. "Those shoes—is there any point in asking around the shoe shops to see if a black woman bought those sort of shoes recently?"

"It can't do any harm," said Wexford, "though she's not likely to have left her name and address on their mailing list, is she?"

"Meanwhile, we've got all this new stuff but we're no nearer knowing who she was, are we?"

"We probably are but we don't know it yet. For instance we know the motive behind the attack on Oni. Someone wanted to stop us getting that information about Sojourner out of her."

"Then why not do it two weeks ago?" Burden objected.

"Very likely because although he, whoever he is, knew Oni Johnson had that information, he never supposed we would run her to earth. He never imagined we'd get to speak to someone whose tenuous connection with Sojourner was merely that she happened by chance to ask her the way in the street. But last Thursday he realized he was wrong. *He saw Karen and me talking to Oni outside the Thomas Proctor.*"

"He?"

"He or she, or let's say, his or her agent. Someone in the know saw us. The rest was guesswork and he had just about an hour in which to get to Castlegate and wait at the top of those stairs. We're going to do a house-to-house, Mike. We're going to question every householder in Kingsmarkham north of the High Street."

At the Benefit Office they found themselves asking the same questions that Barry Vine had asked an hour before. But Barry had only conjectured that Sojourner had been there, without knowing when; Wexford was almost positive that she had come into the building on Monday, July 5, no later than four o'clock in the afternoon.

"Looking for work," he said to Ingrid.

"Aren't they all?" Ingrid turned the blue beam of her eyes on him and lightly lifted her shoulders. "I *wish* I'd seen her, I really do." The implication was that she wished it for his sake, so that she could please him. "But I *would* remember on account of seeing Melanie Akande next day. I'd have thought when I saw Melanie, Wow, look at that, how odd, another black girl I've never seen in here before." She gave him a rueful smile. "But I didn't see her."

"She may have lived near you," Wexford persisted. "In Glebe

Lane or at Glebe End. If you didn't see her in here that day, do you think you ever saw her near where you live? In the street? Looking out of a window? In a shop?"

She looked as if she pitied him. He had this onerous task to perform, this quest to make, this job to do, and she was so sorry. . . . If only she could help, if only there was something she could do to make his burden lighter. Her head was a little on one side, a characteristic gesture. He thought how it would be if he were, say, twenty-five again, and there was this girl that he was obliged to keep meeting, a girl who was spoken for in a way, but only in a way, and he wondered how he would have gone about cutting Jeremy Lang out. Not "if" but "how," for he was sure he would have attempted it, if only for the bluest eyes on earth. . . .

"I've never seen her in all my life," Ingrid said, and suddenly brisk again, she pressed the buttons on her machine that would light up the next client's number above their heads.

Deep in thought, Wexford made his way back through the Job Center area and the freestanding advertising on which potential employers offered what situations were vacant. Most of them gave no names and no locations, stating only pitifully low wages and curious trades, some of which he had never before heard of. He was momentarily distracted and let his eye run down the ranks of cards. In fact, there were few jobs here that anyone, however desperate, would want to apply for and a phrase came into his mind: "needy nothing trimmed in jollity . . ." Inadequate salaries were offered to those willing to care full-time for three children under four or combine twenty hours a week assisting in a boarding kennel with keeping house for a family of five.

He didn't know why an advertisement for a children's nanny (no previous experience required) while the parents were abroad on business seemed to ring a bell in his mind. But he knew his intuition was usually sound and he was searching back in his memory, trying to find a link, when he went outside to find Burden.

The boys sitting on the wall outside had already been shown Sojourner's photograph by Barry Vine. "That other one," was how the short boy with the golden hair described him. The boy with the ponytail seemed to be doing his best to get through his packet of twenty cigarettes by lunchtime, for eleven stubs lay in the ash round his feet. Burden pinned his hopes on their ability now to be more specific.

"On a Monday afternoon," he said. "The first Monday of July. At about four."

The shaven-headed boy with the range of T-shirts—he was in a faded red one today with Michael Jackson's face on it—looked at the photograph and, armed with these new details, said as if squeezing the statement out, as if it was the result of tremendous intellectual effort, "I might've."

"You might have seen her? You might have seen her go into the Benefit Office?"

"The other one asked me that. I don't mean that. I said I never see her go in there."

Wexford said quickly, "But you did see her."

A glance at ponytail and, "What d'you reckon, Danny? It's a long time back."

"I never seen her, man," said Danny, stubbing out his cigarette and coughing. With nothing to do with his hands, he began picking at the skin round his fingernails.

The boy with the golden hair said, "I never see her neither. D'you reckon you saw her, Rossy?"

"I might've," said the one in the T-shirt. "I might've seen her across the road. Standing over there looking. There was me and Danny and Garry and a couple of other kids, don't know what they call them, we was all on the steps like now, only more of us, and she was over there looking."

He had said so before, Burden remembered now. In the early days of the hunt for Melanie Akande, he had mentioned seeing a black girl on the Monday. "And that was on July the fifth in the afternoon?" he asked, full of hope.

But if it had been that Monday he had now forgotten. "Don't know about that, don't know the day or the *time*. It was hot, I do know that. I took me top off to get a bit of sun and this old bat come along and says to me, That's the way to get skin cancer, young man. I told her what she could do, silly old cow."

"The girl on the other side, do you think she wanted to go into the Benefit Office?"

Danny spoke while still picking bits of his cuticles, "If she'd wanted to, why'd she never cross the road? She'd only to cross the road."

"But you didn't see her, did you?" Burden asked.

"Me? No, I never see her. But it stands to reason, she'd only to cross the road."

"She never did," said Rossy, and losing interest, "Give us one of your fags, Dan."

Half an hour before, standing on the same spot, Diana Graddon had said to Vine, "Do you mind if I smoke?" They were about to get into his car.

"I'd rather you waited till we've got you home."

She shrugged and compressed her lips. He was fascinated by her resemblance to Annette Bystock. They might have been sisters. This woman was the younger by a few years and she was slimmer than Annette, less voluptuous, but they had the same dark curly hair, similar bold features, big mouth, strong nose, and round dark eyes, only Annette's had been brown and this woman's were a bluish-gray.

Asked about Snow, she had made no attempt to deny the relationship, though she showed considerable surprise. "It was ten years ago!"

"D'you mind telling me if it was you introduced him to Annette Bystock?"

Surprise was renewed. She was incredulous. "How could you possibly know?"

Vine, of course, was well practiced in parrying such inquiries. "The relationship hadn't lasted long, I'd guess."

"A year," said Diana Graddon. "I found out he'd got children.

The youngest was only three. Funny, how it all comes back. I haven't thought about any of this for years."

"But you didn't split up then?"

"We started having rows. Look, I was only twenty-five and I didn't see why I should settle for him sneaking round for an hour in the evening and then not hearing a word for a week and then a phone call and another bang-bang, thank you very much, sir. He did take me out but only once in a blue moon. I didn't want him permanently either, I mean I wasn't thinking marriage or anything like that. I was young but I wasn't daft. I could just envisage what that'd be, living with a guy who'd got three kids and a wife to keep and a possessive wife by all accounts."

She drew breath and Vine, drawing up outside the house in Ladyhall Road, was wondering how much more of this he wanted to hear when she said, "He came round one evening when Annette was there. Oh, I knew he'd come, he always phoned first, but I thought, So what? We'll have a *social* evening for once, we'll actually manage to meet without having sex, see what he thinks about that, though I could imagine. Funny how it all comes back, isn't it? Annette didn't know who he was or—well, what we were to each other, if you see what I mean." An unpleasant thought seemed to strike her. "You don't mean you think he did it? Killed her, I mean?"

Vine smiled. "Can we go into the house, Miss Graddon?"

"Oh, yes, sure." She unlocked the door. Helen Ringstead appeared not to be at home. They went into the living room. "I mean," she said, "he and Annette, they hardly knew each other. I don't suppose they ever met again."

So she didn't know. . . . He was amused. Odious though Snow might be, you had to hand it to him, he had it all worked out. Vine was going to ask another question but he didn't have to.

"He broke things off soon after that. He told me his wife had found out. Someone she knew had seen us together in a restaurant on one of the *rare* occasions he gave me dinner. This woman had heard him call me Diana. He confessed it all to her, threw himself on her mercy, or so he said."

"Was it about then that you told Annette there was a flat for sale opposite?"

"It must have been. She'd got divorced a little bit before that. We were still friends then." Diana Graddon lit the cigarette Vine had denied her in the car. She drew in a long inhalation. "The fact is, I don't know why we stopped being friends. You'd think we'd have been in and out of each other's houses, living more or less opposite, but we sort of drifted apart, and I think it was her doing. She sort of withdrew into herself. And what's more, I don't think she's had a boyfriend since she split up with Stephen. But I'm just amazed when you say you suspect Bruce."

He hadn't said it. Vine marveled at Snow's structure of deceit and double-dealing. However much as a human being he deplored Snow's behavior, as a man he could not fail to admire his chicanery. He had kept his affair with Diana a secret from Annette and his affair with Annette a secret from Diana, and if he had not succeeded in keeping Diana a secret from his wife he had lulled Carolyn for nine years into the belief that her marriage was inviolable. Had Annette's move to Ladyhall Gardens, opposite Diana, dismayed him? Or had it rather given him the perfect reason for his new relationship to remain on the level of a simple sexual transaction, continually repeated? It was obviously unwise to entertain a girlfriend in a restaurant and indiscreet to go to her home, so he was protected against closer involvement.

What had he said to Annette? Don't be too friendly with Diana, she knows my wife? Or even, She's quite capable of getting in touch with my wife? The best liars stick as close to the truth as mendacity allows.

"I mean, Bruce would have had to know her," Diana persisted. "He'd have had to have a motive, wouldn't he? Believe me, I'd have seen him if he'd ever been to see her here and I never did. I mean, I saw everyone Annette knew, I must have seen everyone who ever called there." She hesitated, coughed a little. The cigarette trembled in her fingers. "It's funny, but I was sort of fascinated by her. I wonder why that was? I don't know why I'm asking you, you're not a psychologist, but I wonder if a psychologist would say it was because she—well, she rejected me really, didn't she?"

Vine, who knew Wexford's methods, waited in silence. He might not be a psychologist but he knew what psychotherapists did. They put the patient or client or whatever on a couch and they listened. A word uttered at the wrong time might be fatal. He would listen, though he didn't know what he was listening for. Nor did Freud, he thought.

"I suppose I resented that. I used to say to myself, Who does she think she is, giving me the cold shoulder? I saw her come in with that pretty girl once or twice, the one from the employment office that she worked with, and she was a bit pally with Edwina what's-her-name. But, d'you know, that was all. Well, I saw her cousin there once or twice, a Mrs. Winster, I can't remember her first name. Joan, Jean, Jane. No man ever set foot in the place, it was like a nunnery. I mean, the idea of Bruce going in there, it's a laugh really." She smiled a little at the absurdity of the notion. "Old Bruce," she said. "What's he up to these days? Apart from murdering women he doesn't know?" The smile split into laughter.

Disappointment slumped Vine's shoulders. She had nothing to tell him. It was all over. He thought of revealing all to her in the hope that disbelief, the slow dawning of enlightenment, the subsequent rage, would bring forth revelations. But if there were no revelations to deliver? He said idly, preparing to go, "You told me you last saw her on the Monday evening?"

"Yes, I was going away to stay with my boyfriend in Pomfret." She gave a sidelong smile, glad of the opportunity to tell him Snow had a successor. "It was always a bit awkward, you can imagine, Annette and me, we sort of avoided each other, but we happened to look across the road at the same time. She said hallo and I said hallo and then I remembered I'd left a sweater I wanted behind, so I went back.

"When I came out again—oh, it was no more than two minutes, if that—she'd gone into the flats and there was this girl standing outside the door, the front door of Ladyhall Court, I mean.

Well, Annette must have gone straight into her bedroom to open the window. She leaned out and saw the girl and the girl—she was a black girl, incidentally—she went over to the window and said something and that—well, that was the last time I ever saw Annette."

nineteen

W hich way is it to find work? She had asked Oni Johnson this in an obscure language because there was something about Oni that told her this woman was Nigerian too.

And Sojourner had done what she was told and walked on, southward to the High Street, fearful of some pursuer, but reaching there unscathed, reaching the Benefit Office too. Instead of going in, she had waited on the other side of the street, staring. Why hadn't she crossed the road, as Rossy suggested, and gone in?

"Men," said Wexford. "She was scared of men. Yes, okay, I know Rossy and Danny and co don't seem very intimidating to us, but neither you nor I is a seventeen-year-old and, I suspect, extremely unsophisticated black girl. She's got an inbuilt fear and distrust of whites anyway. Some man had been beating her and she was going to tell Oni about it but just at that moment Oni was distracted when someone wanted to park a car in the wrong place.

"Men are more frightening to women than other women are. Yes, they are, Mike, whether you like it or not. And here are this lot, one of them stripped down to nothing but his jeans, sitting there, more or less barring the door. And to crown it all, when a woman comes along and speaks to one of them he shouts at her, gives her some obscene instruction, calls her a silly old cow—or worse. That's what he tells *you* he calls her."

The house-to-house inquiries had begun. With a street plan of north Kingsmarkham in front of him, Wexford was beginning to see how enormously the town had expanded since first he came there. Estates as big as villages had been built on the northern outskirts. In the inner areas old houses had been pulled down, as in Ladyhall Avenue, and each one replaced by a dozen small ones and yet another block of flats. The ward in which he would vote in the council election had once comprised the whole town; now it was a small section of it. He looked up from the map as Burden said, "So Sojourner hangs about on the opposite pavement—what for? Just in the hope that they'll go away?"

"Or that someone will come out. She'll have seen clients go in and come out again but no one after about three-thirty, remember. No one signs on on a Monday and the new claims advisers have their last appointment at three-thirty. So anyone who comes out at four-thirty is going to have to be working there."

"You're saying she followed Annette home?"

"Why not?"

"You mean it was just chance she picked Annette?"

"Not quite," said Wexford. "Most of the other people that work there have cars parked in the car park at the back. They wouldn't come out the front way."

"Stanton doesn't take his car to work," Burden objected. "Nor does Messaoud. His wife has it in the day."

"They're men. Sojourner wouldn't have followed a man."

"All right, she follows Annette across the High Street, down Queen Street over there"—as if Wexford hadn't a street plan in front of him—"along Manor Road and into Ladyhall Gardens. It's then that Diana Graddon sees her. Or, rather, she sees Annette and when she comes out a second time, she sees Sojourner at the front door of Ladyhall Court."

"To be precise, she sees Annette leaning out of the window talking to Sojourner. Did Annette let her into the house? Did she want to be let in?"

"Annette must have told her that if she wanted work, or
wanted the dole, her only course was to come to the Benefit Office
next day, the Tuesday. Maybe she said to ask for her and gave her
her name but didn't let her in. She wasn't very free about letting
people into her flat."

"So what did Sojourner say that made Annette wonder if she
should tell the police?"

"You think that's what it was? It was Sojourner that told her
that, whatever it was? This was twenty-four hours, more than
twenty-four hours, before she spoke on the phone to cousin Jane
on Tuesday evening."

"I know, Mike. I'm guessing. But look at it this way. Sojourner
said something to Annette that she didn't like or made her suspicious. What it was we don't know, very likely what she was going
to tell Oni but never did, something about the man who beat her
and maybe where he lived. However, we do know that Sojourner
never took the advice Annette presumably gave her, to come to
the Benefit Office the next day.

"When she didn't come, don't you think it likely that Annette
became uneasy? Perhaps she wanted to discuss whatever it was
with Sojourner before she took any steps. But by that time Annette was feeling unwell. She went home, went to bed, was ill
enough to tell Snow she couldn't see him the next day but was still
worried enough to pass her worries on to her cousin.

"As to why I think the something the police should know
came from Sojourner, well, she *died* that night, didn't she, she was
murdered that night. She couldn't go to the Benefit Office because
she was dead. And her failure to come must have compounded
Annette's fears—only with that virus, believe me, for the time
being you're not thinking about anyone but yourself."

"So on the Monday evening, Annette just sent Sojourner back
home, wherever that was?"

"She behaved, no doubt, as anyone would in the circumstances. Probably she didn't give any advice at all beyond telling
her to come to the Benefit Office. Unfortunately, tragically, So-

journer had nowhere else to go but home. What happened next we've no idea, but we can make a reasonable guess that someone at home, father, brother, husband even, some male relative, shall we say 'punished' her for running away?"

"The person she was afraid was pursuing her?"

"Oh, yes."

"How did he know about Oni Johnson? How did he know about Annette?"

"She told him, don't you think?"

Burden looked as if he would like to ask why but he didn't. "You said Sojourner 'told him.' Told who? Her father? Her brother? Husband? Boyfriend?"

"Husband or boyfriend, it would have to be. We know all the black people here, Mike, we've found them all, we've talked to them. But she may have had a white boyfriend."

All the while he talked he had been thinking, inescapably, of Dr. Akande. It sometimes seemed to him that all roads led back to the Akandes and that, conversely, every route he took he found one or another of the Akandes there. He picked up the phone and asked Pemberton to come up.

"Bill, I want you to get on to Kimberley Pearson's family and find out everything you can about them."

Pemberton attempted to disguise his incomprehension and failed. "Zack Nelson's girlfriend," said Burden.

"Yes. Oh, sure. What, parents, d'you mean? Where are they?"

"I don't know. I haven't the faintest, somewhere within a radius of twenty miles, say. There is, or was, a grandmother. I want to know where she lived and when she died." He paused. "And Kimberley's not to know. I don't want a hint of this reaching her."

With a flash of insight that surprised Wexford and pleased him, Pemberton said, "Do you reckon Kimberley's life's in danger, sir? Is she the next girl he's after?"

Wexford said slowly, "Not if we keep away from her. Not if he—or she—thinks we've done with her. I'm going back to the hospital. I want to talk to Oni again." He added, remembering what Freeborn had accused him of, "But I'm not even going to drive down Stowerton High Street, I'll go the long way round."

Mhonum Ling was there. If there were to be a competition for the most overdressed woman in Kingsmarkham, Wexford thought, it would be hard choosing between Oni's sister and Anouk Khoori. Mhonum's ankle-length pink skirt was just short enough to disclose her jeweled sandals. The T-shirt she wore was a far cry from Danny's; it had sequins on it. He held Oni's hand for a moment and she gave him one of her tremendous smiles.

"I'm going to take you through all that again," he said.

She made a mock face of horror but he thought she enjoyed it really. Raffy walked in, carrying a ghetto-blaster, mercifully not on. Wexford he was used to by now but he gave his aunt the sort of look more likely to be on the face of someone who has seen a lioness on the loose. When Oni repeated the things Sojourner had said in Yoruba, Mhonum shrugged her shoulders and turned her head to look Raffy up and down.

"When she'd gone out of sight," Wexford said, "did the children start coming out? Or did a lot of parents arrive before that?"

"Mothers and fathers, mostly mothers, they start coming five, ten minutes before children come out. That one in the car parked right by my feet, the one I moved on, she was the first. Then all the others start coming."

"I'd like you to think carefully about this, Mrs. Johnson. Did you get the impression she ran away from you because she was afraid of *one of the parents seeing her?*"

Oni Johnson tried to remember. She screwed her eyes tight shut with the effort of concentration. Mhonum Ling said, "You know her name yet?"

"Not yet, Mrs. Ling."

"What you bring that radio in here for, Raffy?" she said to her nephew and without waiting for an answer, "You go down the drinks machine and fetch a Diet Fanta for auntie and one for your mummy." She produced a handful of change from her pink patent leather bag. "And have yourself a Coke, good boy, hurry up now."

Opening her eyes, Oni said, "No good, I don't know. I never did know. She frightened, she in big hurry, but I don't know what she frightened *of*."

He went down the stairs with the silent boy pattering along in front of him. Raffy stopped at the drinks machine, stared hopelessly at the keys and the pictures above them. Diet Coke he could wrest from it. Fanta presented more of a problem. Wexford put out a finger as he passed, tapped the relevant key, and walked on out to the car park. At least a hundred cars had arrived since he left his. He was remembering how he had told the Chief Constable and a good many other people besides that he would have this case solved by the end of the week. Early days, though, it was only Tuesday.

Turning out of the hospital gates and into the roundabout, he nearly took the first exit. Then he remembered he had to avoid the High Street and drove round to the third. Perhaps he was being overscrupulous. No one was following him, the idea was ridiculous, it wasn't as if he intended to stop outside Clifton Court, still less call on Kimberley Pearson, but he took the third exit just the same. He might have saved Oni Johnson's life but he had terribly endangered it first.

This devious route took him along Charteris Road and into Sparta Grove. He hadn't been along that street since the little Epson boys were taken into care and he had only gone there then to say a few words into the television cameras about parents who went off on holiday and left their children at home unattended. Now he tried to remember which of this three-story Victorian row was their house. Not a slummy house at all, the Epsons weren't poor, if they didn't want their children with them they could easily have afforded to pay a child-minder.

He was driving slowly. Ahead of him a man came out of one of the houses, closed the front door behind him, and got into a pink car parked at the pavement edge. Wexford pulled in and switched off the engine. The man was tall and heavily built, fair-haired, young, but he had his back to him and Wexford couldn't see his face. He wasn't Epson. He was too young and Epson was black, a Jamaican.

The car moved off, gathering speed very rapidly, tearing round the corner into Charteris Road. He had seen that man in that car very recently and he had an idea the circumstances were somehow distasteful or that he wanted to avoid thinking about them. That, no doubt, was the reason he couldn't remember.

He sat there for a moment or two but memory had deserted him. His route home took him through the industrial estate, a stark and deserted place, half the factories boarded up or to let. A narrow country lane led back on to the Kingsmarkham Road and ten minutes later he was in his own house.

The answer to things had sometimes in the past come to him, directly or indirectly, from Sheila; from a remark she made or her latest interest or passion, or something she had given him to read. Whatever it was, it had set him on the right road. He needed her now, a word or two from her, a pointer.

But it was his other daughter visiting him this evening with Ben and Robin, having arranged to meet Neil in her parents' house after his job club session. Her indulgent mother had invited them all to stay for supper. Even as he digested this, Wexford thought how much Sylvia would hate being termed, even in his secret mind, his "other daughter." No father ever struggled so hard not to show the preference he felt and no father, he thought, so signally failed. As soon as he walked in the door he had realized he must resist phoning Sheila while Sylvia was there, or at least while Sylvia was in earshot.

The evening was warm. They sat outside, a ring of chairs round the sunshade table, and Sylvia's suggestion that they eat there was met, inevitably, by a version of her older son's favorite phrase.

"Mushk eler."

"Well, it's a problem for me," said Wexford. "You know I can't stand al fresco eating, all those mosquitoes. It's the same with picnics."

The boys and their grandmother immediately engaged in argument about the merits and demerits of picnics. Sylvia, ignoring them, lay back in her chair, half closed her eyes, and began to talk about her counseling course, how completely different was the approach from when she did her social sciences degree, how the emphasis here was on people, on human interaction, on enabling and personal interdependence . . . It was ridiculous, Wexford thought, the way he was behaving, afraid to phone Sheila secretly, lest she had her answering machine on and would therefore ring back after an hour or two. How soon would Sylvia and family go? Not for hours. Neil wasn't expected for an hour.

Dora took the boys with her into the house. Robin was to set the table, she said. The expected response didn't come, presumably because it *was* a problem.

"Would you like a drink?" he said to Sylvia, as much to stem the tide as because he wanted one.

"Sparkling water. Mostly we'll be dealing with depression and anxiety states. But there's always a lot of domestic violence and you have to bear in mind the secrecy imperative in creating confidence in the client. We shall counsel each other, I mean, of course, initially . . ."

When Wexford came back with her water and his beer she was still talking. She seemed to have reached the physical abuse by strong people of other, weaker people. Her eyes were shut now and she was staring up through her closed lids at the blue summer sky.

"Why do they do it?" said Wexford.

He had interrupted her in mid-flow. She opened her eyes and looked at him. "Do what?"

"Men beat up their wives, people mistreat their kids."

"Are you really asking me? Do you really want to know?"

A pang, a guilty wince, was the effect on him of these questions. It was as if she was amazed that he wanted to know anything she could tell him. She would talk, she would assert herself, on and on, relentlessly, but not to entertain or inform. To get back at him, to show him. Now he sounded as if he really wanted to know. Her tone was one of incredulity—you're asking *me?*

What he really wanted was to find a way of escape and phone Sheila. Instead he said, "I'd like to know."

She didn't answer directly. "Have you ever heard of Benjamin Rush?"

"I don't think so."

"He was the Dean of the Medical School at the University of Pennsylvania. Oh, nearly two hundred years ago. He's known as the father of American psychiatry. Of course there was slavery then in the United States. One of the things Rush maintained was that all crimes are diseases and he thought not believing in God was a mental disease."

"So what's he got to do with physical abuse?"

"Well, I bet you've never heard of this before, Dad. Rush made up something called a Theory of Negritude. He believed being black was a disease. Black people suffered from congenital leprosy but in such a mild form that pigmentation was its only symptom. Do you see what holding a theory like that means? It justifies sexual segregation and social maltreatment. It means you've got a reason for ill-treating people."

"Wait a minute," said Wexford. "What you're saying is that if someone is an object of pity you're going to want to use physical violence against them? That seems cockeyed. It's the contrary of everything social morals teach us."

"No, listen. You *make* someone into an object of—not so much of pity as of weakness, sickness, stupidity, ineffectiveness, do you see what I mean? You hit them for their stupidity and their inability to respond, and when you've hurt them, marked them, they're even more sick and ugly, aren't they? And they're afraid and cringing too. Oh, I know this isn't very pleasant, but you did ask."

"Go on," he said.

"So you've got a frightened, stupid, even disabled person, silenced, made ugly, and what can you do with someone like that, someone who's unworthy of being treated well? You treat them badly because that's what they deserve. One thinks of poor little kids that no one can love because they're dirty, covered in snot and shit, and always screaming. So you beat them because they're hateful, they're low, they're *subhuman*. That's all they're good for, being hit, being reduced even further."

He was silent. She mistook his silence for shock, not at the content of what she had said but because she had said it, and quick to make amends, said, "Dad, it's horrible, I know, but I do have to know about these things, I have to try to understand something about the doer as well as the done-to."

"No," he said. "It's not that. I know that. I'm a policeman, remember? There was something else you said, it struck a chord. One word. I can't remember . . ."

" 'Subhuman'? 'Ineffectiveness'?"

"No. It'll come to me." He got up. "Thank you, Sylvia. You don't know how you've helped me." Her look went to his heart. For a moment she looked like her son Ben. He bent over and kissed her forehead. "I know what it was," he said, half to himself. "It's come back to me."

Upstairs, at his bedside but as yet unread, were the leaflets and brochures Sheila had sent him, the literature of her latest passion. He would read them as soon as Sylvia had gone. But he had also remembered something about the man who came out of the Epsons' and had been driving the Epsons' car. He hadn't seen his face. And he hadn't seen the face of whoever was driving that car when a little boy had come out of the Thomas Proctor gates and got into it.

Wexford could see that little boy quite clearly, a brown boy with brown curly hair, who could have been that man's son but only if his mother was black and only if he had fathered him when he was a boy himself.

Was this the man Sojourner had been running to escape a fortnight before?

No, Wexford thought, that wasn't the way it was at all . . .

twenty

The usual call on the Akandes must be postponed. If Wexford's guess was right, he would be in no mood to face them with this at the forefront of his mind. And what was there to say? Even the common pleasantries, weather commentary, inquiries after their health, would come stiltedly. He thought of how he had tried to prepare them, telling them to abandon hope, and he remembered Akande's optimism, flaring one day, dying the next.

He drove himself to work, passing the Akandes' house but keeping his eyes on the road ahead. Reports awaited him on the progress of the house-to-house inquiries but they were negative, they had yielded nothing apart from racism among unlikely householders and an unsuspected liberal attitude where prejudice was most anticipated. When it came to human beings, there was no knowing. Malahyde, Pemberton, Archbold, and Donaldson would keep on all day, ringing doorbells, showing the photograph, asking. If Kingsmarkham produced nothing, they would begin on the villages, Mynford, Myfleet, Cheriton.

Wexford took Barry Vine with him to Stowerton. They avoided the High Street and went by way of Waterford Avenue where the Chief Constable's house was. The neighborhoods changed very quickly in Stowerton and it was a long stone's throw to Sparta Grove. Wexford smiled to himself as they passed the house, thinking how near Freeborn had been to it all, this—well, conspiracy, wasn't it?—going on under his nose.

The pink car was parked in the road, back where he had first seen it the night before. In the broad daylight of a sunny morning it looked very dirty. A finger graffitist had written "Clean me now" in the dust on its boot lid. Not a window in the house was open. It looked empty—but the car was there.

The doorbell wasn't working. Vine banged smartly on the knocker and remarked, looking up at the closed windows, that nine in the morning was early for some people. He knocked again and was about to bellow through the letter box when the sash of an upstairs window was raised and the man whose back Wexford had seen the evening before and had been unable to identify put his head out. It was Christopher Riding.

"Police," said Wexford. "Remember me?"

"Should I?"

"Chief Inspector Wexford, Kingsmarkham CID. Come down and let us in, please."

They waited a long time. Scuffling noises came from inside and the sound of something made of glass being dropped and broken. A string of muffled curses was followed by a dull thump. Vine suggested wistfully that it would be a good idea to kick the door down.

"No, here he comes."

The door was opened cautiously. A child of about four put his head round it and giggled. He was peremptorily pulled back and the man whose face had appeared at the window stood there. He wore shorts and a heavy, very dirty, Aran sweater. His legs and feet were bare.

"What d'you want?"

"To come in."

"You'll need a warrant for that," said Christopher Riding. "You're not coming in here without one. It's not my property."

"No, it's the property of Mr. and Mrs. Epson. Where are they this time? Lanzarote?"

He was a little disconcerted, enough to step back. Wexford, who had the edge on him as far as height went, if not youth, gave him a shove with his elbow and pushed past him into the house. Vine followed, shaking off Riding's detaining hand. The child began to wail.

It was a house of numerous little rooms, a steep staircase climbing up its center. In the middle of the staircase stood an older child, a grubby soft toy trailing from one hand. It was the brown boy with brown curly hair Wexford had seen come out of the Thomas Proctor. When he saw Wexford he turned tail and fled upstairs. The sound of a radio came from behind a closed door. Wexford opened it quietly. On all fours on the floor, a girl was picking up broken glass—no doubt the remains of the object which they had heard dropped—and putting the pieces onto a folded newspaper. She turned her head at the sound of his careful cough, sprang to her feet, and let out a cry.

"Good morning," Wexford said. "Melanie Akande, I presume?"

His coolness belied his true feelings. Extreme relief at finding her alive and well and living in Stowerton fought in his mind with anger and a kind of appalled fear for her parents. Suppose Sheila had done that? How would he have felt if his daughter had done that?

Christopher Riding leaned against the fireplace, a cynical half-amused expression on his face. Having looked at first as if she was going to cry, Melanie had controlled her tears and now sat in an attitude of despair. In her surprise she had cut her finger on one of the pieces of glass and it bled unheeded. Blood trickled onto her bare feet. From upstairs one of the Epson children began to wail.

"Go and see what he wants, will you?" Melanie spoke to Riding as if they had been married for years and not too happily.

"Christ."

Riding shrugged his shoulders with great drama. The younger boy got hold of his jeans and hung on, burying his face in the back of the man's knees. Christopher walked off, dragging the child behind him, and banged the door.

"Where are Mr. and Mrs. Epson?" Wexford said.

"Sicily. They're coming back tonight."

"And what were you planning to do?"

She sighed. "I don't know." The sight of her finger brought the tears back once more to her eyes. She started wrapping a tissue round it. "See if they'll keep me on, I suppose. I don't know, God knows, sleep on the streets."

She was dressed exactly as, according to the missing person description, she had been on the day she vanished, in jeans, a white shirt, and a long embroidered waistcoat. The look on her face was one of utter disenchantment with the life she found herself in.

"Do you want to tell me about it here or shall we go to the police station?"

"I can't leave the kids, can I?"

Wexford thought about it. There was a funny side that he might come to see later on. Of course she couldn't leave the kids. The Epson children were on the Social Services register and had been since their parents were given suspended prison sentences for leaving them in the house alone for a week. But he didn't fancy fetching out a child care officer, getting a care order made, setting the whole machinery in motion for the sake of removing Melanie Akande for one day. No doubt the Epsons, considerably frightened by what had happened last time, had more or less properly engaged her to look after their two sons.

"What did you do? Answer an ad in the Job Center?"

Melanie nodded. "Mrs. Epson, she said to call her Fiona, she was in there. I'd been talking to the new claims officer and when I was done I sort of wandered over into the jobs part and there was this woman standing by the board that advertises jobs for nannies and minders and whatever. I'd never thought of that sort of work but I was looking at it and she said did I want to come and work for her for three weeks.

"Well, I knew you weren't supposed to go with people who

offer you jobs like that but a woman seemed different. I mean, it's because of sexual harassment, isn't it? She said, Why not come and see, so I went with her. She had a car in the car park and we went out the side door—that car you saw outside."

"That's why those boys outside never saw you leave," said Vine.

"Maybe." A thought struck her. "Have my parents been looking for me?"

"The whole country's been looking for you," said Vine. "Didn't you see the papers? Didn't you see the telly?"

"The TV broke down and we didn't know who to get to come and see to it. I never saw a paper."

"Your mother thought at first you were with Euan Sinclair," said Wexford. "She *feared* it was possible. Then she thought you were dead. Mrs. Epson brought you here, then? Just like that? She didn't ask if you wanted to go home first, if you wanted to fetch your things?"

"They were going away the next day. They'd more or less decided they'd have to take the kids. I can understand they didn't want to. They're *awful* kids."

"Not surprising, is it?" said Vine, the conscientious father.

Melanie lifted her shoulders. "I said to Fiona that I could stay if she wanted. I'd got my things with me, you see—well, I'd got enough on account of I'd been going to Laurel's. But I didn't want to go there. I had a date with Euan first but I didn't want to meet him, I didn't want to hear any more of his lies. This house and being here was just what I wanted. Anyway, I thought so. I'd earn some money that wasn't a grant or *pocket money* from Dad. I thought I'd be alone and that was what I wanted, to be alone for a bit. But you're not alone with kids."

"Christopher Riding wasn't with you all the time?"

"I don't know where he was. I didn't know him very well—not then. It was—it was after I'd been here about a week. I was nearly giving up, those kids are so terrible, I had to drive the big one to school, that's why they left me the car, and Chris saw me, he recognized me, and he—he followed me back here."

After she had been there about a week, Wexford thought. That would have been the day or the day after he had talked to Christopher Riding and asked him about Melanie. At least he had been telling the truth then.

"He thought it was funny," Melanie said. "I mean, the whole setup. It sort of fascinated him. He stayed a bit." She looked away. "I mean, he came and he went. He helped me with the kids. They *are* awful kids."

"And were you an awful kid, Melanie?" said Vine. "It's a pretty awful daughter, isn't it, that goes off, disappears, without a word to her parents? Lets them think she's dead? She's been murdered?"

"They couldn't have thought that!"

"Of course they did. What stopped you making one phone call?"

She was silent, looking down at the blood-soaked tissue on her finger. Wexford thought of all the people who must have seen her and who did nothing about it, who did nothing because she was always with two black children they took to be her children. Or saw her with Riding, that they took to be the father of the children with them. Wexford had thought a missing black girl should be easy to find because black people were rare here, but the reverse was true. It was for that very reason that she had failed to be recognized.

"They wouldn't have let me stay here," Melanie said in a voice not much above a whisper. Christopher, who had come back into the room, got a sidelong unhappy look. "My mother would have called it being a servant. My father would have come and fetched me home." Her voice rose and there was a hysterical edge to it. "You don't know what it's like at home. No one knows." She gave Christopher a bitter look. "And I can't get away if I haven't got a job and a—a roof." She said to Wexford, picking him for some reason, "Can I talk to you alone? Just for a minute?"

A shattering scream split the air. It came from upstairs but it might have been in the same room. The scream was followed by a violent crash. Melanie shouted, "Oh God!" and "Go and see what he's doing, Chris, *please.*"

"Go yourself," said Christopher, laughing.

"I *can't* go. They want me here."

"For Christ's sake, I've had enough of this. I don't know what the attraction was in the first place."

"I do!"

"It's wearing thin now at any rate."

"I will go," said Barry Vine in stern admonitory tones.

Wexford said to Melanie, "We'll go into one of the other rooms."

A bleak place that no one seemed to use with a dining table and chairs around it and a bicycle in one corner. A green window blind was pulled down to its fullest extent. Wexford motioned the girl to a chair and sat down opposite her.

"What did you want to say to me?"

"I thought of having a baby," she said, "just so that the council would give me a place."

"More likely put you up in one of their famous bed and break-fasts."

"That would be better than Ollerton Avenue."

"Really? What's so bad about it?"

She relaxed quite suddenly. She put her elbows on the table and gave him a look that was conspiratorial, secrets-sharing. Her wry smile made her enormously attractive. She was at once pretty and charming. "You don't know," she said. "You don't know what they're really like. You just see the hardworking kindly GP and his beautiful efficient wife. They're fanatics, those two, they're ob-sessed."

"In what respect?"

"They're probably better educated than almost anyone in this place. That's for a start. My mother got a science degree before she started nursing and she's just about everything you can be as a nurse, she's got qualifications in *everything*. Medical and psychiat-ric, you name it, she's got it. When we were kids, Patrick and me, we never saw her, she was off all the time getting more certificates. Our gran and our aunties looked after us. My father may be just a GP but he's a surgeon too, he's a Fellow of the Royal College of Surgeons, he can do all sorts of surgery, not just take out an appen-dix. He could easily be as good as Chris's dad."

"So they were ambitious for you?"

"Are you kidding?" said Melanie. "You know what they call people like them? The Ebony Elite. The black crème de la crème. Our futures were all mapped out for us before we were ten. Patrick was to be the great consultant surgeon, a brain surgeon probably— yes, really, that's not funny to them. And it's all right for him, that's what he wants, he's heading that way. But me? I'm not all that bright, I'm just average. I like singing and dancing, so I did my degree in that, but my parents *hated* it because it's what successful black women do, you see. They were glad when I couldn't get a job, they wanted me to go back to college so long as I could live at home. Or I'd be permitted to get office work and study for business management in the evenings *from home*. They talk about careers and training and degrees and promotion *all the time*. And they're too civilized to actually say it, but they're both bursting with pride because they found out that the people who wouldn't live next door to us both left school at sixteen.

"If I got away they thought I'd get back with Euan or someone like him." She twisted her mouth into a bitter shape. "And maybe I will now. I can't have a baby if I haven't got a man, can I? I wouldn't let Chris go that far, though that's what he came for, whatever he says. He only fancies me because I'm black. Charm-ing, isn't it? I've had to fight him off."

"Your parents shouldn't be kept in ignorance any longer. Not for an hour. They've been through a lot. Nothing they've done could justify that. They've suffered intensely, your father has lost weight, he looks an old man, but they've carried on with their work . . ."

"They would."

"I'll tell them you're safe and then you must see them. Bring

the children with you, you haven't much choice." He thought of
the waste of police time and resources, the cost of it all, the misery
and pain and abuse, her brother's recall from his Asian journey, his
own shame and self-justification. But he relented. Mawkish and
sentimental it might be, but he was sorry for her. "When do the
Epsons get home?"

"She said nine or ten."

"We'll send a car for you at six." He got up, preparing to leave,
but remembered something. "One good turn deserves another. I'll
want to talk to you again. All right?"

"Yes."

"I suppose it was you talked to my officer on the phone when
we rang up to inquire about the dead girl?"

She nodded. "It gave me a fright. I thought that was *it*."

"You'd better see to that finger. Have you any plasters in the
house?"

"Thousands. That's top priority. Those kids are always wound-
ing themselves and each other."

Two reports from Pemberton were on his desk waiting for him.
The first told him that the Kingsmarkham shoe shop that sold
black cloth and rubber half-boots kept close records of their sales.
In the past six months four pairs had been sold. An assistant remembered selling one pair to John Ling. She knew him because he
was one of only two Chinese men in the town. Another pair had
gone to someone she described as a "bag lady," who had come into
the shop carrying two bulging carrier bags and looked as if she slept
on the street. The purchasers of the other pairs she couldn't remember. Wexford gave the second report a quick glance and said,
"I want Pemberton here too."

The phone in his hand, Burden said, "You've gone quite red in
the face."

"I know. It's excitement. Listen to this. Kimberley Pearson's
grandmother did die at the beginning of June but she didn't leave
any money, still less any property. She'd been living in one of

those council bungalows in Fontaine Road, Stowerton. Mrs. Pearson, who was her daughter-in-law, knows nothing about any money coming to Kimberley, not family money that is, there *is* no family money, they're all as poor as church mice.

"Clifton Court, where Kimberley moved, after Zack was put on remand, is a block of rented flats—or apartments, as Pemberton mysteriously calls them. And who do you think the company is who owns the freehold of the block?"

"Just cut the suspense and tell me."

"None other than Crescent Comestibles, or in other words, Wael Khoori, his brother, and our local council candidate, his wife."

Pemberton came in. "You can rent those flats with an option to buy," he said. "Forty pounds a week and they claim that when the transfer's made mortgage repayments will amount to the same. Of course, I haven't talked to Kimberley, I asked her mother not to say a word about any of this. Her mother says she went over to Clifton Court the minute Zack was banged up, put down a deposit, and fixed up to move in next day. She's bought a whole lot of furniture since then."

"Is she going to buy?"

"According to her mother, she's already got a solicitor doing the conveyancing. They were squatting in that cottage at Glebe End, by the way, only nobody cared. It's no use to the owner, is it? It needs fifty thousand spent on it before anyone would buy it."

"And Crescent Comestibles owns that block of flats?"

"So the managing agents told me. It's no secret. They're building all over Stowerton, wherever there's a bit of land going or an old house knocked down. It's the same process everywhere. The flats are cheap by today's standards. You pay rent while you're waiting for your mortgage to come through and the mortgage is a hundred percent with no deposit. Your mortgage repayments are the same as your rent."

"In accordance with Mrs. Khoori's own political standpoint," said Wexford slowly. "Help the disadvantaged to help themselves.

Don't give it to them but give them the chance to be independent. Not a bad philosophy, I suppose. I wonder if the day will come when someone starts a political party called Conservative Socialists."

The doctor was told between seeing patients at the Medical Center; his wife was called to the phone in Intensive Care. Wexford came to the house as Dr. Akande arrived home and the pain in his face was as bad as when he thought his daughter was dead. It would be worse if she were dead, immeasurably worse, but this was very bad. To learn that your child is prepared to put you through this, is indifferent as to whether you go through it or not, that is made bearable only when filtered through anger and Raymond Akande wasn't angry. He was humiliated.

"I thought she loved us."

"She acted impulsively, Dr. Akande." He hadn't said anything about Christopher Riding. Melanie could do that.

"She was in Stowerton all the time?"

"It looks like it."

"Her mother works just down the road. I was there making my rounds."

"The Epsons left her a car to do the shopping and take the child to school. I don't suppose she went out much on foot."

"I ought to be down on my knees thanking heaven for all its mercies, I ought to be in a seventh heaven—is that what you're thinking?"

"No," said Wexford, and boldly, "I know how you feel."

"Where did we go wrong?"

Before he could answer—if he had felt able or inclined to answer—Laurette Akande walked in. Wexford's first thought was that she looked ten years younger, his second that she was brimming with happiness, and his third that she was the angriest woman he had seen in years.

"Where is she?"

"A car will bring her at six. She'll have the children with her. It was either that or making some care arrangement and since the Epsons return tonight . . ."

"Where did we go wrong, Laurette?"

"Don't be silly. We didn't go wrong. Who is this woman, this Mrs. Epson, who leaves her children in the care of a totally unqualified person? I hope someone's going to prosecute her, she should be prosecuted. I am so angry I could kill her. Not Mrs. Epson, Melanie. I could kill her."

"Oh, don't, Letty," said the doctor. "We thought someone *had* killed her."

The car brought Melanie and the boisterous Epson boys a couple of minutes after six. She walked defiantly into the room, her head held high. Her parents, who were sitting down, remained seated but after a moment or two of silence her father got up and came toward her. He put out a hand and took hers. He pulled her a little toward him and kissed her cheek tentatively. Rather than responding, Melanie allowed this.

"I'll leave you," Wexford said. "I'll see you here tomorrow, Melanie, nine in the morning."

None of them took any notice of him. He got up and went toward the door. Laurette found a strong determined voice. She no longer seemed angry but only decisive.

"Well, Melanie, we'll hear your explanation and then we'll say no more about it. I think you'd better apply to do a degree in business studies. You might get in in October if you're quick about it. The University of the South does a good course and that would mean you can live at home. I'll send away for the forms for you tomorrow and meanwhile Dad might let you temp for the receptionist at the . . ."

The younger Epson boy began screaming. Wexford let himself out.

twenty-one

In the seclusion of the booth he made a cross on his voting paper. There were three names: Burton K. J., British Nationalist Party; Khoori A. D., Independent Conservative; and Sugden M., Liberal Democrat. Sheila said the Lib-Dem didn't stand a chance and the only way to keep out the BNP was by drumming up big support for Anouk Khoori.

But Wexford now had serious reasons against voting for Mrs. Khoori and he made his cross next to the name of Malcolm Sugden. Maybe it was a wasted vote but he couldn't help that. He folded his paper in half, turned round, and dropped it through the slot in the ballot box.

Since he had entered the Thomas Proctor Primary School some five minutes earlier, Anouk Khoori had arrived in a car driven by her husband, a gold-colored Rolls-Royce. Burton of the BNP was already there, standing on the asphalt forecourt, surrounded by ladies in silk dresses and straw hats, the former vanguard of the Conservatives, seduced away by the attractions of the far right. He was smoking a cigar, the fumes of which hung heavily and reached distantly, on this warm still morning. Mrs. Khoori stepped from the car like a royal personage. She was dressed like one, but of the younger set, in a very short white skirt, emerald-green silk shirt, white jacket. Her hair hung like a yellow veil from under her white hat brim. When she saw Wexford she put out both hands to him.

"I knew I should find you here!"

He marveled at the confidence that enables someone who is almost a stranger to speak in the tones of a lover.

"I knew *you* would be among the first to vote."

Her husband materialized behind her, smiled a big broad studied smile, and thrust his hand in Wexford's direction. The thrust was strong, like he imagined a boxer's might be, but the handshake was limp and it was as if his own hand held a wilted lily. He withdrew it and remarked that they had a fine day for the poll.

"So English," said Mrs. Khoori, "but that's what I love. Now I want you to promise me something, Reg."

"What would that be?" he said, and even in his own ears his voice sounded off-puttingly grave.

She was quite undeterred. "Now that County Councils are disappearing, this little authority of ours is going to expand and become very important. I am going to need an adviser on crime prevention, on public relations, on my approach to the *people* of this sleepy old town—right? You will be that adviser, won't you, Reg? You'll help me? You'll give me the support I'm going to need more than I've ever needed support all my life. What do you say?"

Wael Khoori was grinning all over his face, as well he might, but this was a genial empty smile directed at whoever passed. Wexford said, "You'll have to get in first, Mrs. Khoori."

"Anouk, *please*. But I am going to get in, I know it, and when I'm there you'll help me?"

It was absurd. He smiled but said nothing, avoiding the direct snub. The time was five to nine and Raymond Akande's morning surgery started at eight-thirty. Laurette would have left in time to start the day shift at eight. In the five minutes it took him to drive to Ollerton Avenue, Wexford thought of all those visits he had paid to this house, the doctor's misery, the boy's tears. He remembered taking those parents to the mortuary and Laurette's hysterical rage. There was nothing to be done about all that. He could hardly charge any more people with wasting police time as that itself was a waste of police time.

The chances were he would never come here again. This was his last visit. Even after yesterday, after identification and explanation, it was a shock to see the photographed face, the dead face, alive. She opened the door to him and for a moment he was silenced by the very fact of her, her existence.

"There's no one here but me," she said.

"Christopher would hardly be welcome, I suppose?"

"He's gone back home. I don't ever want to see him again. It was his sister that was my friend, it was Sophie, not him."

Wexford followed the girl into the living room whose walls had heard her parents ask if there was any hope of her being alive. She smiled at him, tentatively at first, then serenely.

"I'm feeling happy, I don't know why. It must be getting shut of the Epson kids."

"How much did they pay you?"

"A hundred. Half before they left and the other half last night."

Wexford showed her the photograph of the dead Sojourner.

"Have you ever seen her?"

"I don't think so."

This expression, of course, means no, but a not entirely unqualified no.

"Sure?"

"I've never seen her. Are you allowed to take photographs of dead people and show them around?"

"What alternative would you suggest?"

"Well, records kept of everyone with photos and fingerprints and DNA and whatever, a central computer with details of everyone in the country on it."

"Our job would be a lot easier if we kept records like that but we don't. Tell me what you did the day before you went to the Benefit Office and met Mrs. Epson."

"What do you mean, what I did?"

"How you spent the day. Your mother said you went for a run."

"I go for a run every day. Well, I couldn't when I had those kids to look after."

"All right. You went for a run—where?"

"My mother doesn't know everything, you know. I don't always go the same way. Sometimes I go up Harrow Avenue and along Winchester Drive and sometimes I take Marlborough Road."

"Christopher and Sophie Riding live in Winchester Drive."

"Do they? I've never been to their house. I've told you, I'd only seen him a couple of times before he followed me back to the Epsons'. I knew Sophie at college."

If she had been happy five minutes earlier, she now looked disproportionately distressed. He wondered what would become of her, if the bullying tactics of that domineering mother would drive her to seek out Euan Sinclair again. He eased the subject back to the route she had taken while out running.

"So which was it that day?"

Melanie seemed pleased to cross him. "I didn't go there at all that day. I went across the fields to Mynford. By the footpaths."

He was disappointed, though he hardly knew why. By asking these questions, whose significance he felt rather than knew, he had hoped to intuit something.

She fixed her eyes on him the way her father did. "I went nearly to Mynford New Hall. It gave me a bit of a shock, seeing the house. I didn't know I was so near it." Her gaze bored into him mesmerically. "That was the day I went to the Benefit Office. You are talking about that, aren't you?"

"It's the day before you went to the Benefit Office I want to know about." He tried to keep his patience. "The Monday."

"Oh, the Monday. I'll have to think. I went along the Pomfret Road on Saturday, and then on Sunday—it was the same Sunday and Monday, along Ashley Grove, up Harrow Avenue, along Winchester Drive, and into Marlborough Road. It's nice up there, nice air, and you can look down and see the river."

"While you were out on these runs you never saw this girl?"

He had the photograph out again and she looked at it again, but quite dispassionately this time.

"My mother said you got them to identify a corpse as me, only it wasn't me. Was it her?"

"Yes."

"Wow. Anyway, I never saw her. I hardly ever saw anyone on foot. People don't walk, do they? They go in cars. I bet you'd be suspicious, wouldn't you, if you saw someone walking up there? You'd stop them and ask what they were doing."

"It hasn't come to that yet," said Wexford. "You never saw her face at a window? Or saw her in a garden?"

"I've told you, I never saw her."

It was hard to remember Melanie Akande was twenty-two. Sojourner at seventeen, he was sure, would have seemed older. But Sojourner, of course, had suffered, had been through the mill. The Akandes had kept their daughter a child by treating her as an irresponsible person, fit only to be controlled and directed by others. It made him shudder to think of her having a baby in order to escape.

The house-to-house was over. Nothing had come out of it, so when he said that they were off to Ashley Grove, Burden wanted to know what was the point of that.

"We're going to pay a visit to an architect," he said to Burden when he had told him of the interview with Melanie. "Or perhaps an architect's wife before she goes out doing good works in the parish."

But this was not Cookie Dix's day for taking reading matter to the sick. She was at home with her husband, though it was neither of them that admitted Wexford and Burden to the house.

And what a house! The hall, which was circular and from which a white staircase arced up, bulging like the prow of a sailing ship, had a marble floor on which lemon trees in pots flowered and fruited simultaneously. The trees grew in the soil itself, of which beds had been created, ficus with rustling leaves and feather-leaved alders, pen-thin cypresses and silver willows with distorted trunks, all reaching up to the light from the glass dome high above them. The maid, black-haired, black-eyed, and sallow, kept them waiting under the trees while she went away to announce their presence. She was back within thirty seconds and led them through a pair of double doors—Wexford had to duck under a branch—through a kind of anteroom, stark black and white, and another pair of doors, into a yellow and white sun-flooded dining room where Cookie and Alexander Dix sat eating their breakfast.

In a reversal of the usual order of things, Cookie got to her feet while her husband remained seated. He had *The Times* in one hand and a piece of croissant in the other. In response to their good morning he said nothing but called out to the departing servant, "Margarita, bring some more coffee for our guests, will you?"

"We are rather late getting started this morning," said Cookie. If she had been questioned the day before by Pemberton or Archbold she said nothing about it. She was wearing a dark green satin garment, more like a dressing gown than anything else but not much like one, being extremely short and tied round the waist with a jeweled cummerbund. Her long black hair was fastened onto the top of her head, where it sprouted in fronds rather like the top of a frost-blackened carrot. "Do sit down." She waved a vague hand at the other eight chairs ranged round this glass-topped table with its verdigris-encrusted legs. "We were out on the toot last night—well, at a party. It was the small hours—the tiniest of hours—when we got home, wasn't it, darling?"

Dix turned the page and started reading Bernard Levin. Something made him laugh. His laughter was the sound sappy wood makes when burning, a crackling and spitting. He looked up, still smiling, watched Wexford sit down, then he watched Burden, and when they were in chairs opposite each other, said, "What can we do for you gentlemen?"

"Mr. and Mrs. Khoori are friends of yours, I believe?" Wexford said.

Cookie glanced at her husband. "We know them."

"You were at their garden party."

"So were you," said Cookie. "What about them, anyway?"

"At that party you said Mrs. Khoori had a maid who had recently left her and that she was the sister of your maid."

"Of Margarita, yes."

Wexford felt a pang of disappointment. Before he could say any more, Margarita came back with the coffee on a tray and two cups. It was impossible to imagine her and Sojourner being related, still less sisters. Cookie, who was very quick off the mark, said something to her in rapid fluent Spanish and the answer came back in that language.

"Margarita's sister went home to the Philippines in May," Cookie said. "She wasn't happy here. She didn't get on with the other two maids."

Having poured the coffee and held out the milk jug and sugar basin to each of them in turn, Margarita stood passively, her eyes downcast.

"They came over together?" Wexford asked and at Cookie's nod said, "On the six-months-stay allowance, or for twelve months because their employers were living here?"

"Twelve months. That's renewable—I mean, the Home Office—is it, darling? They'll—what will they do, Alexander?"

"She will apply to have her stay extended by successive periods of twelve months and after four years, if she wants to remain longer, she can apply to stay indefinitely."

"How did you and the Khooris come to have sisters working for you?"

"Anouk went to an agency and told me. There's this agency that recruits women in the Philippines." She said something in Spanish and Margarita nodded. "She can speak English quite well if you want to talk to her. And she can read it. When she and her sister came into this country they had to be interviewed by the entry clearance officer and they were given a leaflet explaining her rights as a—what is it, darling?"

"Domestic entering the United Kingdom under the Home Office Immigration Act 1971," said Dix without looking up from Levin.

Overnight Wexford had read it all up from Sheila's literature. He said to the waiting woman, "Was there anyone else working with your sister apart from . . . ?"

"Juana and Rosenda," said Margarita. "Those two not nice to Corazon. She cry for her children in Manila and they laugh."

"But no one else?"

"No one. I go now?"

"Yes, you can go, Margarita. Thank you."

Cookie sat down and helped herself to coffee from the new pot. "My head's a bit rough this morning." Wexford would never have guessed it. "Corazon has four children and an unemployed husband at home. That's why she came to work here, for money to send home. Margarita hasn't children and she isn't married. I think she came—well, to see the world, don't you, darling?"

Dix's laughter might have derived from her rather inane inquiry or from the article he was reading. He reached over and patted her hand with a scaly claw of the kind usually seen in the Natural History Museum. Cookie shrugged her green satin shoulders.

"She gets around a bit, has herself some fun. I think she's found a boyfriend, hasn't she, darling? We don't exactly keep her locked up like some do."

There was a pause. "Such as the Khooris," said Alexander Dix with devastating timing.

Burden set his coffee cup back in its saucer. "Mr. and Mrs. Khoori keep their servants locked up?"

"Darling Alexander does exaggerate, but yes, you could call them rather restrictive. I mean, if you live at Mynford Old What-sit, you can't drive and there's no one to drive you—*ever*—and you've got the whole of that huge house to keep spick and span—what on earth do those words mean, I wonder, 'spick' and 'span'?—never mind, we all get the sense of it, if you live like that, what can you do if you *are* let out, but walk across the fields into the outermost reaches of Kingsmarkham?"

Involuntarily Burden glanced at Wexford and Wexford glanced at him. Their eyes met for an instant. "They've had no other servants?"

"Not so far as I know," Cookie said, wavering.

"Margarita would know," said Dix, "and she says not."

"But Margarita never actually went there, darling." Cookie pursed her lips and gave a silent whistle. "Are you looking for someone shut up in the house? A sort of madwoman in the attic?"

"Not quite that," said Wexford and he said it sadly.

Dix must have picked up the note in his voice, for he said in a hospitable way, "Is there anything else we can get you?" He surveyed the table and found it wanting. "A biscuit? Some fruit?"

"No, thank you."

"In that case, perhaps you'll excuse me. I have work to do." Dix got up, a very small diplodocus on its hind legs. He made a small bow to each of them, then to his wife. He would perhaps have clicked heels had he not been wearing sandals. "Gentlemen," he said, and, "Cornelia," thus answering one of Wexford's unspoken questions.

Cookie said confidingly when he was out of earshot, "Darling Alexander is so excited, he's starting a new business. He says we're about to see the dawn of a new Renaissance in building in this country. He's found this marvelous young man who's going into partnership with him. He advertised and this brilliant person answered just out of the blue like that." She smiled happily. "Well, I do hope I've been of help." Wexford marveled at her disconcerting habit of seeming to read his thoughts. "You won't find Anouk at home today, you know. She'll be riding about on a float, *exhorting* the populace to vote for her."

From the front drive they looked back at the house, an intricate arrangement of glass panels, black marble panels, and sheets of what looked like wafer-thin alabaster.

"You can't see in," said Burden, "you can only see out. Don't you think that's claustrophobic?"

"It would be if it was the other way about."

Burden got into the driving seat. "That woman, Margarita I mean, she seemed happy in her work."

"Sure. There's no objection to people employing servants if

they treat them properly and pay them what they're worth. The laborer is worthy of his hire. And the Act's all right, Mike, as far as it goes. In fact, on the surface it looks very good, it looks as if it deals with all contingencies. But it's open to terrible abuses. Domestic workers coming into the country aren't given immigration status independent of the household they work for. *They may not leave and they may not take up any other form of work.* That's what we're looking for, something of that sort."

Instead of Anouk Khoori, it was the BNP's float that passed them as they came back into the High Street. Ken Burton, the candidate, unself-conscious in black jeans and a black shirt—was its significance largely lost on observers?—rode standing up where the passenger seat should have been, blasting out his manifesto through a megaphone. He might be of the *British* Nationalists but, with some subtlety, it was England for the *English* that he was promoting in this sweet warm corner of Sussex.

Posters plastered over the back of the van exhorted the electorate not only to vote for Burton but also to join the march of the unemployed that was scheduled to take place from Stowerton to Kingsmarkham on the following day.

"Did you know about that?" Burden asked.

"I've heard rumors. The uniformed branch have it all sewn up."

"You mean they're expecting trouble? Here? Here?"

"In this green and pleasant land? Well, Mike, there *are* a lot of people out of work. It's much higher than the national average in Stowerton, something like twelve percent. And tempers do run high." He paused. "It's time to pay a visit to Mynford New Hall, I think."

"She won't be there, sir. She's out drumming up defaulters."

"So much the better," said Wexford.

"You mean we talk to the servants?"

"It's not a servant we're looking for, Mike," Wexford said. "We're looking for a slave."

twenty-two

This was the long way round, by the road that took in Pomfret and Cheriton. You could walk it across the fields from Kingsmarkham in forty minutes or run it in twenty-five, it was only about two miles, but seven this way. Burden, who was driving, had never seen Mynford New Hall before. He asked if it was as old as it looked but, on hearing building had barely been completed at the time of the garden party, lost interest.

Wexford had expected election posters, even though Mynford was outside the ward for which Mrs. Khoori was standing. But there was nothing on the gateposts and nothing in the windows of the mock-Georgian house. Someone had planted full-grown, fully blooming geraniums in the beds that had been bare a fortnight ago. A bellpull had been added since his first visit and a pair of the biggest and most elaborate carriage lamps he had ever seen.

But he doubted if the bellpull was connected, either that or there really was no one at home. It was Burden who looked up and saw the face looking down at them, a pale oval face and head whose black hair was invisible in the blackness behind it. Wexford, who had rung that bell four times, called out, "Come down and let us in, please."

Obedience was not prompt. Juana or Rosenda continued to stare impassively for some moments. Then she gave a little nod, a bob of the head, and disappeared. And when the door was finally opened it was not she who opened it but a woman with brown skin and Asian features. Wexford had not exactly expected a uniform, but he was surprised by the pink velvet tracksuit.

It was very cold in the house, with the same feel that you get when entering the chilled food area in a supermarket. Perhaps they had the same air-conditioning system as that installed in the perishable food departments of Crescent Stores. He and Burden produced their warrant cards. The woman looked at them with interest, apparently deriving some amusement from a comparison between the photographs and the living men.

"You got old since this one," she said to Wexford with a scream of laughter.

"What's your name, please?"

The laughter was switched off and she looked at him as if he had said something very impertinent.

"Why you want to know?"

"Just give us your name, please. Are you Juana or Rosenda?"

The change from affront to sullenness was rapid. "Rosenda Lopez. That one Juana."

The woman whose face had stared down at them had come silently into the hall. Like Rosenda she wore white trainers but her tracksuit was blue. Her accent was the same as Rosenda's but her English was better. She was younger and might almost have given justification to Dix's *Mikado* parody that the Khooris' maids were barely out of their teens.

"Mr. and Mrs. Khoori are not at home." Her next words sounded like a phone answering machine. "Please leave a message if you would like to."

"Juana what?" said Burden.

"Gonzalez. Now you go. Thank you."

"Ms. Lopez," said Wexford, "Ms. Gonzalez, you have a choice. You may either talk to us here and now or else come with us back to Kingsmarkham to the police station. Do you understand what I'm saying?"

It was necessary to repeat this several times, for him to repeat it and for Burden to put it into slightly different words, before there was any sort of response. Both women were mistresses of the art of silent insolence. But when Juana suddenly said something in what he took for Tagalog and both broke into giggles, Wexford thought he could understand the misery of Margarita's sister Corazon who had been laughed at for missing her children.

Juana repeated the incomprehensible words, then apparently translated them. "No problem."

"Okay. All right," said Rosenda. "You sit down now."

There seemed no need to penetrate farther into the house. The hall was a vast chamber, pillared, arched, alcoved, the walls paneled and with recessed columns, very much the kind of room guests must have been welcomed into at a Pemberley or a Northanger Abbey. Only this was new, all new, barely finished. And even in the early nineteenth century, even in winter, no great house would have been as cold inside as this one. He sat down on a pale blue chair with spindly gold legs but Burden remained standing as did the two women, side by side, enjoying themselves.

"Did you work for Mr. and Mrs. Khoori when they were in the Dower House?"

Burden had to take them to a window and point out the woods in the valley, the invisible roofs. Nods encouraged him.

"And again, of course, when they came here in June?" More nods. He remembered what Cookie Dix had said about shutting people up. "Do you go out much?"

"Go out?"

"Into town. Go and see friends. Meet people. Go to the cinema. Do you go out?"

From the vertical, their heads moved horizontally. Juana said, "Don't drive car. Mrs. Khoori go shopping and we don't want cinema, have TV."

"Was Corazon with you at the Dower House?"

His very anglicized pronunciation of the name had them in giggles again and the way he said it was repeated by each of them. Then, "She was cook," said Juana.

Memory returned. The Medical Center and a woman who broke the no smoking rule. "She had to have the doctor? She was ill?"

"Always ill she was. Homesick. She went home."

"And that left the two of you," Wexford said. "But there was another servant, at the same time as Corazon or perhaps after?"

It was hard to tell if they were blank or wary. He sought political correctness, saying carefully, "A young girl, seventeen or eighteen, from Africa."

Almost shivering from the cold, Burden showed them the photograph. The effect was to stimulate more laughter. But before Wexford could decide whether they were laughing from race prejudice, simple wonder that anyone could suspect them of an ability to identify this girl, or from a kind of pleasurable horror—Sojourner's face seemed to look more deeply dead each time he produced the photograph—the front door opened and Anouk Khoori came in, immediately followed by her husband, Jeremy Lang, and Ingrid Pamber.

R eg," she said, not a bit discomposed, "how lovely! I had a feeling I might find you here." She held out both hands to him, one of them holding a cigarette. "But why didn't you let me know you were coming?"

Wael Khoori said nothing. His was invariably the manner of the highly successful millionaire businessman who puts on a genial, smiling, silent front, while seeming to be quite elsewhere, preoccupied by distant things, high finance, perhaps the Hang Seng index. He smiled, he was patient. He stood waiting.

"We have come home for lunch," said Mrs. Khoori. "Electioneering is very hard work, I can tell you, and I'm famished. Isn't it lovely and cool in here? Of course you must stay to lunch, Reg, and you too, Mr. —?" She addressed Rosenda in exactly the same friendly, rather breathless way, "I do hope you can put on something delicious and *quick,* please, as I have to get back to the *fray.*"

Khoori spoke. He ignored everything his wife had said. She

might not have said a word. "I'm quite aware of what you're here for."

"Really, sir?" said Wexford. "We'll talk about it then, shall we?"

"Yes, of course, after lunch," said Anouk. "Come along, into the dining room, everyone, and quickly because Ingrid has to go back to work."

Again she was ignored. Khoori simply stood his ground while she swept up Jeremy and Ingrid, an arm round each of them, and propelled them across the hall. Ingrid, pinched and pale in her sleeveless dress, nevertheless turned to give him one of her flirtatious looks, arch, tantalizing. But she was changed, the blue glance had lost its power. Her eyes had lost their color and for a moment he wondered if he had imagined that brilliant azure, but only for a moment, for Khoori was saying, "Come with me. In here."

It was a library but a quick glance round showed him it was not of the kind one would use for reference or wish to spend much time in. The Khooris had perhaps said to a firm of interior decorators, Put shelves all over the walls and fill them with suitable books, old ones with handsome bindings. So *The Natural History of the Pyrénées* in seven volumes had been supplied and Hakluyt's *Voyages* and Mommsen on Rome and Motley on the Dutch Republic. Khoori sat down at a reproduction desk. Its green leather inlay had been made to look as if quill pens on parchment had been scratching at it for centuries.

"You don't seem surprised to see us, Mr. Khoori," said Wexford.

"No, I'm not, Mr. Reg. Annoyed but not surprised."

Wexford looked at him. This was very different from Bruce Snow's assumption that they were traffic police. "What do you suppose this is about?"

"I suppose, I *know*, that those women or one of them have not applied to the Home Office for an extension of their stay. This, despite their extreme desire to stay and my having had the applications typed for them. And their knowledge that they can only stay under the provisions of the Immigration Act of 1971. All they have to do is sign the letter and take it to the post. I know because this is what happened last time, when they first came to us and had been granted an initial stay of six months. You have to keep a constant eye on these people and I haven't the time to be as vigilant as I should be. So, very well, that's that. What do we do to put matters right?"

A little subterfuge would do no harm, Wexford thought. "Simply reapply, Mr. Khoori. A mistake was made but made in good faith, apparently."

"So I reapply and this time make sure the application gets to its destination?"

"Right," said Burden, transforming himself into an Immigration official. He began inventing with a facility Wexford could only admire. "Now, this woman Corazon, we understand she wanted to change her employment, which is of course illegal. Under the provisions of the Act she's only permitted to work for the employer whose name is on the stamp in her passport."

"There was some story about the other servants ill-treating her—well, being unkind to her. She was always in tears." Khoori shrugged. "It wasn't very pleasant for myself and my wife."

"So, understanding she wasn't permitted to work elsewhere, she went home? When would that have been?"

Khoori put up one hand and smoothed his casque of white hair. It fitted him like a wig but it plainly was not a wig. The hand was long, brown, exquisitely kept. He frowned a little while he thought. "About a month ago, maybe less."

And it was exactly four weeks to the day since Wexford had first encountered Anouk Khoori at the Medical Center. She still had a cook then, a servant who had perhaps fallen ill through homesickness and the cruelty of others.

"Would you mind telling me, sir," Wexford said, "where the money came from for her return flight?"

"I paid, Mr. Reg. I paid."

"Very generous of you. Just one other thing. I'd like you to set me right on this question. Would you say it was true that in the Gulf States the labor laws don't recognize domestics as workers but treat them as family members?"

Suspicion that this might be a trap flicked in Khoori's eyes. "I'm not a lawyer."

"But you're a Kuwaiti national, aren't you? You must be aware if this is so or not, if it is in fact taken for granted."

"Broadly speaking, I suppose it's so, yes."

"So that families from the Gulf States do bring in servants *as family members or friends*, having no status as domestics and therefore no protection from abuse? And although it's clear they are coming in not on holiday but to work they are allowed to stay as visitors."

"Possibly. I've no experience of it."

"But you know it happens? And that it happens because refusing entry to domestics either as workers tied to one employer and restricted to twelve-month stays, or as family members or friends and ostensible visitors, might discourage wealthy investors like yourself from coming here at all?"

Khoori gave a loud braying laugh. "I'm damned if I'd be here if I had to wash my own dishes."

"But you have never personally brought anyone in under those special circumstances?"

"No, Mr. Reg, I have not. You can ask my wife. Come to that, you can ask Juana and Rosenda."

He led them into a vast cold dining room with ten windows down one wall and a painted ceiling. Some ten feet under the depicted cherubs, cornucopias, and lovers' knots, Anouk, Jeremy, and Ingrid sat at a mahogany table big enough for twenty-four, eating smoked salmon and drinking champagne.

"We are celebrating my victory in advance, Reg," said Anouk. "Do you think that a very foolhardy thing to do?"

Her husband whispered something to her. It evoked a tinkle of laughter, not however a happy sound. The repulsion she held for Wexford came back and he turned instinctively to look at Ingrid, beautiful fresh young Ingrid whose hair was still crisp and smooth and skin glowing with health but whose eyes had become as dull as stones. As he looked she took a pair of glasses from her bag and perched them on her nose.

If she had changed, it was nothing to the change that had come over Anouk Khoori. Under the makeup she had gone bright red and her features seemed to knot up with tension. "It's that girl who was murdered, isn't it? That black girl? We've never seen her." Her carefully modulated voice grew shrill. "We know nothing about her. We've never had anyone working for us here but Juana and Rosenda and that Corazon who left and went home. I think it's awful this happening today. I will not have anything like this happening to spoil my chances!"

As her voice rose to a high note of panic, Juana and Rosenda both came into the room, the former with a carafe of water on a tray, the latter carrying a fresh plate of brown bread and butter. Their employer's vexation, the sudden angry distress that Wexford at any rate had never witnessed before, caused them a mirth they could barely conceal. Juana had to hold her hand tightly over her mouth while Rosenda's lips twitched as she stood staring.

Wexford had scarcely anticipated her inspired guesswork. Or was it less guesswork than genuine guilt?

"You tell them," Anouk shouted, "you tell them, you two. We never had anyone here like that, did we? You love it here, don't you? No one ever hurt you, you tell them."

Juana's laughter broke free. She was beyond controlling it. "He crazy," she said, gasping. "We never see no one like that, do we, Rosa?"

"No, we never see no one, no way."

"No way we don't. Here your bread and butter. You want more lemon?"

"All right," Wexford said. "Thank you. That's all."

Evidently remembering that he had already voted, Anouk shouted at him, "You can get out of my house! Now! Both of you, get out!"

With a little gasp, Ingrid had got up, clutching her napkin. "I shall have to go. I must get back to the office."

Rosenda was holding the dining room door open, murmuring, "Come on, come on, you got to go now."

"You'll give me a lift, won't you?" Ingrid said to Wexford.

It was Burden who answered. "I'm afraid not."

"Oh, but, surely . . ."

"We're not a taxi service."

Behind them in the dining room Anouk had given way to a crisis of nerves, uttering little staccato cries. Khoori said to no one in particular that it might help to bring the brandy. Wexford and Burden made their way across that desert of a hall to the front door, escorted by both giggling women. The heat outside met them in a wave, a positive sensuous pleasure. They were barely in the car when Ingrid came out followed by Khoori, who handed her into the car they had arrived in.

"I'll bet that's the first time a Rolls like that has ever brought anyone to the Benefit Office," said Burden, starting the engine. "Looks a bit different without her contact lenses, doesn't she?"

"You mean that blue was *lenses?*"

"What else? I suppose she got allergic and had to leave them off."

Perhaps it was from the scent of his aftershave, but Gladys Prior knew it was Burden before he spoke. She even spelled his name out before he spoke, persisting with the joke that afforded her so much amusement. Wexford's inquiry brought fresh gales of laughter.

"Is he in? Bless you, he hasn't set foot outside in four years."

Percy Hammond was at his Mizpah, looking out across his Plain of Syria. Without turning round, identifying them by their voices and their footsteps, he asked, "When are you going to catch him, then?"

Wexford said, earning a surprised and perhaps admonitory

glance from Burden, "Tomorrow, I should think, Mr. Hammond. Yes, we'll catch—er, them, tomorrow."

"Who's going to have that flat opposite?" said Mrs. Prior unexpectedly.

"What, Annette Bystock's flat?"

"That's the one. Who's going to have it?"

"I've no idea," said Burden. "It'll probably go to the next of kin. Now, Mr. Hammond, we'd like a little more help from you . . ."

"If you're going to catch him tomorrow, eh?"

Burden's expression showed all too plainly what he thought of Wexford's wild boast. "What we want you to do, sir, is go back over what you saw from this window on July the eighth."

"And, more important," said Wexford, "what you saw on July the seventh."

It would have been unprecedented, he would never have done it, not actually done it, but Burden *nearly* corrected Wexford. It was on the tip of his tongue to murmur, You don't mean that, not the seventh, he saw no one on the seventh but that girl with the blue lenses and Edwina Harris and a man with a spaniel. It was all in the report. Instead of saying it, he coughed, he cleared his throat just a little. Wexford took no notice.

"On the Thursday morning, very early, you saw this young chap who looked a bit like Mr. Burden here come out of the house with a big box in his arms."

Percy Hammond nodded vigorously. "About four-thirty it was, A.M."

"Right. Now on the previous night, the Wednesday night, you went to bed and to sleep but you woke up after a while and got up . . ."

"To spend a penny," said Gladys Prior.

"And naturally you looked out of your window—and you saw someone come out of Ladyhall Court? You saw a young man come out?"

The old wrinkled face was distorted even more by the effort of remembering. He clenched his hands.

"Did I say that?"

"You said it, Mr. Hammond, and then you thought you'd made a mistake because you definitely saw him in the morning and you couldn't have seen him twice."

"But I did see him twice . . ." Percy Hammond said, his voice dropping to a whisper. "I *did*."

Wexford took it gently, moving with care. "You saw him twice? In the morning—and the night before?"

"That's right. I knew I did, whatever they said. I saw him twice. And the first time, he saw *me*."

"How do you know?"

"He wasn't carrying a box that first time, he wasn't carrying anything. He came to the gate and he looked up and looked straight at me."

It was the last visit he would pay to Oni Johnson. She had nothing more to tell him. By her openness she had saved herself and next day she would leave Intensive Care for a room to be shared with three other women in Rufford Ward.

Laurette Akande came out to meet him. She looked at him and spoke as if the past month had never been. She had never lost a daughter and he hadn't found that daughter, there had been no anguish, no suffering, and no joyful reunion. He might have been a sympathetic stranger. Her manner was light, her voice brisk.

"I wish someone could get that boy of hers to have a wash. His clothes and his hair smell, not to mention the rest of him."

"He'll be gone when his mother goes," said Wexford.

"It can't be soon enough for me."

Oni looked pretty, sitting up in bed wearing a pink satin quilted bed jacket, much too hot for the temperature, the obvious gift of Mhonum Ling. Mhonum was on one side of the bed, Raffy on the other. It was true that he smelled unpleasant, his curious hamburger and tobacco odor battling, and winning the battle, against his aunt's Giorgio eau de toilette.

"When you going to catch him then?" said Oni.

He was fated, it seemed, to be that afternoon the butt of everyone's laughter. Oni laughed and then Mhonum laughed and Raffi
joined in with a sheepish snigger.

"Tomorrow."

"Are you kidding?" said Mhonum.

"I hope not."

I t was developing into a pattern. Sylvia drove the children and
Neil into Kingsmarkham, Neil went to his job club, promising
to meet them later, and Sylvia homed on her parents. Or, more
often, her mother. Wexford never asked how long she had been
there by the time he got home, he didn't want to know, though
later Dora sometimes told him, always qualifying these grumbles
with a prefatory, I really shouldn't talk like this about my own
child . . .

"I don't suppose you've any objection," Sylvia said when he
walked in, "if I take part in the Unemployed March tomorrow?"

He was surprised to be asked—and just a little touched. "It
won't be the kind of event in which arrests are made. There'll be
no setting fire to property and no overturning of cars."

"I thought I ought to ask you," she said in a tone that implied
long-suffering dutifulness.

"Do as you like as long as you don't frighten the horses."

"Will there be *horses*, Granddad?"

Wexford laughed. He thought he was due for a spot of laughter
whose meaning eluded the others. The doorbell rang suddenly. No
one ever came to their door and rang it in the Colonel Bogey
mode: da-da-di-di-di-pom-POM. Such jauntiness was wholly unexpected. Wexford went to answer it. His son-in-law was on the
doorstep, grinning widely, insisting on shaking hands with him.

"Can I have a drink? I need one."

"Of course."

"Whisky, please. I've had a wonderful afternoon."

"I can see that."

Neil took a swig of his drink. "I've got a job. And in my own

line. I'm going into partnership with this old architect, terribly distinguished man, and he's funding it, I'm . . ."

"I do think," said Sylvia, "that it's outrageous you coming out
with that in front of everyone instead of telling me first."

Her father was inclined to agree but he said nothing. He had a
drink too. "Alexander Dix," he said, when the whisky struck
home.

Neil had taken his younger son on his knee. "That's right. The
one offer I answered that was taken up. How did you know?"

"I doubt if there's more than one rich old distinguished architect in Kingsmarkham."

"We're starting with a rather ambitious plan for the Castlegate
site. A shopping mall, if that isn't to degrade what it will ulti-
mately be. A thing of beauty, an asset to the town center, crystal
and gold, with a Crescent supermarket as the pivot of the whole
thing." He caught his father-in-law's eye and misinterpreted the
gleam he saw there. "Oh, without the moons and minarets, don't
worry. It's part of this new government policy to restore commerce
to town centers." He said laconically to Sylvia, "You can stop signing on as from Tuesday."

"Thanks very much. That's for me to decide, I think."

"You might say you're pleased."

"I don't specially want to be part of the kind of society where
the woman is indoors and the man comes home and says he's got a
lucrative new job, so she says, Oh goody, can I have a pearl neck-
lace and a fur coat now?"

"You shouldn't wear fur," said Ben.

"I don't, I can't afford it, and never will be able to."

"*Walang problema,*" said Wexford in Tagalog.

Robin, in his headset, looked up at him pityingly from the
screen in his hand. "I don't do that anymore, Granddad," he said.
"I'm into first day covers with celebrity autographs now. Do you
think you could get me Anouk Khoori's?"

twenty-three

The march of the unemployed was due to begin at eleven in the morning. The marchers were asked to assemble in Stowerton marketplace with their banners and the column would form up from the steps of the old corn exchange. The day was going to be even hotter, but with rain later and the chance of thunder. The local news, which Wexford watched intermittently while getting dressed, told him all this, but it was Dora, who had got it from Sylvia, who supplied the details of the route. The march would proceed through Stowerton to the roundabout, pass along the bleak streets of the industrial estate, rejoin the Kingsmarkham Road, and enter the town by the Kingsbrook Bridge. Its final destination was Kingsmarkham Town Hall.

He had to go back to the news for results in the council election. Voting, however, had been so close between the Liberal Democrat and the Independent Conservative that a recount was taking place. Ken Burton was out, having secured a mere fifty-eight votes. Wexford wondered whether to phone Sheila and tell her the news, but decided against it. She probably had her own means of knowing, anyway.

"Guess what," said Dora. "*We're* invited to Sylvia's for Sunday lunch."

But Wexford only said obscurely, "I hope it's all right," and added, "Neil's job, I mean."

The day was still and sultry, heat hanging under a sky of veiled blue. It was like the beginning of the month when he had been reading by the open French windows and Dr. Akande had phoned with the first mention of Melanie. The air this morning had a scalding feel, and Burden said he'd known cooler steam come out of a kettle. Inside the car the air-conditioning was as efficient as that at Mynford New Hall and Wexford told Donaldson to turn it off and open a window.

"We're very quick to dismiss old people's statements of fact, aren't we?" Wexford said. "If there's the slightest doubt we immediately assume they're senile or their memories are useless or even that they're no longer quite sane. Whereas with a younger person we'd at least listen and even encourage while they sort things out.

"Percy Hammond said he went to bed on that Wednesday evening and to sleep but he woke up, got up, and 'put the light on for a minute.' He turned it off 'because it was so bright.' I think we all know that feeling. He looked out of the window and saw 'this young chap come out with a box in his arms. Or was that later?' he said.

"We didn't ask him to think about it, we didn't say 'think carefully, try to remember the times,' Karen just confirmed that it must have been later, this was in the morning, he saw the 'young chap' in the morning. I was just as much to blame, I let it go too. But, Mike, the fact was that the old man *saw Zack Nelson twice*.''

Burden looked at him. "What d'you mean?"

"He saw him at eleven-thirty or thereabouts on Wednesday and he saw him *again* at four-thirty the following morning. There was no real doubt in his mind about that. The only doubt was whether Zack was carrying the 'box' at night or in the morning. And that first time, on the Wednesday night, Zack saw *him*. He saw a face looking at him from the window. D'you see what that means?"

"I think so," Burden said slowly. "Annette died after ten P.M. on the Wednesday and before one A.M. on the Thursday. If Percy Hammond saw him for the first time at . . . But that means Zack killed Annette."

"Yes, of course. The doors were open. Zack went in at, say, eleven-thirty, and found Annette asleep in bed. She was weak, she was ill, she was probably running a temperature. He looked around for something with which to do the deed. Perhaps he had something with him, a scarf, a cord. But the lamp lead was better. He pulled it out of the lamp, strangled Annette—who was too feeble to put up much of a fight—took nothing, and left. There's not a light on anywhere but a street lamp, there's no one to see him, he's in the clear—until he looks across the road and sees, pressed against the glass, old Percy Hammond's face staring out at him."

"But then surely, the last thing he'd do would be to go back five hours later?"

"Are you sure of that?"

"The last thing he'd want was to draw attention to himself."

"No, that's exactly what he did want. He wanted to draw attention to himself or someone else wanted him to. This is what I think happened. It's guesswork but it's the only possible answer. Zack was scared stiff. The possessor of what is, after all, putting it brutally, quite a frightening face had seen him, had stared long and hard at him. He panics, he needs advice. He realizes fully the enormity of what has happened.

"Who can advise him? Obviously, only one person, the man or woman who has put him up to this, the instigator whose paid hit man he is. It's the middle of the night but never mind that. He's doubtless been told never to contact this person, but never mind that either. He makes his way down the road to the corner shop, outside which is a phone box. He makes his call and the advice comes back from a far clever perpetrator than Zack could ever be: Go back, steal something, make sure you're seen. Make sure you're seen a second time."

"But why? I don't get it."

"He, whoever he is, must have said, They will know the time she died. If you go back at four or later they *will know she must have been dead before you got there*. You will be in the clear as far as murder goes. Of course you'll go to prison for the theft but not for long and it's worth it, isn't it? It was an elderly person saw you, you say?

They'll take it for granted an elderly person was confused about the time."

"We did," Burden said. "We did take it for granted."

"We all do it. We all patronize the old, and worse. We treat them as if they were small children. And we'll be on the receiving end of that one day, Mike. Unless the world changes."

The place was strangely like the interior of the cottage at Glebe End. Kimberley had transported all her possessions in cardboard boxes and plastic carriers and in these containers they remained. They were still to her what cupboards and drawers are to other people. But she had bought furniture: a huge pneumatic three-piece suite of purple and gray tapestry with a gold thread running through it and trimmed with gold braid and gold swags, a crimson table inlaid with gilt, a television set in a white and gold cabinet. There was no carpet, there were no curtains. Clint, who had learned to walk since Burden had last seen him, staggered about the room, wiping the chocolate biscuit he had sucked on any tapestry surface he came into contact with. Kimberley was dressed in black leggings, stiletto-heeled white shoes, and a strapless red bustier. She gave Burden a belligerent look and said she didn't know what he meant.

"Where did it all come from, Kimberley? All this? Three weeks ago you were wondering what'd become of you if you lost that cottage."

She maintained her sullen glare, but taking her eyes from his face, gazing down at her own feet, her toes turned in.

"It came from Zack, didn't it? It didn't come from your grandmother."

She said to her feet, "My nan did die."

"Sure she did but she didn't leave you anything, she'd nothing to leave. What was it, paid to Zack in cash, was it? Or did he open a bank account for you and him and have it paid in there?"

"I don't know nothing about this, you know. It don't mean nothing to me."

"Kimberley," said Wexford. "He murdered Annette Bystock. He didn't just steal her TV and her VCR. He murdered her."

"He never!" She looked up and sideways, her shoulder hunched, as if trying to protect her face from a coming onslaught. "He nicked her things, that's all he done." The child, back at his favorite occupation of removing articles from one cardboard box and putting them into another, now fished out an unopened packet of teabags and trotted over to his mother with his find in his hands. She snatched him up and set him on her lap. It was as if she made him into a shield for herself. "He told me, he just nicked her telly and stuff. If he's got money in the bank, why shouldn't he have? Okay, it was his family it come from, not mine. He said to say my nan, on account of she died. But it was his family it come from. His dad's got money. Don't tear that open, Clint, you'll have the tea all out."

The child took no notice. He had torn the cardboard and found the teabags. He was immensely content. Kimberley held him tightly, her arm clamped round his waist. Her voice was fierce: "He never done no murder. Not Zack. He never would."

She was telling the truth, Wexford thought, insofar as she knew it. He was almost sure she didn't know. "Zack told you there'd be money in the bank, did he, before he went away?"

She nodded vigorously. "In my bank account. He put it in there for me."

Clint had a teabag gripped in both hands, his face growing red with the effort of tugging at it.

"Why this flat, Kimberley?" said Burden.

"It's nice, in't it? I liked it, I fancied it, in't that enough for you?"

"Wasn't it because you didn't have to make any effort? It belongs to Crescent Comestibles, doesn't it, and that's Mr. Khoori? You didn't have to do a thing. Mr. Khoori put you in here and gave you the money to get what you wanted."

It was plain to Wexford that she had no idea what Burden meant. She was no actress. She was simply ignorant and these

names signified nothing to her. The child on her lap had succeeded in his endeavor, had split open the teabag and was scattering tea over her leggings and the floor. But she was oblivious to it.
She stared in bewilderment and said at last, "You what?"

Wexford saw no point in explaining. "What did happen,
Kimberley?"

She brushed the blackish grains off her legs and gave Clint a
halfhearted shake. "I was walking down the High Street here with
him in the buggy and I saw that written up about flats and mortgages and whatever and I thought why not, there's all that money
Zack says is mine now, and I went in and saw this feller and said I
got the money, I could give him the cash or a check and when
could I move in. And that's what I done, moved in. And I don't
know nothing about any Mr. Coo—what you said, I've never
heard of him."

Of course, she must know that the source of this unexpected
accession of cash was suspect. Legitimately earned money, no
doubt many thousand pounds, does not find its way miraculously
into the bank accounts of such as Zack Nelson. Families such as
the Nelsons have no private fortunes, set up no trusts, to assist
their humbler scions. She knew that as well as they did. But Wexford was aware she would never come out with it, she would never
say she knew this gain must be ill-gotten but her desire for better
accommodation was so great that she conveniently overlooked
that fact. She would only come up with wilder and wilder explana-
tions and excuses.

"The main thing," he said to Burden when they were outside
in Stowerton High Street, "is that she doesn't know where it came
from. Zack Nelson, in his wisdom, never told her. Or, rather, he
told her a lie that he knew she would know was a lie but would
accept. He meant her to be safe and she is safe. We needn't have
made detours to avoid the High Street."

"*He* knows, though."

Wexford shrugged. "And do you think he'll say? At this stage?
Okay, we can go along to the remand center and ask him and he'll

trot out all that stuff about Percy Hammond being senile and Annette being dead long before he ever went into Ladyhall Court. And that's what we can't prove, Mike. We'll never prove Percy Hammond saw Zack twice. If Zack keeps his mouth shut now, and he will, the worst that can happen to him is he'll go down for six months for burglary."

They were walking along the street, just walking and quite aimlessly, the heat making for slow idle steps, yet they were at the Market Cross almost before they knew it. Banks are always together in whatever part of a town is given over to them and passing first the Midland, then the NatWest, made Burden say, "This bank account Zack opened. He must have done that before killing Annette. As soon as he agreed to do it, on the Tuesday or the Wednesday at the latest. We can find out whose big check or banker's draft or whatever was paid into that a couple of days later."

"Can we, Mike?" Wexford said it almost wistfully. "On what grounds are we going to take a look at a bank account in Kimberley Pearson's name? She hasn't done anything. She hasn't even been charged with anything. She doesn't know where the money came from, but she's probably convinced herself by now that it came from Zack's rich old granddad. She's innocent in the eyes of the law and no bank is going to let us breach her right to privacy."

"It beats me why Zack Nelson drew attention to himself by having Bob Mole sell that radio in full public view like that, in the market that we make a point of keeping our eye on."

Wexford laughed. "Just for that, Mike. For that reason. It was the same as when he went into Annette's flat, the same drawing attention to himself. That's what he wanted to do, to get it over, get himself charged with theft and banged up, out of harm's way. He even chose the most easily identified item among the stolen goods, that radio with the red stain on it."

They stopped in the square and were about to turn round and retrace their steps, as people do who have been walking aimlessly, when Wexford's attention was caught by the crowd that had gath-

ered outside the corn exchange. It was a Victorian building, its pillared entrance approached by a flight of steps. These steps some of
the people who were waiting treated like seats in an amphitheater,
sitting or lounging on them. Up by the entrance half a dozen
seemed to be working on a banner, which suddenly unfurled and
stretched out read GIVE US THE RIGHT TO WORK.

"It's the start of the unemployed march," said Burden. "Who
would have thought that could ever happen here? I mean, you
could imagine it in Liverpool, say, or Glasgow. But here?"

"Who could imagine slavery would ever happen here? But Sojourner was a slave."

"Not exactly that, surely."

"If someone works without wages, or without accessible wages,
cannot leave her employment, is not allowed out, is beaten and
abused, what is she but a slave?

> Slaves cannot breathe in England, if their lungs
> Receive our air, that moment they are free;
> They touch our country and their shackles fall.

"I got that out of a book, I don't suppose it'll stay in my memory for long. The point is, it may have been true once, it isn't anymore." Wexford took a piece of paper from his pocket. "I copied
this down. It's a case history and it didn't happen in the eighteenth
century or the nineteenth but six years ago:

" 'Roseline,' " he read, " 'is from Southern Nigeria. At the age
of about fifteen she was 'bought' for £2 from her impoverished father, who was led to believe he would be paid that sum regularly
every month to help feed his other five children. Roseline, he was
told by the couple, was to stay as their guest and be taught domestic science. They brought her to Sheffield, where the husband
worked as a doctor. She was kept as a servant, not allowed out,
slept on the floor, and was made to kneel on the floor for two hours
if she fell asleep before being allowed to go to bed. Her working day
started at 5:30 A.M. and lasted for eighteen hours. She cleaned and

washed for her employers and their five children. She was caned and kept short of food. On one occasion, in desperation, she wrote a note intended for the next-door neighbor offering sex for a sandwich. The note was discovered and she was further punished. In September 1988, while her abusers were away for a week, she gathered enough courage and spoke to a regular passerby who had often seen her staring out of the window, and beckoned to her. This neighbor helped her to escape, and she took her former employers to court. She was awarded £20,000 in damages. However, she had only been given leave to stay for three months, and her employers had kept her for over three years. She was an illegal overstayer and thus liable to immediate deportation.' "

Burden was silent for a moment. Then he said, "Sojourner tried to escape and was further punished—is that what you're saying?"

"They went too far with their punishment. No doubt, they were afraid of the publicity and of having damages awarded against them. They made sure that wouldn't happen. They made very thoroughly sure by killing Annette, who perhaps had it in her power to reveal their identity and whereabouts, and tried—twice—to kill Oni, who might have been told where they lived."

"You think she was allowed in like this Roseline as a visitor? She was allowed three months or six months but overstayed?"

"Who's to know if she's never allowed out and no one sees her? If visitors to the house never see her? In fact, an employer has only to say to her that if she's discovered she'll be deported to wherever it is, the Gulf probably, for her to collude in this breaking of the law."

"If conditions are that bad for her wouldn't she want to be deported?"

"That depends on what awaits her. There are a good many parts of the world where all that's left for a homeless destitute woman is prostitution. In any case, Sojourner only colluded so far. She is supposed to have been told her rights *before* she left to come here, she's supposed to have been given the pamphlet to read, explaining the Immigration Rules Concession and what to do if she's ill-treated. But that's good only so far as it goes. If, as I think, Sojourner came in as a visitor with the family, as a *guest*, she wouldn't have any rights and, for all we know, she couldn't read. She very likely couldn't read English, anyway.

"Probably she knew very little about the outside world, this England, Kingsmarkham. She was black but she never saw another black person. And then, one day, looking out of a window, she saw Melanie Akande out running . . ."

"Reg, that's pure fantasy."

"It's intelligent conjecture," Wexford retorted. "She saw Melanie. Not once only but many times. Nearly every day from the middle of June onward. She saw a black girl like herself out there, a Nigerian like herself, and maybe she sensed Melanie's African origins."

"Allowing that that's true, which I'm not sure I can, so what?"

"I think it gave her confidence, Mike. It showed her that escape might be possible and the world wouldn't be entirely alien. So she ran away, in the dark, knowing nothing else . . ."

"No, that won't do," Burden said. "That can't be so. She *knew about the ESJ*. She knew it was where you went to find work or get money if there was no work . . . look—the march is starting."

A hundred of them? Like most people, Wexford wasn't much good at calculating numbers from a rapid glance. He would have to see them in sets of four or eight before he could tell. They were forming up now, four abreast, with a chosen two in the vanguard, holding the banner, both men and both middle-aged. Burden thought he recognized one of them from frequent visits to the Benefit Office. It was then that he had his first sight of the two officers from the uniformed branch, two of whom had suddenly appeared on the corn exchange steps.

They were a procession now and they began to move. What signal set them off was hard to know. A whispered word perhaps, traveling down the line from one to another, or the banner suddenly upraised. The two officers on the steps went back to their car, parked on the market square flagstones, a white Ford with the scarlet stripe and eagle crest of the Mid-Sussex Constabulary.

"We'll follow them too," said Wexford.

They stood back to let the column pass. Marching was rather slow, as it always is at the start. Speed would pick up when they came out into the main road to Kingsmarkham. Nearly everyone wore jeans, a shirt or T-shirt, trainers on the feet, the ubiquitous uniform. The oldest person there was a man well into his sixties who could not have hoped for work and must be marching out of public-spiritedness or altruism or even for the fun of it. The youngest was a baby girl in a pushchair, her mother a twin of Kimberley Pearson before she came into a fortune.

A second banner brought up the rear: JOBS FOR ALL. IS IT TOO MUCH TO ASK? Two women carried it, a pair who looked so much alike they must have been mother and daughter. The column proceeded up the High Street, the police car crawling behind it. Wexford and Burden got back into their car and Donaldson moved out behind the white Ford.

"Someone must have told her," said Wexford stubbornly, answering Burden's rebuttal as if there had been no break in their conversation. "There must have been someone who went there or someone she met who told her the ESJ was the place."

"Like who?" Burden was very sure of his ground. "And if so, why didn't this person tell her where it was? Help her to escape, come to that? Tell her how to have recourse to the law?"

"I don't know."

"If this person told her about jobs and benefit and how to get away, why hasn't he or she come to us?"

"These are minor things, Mike. These questions will be answered. At the moment we don't know where this beating-up happened, where her death happened. But we do know why. Because, getting no help from Annette, she had no choice but to go home. Where else could she go?"

The column turned left into Angel Street and, picking up speed, came to the roundabout. The first exit was for Sewingbury, the second for Kingsmarkham, the third led to the industrial estate where Wexford had been two days before. After passing between the factory sites, it would rejoin the Kingsmarkham Road at the pub called the Halfway House.

"Not much point in that," said Burden. "Half the industry's closed down."

"I expect that is the point," Wexford said.

The sun, which had shone quite brightly while they were in Stowerton marketplace, had gone in, retreating behind a thin veil of cloud. It had grown white and distant, a mere puddle of light, and the cloud was breaking, the little clouds were edged with darkness. But the heat remained, the heat even increased, and two of the young men among the marchers shed their shirts and tied them round their waists.

Reinforcements awaited them on the corner of Southern Drive, half a dozen men and a young woman with a banner of their own, obscurely proclaiming YES TO EURO-WORK. There is perhaps no more dismal sight in social terms than a row of empty factories. Boarded-up shops have nothing on it. The factories, two of them brand-new, had their windows all closed in the heat, their front doors padlocked, and signs offering the buildings either to let or for sale planted in lawns on which untended grass grew long. The members of the column, again at some signal, turned their heads as one to acknowledge these monuments to joblessness as they passed, like a regiment honoring a cenotaph.

Not all the factories were closed. One that manufactured machine parts had remained open and another producing herbal cosmetics seemed to be flourishing, while Burden remarked that the printers on the corner of Southern Drive and Sussex Mile had reopened and its presses were once more operating. It was a good sign, a sign of recession ending and prosperity returning, he added. Wexford said nothing. He was thinking, and not just about economic problems. In accordance with its previous behavior, the column should have cheered but it kept silence. Its members seemed not to share Burden's optimism. Up the long shallow hill the column went. The distance was a mile, at least a mile, and Wexford would have asked Donaldson to pass and go on ahead but passing was impossible. The road became a narrow country lane, a white pathway between high hedges and giant trees.

They met only one car before they reached the turn into the Kingsmarkham Road. It stopped and the white Ford stopped too. But before the officer had his door open, the column's members had shifted, had converted themselves into a single line, the banners held back flat against the hedge. Slowly the car came on and as its occupants came into focus Wexford saw that the driver was Dr. Akande, his son beside him in the passenger seat. Akande nodded and raised one hand in the classic gesture of thanks. The hand went down before he saw Wexford, or it might have been that he didn't see him. The boy next to him had a sullen injured expression. That was a family who would never forgive him for warning them to prepare for a daughter's, a sister's, death.

Traffic on the Kingsmarkham Road wasn't at its heaviest at Friday lunchtime but it wasn't light either. The white Ford went past the marchers and took up its new position at the head of the column. More joined at the point where the Forby Road turned in and they stopped to let a dozen cars coming this way from Kingsmarkham pass by. It was close on a hundred and fifty people now, Wexford calculated. A good many seemed to have decided that this stretch was the place to attach themselves to the marchers, whole families who had abandoned their cars on the grass verges, women with three or four children who looked on this as a fine day out, boys in their teens that Burden said could only be there because they were looking for trouble.

"We'll see. Maybe not."

"I meant to tell you. All this slavery stuff put it out of my head. Annette did make a will and who do you think she left her flat to?"

"Bruce Snow," said Wexford.

"How did *you* know? That's too bad, I was going to astound you."

"I didn't know. I guessed. You wouldn't have been so dramatic if it had been the ex-husband or Jane Winster. I hope he's grateful.

He'll have somewhere to live after his wife's taken him to the cleaners. Won't be very comfortable with Diana Graddon on the other side of the street."

The column was coming up to the outskirts of Kingsmarkham. Like most English country towns, it was approached by roads lined by big houses dating from the mid- and late nineteenth century, "villas" with high hedges and old-fashioned gardens, a subtly different atmosphere from Winchester Avenue and Ashley Grove. Wealth hid inside the walls of these houses instead of flaunting itself, concealed under an indifference that almost amounted to shabbiness.

A woman came running out of one of the houses, down a long flagged path, to join the march. She might have been employer, employee, or unemployed, it was impossible to tell from her jeans and sleeveless shirt. Would Sylvia stay at home now the need had gone? Or would she join the march, generously campaigning for others? Burden, who had been lost in thought, suddenly said, "That case history of yours, does it give the nationality of the employer?"

"No. Presumably, the family was British."

"They might be but Nigerian too." Burden was struggling and Wexford didn't help him. "I mean they might have been Nigerian *before* they were British." He gave up. "Were they black?"

"It's PC, it doesn't say."

Up ahead of them the bridge over the Kingsbrook had come into sight. A massive resistance to the introduction of roundabouts had kept Kingsmarkham town center, at least to a superficial eye, much as it had always been. But the bottleneck caused by the narrow bridge had resulted in so many traffic holdups that the bridge had been widened two years before. It was no longer the shallow stone arch, featured on many postcards, but an uncompromising affair of gray-painted steel, overlooked by the motel extension to the Olive and Dove Hotel. The trees were mostly still there, the alders and willows and giant horse chestnuts.

It was the favored beat of teenage boys who ran among traffic stopped by a red light to clean windscreens. The boys were there today but they gave up their thankless and often unwelcome labors to join the march. This side of the bridge a knot of people, perhaps a dozen, joined the tail of the column. Among them was Sophie Riding, the girl with the long corn-colored hair Wexford had first seen waiting her turn in the Benefit Office and whose name he had learned from Melanie Akande. She and a woman with her were carrying a red silk banner, skillfully made and with the words GIVE GRADUATES A CHANCE cut out in white and stitched to the silk.

The column waited. The policeman on duty waved on the three cars waiting at the lights and when they had passed beckoned the marchers onto the bridge. Wexford saw the drinkers at the tables outside the Olive get to their feet and crane their necks to see the lengthening procession go by. Burden said, "By the way, something else I forget to say, Mrs. Khoori got in."

"Nobody ever tells me anything," said Wexford.

"With a majority of seven. What you might call a close-run thing."

"D'you want me to follow them, sir?" Donaldson asked.

The marchers intended to turn into Brook Road. The banner carriers at the head of the column stopped on the far side of the bridge and one of them held up his hand, pointing to the left. Some consensus of opinion, an invisible wave, must have passed along the quadruple line of people, for the message reached him and the column turned, snaking to the left like a train negotiating a sharp curve in the rails.

"Park opposite the Benefit Office," Wexford said.

Ahead of them, the marked police car did this too. On the walls between which the steps ran up sat Rossy, Danny, and Nige, and Raffy with them. Raffy, without his hat for once, displayed the huge helmet of dreadlocks that crowned his head and tumbled in a cascade down his back. As the procession approached and came to a straggling halt, Danny got down off the wall and stubbed out his cigarette.

"What happens now?" Burden said.

"Some gesture will be made."

As Wexford spoke, Sophie Riding gave up her end of the GIVE GRADUATES A CHANCE banner to the man next to her. She detached herself from the column and walked up the steps. In her hand she held a sheet of paper, a petition perhaps or statement. Rossy, Danny, Raffy, and Nige stared after her as she disappeared into the Benefit Office.

She was inside no more than fifteen seconds. The paper had been handed over and a point had been made. Within moments of her absorption back into the column, the double doors of the Benefit Office opened and Cyril Leyton appeared. He looked from left to right, then directly at the column, which was no longer a column, which had lost its shape and become an amorphous scattered crowd. Leyton scowled. He seemed about to say something and perhaps would have done if he had not, in that moment, caught sight of the police car on the opposite side of the road.

The door swung and swung again behind him as he went in. It was the kind that is made, no doubt wisely in the circumstances, to be unslammable. Apparently at no word of command, like a flock of birds whose leader directs them by silent unknown means, the crowd formed into fours once more, swung round—those in the vanguard had no intention of giving up pride of place—and headed back the way it had come.

The boys from the wall joined on the end. Sophie Riding took up one end of her banner and the woman with her the other end. As the column turned into the High Street, the clock on St. Peter's Church began striking noon.

twenty-four

The heat was like the inside of a rain forest now, or like a sauna. There was no breath of wind. The sun was lost under banks of frothy whiteness that overlaid a sky of dark gray cloud. Thunder had begun to roll but so distantly that its rumblings were lost behind the throb and beat of traffic noise.

The march occupied the left-hand lane of Kingsmarkham High Street. Here the High Street was fairly wide and there was room for Stowerton-bound cars to creep past but those heading for Stowerton were diverted into Queen Street and the long serpentine southern route. The column passed St. Peter's Church as the final note of the midday clock chimes died away and proceeded northward close to the churchyard wall.

At the point where the diversion began two police officers, a man and a woman, cleared space for the column to pass. It had picked up more people at the churchyard gate, and outside the biggest of the High Street supermarkets a man and a girl who had taken a trolley from the rank on the forecourt abandoned it and tagged onto the end of the procession instead.

The police car with the stripe down its side and the crest on its door had turned back and been replaced by an unmarked Vauxhall, driven by PC Stafford from the uniformed branch with PC Rowlands beside him. Wexford and Burden had left theirs on a

vacant meter outside the offices of Hawkins and Steele, where
Bruce Snow worked, but when Stafford put his head out and offered a lift, Wexford shook his head and said they would follow the
column on foot. Sophie Riding, who had handed in the petition at
the Benefit Office, was two people ahead of them. They were sand-
wiched between her and her banner and the unmarked police car.
That was how they came to witness so entirely what was about to
happen.

The Range Rover was parked on the right-hand side and facing right on a broken yellow band fifty yards or so ahead of them
outside Woolworth's. It was an inconvenient place to have parked
on this morning of all mornings but its positioning broke no traffic
rule. Wexford didn't recognize the Range Rover, any more than he
did the white van behind it and the car in front of it, but he did
note the behavior of its driver and the behavior of the other drivers in leaving vehicles on that particular spot as antisocial. He
noted too its olive green color and a memory came into his mind of
the Women, Aware! meeting and a note passed to him. More interesting at that moment was the sight, far ahead, only accessible
to someone as tall as he, of Anouk Khoori crossing the greensward
outside the council offices, her arms outspread. She wore a loose
flowing garment and she was holding out her arms like a royal personage returning from a goodwill tour, greeting the children from
whom she has been parted for a month.

Wexford was remarking to Burden that he wondered if she
would tell the marchers that she knew they would come, she had
had a feeling they would, when the nearside door of the Range
Rover opened and Christopher Riding stepped down onto the
pavement. The Range Rover was now no more than a car-length
ahead of where Wexford and Burden were. Its offside door opened
and Christopher's father got out. Things happened very quickly
then.

Christopher edged round the front of the Range Rover as his
sister Sophie came alongside. He and Swithun Riding in a con-
certed swift movement seized her by the arms and she dropped the
banner with a cry. They lifted her off her feet, threw back the car

door, and slung her inside. Both tall and powerful, with big hands and muscular arms, they swung her in the air, her bright swatch of corn-gold hair flying out, before throwing her into the backseat.

The marchers in the immediate vicinity fell back, fanning out. A woman screamed. Someone picked up the banner. The column ahead of the girl marched on, unaware of what had happened, but those at its tail stopped to stare. This time Swithun Riding was in the driver's seat, his son squeezing himself between the bonnet of the Range Rover and the car in front of it. There must have been a central locking system, for Sophie couldn't unlock the door and escape. She was beating her fists against the window, she began to scream.

Wexford looked back at the unmarked Vauxhall and cocked his head at Stafford. He lunged forward and grabbed the rear door handle, but finding the door locked as he expected, hammered on the glass. Stafford and Rowlands had both left the Vauxhall. This was not what they had expected, this was unprecedented, this in *Kingsmarkham?*

The driver of the car ahead of the Range Rover, knowingly or unwittingly, now reversed an inch or two. It was a dangerous move and made Christopher let out a bellow of rage and fear. The reversing car nearly crushed him, but the driver had braked just in time. Christopher found himself trapped between its rear bumper and the Range Rover's front fender. The two vehicles made a mantrap that pinned his legs. He stood struggling, waving his arms and shouting, "Go forward, go forward, you bastard!"

The front of the column, unaware of the fracas at the rear, marched on, unperturbed. Like a pantomime horse whose hind legs have given up the game, it broke into an ungainly trot for the last final hundred yards of its progress. The rear guard had scattered into a crowd of fascinated spectators. Burden, with a quick nod to Wexford, slipped round the back of the Range Rover and in front of the white van behind it, walked past the imprisoned screaming girl, and wrenched open the passenger door Riding had unlocked for his son.

"Go back, go back!" the boy was yelling now.

Riding started the engine and had begun to move the automatic shift when Burden put his foot on the step and climbed into the passenger seat. Riding had never seen him before and must have taken him for an interfering member of the public. Without hesitation, he did at once the utterly unexpected, drawing back his right arm like a discus thrower and letting fly with a savage punch to Burden's jaw.

The passenger door swung open. Burden reeled backward through the empty space. He broke his fall by clutching at the door frame but still half-tumbled to the pavement. The girl screamed more loudly. His passenger door swinging, Riding reversed into the white van, hitting it with a reverberating crash. Then he saw the uniformed policemen. He saw Wexford.

Wexford said, "Open that door."

Riding only stared at him. Half the crowd had moved around the Woolworth's side of the van. Someone picked Burden up. He staggered, dazed, put a hand up to his head, and sat down heavily on the low wall in front of the store. Wexford pushed the boy out of the way and, moving between the Range Rover and the car ahead, stepped up inside the swinging door.

"Don't try the same thing with me, will you?" he said.

He unlocked the nearside rear door and helped the girl out. Her face was awash with tears. She held on to him, her hands gripping his sleeves. A stream of invective pouring from Riding made her tremble. He thrust his face at the open door, shouting in Burden's direction, "What's it to you if I stop my own daughter making a foul exhibition of herself? What business is it of yours, for Christ's sake?"

The girl shook. Her teeth had begun to chatter. Christopher, now free and rubbing his crushed legs, stood up and put out one hand to her in a gesture of appeasement. She screamed at him, "Get away from me!"

Wexford said, "All of you are coming to the police station *now*."

Blood was running down Burden's face. He mouthed something, while holding on to his head. The howling siren of an ambulance, summoned by Stafford, sent the crowd falling back, splitting now into two distinct groups, one solidly behind Burden, the rest spectators by the churchyard wall. The ambulance came out of York Street and blocked the road, parking where the column had marched. Ahead the marchers had gone out of sight and with the appearance of the paramedics, two of them with a stretcher Burden scowled at, the first drops of rain began to fall.

Riding had unlocked his driver's door. His face dark red, he stepped down and said to Wexford, "Look, what I did was entirely justifiable. I told my daughter I'd stop her if she joined that march, she knew what was coming to her. That chap seemed to think he was making some sort of citizen's arrest . . ."

"That chap is a police officer," Wexford said.

"Oh God, I didn't . . ."

"If you'll get into the car we'll go to the police station. You can do your explaining there."

The girl was tall and strong and straight. She looked what she was, the product of twenty-two or -three years of top-grade feeding, fresh air, care, and attention, the best of schools. Wexford didn't know when he had seen a more vulnerable face. There was no bruising on it but still it looked bruised. The skin was soft beyond belief, almost transparent, the eyes puffy, the lips chapped and that in high summer. Her hair, the color of the ripe barley they had been cutting in the fields up at Mynford, looked unnatural framing that suffering face, it looked like false hair worn by an actress miscast for her part.

She said to Karen Malahyde, "I can go home if they're not there."

"Well," said Karen, but she said it kindly, "just at the moment you aren't going anywhere. Would you like a cup of tea?"

Sophie Riding said she would. Carefully, Wexford said to her, "We won't go in the interview room. They aren't very pleasant places. We'll go up to my office." Suddenly, he thought of Joel

Snow and he knew Karen was thinking of him too. This was different, of course it was—wasn't it? Joel too had been unwilling while this girl knew it was the only way. He said to her in the lift, "It won't take long."

"What do you want me to do?"

"Something I wish I'd been able to ask you to do two weeks ago."

They went into his office. The rain was heavy enough to blind the windows and make it dark. Karen put on lights and the sky outside the window turned to a streaming twilight.

She gave Sophie a chair.

Wexford sat down behind his desk. "It was you sent me that question about a rapist at the Women, Aware! meeting?"

She was eager to talk but she was afraid too. "Oh, yes! I wanted to come round afterward, like you said. I would have done if I could, I hope you believe me."

Suddenly, preceding the thunder by seconds, a brilliant zigzag of lightning expelled everything, seeming to hold the streaming water suspended, making the dark sky invisible, until the crash came and the world went on. Sophie shuddered and made a little sound, like a protest. There was a tap at the door and Pemberton came in with tea. She covered her face with her hands for a moment, then took them away to show the tears flowing down her cheeks. Karen pushed the box of tissues at her.

"I believe you," Wexford said. "I understand what stopped you coming to me."

Sophie took a tissue. "Thanks." She said to Wexford, "What do you want me to do?"

"Make a statement. Tell us about it. It won't be difficult, practically speaking. It may be difficult emotionally."

"Well," she said, "I can't go on like I have been. It has to stop. I can't go another day, not another minute."

He said fairly, "There are other ways. We'll manage without your statement. You don't have to do it. But if you don't, I'm afraid—well, there may be more . . ."

She gave a little cry that cut off the end of his sentence. She looked away, said, "I'm ready. What do I do?"

Karen said into the recording device, "Sophie Riding at Kingsmarkham Police Station on Friday, July thirtieth. The time is twelve forty-three P.M. DCI Wexford and DS Malahyde are present . . ."

When it was over and he had heard it all, Wexford went downstairs to where Sophie's father sat in Interview Room One with DC Pemberton. He looked chastened. His face had resumed its normal color. The twenty minutes he had waited down here had no doubt brought him to regret his hasty behavior. A man who has hit another man is always aghast to discover that other is a policeman.

He got up when Wexford came in and began to apologize. His reasons for behaving as he had came out with easy fluency and they were the excuses of the man who has always been able to buy or talk his way out of trouble.

"Mr. Wexford, I can't tell you how sorry I am about all this. Needless to say I wouldn't have struck your officer if I'd had any idea. I took him for a member of the public."

"Yes, I expect you did."

"This doesn't have to go any further, does it? If my daughter had been reasonable and got into the car—after all, she'd completed the best part of that damn-fool march—if she'd done that none of this would have happened. I'm not a harsh father, I adore my children . . ."

"Your treatment of your children isn't in question," Wexford said. "Before you say any more I should warn you that anything you do say will be taken down and may be given in evidence . . ."

Interrupting, Riding shouted, "You're not charging me with hitting that chap!"

"No," said Wexford. "I'm charging you with murder, incitement to murder, and attempted murder. And when I have done that I shall go into the room next door and charge your son with rape and attempted murder."

*   *   *

W ithout Sophie Riding's statement," Wexford said, "I doubt if anything could have been made to stick. We had no evidence and no proof, no more than conjecture."

Burden's face was swollen like a Victorian cartoonist's image of a man with toothache. "Assault on a police officer is the least of his worries, I suppose. Odd, isn't it, I was the one most impressed by what Mavrikiev said about killing someone with your fists and it was me who really had it brought home to me.

"It's a funny thing, you see these characters in films, Westerns and that sort of thing, they knock each other around but it never seems to have any effect, they get a great swingeing blow to the jaw but they're up again in a flash and hammering away at the other one. And you see them in the next scene with not a mark on them, all spruced up with a girl on their arm, taking her out for a night on the town."

"Hurts, does it?"

"It's not so much that it hurts. It feels so enormous. And it doesn't feel as if it'll ever *work* again. At any rate he left me all my teeth. So, are you going to tell me about it?"

"Freeborn'll be here in half an hour and I'll have to tell *him*."

"Well, you can tell me first," said Burden.

Wexford sighed. "I'll play you the tape of Sophie Riding's statement. You realize, of course, that Sojourner knew of the existence of the Benefit Office through Sophie. She'd heard Sophie talking about it, about going there and signing on and so forth, though she didn't know where it was."

"What, talking about it to her parents?"

"And her brothers and her little sister, no doubt. Sojourner waited on them, she'd always have been in and out, though never out of the house."

"How did they get her into the country in the first place?"

"Sophie doesn't know. She wasn't there, she was already at Myringham Polytechnic that's now Myringham University and before that she'd been at boarding school here. But she'd seen Sojourner at their home in Kuwait when she was there in the holidays and she remembers when Sojourner first came. Her idea is that she was brought here as the boy's girlfriend. In a hideous kind of way, she *was*, if 'girlfriend' is one definition of the woman you have forcible sexual intercourse with."

"*That* was going on?"

"Oh, yes. The father too, I daresay, though I don't know—yet. Listen to Sophie."

Wexford wound the tape on, pressed "play," reversed, and got the point in the statement he wanted. The girl's voice was soft and plaintive, yet outraged too. It came over as a cry for help, yet there was no appeal in it.

"My mother told me a Kuwaiti man bought her from her father in Calabar, Nigeria, for five pounds. He meant to educate her and treat her like a daughter but he died and she had to be a servant. My mother talked as if we'd done her a great favor, as if it was the best thing in the world for her finding a 'good home' with us. 'Good home' is the expression they use about dogs that get rescued, isn't it? I think she was about fifteen then.

"I never thought much about it. I know I should have, but I wasn't at home with them very much. I liked it here in England, I was always longing to get back to England. When the Gulf War started they came home. It wasn't a problem for my father, he could work anywhere, he's a brilliant pediatric surgeon. I don't like saying it, I wish I didn't have to, but it's true. He loves babies, you should see him with a baby, and he loves all of us, his family, his children. But we're different, as far as he is concerned, we're what he calls the upper crust. He says some people are destined to be hewers of wood and drawers of water. I think that comes from the Bible. For him some people are born to be slaves and wait on others.

"I must have been very naive. I didn't know what the bruises on her were—well, the bruises and cuts and all the other marks. In Kuwait I'd thought she was pretty to look at but she wasn't pretty in England. I'd graduated and I was home all the time and it was all a mystery to me. I never saw anyone hit her but I could tell she was frightened of my father and my brother. And my other brother David when he was at home, though mostly he wasn't, mostly he's away at college in America. The bad part—for me, that is—the bad part was that I thought she was stupid and clumsy, I could even see what my mother meant when she said she wasn't fit to sleep in a proper bedroom."

The machine on pause, Wexford went on, "Psychologists say that someone ugly and dirty is a ready candidate for abuse. That your own abuse has resulted in the ugliness makes no difference. The reasoning behind it seems to be that ugliness deserves punishment, and dirt and neglect of personal hygiene even more so. It got to a point where Sojourner was being beaten and struck for every small fault. She worked twelve or fourteen hours a day but that wasn't enough. Susan Riding told me herself they had six bedrooms in that house but that didn't mean they had one for Sojourner. She slept in a small room off the kitchen. All the rooms on the ground floor at the back have bars at the windows, to keep out burglars no doubt, but very convenient if you want to prevent someone escaping.

"I've just been to the house, I've seen it. It used to be a dog's room and they've got a dog in there now. Susan Riding says it was more 'appropriate,' her word, for Sojourner to be in there, 'in case they wanted her to do anything for them in the night.' The mattress on the floor was apparently 'what she'd been used to,' she 'wouldn't know what to do with a bed.' Here's Sophie again."

The girl's voice sounded clearer and more confident this time. "I needed a job, so I did the obvious thing, I went to the Job Center and I signed on, only it wasn't the obvious thing to my parents. My father said it was a disgrace, that was for the working classes. He was quite prepared to keep me. Education wasn't *for* anything, he said, it was to make you a finer better person. He'd make me an allowance. Hadn't he always kept me? My mother actually said they would keep me *until I got married*. We argued about this a lot and that poor girl overheard. Her English was never brilliant but she'd have understood that. She'd have known there was a place nearby you could go to and ask them to find you work and if there wasn't any work they'd give you money.

"It was the beginning of July, the first or the second, when my brother Christopher asked her to wash his running shoes for him— well, told her to. They were white trainers. She made a mess of it, I don't know what she did, but she was terrified. Anyway, he beat her up for it. That was when I first realized what went on. It sounds absurd, I know, that I didn't know before, but I suppose I just didn't want to believe that of my own brother. I love my brother, or I did love him, he's my twin, you know.

"I saw Christopher go into her room and come out again after about twenty minutes. I'd have gone in but she didn't make a sound, not through all that beating she never made a sound.

"But when I saw her next day I knew. I asked my brother and he denied it. She was clumsy, he said, I should know that, she always had been, she wasn't really fit to live in a civilized house. He made a lot of remarks about mud huts and he said she couldn't cope with furniture, she was always knocking into furniture. Well, I wasn't satisfied, I told my father but all that happened was he flew into a rage. If you haven't seen him in a rage you can't know what I mean. He's terrifying. He accused me of being disloyal to my family, he wanted to know where I'd 'picked up these ideas' and was it from my 'Marxist' friends I'd met at the Job Center.

"I know I should have done more. I have a lot of guilt about that. Somehow, then, I knew what I'd been hiding from myself all this time, that Christopher had raped her too, over and over, there had been all the signs I pretended not to see. All I did was send you that question at the meeting and that was worse than useless.

"On the Monday after the beating she disappeared. My father was at the hospital and Christopher was in London at a job interview, of all things. I guessed she'd run away and my mother thought she had but we didn't know what to do and in the evening my mother had to go out to a committee preparing for that Women, Aware! meeting. She left a note for my father. I said we ought to tell the police but my mother flew into a panic at that. Of course I can understand why now. I had a date and when I got in at about eleven-thirty my mother was in bed and Christopher was out but my father was there. He said he didn't know what we were in a flap about, he'd told my mother. He'd sent the girl home, she was worse than useless and it made him sick seeing her about the house. He said he'd sent her back to Banjul on British Airways but there isn't a BA flight to Banjul on a Monday, the only flights are on Sundays and Fridays, I checked. My brother was out all that evening and my father told me and my mother he was driving her to Heathrow but he can't have been because there wasn't a flight.

"I didn't believe any of it. For some reason I thought she'd be in her room. They'd have beaten her up when she came back and she'd be in there lying on her mattress. I tried the door but it was locked. Well, you know, in a house like ours—a house like *theirs*— all the inside keys fit all the locks. I got another key and unlocked the door and everything was gone. She hadn't got much, just the two dresses that were my mother's castoffs from years back and those awful black lace-up canvas boot things my mother bought her, the cheapest you can get. But it was all gone, all but the mattress and her headcloth. I don't know why they didn't find it when they cleaned the blood up but they didn't. It was on the mattress and the mattress was sort of red and blue. Well, the cloth was blue and red—red with the blood on it.

"I've kept it. It was like a kind of madness, keeping it. I longed to throw it away but I couldn't. Even then it didn't occur to me that she might be dead. My brother was out that night for hours. I heard him come in, it must have been two-thirty or three, and he went off on his holiday to Spain next morning, so I never had a chance to talk to him. Anyway, I was afraid to talk to him, this wasn't my brother, this wasn't Chris that had been closer to me than anyone. Then I found his sweater in the wash with blood all over it.

"I thought maybe my father had got her taken to hospital secretly because my brother had gone too far. My father has a lot of influence, I don't know if he could do that, but I thought he could.

All I could think of then was my brother raping her, my brother raping *anyone*. I didn't blame my father much then, I thought maybe he was just protecting his own son, I went to the Women, Aware! meeting with him and I wrote that question to you on an impulse. My father didn't see what I'd asked. I told him I'd asked whether it was legal to carry a CS gas canister. But I couldn't come up afterward and explain, I couldn't get away from him."

Chief Constable Freeborn seemed to have forgotten about Wexford's "carousing" picture in the paper. If the three weeks it had taken to catch the murderer of the two women still rankled, he gave no sign of it. He was all affability. To the old "snug," a tiny room containing a table and three chairs, in the deepest recesses of the Olive and Dove, a barmaid brought the three beers he had ordered. Wexford sat down in the chair with the arms. He thought he deserved it.

"You have to remember," he began, "that she knew nothing about what rights she had under the Immigration Act, she didn't know there *was* an Immigration Act. She knew she wasn't allowed to work but 'work,' it had been explained to her long ago, was what you got paid for and she was never paid, she was simply given 'a good home.' Susan Riding called her the 'au pair'—or that's what she called her to me after Sojourner was dead. To do Mrs. Riding justice, and I suppose everyone merits justice, I don't think she knew much about Sojourner's fate. She let her sleep on a mattress on the floor in the 'dog's room' because she's that sort of woman, the kind that used to talk about the poor keeping coal in the bath if you gave them bathrooms. In buying Sojourner the cheapest footwear she could get, she probably thought she was being very bountiful. I wonder what she'd say if she knew the shop assistant put her down as a bag lady who slept on the street?

"But she knew nothing about the rape or the violent assaults, and if she suspected she shut her eyes to it, told herself not to let her imagination run wild. That evening when she came home from the committee meeting, her husband told her he'd sent the girl home and Christopher was out driving her to the airport. According to Mrs. Riding, Sojourner had become 'dirty and lazy' and was worse than useless. Except that she needed help in the house, she was glad to see the back of her.

"What had in fact happened was that Sojourner ran away on the Monday afternoon. Riding was out, the boy Christopher was in London, and the young sister was at school. She didn't know where to go, she had never been out before, not out of their grounds, that is, but she knew there was a place where you went to find a job. She must have reasoned that anywhere she could find work couldn't be worse than what she'd left behind."

Freeborn interrupted. "You say she didn't know where to go. Winchester Avenue's a good way from the what-d'you-call-it, ESJ, how did she know the way?"

"She didn't, sir. Perhaps she followed the river. You can see the Kingsbrook if you look down from there over the gardens. Melanie Akande liked to look at it while she was out running. Maybe some instinct led Sojourner toward the river, downhill, maybe she knew a town is often on a river. Her instinct led her to Glebe Road and she encountered Oni Johnson, who directed her to the Benefit Office. The rest you know, how she followed Annette home and, failing to get the help she wanted from her, she had no choice but to return to where she had come from."

"Pity this Annette didn't send her to us," said Freeborn.

The understatement of all time, Wexford thought, but of course he didn't say so. "She doesn't seem to have gone home at once or perhaps it took her a while to find her way back. At any rate, she didn't get there until Susan Riding and Sophie had gone out. Let us take it that she went in the back way and into her room where Swithun Riding found her.

"I don't say he meant to kill her. There seems no reason why he would. He asked her where she had been and when she told him he asked if she had spoken to anyone. Yes, the woman who takes the children across the road and this woman from the place where they give you jobs or they give you money. What's her name and where does she live? She tells him and it all comes out. Riding's daughter has described his rages. He flew into one then and set about her with his fists. Mike knows what his fist feels like and she was a young girl, thin and frail. They fed her pretty badly. Even so, she didn't die from his fists but from striking her head against the steel frame round the window bars. When you're in that room you can see how it happened."

"So he got his son to help him dispose of her," said Burden. "Young Christopher took the body to Framhurst Woods and buried it, did he?"

"That was when he was supposed to be driving their erstwhile slave to Heathrow. I doubt if he knew where to do the deed, just drove out into the country until he found somewhere suitable. The road isn't busy and he'd have waited till dark."

"And after that Riding had to make up his mind what to do about Annette and Oni."

"I don't think he meant to do anything about Oni. After all, the Oni connection was a bit tenuous. Oni wouldn't go to the police, she had nothing to go *with*, but Annette was different. He must have gone nearly mad wondering what Sojourner had told Annette. He wouldn't have got much sleep that night. Just after Annette made her phone call to the Benefit Office next day a man phoned and asked for her. Ingrid Pamber thought it was Snow but it wasn't, it was Riding. And he got an answer that gave him a little breathing space. Annette was at home ill in bed."

"How did he know her name?" Freeborn wanted to know.

"Sojourner got it off the plate above the bell at Ladyhall Court. His next move was to get hold of Zack Nelson. Nelson owed him one, you see. It was Riding who performed the operation on Zack's son when the child was found to have some kind of heart malformation at a few weeks old. No doubt, Nelson had made extravagant promises at the time—'Anything in the world I can do for you, Doc, any time, you only have to ask,' you can imagine the kind of thing.

"Zack needed money too. He needed somewhere for his girlfriend and their child to live. But Zack botched it up, he let Percy Hammond see his face and he had to go back on Riding's instructions for a somewhat less venal offense—burglary. He knew he'd go down for that, he *wanted* to go down for that, so he got Riding to pay the blood money into an account he opened for Kimberley Pearson.

"So it looked as if Riding and his son were in the clear, until that is our treasure-seeking plumber dug up the body. Even then it must have been clear to Riding no one had the faintest idea who Sojourner was. The real fear started when he was picking up his younger daughter from the Thomas Proctor School and he saw me homing on Oni Johnson.

"I saw the Range Rover pull away from outside the Thomas Proctor the day of the attack on Oni but of course I didn't make the connection. I thought it was her son Raffy we wanted to talk to, not Oni. Riding easily got to the Castlegate before she got home—or else his son went. Christopher may also have seen me, for he was there in the Epsons' pink Escort, picking up the Epsons' older child. By the way, unpleasant though it is to contemplate, I think Christopher followed Melanie to Stowerton on that previous occasion because he had acquired a taste for black girls, it was black girls he fancied. Luckily for her, Melanie didn't fancy *him* and he was no doubt afraid to attempt the rape of a free and independent young woman.

"I don't yet know which of them made the attempt on Oni's life. We shall find out. I do know that it was Riding who went into the Intensive Care Ward next day and—with very little time or privacy at his disposal—pulled the IV line out from Oni's arm. It didn't work but it was worth a try."

"Who picked the Riding child up from school the day Sojourner ran away?" Burden speculated. "Not Riding or his wife obviously. A friend probably, they very likely had a rota system. Because if he'd done it or his wife had done it they'd have caught Sojourner before she got to Annette or Oni and none of it would have happened. I wonder if he thinks of that now?"

Freeborn, who had finished his drink in one single long swig, said irritably, "Why do you call her that? What does it mean?"

"She was a poet," Burden said, and then added doubtfully, "wasn't she?"

"A *what?*"

Wexford was too angry to explain. He was shaking with anger and hoped it didn't show. Evoked by the Riding family, it had nothing to do with Freeborn but he was tempted to vent it on this Philistine, this insensitive poker face who stared at him with a kind of disgusted incredulity.

Making a supreme effort at self-control, he said laconically, "I didn't fancy Miss X. We hadn't a name for her."

"Well, you know it now, presumably?"

"Oh, yes," said Wexford. "I know it now." He thought of her youth for a moment and her fate and, as quickly, crushed those thoughts. Here was not the place for them and this was not the time. "If she ever had a surname no one seems to remember it. Sophie never forgot the first name she gave them when she was handed over from the man who died, but the others had forgotten it." The careful pronunciation he attempted might be right and might not. "She was called Simisola." He got up. "Shall we go?"